GUARDIAN *of* SECRETS

a Library Jumpers novel

Also by Brenda Drake

The Fated Series
Touching Fate
Cursing Fate

Also in this Series
Thief of Lies

GUARDIAN *of* SECRETS

a Library Jumpers novel

·BRENDA DRAKE·

ENTANGLED PUBLISHING, LLC

Entangled Publishing, LLC
2614 South Timberline Road
Suite 109
Fort Collins, CO 80525

Entangled Teen is an imprint of Entangled Publishing, LLC.

Visit our website at www.entangledpublishing.com.

Edited by Liz Pelletier and Stacy Abrams
Cover design by Anna Crosswell, Cover Couture
Interior design by Toni Kerr

ISBN: 978-1-63375-591-8
Ebook ISBN: 978-1-63375-590-1

Manufactured in the United States of America

First Edition February 2017

10 9 8 7 6 5 4 3 2 1

For those not afraid to jump into love.
And to Rich, my love, who took the plunge with me.

CHAPTER ONE

If you could drown in boredom, I was about to gulp my last bit of air.

I leaned against the tree I sat under and pulled my knees up to my chest, watching the frail-looking neighbor girl clamber up the porch of our newly purchased home on Pine Orchard Road. She handed a plate of something to Pop. They exchanged pleasantries before she pirouetted, scrambled back down the steps, and headed down the long driveway. She resembled Snow White, with her dark hair and pale skin. The widow's peak on her forehead and her sharp chin made her face look like a pasty heart.

You'd think I'd be happy for quieter times after accidently jumping into a gateway book in Boston and transporting through a portal to a library in Paris. That's right. I had jumped into a book—long story for another time. Not to mention, my normal life had changed drastically. Being a Sentinel, which was just a fancy word for a magical knight, and able to fight unfathomable beasts would be cool if it weren't real life and was just a video game. In real life, people died.

Permanently.

I wondered if Conemar and his band of rogue Mystiks—yep, the worst bad guys ever—would give up searching for us. Uncle Philip had said I shouldn't worry and that there wasn't a threat anymore, but I seriously doubted it.

Unfortunately, even after defeating Conemar, I *still* had to go into hiding with my family and friends just in case his followers wanted to seek revenge. Having a price on your head would be bad enough in the human world, but having one in the Mystik's realm was more than terrifying.

I glanced at the fancy new phone Pop had bought me so I could video chat with everyone I missed back home. Which was mostly my best friend, Afton, since Nana's cell phone was from the Stone Age and didn't have the video feature. I found Afton's name in the recent calls section, tapped the call button, and waited for her to answer.

Stuck in Branford, Connecticut, alone without my boyfriend, Arik, and the other Sentinels for two weeks was getting to me. My other best friend and newly discovered cousin, Nick, moved into a home down the street with his parents four days ago, but I hadn't spent much time with him. He was too busy helping his parents get their restaurant ready for its big opening.

Afton's face popped onto the phone's screen. The awkward video angle made her large brown eyes look kind of buggy over the phone. "You know I love you, Gia, but this is the third time in less than an hour." Another call beeped through and I ignored it. I really needed my best friend. "I'm at work," she was saying. "I can't chat right now. I promise I'll call you as soon as I'm off."

"Okay, I'm sorry…it's just…well, I miss you."

I waved at Pop zipping down the street in his Volvo. With his focus fixed on the road, he didn't see me.

"I miss you, too." Afton leaned back, glanced over both shoulders, and brought her face close to the screen. "Why don't you hang out with Nick?"

"Cause Deidre's with him again. Those two never separate. It's sickening—" I stopped when I noticed the disappointment cross her face. "Shit. I didn't mean…"

"No worries. I'm fine," she said over a slurping espresso machine somewhere off screen. I knew every one of her expressions. The forced smile and sad eyes told me she was lying. "I had my chance. He's moved on. Anyway, why don't you go to a movie or something?"

"I just got back from one. This has to be the longest Saturday *ever*."

"Hey, I've got to go. Customers. Talk to you later." She hung up, and the screen went dark. I pushed the end button.

Though I was lonely, I kept to myself out of fear of saying something I wasn't supposed to about the Mystik world. I needed to talk to someone who knew about the ridiculous stuff going on in my life. Someone to listen and assure me I would be okay. I needed my friends, but Nick and Afton were too busy.

The neighborhood girl strolled along the side of the road in my direction. She hadn't noticed me earlier when she passed on her way to my house, so I hoped she wouldn't again on her way back to hers, which was a lot bigger than ours was. Still, we had more than three thousand square feet in our gray Victorian home that needed some serious renovations. It had a pointy turret and sat on an acre lot at the end of a quiet road with a crooked street sign.

When the girl neared, she spotted me in the shadows of the tree and practically skidded to a stop.

Please don't come over. Please don't come over. Shit. She's coming over.

She stepped cautiously across the browning grass as if worried she might kill it. Before long, she hovered over me.

"Hi, Deidre," she trilled. "Did you get my text?"

She thought I was my "pretend twin." Having my Changeling around was like having a walking mirror around all the time.

I stood, the fall leaves crunching under my feet. "Um, Deidre's my sister. I'm Gia."

"Oh, right, she did say she has a twin. You're identical."

This one's observant.

"We are."

She smiled. "I'm Emily... Emily Proctor. I live next door."

"I know. I saw you with your dad yesterday."

Her smile slipped, and she looked down at her hands. "He's my uncle. My parents are gone. The house used to be my grandparents' home."

"I'm sorry," I said uncomfortably.

When she looked up, the sun hit her light blue eyes and glistened against the tears gathering on her bottom eyelashes. "Thanks. It's been a few years now, so, you know..."

No matter how long or how young you were at the time, when a parent passes away it leaves a wound. One that is always gaping, leaving you vulnerable to attacks of emotions at the most awkward moments. Like now. "Yeah, I do," I said softly. "My mother died when I was four."

She smiled again. "Now *I'm* sorry. That sounds insensitive, right? I never know what to say in this kind of situation."

"How do you know Deidre?" I asked, hoping to change the conversation to something less depressing.

"She's in my biology class."

"Oh, right—" A loud motor cut off my words. As if on cue, Nick's junkyard special pulled up, dark exhaust coughing out of the pipes in the back. I plugged my nose to block the burnt oil smell.

My heart almost burst at the sight of him, but I forced myself to act unaffected by his arrival. We were supposed to pretend there wasn't a long history between us.

Nick got the motorcycle even though his parents protested. Nothing said *we're sorry for lying to you* all *your life about being adopted and about being the Antichrist aka Conemar's son* than turning a blind eye to his new rebel attitude.

Deidre swung her leg over the seat and hopped off the bike. She removed her purple and black helmet, and I wasn't sure if it was me, or Emily, or both of us who gasped. Her long brown hair was gone. The new style was bleached and short, with long lavender bangs hiding one eye.

"Oh my *gosh*," Emily squealed. "I love your new hairstyle. You look so…um…couture."

Nick unsaddled himself from the bike. "She looks biker chic to me."

I lowered my head and rolled my eyes at his comment. Nick was too lovesick to notice. It was obvious what Deidre was going for—the complete opposite of me. Who could blame her? After all, she was a Changeling and born to be me, and finding that out had to have messed with her head.

"You look amazing." I feigned excitement in my voice. There I went again, trying hard to bond with her, and she ignored my effort. Having to share a room with her was awkward and somewhat quiet. I did all the talking and she'd give me quick, simple answers. At the rate it was taking Pop and Carrig to renovate the other rooms in our house, we'd be roomies for a lot longer than I'd like.

Nick cocked a brow at me and gave me a look that spoke more than words. That he knew I was faking it.

I gave him a wide grin. "What's up?"

"Not much," he said. "Just dropping off Deidre."

Deidre stared into the bike's rearview mirror, fixing her helmet hair. "You and Nick have some sort of meeting with Pop."

"Really? Pop just left. Why didn't he take me with him?"

"He said he couldn't find you." She frowned at her reflection. "He had to overnight a package before the post office closed. You can go with Nick and I'll hang out with Emily." She looked over at her. "If you're not busy, anyway. I'd love to do some shopping today, and I like your style."

Emily beamed. "I'd love to."

"I'm not riding that thing." I nodded my head toward the rusted metal.

Nick patted the cracked seat. "It looks like shit, but it runs."

"But is it safe?" I gave the bike a curious eye. "I'd rather walk."

Deidre threw down a gauntlet. "What, are you scared? I rode it."

I wasn't one to pass up a challenge. I snatched the helmet from her and put it on. "If you wreck, I'll kill you," I said to Nick as I straddled the bike.

"See you later, babe," Nick said, and planted a firm kiss on Deidre's lips. "Later, Emily."

"It was nice chatting with you, Gia," Emily said and frowned.

Did she see me roll my eyes at Deidre's hair? Or see Nick and I exchange looks?

"Yeah, it was great," I finally answered.

Nick revved the bike, and I quickly wrapped my arms around his waist before he sped off.

"Where are we going?" I yelled over the loud motor.

He turned his head to the side and yelled, "The library. The new librarian arrived Friday. She's a plant"—he adjusted himself on the seat—"from the Wizard Council. She's here to monitor the gateway book."

The thought of entering a library again made my stomach clench. Libraries had once been my escape, but now they were a doorway to my nightmares. To the Mystik world.

Nick took a corner fast, the tires squealing, and I gripped him tighter.

"Hey, easy there!" he said. "You'll crack a rib."

"Stop complaining. You're such a baby!"

Nick sped the bike around another corner, revved the engine, and released the throttle, obviously to freak me out, which worked. I squeezed him tighter, and he winced.

After another horrifying turn, we ended up at the James Blackstone Memorial Library adjacent to the town square. Made out of white marble and with four pillars holding up an overhang draping the porch, the place resembled a state building. It looked like some Greek architecture Afton had showed me in one of her books. Nick slowed the bike into an open parking spot.

I yanked off the helmet and shoved it at him. "What were you thinking? You could have killed us."

"I had it all under control." He lifted the seat and packed in the helmets.

"You're an ass."

He snickered and slammed the seat down. "Yeah, but you love me anyway."

A big stupid grin spread across my lips. He was right, but I'd never admit it. Nick and I were like brother and sister. We didn't do mushy. "I'm glad we finally have some alone time," I said.

"Me too," he said.

Pop pulled his Volvo into a space down the row from Nick's bike. He swung open the door and crossed the parking lot, meeting us at the steps. Beyond the opened bronze doors was a rotunda. The walls were pink marble, with varnished wood doors and frames. I gazed up at the dome above our heads, my mouth dropping in awe. Eight large paintings with scenes illustrating some sort of history timeline adorned the inside, and medallion-shaped portraits of important-looking people created a circle between arches exposing the balcony just below it.

A draft from the open door swirled around me, raising the hairs on my arm. An uneasiness settled around me, and I absentmindedly reached for my sword. Of course, it wasn't there. This wasn't a mission. We were just there to meet whoever it was Uncle Philip sent to watch over the gateway book.

"Isn't it beautiful?" A young woman wearing black-rimmed glasses that matched her thick, straight hair stood next to me. "The paintings depict the history of bookmaking. The portraits are of famous authors. Harriet Beecher Stowe"—she pointed each one out as she named them—"Nathaniel Hawthorne, Ralph Waldo Emerson—"

"Are you Kayla Bagley?" Pop interrupted her.

"Oh… N-no, sorry, I'm Maira. I volunteer here. Miss Bagley is new. She's filling in for a librarian who's on a leave of absence. Maybe I should get someone with more experience to help you?" She looked nervous about what she had said and quickly corrected herself. "I mean, Miss Bagley is still acquainting herself with how things run around here."

"They understand what you meant, Maira," an overly sweet voice came from behind us. "You may continue with whatever you were doing. I'll take care of our guests."

"Yes, Miss Bagley," Maira muttered.

Miss Bagley was a ginger in her mid-thirties. Smaller than what I was expecting. Her apricot-colored hair was pulled back in a bun. Her plain white shirt, loose gray pants, and sensible chunky shoes said she wasn't obsessive about her appearance, which apparently Pop didn't mind. He was giving Miss Bagley that awkward smile he gets when he likes someone.

Look away. I stared back up at the frescoes on the ceiling, feeling uncomfortable for Pop.

"It was nice meeting you," Maira said, and shuffled away.

"Mr. Kearns, I assume," Miss Bagley said through nude-colored lips. "And you must be Gianna?"

"It's just Gia."

"Oh, that's right. Sorry. Your uncle… I mean, Professor Attwood did a wonderful job describing both of you." She pulled out a tube of lip balm from her pocket and applied it. "Sorry, my lips get so dry, and I hate wearing lipstick."

A woman after my own heart. I preferred my root beer–flavored Lip Smacker, too.

Pop turned a bright smile on for her. "Please, call me Brian."

She smiled back and it was like the sun came out to blind us. "And you may call me Kayla." They were totally flirting in front of us.

Ugh. As much as I wanted Pop to have someone special in his life and be happy, I didn't need to be a witness to it.

"I'm Nick," he said, elbowing me and nodding at Pop and Miss Bagley. He had noticed the flirting, too.

"Well, if I knew I would be working with such handsome men, I would have dressed better." She winked at Pop. She actually *winked* at him.

"How old are you?" I blurted out.

"Gia…" Pop gave me that glare again.

"No, it's fine. I just turned thirty-six," she said.

That could work, so I decided to offer, "Pop's forty-two.

He'll be forty-three in a month."

"You don't say? You look so much younger."

Miss Bagley turned, and Pop gave me the warning eye again.

She headed for a door that must have been freshly polished. A lemon scent hung in the air. "Shall we get your library cards?" she asked. "Then I'll give you a tour. We just received a new reference book this morning. It contains photographs of the world's most beautiful libraries. You simply must see it."

"That will be fantastic," Pop said, and then mouthed to me behind Miss Bagley's back, "Behave."

"Dude, you're in trouble," Nick whispered to me.

"Shut up," I hiss-whispered back. "Why were you smirking, anyway?"

"Did you see them? Your pop likes librarians."

I wrinkled my nose at him. I didn't want to think about Pop and his possible fantasies. "Please stop. Besides, she's not a real librarian. You do know that, right?"

He laughed. "Well, your pop forgot."

I elbowed him. "I will cut you."

"You could try."

Pop scowled at us over his shoulder.

I couldn't shake my bad mood. It had started that morning and just kept growing. And Nick's teasing wasn't helping.

At her desk, Kayla issued us library cards, then took us on a tour of the library.

She guided us to a room off the rotunda, with book stacks and a staircase leading to a balcony. "This is the reference room where I put the gateway book." She pulled a familiar-looking leather-bound book from a case behind the stairs. "I'll keep track of it, so it will be here whenever you need it." She slipped it back into place. "There's a quiet study area in the mezzanine. Follow me."

She went up a staircase with Pop right behind her. Witnessing Pop check her out was more than uncomfortable. I glanced at Nick, and he was holding back a snicker.

Nick mouthed, "Nice butt."

"Really?" I hissed at him, holding onto the wood railing as I climbed.

"Hey, what can I say," he whispered through a smirk. "I'm a proponent of well-formed structures."

"Is that right?" Kayla said from above us. "I'm always impressed when kids appreciate historical landmarks and architecture."

"Oh, I appreciate it," he said.

I rolled my eyes at him and stepped onto the landing. Directly off the stairs was a long desk. It was a circular space with tables against the curved wall, facing the many windows looking outside.

"You could make your jumps here if you want," she said.

"This is a great spot," I said.

"You'll have to make sure it's vacant before jumping." She leaned toward us, lowering her voice. "The reason I summoned you today, was not only to familiarize you with the library but also to give you this." She handed me a small silver box that resembled Pop's old pager from the nineties that he kept in a junk drawer in our kitchen.

"What's it for?" I turned it over in my hand. On one side, a crystal button stuck out in the center.

"Push the crystal when you need access to the library," she said. "It will send an untraceable signal to its match, which I have. Once received, we'll meet here within fifteen minutes."

"What, no bat signals?" Nick said.

"I don't understand," she said.

"It's a spotlight. They point it at the sky to call—"

I stopped Nick with a sharp elbow in his side.

"*Stop.*" He shrugged away from me. "You're always doing that."

Miss Bagley gave him a curious look. "I don't think a spotlight is a good idea. It would draw too much attention."

Nick stifled a laugh, and Pop gave him a warning look.

"Anyway, for an emergency, hit it twice and it will flash red. Any questions?" she asked.

"Can't think of any." I glanced to Nick. "You?"

"No," he said, amusement hanging in his voice.

She went to the stairs. "Shall we continue?"

"Lead the way," Pop said in that swoony tone that was sure to make the movie popcorn I consumed earlier come up and be the feature presentation on the library floor.

"We'll stop by my office on the way out," she said, stepping off the last stair. "I'll give you a brochure with the times of operation. Also, I'll write down my cell number for non-emergencies."

Pop stalked after her like a lost puppy. He hadn't dated much. I think he worried about disrupting my life or something heroic like that. Maybe Miss Bagley would be a good thing for him. I wasn't going to be around him forever, especially if I made it into New York University. It was time for Pop to find someone special.

"You okay?" Nick asked.

I gave him a sideways look. "You weren't helping."

"Come on," he said. "It was cute. Your pop. Miss Bagley. I can see it now. A big wedding in a library."

"Why do you have to be so irritating?"

Two girls about our age walked by. They could have been younger, but with all the makeup, revealing clothes, and expensive-looking accessories, it was hard to tell.

"We should catch up to Pop and Miss Bagley," Nick said, trailing off.

"You're hopeless," I said to his back.

"I prefer the athletic type to pompous peacocks like them," Arik's voice came from the other side of a bookcase.

I gasped and reeled around. Every whisper and soft footstep in the library quieted, and all I could hear was my pulse, quick and loud in my ears. The bookcase between us blocked my view of him, except for his lopsided smile and his almost perfect teeth.

Am I dreaming?

I took a step forward and placed a nervous hand on the top of the books lining the shelf.

He grasped it.

"It *is* you," I said.

CHAPTER TWO

I darted around the bookcase. "Pompous peacocks are males," I said, a little breathless, but not from exertion. Arik leaned casually against the wall, his arms crossed, with a mischievous grin pulling across his beautiful face. His brown hair was longer than he normally wore it. A loose strand hung over one of his heavy brows.

It was strange to think of Arik as my boyfriend. I thought I'd lost him after he was seriously injured jumping into a library to stop Conemar from hurting Afton. He'd landed head first on the marble floor. He'd been unconscious for a week, and I worried he would die. But he'd pulled out of it, and we've been together ever since.

"Details," he said, his dark eyes watching me intently.

"Well, if you're going to insult someone," I whispered, "you should get it right." I took a few uncertain steps forward. I wanted to throw myself at him, but I kept calm. "Females are peahens and not colorful at all. They're more like me."

"Then I shall be quite happy with my peahen." He met my steps. We were so close I could smell him—woodsy and freshly showered. He pulled me to him, and I tilted my face up to meet his lips. I'd missed their softness. My fingertips glided across his chest and he shivered. Before I knew it, he had backed me up against a shelf and the case rocked, the wooden edge digging into my lower back, reminding me we were in the library. And Pop and Nick were just down the hall with Miss Bagley. I pushed him away.

"What are you doing here?" I glanced at the entrance to make sure no one was around.

Amusement lit his eyes. "I like how you respond to my kisses."

My cheeks warmed. "You didn't answer the question."

"I just arrived a few hours ago, and thought I'd pop over and see you." He tugged me back into his arms and kissed my neck. "We're not officially to *meet* until my first day of school, and Monday morning seems like an eternity away."

"How'd you know we were here?"

"Your cell phone has a tracking device. Carrig knows both your and Deidre's whereabouts at all times."

I wondered if Carrig was doing that because he was the leader of the Sentinels or because he was trying to be a good father. The thing was, I had a father. Maybe Pop wasn't biological like Carrig, but that didn't matter to me. Pop was the only father I'd known. And honestly, Carrig was growing on me, but I just didn't want him stepping on Pop's territory.

"Wonderful," I said. "I already feel like a prisoner here. Now they're monitoring me?"

"It's only for your protection."

I darted another glance behind me. "I'd better catch up to the others." Though I hated that we had to pretend we didn't know each other, I understood the reason. It might raise suspicion with the people in town that my and Nick's families, not to mention the Sentinels at the Academy, knew one another before coming to Branford. There was no telling which residents could be Mystiks masking their forms with glamour or concealing their magical abilities while living among the humans. We couldn't risk it. Any one of them could have ties to Conemar.

"I will agonize until then," he said and gave me a quick kiss. "I'll wait here until all's clear."

"I'll see you Monday." I walked off with a spring in my step, peeking over my shoulder several times to catch a few final glimpses of Arik. I blew him an air kiss. An *air* kiss. I wanted to kick myself, but then Arik caught the invisible token and touched his fingers to his lips. I chuckled and ducked around the corner.

"What's up with you?" Nick asked, eyeing me suspiciously. "You're never this happy unless—"

"Nothing." I gave him a warning look as I yanked open the door leading outside. "I just *love* libraries."

"Thank you again, Miss Bagley," Pop said, holding the door open, his awkward smile back.

Her lips slowly pulled into a smile as she held Pop's stare. "Uh-uh, it's Kayla, remember?"

Pop rubbed his forehead. It was a sure sign he was nervous. "How could I forget? Listen, I'd love to take you for coffee sometime."

"It's a date." She'd said it like slow-moving molasses— sweet and drawn out.

Deciding I was over watching Pop swoon all over Kayla, I bounded down the steps.

"Hey, slow down," Nick called after me.

I stopped beside his motorcycle.

"So you can hitch a ride with your pop, right?" He swung a leg over the seat. "Cause while you were *chilling* in the book stacks, Deidre sent me a text asking me to meet her and Emily for dinner."

"Happy to." And it was the truth, because I'd ride a Billy Goat before getting on his bike again. "Catch you tomorrow."

He raised a leather-gloved hand and sped off, smoke spurting out his muffler.

The entire ride home, Pop gushed about how amazing Miss Bagley was while I stared out the window. When he stopped the Volvo in the driveway, I scrambled out and half jogged to the door. The scent of something odd coming from the kitchen almost knocked me over.

"What's that smell?" Pop asked, closing the front door.

"Faith must be cooking again." We had a new mission in life: one of us tried to get to the kitchen before Faith had a chance to. Being a Laniar, she was used to only eating raw meat. After discovering human cuisine, she gained a passion for cooking...and a few extra pounds.

Though assigned to protect our home, Faith was more of a friend than a guard, and we hung out a lot. Or at least, we did when one of us wasn't sleeping. It sucked that Laniars slept during the day. It only gave us a few hours together at night before I went to bed. With her odd appearance—a Mystik creature that looked like a human-greyhound cross with long limbs and a wide chest—she had to hide from our new neighbors. Which meant we spent most of our time in the attic we'd converted into a living space for her.

I peered around the doorframe of the kitchen. Steam rose from a pot on the stove and something sizzled in a frying pan.

"What are you cooking?" I asked, not wanting to enter.

Pop squeezed past me. "Smells...interesting."

"Oh wonderful, you're home." She flipped something in the pan. "Peanut butter fish with lemon noodles."

My stomach churned. "Um, remember? I don't like fish?"

"Drat. I forgot." She stared at the fish sizzling in the pan. "I've made too much. Where're Deidre and Nick? They'll eat some."

"They went out to dinner."

Pop was reading a text with a wide smile on his face.

"You never get texts," I said, finally entering the kitchen of doom. "Actually, I didn't even know you knew how. Who sent it?"

"Kayla. She can make coffee tomorrow."

Faith sighed. "I just hate wasting food."

"Don't worry, Faith. Pop loves fish. He'll eat my serving."

He shot me a what-are-you-saying look.

I grinned widely at him and sat down at one of the place settings at the table. If Faith couldn't cook, she could definitely set a fancy table. She placed a plate in front of me with the lemon pasta and a burnt roll. Pop's plate had two grayish-looking fish, their heads attached and their eyes murky and dead, with melted peanut butter oozing out of their chest cavities.

"Bon appétit," Faith chirped, and walked off to get herself a plate.

I stabbed some pasta with my fork. "Hey, maybe your new girlfriend can hook Faith up with some cookbooks?" I shoved a forkful of pasta into my mouth and crunched on it. Faith's version of *al dente* was on the brittle side.

"Funny." Pop removed some bones from his fish.

Faith plopped down in a chair across from me and took a big bite of fish. Her eyes widened.

I laughed at her expression. "Takeout?"

She nodded exaggeratedly, spitting her mouthful onto her plate. Obviously, she was in need of a Miss Manners class.

The front door flew open and banged shut. Deidre pounded up the stairs and slammed the door to our bedroom.

The three of us just sat there, waiting for the other ones to make a move.

Pop looked at me. "Maybe you should go check on her?"

"Uh-uh, not me. She hates me."

"And she definitely doesn't like me," Faith added before Pop could ask her.

Pop scooted his chair out. "It's because you alienate her. You could include her once in a while, you know?" He plodded off upstairs after her.

Faith and I stared at each other, stunned.

"He's got it all wrong," I said. "How many times have we invited her to do things?"

Faith raised her eyes to the ceiling, thinking.

"That was a rhetorical question. You don't have to *actually* figure out a number."

"Oh, then, it's too many times to count," she said. "So what shall we order for dinner? Chinese?"

"Definitely."

The doorbell rang, and when I opened the door, I was surprised to find Mrs. D'Marco standing there wringing her hands. Worry hung on her face and she had dark circles under her golden brown eyes. I hadn't really seen her much since finding out she and Mr. D'Marco had adopted Nick. They'd even hidden it from their son, and Nick wasn't handling the news too well.

"Is Nick here?" she asked, worry lacing her words.

"No." I opened the door wider. "Please, come in."

She took a few steps forward but didn't come fully inside.

"What's wrong?" I pressed.

Her eyes darted around the entry and up the stairs. "He came home angry. He punched the wall. His father yelled at him, and he took off on that…that bike."

I grasped her shaking hands. "It'll be all right. He's just going through a lot."

"I know. I just worry he'll hurt himself." She sniffled. "Maybe Deidre knows something? Is she here?"

"I'm here," Deidre said from top of the stairs. "We fought. All I said was that he resembled his biological father. He blew up in front of Emily. We didn't even make it into the restaurant. It was so humiliating."

What the hell? Of course Nick wouldn't want to look like Conemar. The man was evil. He had killed Nick's birth mother. Nick hated him. Deidre lacked a sensitivity chip. I was about to tell her just that, but her eyes were puffy and red, so I decided against it. "Do you know where he went?" I asked instead.

"When he gets like this, he goes to Stony Creek Beach." Deidre looked directly at Mrs. D'Marco. "I'm so sorry."

"It's all right, dear," Mrs. D'Marco said. "He just needs time to adjust to everything."

"So who knows how to get to this beach?" I asked.

"I'll drive you," Emily's voice came from the porch.

I spun around. "Where did you come from?"

"My car. I was worried about Deidre. She left her sweater behind." She held up Deidre's loose-knit black sweater that couldn't possibly offer any kind of warmth.

"Okay, but I've seen how fast you drive down our street. Could you *not* kill us, please?"

"I don't drive fast," she said.

She totally did. When we first moved here, we drove up with the moving van, and she sped by us as if she were on a racetrack.

"Don't listen to her, Emily," Deidre called down. "If you don't drive five under the speed limit, she gets nervous."

"It's better to be safe than sorry. Come on, Emily." I headed down the sidewalk for her car. "Mrs. D'Marco, we'll get him home soon."

"Thank you, and thanks, Deidre." Mrs. D'Marco followed us down the sidewalk to her car.

Emily guided her white Civic down our street a lot slower than she normally drove. "Nick and Deidre are pretty hot for each other."

"Yeah...I suppose so."

She raised an eyebrow, easing the car around a corner. "I've never experienced that kind of passion before." Oncoming headlights lit up her teal-colored eyes. "Who's the lady living with you guys?"

"My aunt."

"How come she never comes out?"

"She has a skin condition. It's rare."

"What's it called?"

What is up with all the questions?

"It's Xeroderma Pigmentosum." I stumbled on the pronunciation.

"Oh, that does sound bad." Another car passed, illuminating the inside of the car. "Your family seems close. I can sort of see you having dinner from our kitchen window." Her head snapped in my direction. "It's not what you think. I'm not a stalker, I swear. I can't really see you all that well. Your house is too far away."

I grasped the grip handle above the door. "Eyes on the road."

I sound like Nana. Ever since my mom died while saving me from traffic when I was four, driving and crossing busy streets scared the crap out of me.

She smiled and returned her attention to her driving. "Anyway, you all have fun. Meals at my home are too quiet and boring. My uncle doesn't talk much or play board games like your family does."

"It must be lonely," I said. "You're welcome to come over and play sometime." I wanted to bite my tongue off. If she came over, Faith would have to hide out in her room.

"Thank you," she said. "I'd like that." The bright smile on her face made me glad I'd invited her.

The ocean came into view, and Emily turned onto the road that ran parallel to the water. Directly in front of us, a lightning bolt shot up to the sky. Thankfully, Emily was too busy driving to notice the strike's starting point.

I spotted Nick's bike parked in the grassy area near the beach.

"Pull over here," I said.

"You see him?" Her tires rolled up to the curb as she parked.

"No, not him," I said, opening the door. "But there's his bike. You don't have to wait. Nick can drive me home. Thanks for the ride." I got out and shut the door.

The passenger's side window went down. "Are you sure? It looks like a storm is coming," she said. "I can wait."

"No, thanks, we'll be fine. See you at school."

She shifted the gear stick into drive. "Wonderful, I'd like that. We can hang out at lunch. What time is yours?"

"Eleven-thirty..." I trailed off, my eyes searching for Nick. Another flash of light hit the sky.

"Mine, too," she trilled. "I'll see you then."

It might be good to make new friends. "Sounds great," I said. "See you later."

She did a U-turn and drove off. I sprinted to the area where I spotted the lightning. A shadowed figure sat on a white bench near the water. Another flash of light kissed the sky and illuminated Nick.

Since discovering he was a wizard, Nick struggled with his new magic. And he was careless. Anyone could spot him out here. How would he explain it to someone who was human and not from the Mystik realm? I couldn't imagine how it felt to have that much power. Unlike him, I was a Sentinel.

I had little magic and relied on my battle training to best wizards and other-world creatures. He only needed to shock or electrocute his adversaries.

"What exactly are you doing?" I asked, approaching.

He almost fell off the bench. "*Shit*, Gia. Don't sneak up on a person like that."

"Seriously, Nick? What are you doing? Someone might see you, and then we'd be discovered."

"Just leave me alone."

"I'm not going to *just leave you alone*." I sat down on the bench beside him. A light breeze swept loose strands of my hair across my face. The briny smell of the ocean filled my nose. "Talk to me. You're my best friend, Nick. I'm here for you."

He formed an electric charge on his palm. I created my pink globe and tossed it on his hand, snuffing out the charge.

He made another electric ball and I cast another globe at it.

"Quit doing that."

"You stop it."

"I get it. Your globe is badass. It can counter magic and shield people, but it makes you weak. I can do this all night and wear you out."

"You're not nice."

He buried his face in his hands. The knuckles on his right one were torn, with blood coagulating around the wounds. "I don't know what's happening to me. I can't stop myself. I know I'm being mean to Deidre, to my parents...to everyone."

"You haven't been that mean to me, yet. That has to say something. I'm the most annoying one of the bunch."

He snorted.

"Did you just snort?"

"No." He looked startled. "It was a sneeze."

"I think you snorted."

His face brightened. "I know what you're trying to do. And it's working."

"I'm not trying to do anything. That was a full-on snort." I wrapped my arm over his back and watched the water lap against the retaining wall in front of us. "I know you can't see a therapist for this, 'cause what would you say? That you just found out you're the son of the most evil wizard of the Mystik world and the curers recently released your magic?"

He gave me a half smile. "Yeah, that might not go over too well."

"Or maybe you could. They'd think you were delusional, and you'd score some drugs."

"Drugs make me nauseous."

"Listen," I said. "I was a mess after getting sucked into the gateway book and thrown into the Mystik world. Everything was happening so fast. I was scared and confused. I made so many mistakes. Hell, I was freaked out. I was facing a shit-ton of life-threatening situations. That's a lot for a teenager to handle. But now, with all the training and with Carrig's help, I'm stronger. Both in mind and body. I was born to be this. I just needed the mindset, you know?"

He stared at his hands, and I stared at the water, searching for the right words to say. "This has to be tough for you. I get it. I've been there. It'll take time to adjust. How about I be your counselor? Anytime you feel anxious or angry, you call me and we'll punch some bags or whatever. It always helps me to relax. Plus, my services are cheap."

"Violence would make *you* relax." He was pleased with his retort and laughed, which was followed by another snort.

I chuckled, removing my arm.

"That wasn't a snort… Never mind." He pulled his fingers through his hair. "What is wrong with me? I don't mean what I say, or want to punch things. It's like an out-of-body experience. I see myself doing terrible things, and I can't stop it. I'm not me anymore."

"You're still you, just a little more powerful. It might be the wizard power that's making you snap. You're not used to it." A thought came to me. "How about I ask Uncle Philip if he knows how you can control it?"

He straightened and stared at the water. "Do you think Professor Attwood would?"

"He told you to call him Uncle Philip," I said.

"I keep forgetting."

Nick and my long-lost uncle had become fast friends. Uncle Philip had been in love with Nick's birth mother, Jacalyn, before Conemar killed her. The two spent many hours together as Uncle Philip shared stories, letters, and pictures of her with Nick. I was certain my wizard uncle would want to mentor Nick.

"It won't hurt to ask him for help," I said.

"Okay, let's try."

"Good." I bumped his shoulder with mine. "I think you have some apologies to make."

"What? Are you my mother now?"

"No. I'm your conscience." I snorted then, and we both laughed so hard we almost fell off the bench.

CHAPTER THREE

The McCabe Boarding Home for Foreign Exchange Students was an old converted condominium building. Worried that authorities would watch the Sentinels too closely, Carrig had convinced the Wizard Council to change their original plan from a home for wayward teens to a boarding house. Several Sentinels from around the world had joined the school.

The inside of the McCabe Fencing Club in the building next door resembled an abandoned warehouse. Concrete columns wrapped in bright blue padding supported the high ceiling. Mats covered the entire floor, and kicking bags hung from hooks embedded in the ceiling.

For the past few weeks, the practice drills were grueling. Arik matched me blow for blow, our dummy swords smacking at each contact. With some effort, I dodged a high swing. Carrig called us to break, and I relaxed, trying to ease my breaths.

Arik cut a glance at me. "Gia, you can't beat me."

"Oh, really? Be ready to get schooled, little boy."

"Hmm…" He grinned, his gaze sweeping over my body. "Will you be wearing a school girl costume while you *school* me? I can imagine it now…"

"Stop being an arse, Arik," Carrig, aka my biological dad and the head leader of all the Sentinels, grunted. "She be taking it easy on you. Now, go again."

Arik got into a fighting stance.

I kept my eyes on Arik's shoulders, waiting for a hint as to what his next attack would be.

A loud bang came from the right of us and my gaze flew in the direction of the noise. Jaran had backed into a weight stand and knocked it over.

Kale and Lei fought on the mat beside us. He'd move forward, and she'd move back. She swung her leg at him, and he ducked. Her long black braid whipped around as she got back into her stance. Their personalities were complete opposites. She was fierce and aggressive, and he was calm and calculating.

Next to Arik, they were the top fighters out of both the past and present Sentinels from our wizard haven of Asile. They'd even won awards at the Mystik Trials. The Mystik world had seven wizard havens, along with creatures from many of the outlying covens, compete in the games. It was much like the human world's Olympics.

Kale dodged Lei's next attack, diving and smacking onto the mat in a forward roll. He was back on his feet fast, but his stance was too wide. She dropped into a squat and swept her outstretched leg against his shins. His legs buckled, and he collapsed to the floor.

Arik caught me off guard as I laughed at the shocked expression on Kale's face. His padded wooden sword landed on my shoulder. I yelped and fell spread eagle onto the mat.

"Bloody hell. Why didn't you block me?" Arik looked at

me with concern in his eyes.

A few of the foreign Sentinels fighting nearby snickered.

I glared at them.

"Didn't you hear the command from Carrig?" Arik reached his hand out to me.

"No...maybe." I huffed, grabbing his hand. "Didn't you notice I was distracted?"

"How would I notice? You were facing me and seemed ready for my attack. You can't be distracted in a battle."

"We're done here," Carrig shouted over exerted grunts and the *clunks* of wooden swords banging together.

Arik yanked me to my feet, with a smile playing on his sexy lips. "I thought you were going to school me."

"Shut up," I said, pushing him aside playfully and staggering over to the others.

"Grab your bathing suits," Lei said, burying her fake sword into the equipment barrel. "We have an hour to soak our muscles before globe practice."

Sinead, Carrig's wife from the fey nation, had a large pool installed in the backyard of the gym. A wooden deck surrounded it, and on one side were jets to massage our sore muscles.

After I changed into my bikini and pulled on my cover-up, I met Arik at the path that led down the hill to the pool.

"Where are the others?" I hugged two towels, the fall air chilly on my exposed skin.

"I sent them ahead so I could show you something. Come on."

"Where are we going?"

"You'll see."

He took me along a path cutting between tangled trees, my flip-flops crunching over fallen leaves.

"*So*," I said. "My nana sent me tickets to a play in New

York City. I asked Uncle Philip, and he said we could go."

He pushed some twigs out of my way. "I'm not one for stage performances."

"Really?" We didn't know that much about each other. We hadn't been together that long and when we were, we were either practicing or making out. "What do you like to do, then?"

"Play games on Jaran's iPad. Watch pro wrestling with Demos." He ducked under a low-hanging branch, a smile pushing at the corners of his lips. "Romance you."

I wasn't sure if the warmth in my cheeks was because of what he said or from our recent workout.

"The play is an adaption of a novel," I said. "*To Kill a Mockingbird*. Have you read it?"

"I don't read many books."

Wait. Did I hear that right?

"But you've read *The Secret Garden*." I couldn't hide the surprise in my voice. I hadn't realized he didn't read much. Books were like oxygen to me. Without them, I couldn't breathe.

"When Oren died," he said, "the book was among the few items he'd owned. He had read it excessively to me as a boy. To the point of madness, and that is why I had whole passages memorized."

Oren's book? His parent faery. He'd been murdered by a hound. Arik was thirteen and had witnessed the attack. The ground dipped and I focused on my steps. My heart sank in my chest. Though I was disappointed that Arik didn't want to attend the play in New York with me, I was even sadder to find the thing that had bonded us together when we first met wasn't real.

"Why the frown?" he asked.

"I just thought you liked the book as much as I do." It was

strange how I'd never realized how different we were.

"I see," he said. "I do feel as though the libraries are my own secret garden, if that makes you feel any better. And I didn't entirely dislike the story. You must know I was a young boy. I wanted to read about knights and dragons, not about a little girl and her friends."

He had a point.

"Are we better?" He sounded worried.

"Yes, of course," I said.

The path ended at a small cemetery. A broken picket fence surrounded the tiny clearing. Moss covered the chipped stone grave markers. I could barely read the names etched on them: Parker, Jacobs, Howe, and Procter—my eyes stopped on the name. Emily's last name was Procter. I wondered if it was one of her relatives.

"What is this place? A secret burial ground?" I crept around the headstones. "They're old. This one is from 1662."

The moss-covered trees shaded the area covering the grave with an earthy coldness.

Arik went the other way. "This one is legible."

I stopped in front of the one with the fading Procter name etched on it. "This place is sort of creepy." It felt like chilly fingers ran up my spine.

Arik stood behind me, slid his arm around my waist, and rested his open palm on my belly. My stomach fluttered under his hand. He moved my hair away from my shoulders with his free hand and kissed my neck. I shivered.

"You're cold," he whispered, his lips moving against my skin. It was a statement, not a question, but his body was questioning. As if he was asking to continue. There was no way I would make out with him in the middle of a graveyard.

"Let's go." I stepped away from him.

"I thought you would like this place. Somewhat ancient,

isn't it? Sort of like that burial ground outside the library in Boston you enjoy."

I turned to face him. "Normally, I would love something like this, but this place feels wrong." I glanced at the light shifting between the branches of the trees. Something glinted in the leaves at the foot of a tree. I picked it up and examined it.

"It's an arrowhead." I passed it to Arik.

"A modern one," he said, turning it around in his hand. "There isn't any rust."

I inspected the tree and touched the many cuts in the bark. "Someone's been using this tree for target practice."

"A hunter or an archer must have practiced here recently," he added.

"Must be." We were in a part of the woods open to the public. Anyone could come out here and do whatever they wanted.

"Come on," he said, taking my hand. "We should join the others."

I followed him down the hill to the pool and shrugged off my cover-up. The warm water lapped against my chin as I sank down onto a seat in the pool. Arik sat beside me and gave me a devilish grin. "Come here, you."

I slid closer. It felt good to be with him, lost in our own world, away from the others splashing around on the other side of the pool.

Arik drew me onto his lap and kissed me, my disappointment about him not wanting to go to the play disappearing. I wrapped my arms around his neck, and our kisses got hungrier. He slipped his hands down my back, and goose bumps erupted across my skin even though the water was warm, nearly hot.

Something exploded in the pool beside us and water smacked hard against my back. Demos popped up from the depths, grinning. He shook the water from his drenched blond hair. Out of all the Sentinels from Asile, Demos goofed off the most.

"Did you see how high that splash went? Blinding show, wasn't it?" He swam to the side of the pool and climbed out.

I glanced at the group across the pool, and Lei smirked at me. I moved away from Arik, bending my knees and pushing my feet against his chest, and shot off like a missile in the water. Bobbing a few feet from him, I admired his wet skin glistening in the light. I wanted to soar back to him but knew I wouldn't be able to control myself, and we had an audience.

"Now who's the tease?" He grinned and shot after me, catching my foot before I could swim away. He towed me back to him, wrapping his arms around me. "I want to stay here forever with you." He placed his lips on mine and spun me around in the water, his tongue searching mine. When his hands started roaming, I pushed away again.

I sank down into the water to keep warm, the scent of chlorine filling my nose, the wake from our movements slapping my cheeks. "You're dangerous," I said, with my lips just above the water.

"I'm dangerous?" He waded toward me. "You are. I'm just an innocent male, helpless to your charms."

"Don't come any closer," I warned, but so wanted him to.

He inched closer. "Come back here, and let me show you just what you do to me."

I squealed as he chased me. I pushed through the water to the other side of the pool, with him close behind, reaching the others first. Lei and Kale were huddled together in a high-bubbling area, and Jaran floated in front of them as the three talked.

Demos cannonballed into the water again, drenching everyone. The Sentinels sitting on the edge of the pool soaking their feet, cussed at him in different languages and accents.

"That was weak," Pia, one of the twins from the Santara haven in Spain, teased.

Her twin, Reya, nodded. "You weigh as much as a twig, Pia, and you could do better than him."

Demos laughed as he splashed to the steps. "I'd like to see you try."

I leaned back and floated, the water flooding my ears and muffling the others' conversations. It was times like this when I thought about Afton, Nana, and Uncle Philip. What were they doing at this very moment?

It was also during these quiet times that Bastien would enter my mind. I'd heard he was completing his final magic tests. What did a novice have to do to graduate to senior wizard? And was he okay? His deep blue eyes and confident smile played across my mind.

He definitely had a rock-star appeal, as Lei had claimed the first time I met him. It was also then that I discovered we were betrothed to each other before I was born. The Wizard Council had put into law the betrothal system to prevent the birth of a child with two Sentinel parents that would bring the coming of the end. I was that child.

The end of what? People believed both the human and Mystik worlds, but not my Uncle Philip. He thought it meant the end to an evil that had been simmering under the surface of our worlds for centuries—the Tetrad. An apocalyptic monster that could control the elements and bring about biblical-level destruction. Conemar wanted to control the monster. But we had stopped him.

I hadn't seen Bastien since we'd fought Conemar together and sent him to another realm—and not since Bastien had declared his feelings for me. I had hoped we could be friends.

But mostly, I worried I wouldn't see him again, and that scared me. I closed my eyes tight and made the thought go away.

The sun played on my eyelashes, reminding me of the light blinking through the trees that surrounded the graveyard. The headstone with *Proctor* on it haunted me. Was it for someone in Emily's family? Why was the cemetery so far from the city?

Arik glided up to my side of the pool and said something.

I popped my head up. "Huh?"

"Are you ready for the next practice?"

I straightened, my feet hitting the pool floor. "Is it time already?"

"I'm afraid so."

After we changed back into our gear, we met Carrig and Sinead on the secluded field past the pool for battle globe practice.

Sinead taught us to retract our minds back into our subconscious selves and feel our globes from where they originated within our inner beings. She said it would help us control them better. It took several days for all the Sentinels to grasp this exercise.

I threw my pink globe so far I couldn't see where it landed. No one else in the group even came close to that distance. Sinead took me aside to help me learn accuracy in my throws. Before long, I was lobbing my globes, wherever my eyes focused. During practices, we discovered the bigger the globe I made, the more energy it sucked from me, so I created small spheres in my palm and threw them. Once they connected to an object, they exploded and covered it in a pink membrane, protecting or immobilizing its victim.

Only one other person had had the same type of globe as I did, a boy who lived many centuries ago. He died before his thirteenth birthday from the plague. It was a protection globe, but apparently, it didn't protect its owner from human diseases.

Arik threw his fire globe. It landed against a tree trunk across the field and flames licked up the trunk. Jaran tossed his water globe and put the fire out; blue steam hissed from the bark. Demos ran out and lobbed his green wind globe. The blast of air hit the tree and knocked it over.

"Hey, guys, be nice to the trees!" I yelled at them.

Arik lobbed another globe at the tree. "Not to worry. It's a fake."

Lei raised her palm and shot lightning from her white globe, and Kale stunned the flash in mid-air with his, turning the bolt purple.

"All right, Gia, your turn." Carrig stood behind me and watched me throw a few globes.

"Has your truth globe returned?" he asked from behind me.

I glanced at my hand. Each Sentinel had a magical globe they used in battle. But because both my parents had the Sentinel gene, I could conjure two—one that could test if someone was truthful and another that removed spells and protected whoever was inside its bubble. And now one was gone.

My truth globe. With a drop of someone's blood on its silvery sphere, it could tell me if that person was untruthful. I'd lost it when Lorelle, a faery on Conemar's side, had cast an ancient spell on me.

"No." I lobbed a pink globe over Kale's head.

Kale spun around. "Hey, I said to stop that. You might miss or something."

I shrugged. "It's not like my globe kills people. It just undoes charms and shields things."

"And disables my globe," he added.

"It comes back after a few minutes." I threw a curve globe around him.

"Jaysus," Carrig said. "Grand throw."

Lei shot another bolt from her globe. It zapped across the field and landed just before the line of trees, illuminating a large figure in the shadows.

"Who's that?" I said, squinting.

Carrig and Arik sprinted across the field toward the figure. Whoever it was tore off into the woods. My muscles tightened and I couldn't move. Was it a spy? One of Conemar's creatures? I shook off my fear and dashed after Arik, my heart beating fast in my chest. Branches and twigs snapped in the distance. My boots slipped down the hills. Lei came up from behind and passed me, easily descending the hill.

I slid several times going down, bracing my hand against the ground, my fingers sinking into the cold dark soil. Carrig and Arik reached the street first, with Lei and then me after them. We searched both directions, but no one was there.

"Could it have been an animal?" Lei scanned the trees. "Or a trick of the light?"

"It be difficult to tell with the shadows," Carrig said, combing his fingers through his hair as he searched the trees. "It might've been an animal. No one could get through the charms around this place."

"A powerful wizard could," Arik said. "If we've been found, we should flee."

"Maybe we should contact Asile," Lei said.

Feet crunching on the gravel sounded behind us, and we all turned. Demos and Kale dragged a man dressed in all black who looked like he'd been stunned. Most likely from Kale's globe.

"Here's your culprit," Demos said, with a smug expression on his face.

Carrig removed a leather rope from his belt and unraveled it. "Remove the stun," he said.

After Kale tossed a purple globe on the man to release him, Carrig whipped the rope at him. The leather sparked to life and wrapped around the man's arms. He fought against its grips, the charge crackling with each of his struggles.

"What is that?" I asked.

"It's a spelled whip," Lei said. "The energy's charge can be quite painful when tightened."

The man's thick shoulders and large body looked like it could wrestle a bull and win. He glared at me with white-marbled eyes. I recognized him. He was the hunter who chased us through the *T* after we accidently jumped through the gateway book that first time.

"You're that hunter," I said.

The man growled at me. He actually bared his rotting teeth and *growled*.

Arik gave me a baffled look and shot his eyes at the man. "Hold on there, it is him. I thought he was Conemar's hunter." He got down in the man's face. "Who sent you?"

"What hunter?" Lei looked from me to Arik.

"The one who chased us in the Boston subway," Arik said, "just after Gia and the others accidentally jumped through the gateway to Paris."

The man's vacant eyes landed on me, holding my gaze. I couldn't move or breathe, and everything around me blurred. A vision overtook me. The version of me in the image was cold and broken, lying face down on a ground covered in ice and snow. *Am I dead?* I wanted to scream but all that came out was a choking sound.

"Don't look in his eyes!" Arik dragged me away from the man and blocked my view with his body. "He's compelled."

The vision vanished and my head stopped throbbing.

Carrig tightened the slack on the electric rope, and the man shook under its power. "Hurts, doesn't it? I can be nice and keep it slack, but you need to behave yourself. I'm sure you can understand me, right?"

"What was that?" I felt like I was trying to balance on the floor of a turbulent plane. My knees buckled before Arik tightened his arms around me, keeping me upright.

"The wizard compelling him was working your mind." He held me close to his chest. "To weaken you."

"This is a very unfortunate development," Kale said.

"I'd say." Demos paced in front of the man, staring him down. "We won't get any information from him."

Arik glanced down at me. "How are you feeling?" he whispered.

"Better." The shakes had stopped, but my head still ached.

Carrig's eyes followed Demos's frantic pacing. "Will you stop that, already? You make a man dizzy with all your back-and-forthing."

Demos stopped and gave him a smirk, then started pushing rocks around with the toe of his boot. Asking Demos to stop moving was like asking a bee to stop buzzing. Wasn't going to happen.

"There be a way to get something out of him," Carrig continued.

Arik looked over at him. "By what means?"

"The Scryers can read his mind. See what the wizard had learned from the compulsion." Carrig shuffled the man over to Kale and handed him the end of the whip. "Take him to Asile."

"Certainly," he said. "I'm happy to dispose of trash." The man grunted when Kale tightened the cord again.

"What will Asile do with him?" I asked.

"After they get what they need from his mind, they'll send

him to a Somnium prison," Kale said, and tugged the rope for the man to follow him. "Shall we be on our way?"

Demos trotted after them. "I'm coming. You don't get to have all the fun, Kale."

"I'll inform the others so they're not chasing ghosts." Lei climbed back up the hill and ducked under branches on her way.

"What are we going to do?" I withdrew from Arik, swaying slightly as I stood on my own.

Carrig started up the hill. "We heighten security until Kale and Demos return with the report from the Scryers. We must see what be learned from the hunter's mind. Be prepared to move fast if need be." He pushed a branch aside.

Arik took my arm and guided me. "Can you manage it?"

"I think so." I stepped over a log. Every movement made me feel like my head would pop off and roll down the hill. If this was how Arik had felt when attacked by a compelled hunter, no wonder he'd been moody after his encounter. One of them had cornered him on the day I left my home for Asile and a new life. A life full of magic, danger, and Arik.

On my first encounter with the hunter, he had been fierce on the platform to catch the *T*, easily tossing people out of his way and almost toppling the train to get to Afton and Nick inside. The massive man had left destruction in his wake. And he was here.

How did he find us so fast?

My boot sank into a muddy puddle. The mud slurped as I tugged my foot out. I pushed a branch out of my way. "Won't the wizard controlling him know where we are?"

"There be a delay in transmitting information," Carrig said. "We can only hope my lasso broke the connection before the controlling wizard received our location. The Scryers can determine if it had."

"That hunter was previously in Conemar's control," Arik said. "Whoever has hold of the man's mind now must be searching for Conemar's whereabouts."

"That be likely so," Carrig said. "When Professor Attwood comes tomorrow, I'll have him increase the charms around our homes and the club."

I looked over my shoulder as we headed back to the others, half expecting a hunter to jump out at us. I knew we had gone into hiding for a reason, but the reality of it hadn't settled in yet. There were possibly any number of wizards and their hunters searching for us. I no longer felt safe in this quiet ocean-side town.

CHAPTER FOUR

The council's chambers were deep within the labyrinth of corridors in Asile's castle. It resembled a courtroom, except round, with a mosaic copula overhead. Six high wizards sat at a long table elevated on a massive stone slab at the back of the room. One chair was empty, and I assumed it was for Conemar, the missing High Wizard of Esteril.

I fastened the rhinestone clasp on the black silk clutch I'd bought at a secondhand store, worrying the Wizard Council's questions would never end. I'd already given my statement, but they insisted I stay through the entire hearing in case they had any more questions for me. If the session went on much longer, I'd miss the play in New York.

Crossing and uncrossing my legs, I couldn't get comfortable on the stone bench. I'd rather be wearing jeans than the black dress I'd chosen for Broadway.

Bastien sat in the witness box beside the wizards. His steel-blue eyes flitted in my direction, and I adjusted myself on the bench, again, lowering my gaze.

A wizard, ancient-looking and bent over, spoke in a

commanding voice. "You are Bastien Renard, son of Gareth, the former High Wizard of Couve?"

"I am," Bastien answered.

"You said in a previous statement that Conemar had vanished." The man cleared his throat. "Where did he go?"

"As I have told you at the previous inquiry," Bastien said. "I have no idea where Conemar is. The ritual I used is in that ancient spell book. You have it. What does it tell you?"

Merl stood and cleared his throat. His dark hair had more silver in it than when I'd first met him. "As High Wizard of Asile," he said, "I move that we end the proceedings. We aren't learning anything new from these interviews."

A woman with dark hair and darker eyes rose from her seat on Merl's left. "I am Akua, of the Veilig haven in Africa. My husband, Enitan Uba, apologizes for his absence here today. He has been stricken by a mysterious Mystik disease. My people are sickened by it. We have uprisings within all the havens. I vote for Enitan, and therefore, I second Merl's motion. But in hearing the testimonies today, not only do I fear the further spread of disease, but also fear Conemar's followers. They come from the most undesirables in the Mystik realm. I make a motion that we close all entries into the covens."

The rest of the wizards agreed.

Bastien shot to his feet. "You can't close the covens. What about the innocents that reside there?"

"We understand your concern, Bastien Renard," the ancient-looking wizard said. "But there is no other choice to ensure our safety. Aid will be sent to the covens during this time of quarantine."

Uncle Philip stood from his seat in the stand to the right of the wizard council. "I agree with Bastien. This action can only fuel the anger rising in the Mystik world."

"We have noted it," the wizard said. "But the decision has been made. We are done here." He scooted his chair out and hobbled to the steps of the stage.

When we were excused, I waited in the corridor for Bastien.

"Hello," he said, stopping in front of me. The suit he wore fit him perfectly. "I see you couldn't resist waiting for me." He winked.

There was no way I'd admit it. "I was waiting for Uncle Philip."

His gaze passed over me. "He exited through the back door with the high wizards and other council members."

"Are you okay?" I asked.

"I will be fine." He smiled. "I understand their concerns. But they are unfounded, and Couve will fight this order."

"Well," I said, "It's nice seeing you again. We haven't seen each other since..."

"Since I declared my feelings for you."

How could I forget the words he'd said to me? I had pushed them away from my thoughts. *"I'm falling for you, Gianna,"* he had said. *"With time, I'll prove to you we belong together. Go ahead and have your fun with Arik, but it's my arms you'll end up in one day."*

My skin heated, and I hoped my blushing cheeks weren't noticeable. "No. I meant since we fought off Conemar together."

A Mystik with long arms and grayish skin bumped me, knocking my purse from my hand. It hit the floor hard and the fastener popped open, spilling the contents across the tiles.

"Watch where you're going—"

The glare in the creature's large coal eyes stopped me.

"Don't worry about him," Bastien said. "He's angry at the council's order."

"I would be, too," I said, watching the creature stomp down the hall.

Bastien and I bent down at the same time to gather my things from the floor. I snatched up my root beer–flavored Lip Smacker, keys, and pack of tissues. He picked up the two tickets to the play in New York and inspected them.

"*To Kill a Mockingbird*," he said, standing. "A great story. The play is tonight. In fact, within the hour. You should hurry. Arik must be anxiously awaiting you."

I straightened, snapping my clutch shut. "He's not into plays. I'm going alone."

"I enjoy the theater, and I'm dressed for it. Would you like some company?" He held the tickets out for me. Our fingers brushed as I grasped them, my breath hitching in my throat. Amusement lit in his eyes.

Studying the tickets in my hand, I thought about Arik. Would it bother him if I took Bastien? It was innocent. We were only friends. Besides, I trusted Arik and he should feel the same about me.

"I would love the company."

"Good," he said. "We should be on our way, then."

The corridor had mostly emptied of people and Mystiks as we rushed down it. A crowd in the tunnel leading to the Bodleian Library in Oxford, England made me worry we'd miss the play.

Bastien summoned the gateway book and thumbed through it to a photograph of the New York City Public Library. He studied the page to make sure the coast was clear. The images were like windows into the libraries. "You first," he said.

I made my jump into the page. Blackness—dark and cold—surrounded me. I enjoyed jumping through the gateway. I actually looked forward to it now. The chilly air refreshed me and the free fall was a real rush. The faint gray at the end of the portal came into view. I leaned back to slow down. The book flew off the shelf at the same time I came out of it, and I landed with almost no sound on the tiled floor. A few minutes later, Bastien shot out, and we rushed to the exit.

Barely making it to the theater in time, we found our seats just as the lights dimmed. I snuck glances of Bastien's face during the performance. I could see what Lei meant when she had said he was like a rock star. With his strong jaw and confidence, he could definitely earn himself a fan base of admirers. But there was more to him than that. He empathized with others, and I bet he would never give up the fight for the Mystiks.

When the play finished, we returned to the library and found the gateway book in the Rose Room.

Before jumping into the book, I turned to him. "Thank you for going with me. It would have been boring by myself."

"I've been to many plays," he said. "This one was done well. But my favorite is still *Anna Karenina* in London. Have you read the book?"

"No. I've wanted to but never got around to it."

He held his hand up and chanted something under his breath that I couldn't decipher. Several seconds later, a book flew to him, its pages flapping in the air. He caught the novel and handed it to me.

"Read it and we can discuss the story sometime," he said.

The green linen cover was worn, and the smell of antique pages filled my nose. "I can't take this. It's not checked out."

"Go ahead. My spell has checked it out for you. Return it when you're done." His eyes studying my face made me nervous. "What is your favorite book?"

"*The Secret Garden*, I suppose." *I suppose?* I've never felt negative about that book before, but hearing Arik say he only read it because of Oren, and not because he'd chosen to read it on his own, nagged at me.

"I haven't read that one. I'll have to give it a look sometime." He glanced at an expensive-looking watch on his wrist. "I must be off. My Sentinels are waiting for me. We are bringing provisions to a Mystik coven that has fallen on hard times."

"Yeah, I should get back, too," I said. "I have a meeting with Nick and Uncle Philip."

"You go first," he said.

I found the page to James Blackstone Memorial Library in Branford. "Thank you, again," I said and spoke the charm.

As the book tugged at me, Bastien nodded. "Entirely my pleasure."

After changing, I met Nick back at the library to search for Chiavi. Coming out of the book in The John Rylands Library in Manchester, England, I landed on a red carpet runner. Nick careened out of the pages, his arms flailing as he tried to keep his balance. He stumbled until he righted himself.

I adjusted my breastplate and smirked at him. "Well, that was graceful."

"Ha-ha." He gave me a biting look. "I hate going through that damn thing."

"If you don't struggle, it's actually fun."

"Where were you tonight?" he asked. "And why all the makeup?"

I had rushed home after leaving Bastien, quickly changed into my Sentinel gear, and forgot to wash my face. I leaned over and snapped the strap securing my dagger inside my calf-high boots. My brown leather cargo pants were still wet from Faith washing them.

On the hilt of my sword was a silver tiger head with sapphire eyes. My helmet, scabbard, and shield matched it. The helmet was shaped like a cat's head and covered half my face like a Batman mask. I carried it with me but hardly ever wore it because it was uncomfortable.

I straightened and rested my hand on my scabbard. "I went to a play. How was your date?"

"Same. Dinner. Movie. Made out." He shrugged. "Typical date."

"Do you and Deidre like the same things?"

"Of course we do," he said. "She loves riding fast on my bike. We're both into superheroes and Anime. Why do you ask?"

"I'm not sure Arik and I like the same things."

His eyebrow rose slightly. "Sure you do. You both like to fight."

I tied my hair up in a ponytail. "Yeah, fighting and making out."

"Maybe once you guys can go public at school like Deidre and me, you'll discover more things you have in common with him."

Nick and Deidre had gotten together once his family moved into their house, causing a bunch of questions about their instalove status around the neighborhood and at school. To avoid calling attention to our group, it was decided that Arik and I would wait to go public. That way it would look as though we'd just met and our relationship had grown naturally over the past few months.

"Maybe." I shrugged a shoulder and decided to direct the conversation away from my frustrating love life. "So how's your schoolwork going?"

"Nice." He gave me one of his knowing smiles. "I see what

you did there. Deflecting the subject away from you and Arik. We've been at school for a few weeks now, and you haven't asked how I was doing once. What's up with you two? It's more than not liking the same things."

"No it's not," I said. "Drop it. Let's talk about something else."

"Okay. Do you ever wonder if the security systems and cameras really go off when someone enters through a gateway book?" Nick paced. "I always expect to get rushed by guards with guns."

"I don't think they carry guns." I glanced around the ceiling. Now I was worrying.

We both spun around when suddenly, the five-bulb light fixtures on the walls burst to life, revealing the gothic-style reading room. I pulled my sword out of its sheath. The amber light illuminated an extremely high, arched ceiling with clerestory windows. Uncle Philip lowered his hands and cleared his throat. Red carpet runners flanked a row in the center containing tables, statues, and display cases. He headed down one of the carpets to us, passing large reading alcoves bordering the room. The galleries above the alcoves spanned the entire length on both sides.

Uncle Philip wore a leather jacket and jeans. His reddish-brown hair looked like he'd just woken up. "Are you quite finished quarreling? I don't have all evening. I do like to sleep on occasion."

I laughed and put my sword away before throwing my arms around him. "I missed you so much!"

"And I've missed you, as well." He squeezed me before pulling away to let Nick give him one of those one-armed guy hugs.

"Good to see you, man," Nick said, clapping his back.

Uncle Philip took a step back, his eyebrows pinched

together as he studied Nick. "How are you managing your emotions? Have our exercises helped level them?"

"Well, I don't know about the exercises," Nick said, and pulled something out of the front pocket of his jeans. He unfurled his fingers to reveal a clear, egg-shaped crystal resting on his palm. "But this mood crystal you gave me is awesome."

I leaned over to get a better look at it. "What does it do?"

"When I hold it, a color appears to show my current mood."

"Like a mood ring?"

"Yeah, just like that." Nick flattened out his hand, stretching out his fingers. The crystal slowly turned a rusty yellow color. He raised his hand for me to get a better look. The light sparking between his fingers lit up his brown eyes.

"What's that mean?" I asked.

"He's nervous," Uncle Philip said. "It's probably from jumping through the gateway."

"Now watch this." Nick closed his fingers around the crystal and closed his eyes. The light escaping his fingers turned colorless before disappearing. He opened his hand. "See? All better." The crystal was clear.

"It controls your emotions?"

"Yep. It's euphoric," Nick said.

"That's a fancy word for you."

Nick glowered at me. "Thanks for your confidence in me."

"It's his word, right?" I nodded toward Uncle Philip. "Not yours."

"Yeah, all right, so he said it." Nick shoved the crystal back into his pocket.

"I can wait if you want to row at it some more." Uncle Philip's tone said anything but that he'd wait for us.

"We're not fighting," I said. "It's more like indoor sports to us."

"I have something for you, as well, Gia." Uncle Philip removed a small beige box from his pocket.

I lifted the lid and held up the long, thick chain with a glass locket attached to it. The locket contained a pure white feather rolled up to fit inside. "What is it?"

"It's been spelled with one of Pip's feathers. Merl created the charm so that when you find a Chiave, you won't need a Monitor to unlock the secret. Your brand should no longer bleed."

The Chiavi. It had fallen on Nick and me to find them, since we were the Seventh Wizard's heirs. The seven magical keys, transformed into artifacts hidden in the libraries, unlocked an apocalyptic beast called the Tetrad. Whoever released the being would become the Tetrad's master and could use it to destroy or rule both the Mystik and human worlds.

I fastened the chain around my neck. The locket swung down against my chest, beside my crescent-shaped scar. I'd gotten the mark when Nana Kearns burned a charm into my skin. I don't remember getting it since I was only a baby at the time. She did it to shield me from the havens' Monitors, and she swore she used a numbing spell beforehand. "Thanks," I said, smiling up at Uncle Philip.

"No need to thank me, I'm just the deliverer."

"So what are we doing here tonight?" Nick asked.

Uncle Philip clipped down one of the red carpet runners. "Our lesson this evening will be rather difficult, but it is imperative that you follow my instructions precisely." He glanced over his shoulder at Nick.

I tried to hold in a chuckle as I hurried after Uncle Philip.

"What?" Nick tried to grab my side, and I dodged it. "I know how to listen."

"Between you and Demos, I'm not certain who is more

easily distracted," Uncle Philip said.

"What is this? Pick on Nick day?"

"Oh, I'm sorry." I swung my shield beside my leg. "You're just an easy target."

He tugged the crystal out of his pocket again. It instantly turned a muddy color, and there was no light inside it.

"Come on, really? You're upset at that?" I shook my head. "We've been teasing each other since we learned how to talk. It's our thing."

"Gia, leave him alone," Uncle Philip warned. "We shouldn't tease him in his condition. It takes time to get used to new powers. Growing into it is easier than being thrown in at Nick's age."

Nick tightened his hand around the crystal until it turned clear.

Uncle Philip stopped and faced one of the many alcoves. "Do you feel it?"

Inside the alcove stood a small table and several chairs, with bookcases and a tall multi-paneled window.

"Feel what, Professor?" Nick asked.

"Yeah, I don't feel anything, either."

"Gia," Uncle Philip said. "Remove all metal on you. I don't want you getting a nasty shock."

I unbuckled my belt, removed my scabbard, and placed it with my shield and breastplate on one of the display cases. There was a statue of a man at the end of the row of tables and one of a woman directly across the room from him. Their frozen, plaster eyes stared at each other as if they longed to stand together.

"That's John Rylands and his wife, Enriqueta," Uncle Philip said, noticing my gaze shifting between them.

"It's so sad," I said. "They should be together."

"But then they couldn't look at each other." I was surprised at Nick's observation. The curator was right to put an entire room between them.

"We should get started." Uncle Philip waved his hand in the air with the flare of a royal. "*Scoprire la botola.*"

Uncover the trapdoor. The magical charms were all in Italian. They used to be in Latin before a wizard from the Mantello haven in Italy had converted them for easier use. The rest of the havens had adapted his simpler method as well.

Uncle Philip stretched his hand out in front of him. "Do you feel it?" he asked.

Nick and I gave each other sidelong looks. Nick shrugged and then reached his hand out. I followed his move.

"Clear your mind," Uncle Philip said. "Think of nothing that surrounds you."

Nick pulled his hand back. "Nope. Still nothing."

I was about to pull mine back, too, but a weak charge bit at my fingertips. "It's static," I said. "Must've come from the carpet runner."

Uncle Philip glanced at me. "Don't move. You're not fully in it. Reach farther out."

I hesitated, not because I didn't trust him, but because too many freaky things had happened to me in libraries. The great libraries of the world didn't require a membership card, but they did harbor dangers. Dangers I was getting tired of facing.

"Trust me," he said.

I reached out my hand. Sparks rushed across my skin, snapping like rubber bands against my flesh. I yanked my arm back. Uncle Philip didn't move. He kept his arm outstretched in front of him. The sleeve of his shirt quivered from the charge.

"Where is that coming from?" I rubbed my skin.

"It's a doorway to one of the Somniums." He rotated his

hand. "This door's trap has been removed, and a charm placed on it to keep it closed. Inside, there are barren wastelands. The ones found have been turned into prisons for some of the evil wizards and Mystik criminals."

I stuck my arm out again, energy nipping at my fingers. The shock turned into a cold tingle, as though I'd slathered the entire contents of a jar of menthol cream on my skin.

"Come on, Nick, try it." I pushed my hand in farther and the sensation disappeared. "It's gone."

"Yes, they only appear for short periods of time." Uncle Philip lowered his arm. "The ones we've tagged can be summoned. As I had summoned this one."

"I want to learn that," Nick said.

"Oh, now you're interested." I rolled my eyes. "Mention magic and you're all over it. Don't you want to know how it feels? What if you trip one because you didn't recognize it was there?"

Nick slipped his hand in his pocket as if he was checking to see if the crystal was still there. "So, if I feel static, I'll avoid the area. Simple."

"It isn't as simple as it may appear," Uncle Philip cautioned. "Most people ignore the sensation. It's what comes after the static that will alert you to a trap." He leaned forward and narrowed his eyes on Nick. "This isn't fun and games. If trapped in an untagged one, you'll never return, and the place you find yourself in will be hell. The creatures living in the Somniums will hunt you until they've devoured you."

Nick backed up. "Has anyone ever returned from them?"

"Only one." Uncle Philip straightened. "He's insane now. A killer." The window rod in the top pocket of Uncle Philip's jacket glowed blue and then flashed several times. The devices were used to connect the Mystik and human worlds. Because libraries had magic, both realms could contact anyone in them. It flashed again.

Uncle Philip removed it, pulled the rods apart, and spoke to a woman I'd never seen before.

"Professor Attwood?" the woman's voice vibrated across the rods.

"Yes, Tarah?"

"If at all possible, you are needed back in Asile."

"I'm in the middle of a lesson. Is it urgent?"

She adjusted her screen. "Merl didn't say. He did tell me to mention that he wouldn't call for you if it weren't important." She smiled. "I guess he knew you'd ask."

"All right, then. I'll be there momentarily." He closed the rods. "I'll summon another door for you to examine." He looked pointedly at Nick. "And do make sure you test this one out."

"So I don't get to learn how to summon one?" Nick pressed his lips together and fumbled with the crystal in his pocket.

"We'll schedule a lesson in a few days," Uncle Philip said as he hurried to the gateway book, placed it on the floor, and flipped the pages.

"Really?" Nick beamed. "Cool."

Uncle Philip took a few slips of folded paper out of the inside pocket of his jacket and handed them to me. "I've been studying the chart you wrote down for me."

I unfolded the papers. The first page contained the clues I'd written down from an old textbook authored by my great-grandfather, Gian Bianchi. The clues were a chart to finding the seven Chiavi. He'd left it for his heir, for me, his namesake.

The next page had a list of about twenty libraries around the world.

"See this one here..." He pointed out one of the lines I'd written.

Behind Leopold he stands, one hand resting on a crown

and the other holding a rolled prize. I glanced up after reading it.

He withdrew his finger. "Leopold is a Germanic name. I believe this Chiave must be in one of these libraries in Germany. After you practice, your mission will be to search the listed libraries for it."

"Which one do we check first?" I asked.

"Just pick one in Germany, and if you don't find the Chiave, we'll mark the library off the list. Now, I must go." He waved his hand in the air and said the charm to finding the trap again. "Hurry and practice before it disappears. Good evening, until our next meeting," he said, nodded, and jumped into the book.

I pulled my eyes from the book's pages resting into place. "Okay, Nick, let's do this. Once you get through the shock, it's easy." I plunged my fist into the area Uncle Philip had waved his hand across. I flinched as the power snapped at my skin before changing into the cool menthol feeling.

Nick sucked in a sharp breath. "How can someone miss this sensation? And what about normal people? How do they avoid them?"

I stretched out my fingers, trying to make the tingles fade faster. "It said in one of my text books that humans are immune to it."

"I will never get used to you referring to humans like that." He twisted his hand around, fisting and un-fisting it as if it were asleep.

"Like what?"

"Like humans. As if you aren't one."

"Yeah, it's strange. I probably get it from hanging out with Arik and the others."

"This is easy," he said. "Why do we have to practice this?"

"I don't know. I'm not sure I'd notice the difference

between a normal shock and a trap. Guess we just don't trust any static."

"Well, it's gone now." He dropped his arm. "Now what? I'd like to get back soon. Deidre wants to catch a midnight release."

"We could check one library and go home."

He slipped his hand into his pants pocket again. It was as if that crystal was his security blanket. "Sounds good."

"So how are you and Deidre doing?"

"Well, you know…" Sadness crossed his face.

"No, I don't know. You don't talk about her much, and Deidre doesn't talk to me."

"I've been hard on her. I try not to be, but it's like I can't control anything anymore. Well, that was before Professor Attwood gave me the crystal." He shrugged his shoulder. "I'm trying to make up for things. Not sure if it's too late or not."

"I'm sure it's not too late." But I wondered if it might be. From what I had seen of Deidre the last few weeks, she and Emily were hanging out a lot. The two together attracted tons of attention from the guys.

He bumped my shoulder with his. "Thanks."

"For what?"

"Downplaying it." He bumped me harder this time.

I bumped him even harder. "Stop it. I hate when you do that."

"I haven't done *that* since we were like…twelve."

The gateway book rattled against the carpet.

"Uncle Philip?" I glanced from the book to Nick. "You might not get to go to that movie."

"Shit. Deidre won't be happy—"

A body, clothed in Sentinel gear, flew up from the book and then crashed back down onto it.

CHAPTER FIVE

The guy's head hit hard against the wooden floor beside the carpet runner. A puddle of blood formed underneath him, soaking into the carpet. His dark hair covered his face, but something about him was familiar to me.

I ran to the body, dropping to my knees beside him. Nick just stood there, a shocked expression on his face. I brushed the hair from the guy's face. *Antonio.* The lead Sentinel for the Vatican. Arik and I had illegally jumped into the Vatican Library on the first day I discovered the gateways, and Antonio wasn't very nice about it. Arik had received an infraction on his record because Antonio had filed a report instead of issuing a warning.

Antonio moaned, his eyes focusing on me. "Gianna."

I pinched my eyebrows together. "You remember me?"

"I do. Everyone knows you." He coughed and bloody spit dribbled onto his lips. "You must get out of here. *Fast.*" He coughed again, choking on his blood. "The Red is coming."

"Who's The Red?"

"He's...a very...dangerous Laniar. He's..." He grunted.

"He's searching for Conemar." He swallowed hard and winced under the pain. "He did not believe me... You must go."

"Believe what?" I asked.

"That Conemar isn't imprisoned in the gallows under the Vatican." Something thumped under him. "Hide. He comes." A series of coughs shook Antonio's body, blood now streaming down his chin. The thumping got louder, jerking Antonio's body up and down.

"Gia, come on!" Nick took off in the opposite direction of Antonio and the gateway book.

I froze. "Nick! We have to help him. I don't know what to do."

Antonio's eyes were closed when I looked back at him.

Is he dead? I was pretty sure he was and whoever was trying to jump into the library wanted to make sure of it.

"Nick," I shouted. "We have to jump with him. Get back here." The gateway book was underneath Antonio. I pushed him but couldn't roll him over. I grasped the corner of the book and tugged, but it wouldn't budge. "I can't get it. Help me."

Nick hurried over.

The book bucked again. Harder this time.

"It's too late. Someone's jumping through it. Run." I popped up and ran after Nick. My feet slipped on the wet floor, and I face-planted into Antonio's blood. Scrambling on all fours, I tried to get to my feet.

Nick spotted me struggling over his shoulder and turned back. "Get up, get up, get up!"

Antonio flew into the air behind me, his lifeless body flopping like a rag doll. He slammed against the floor with a sickening, wet *thud*, his arm knocking the book shut before it could fully open.

I made it to my feet and sprinted for Nick.

"You're leaving a trail of blood." He formed fire in his

hands and touched it to the carpet runner. It was like a spark gobbling up a fuse. The fire rushed across the carpet and picked up speed as it grew.

"What are you doing?" I screamed. The fire roared past me, heat licking my skin and heading for Antonio. I formed my globe and pitched it at him. It landed on his stomach and exploded across his body, encasing him in a pink membrane of protection just as the inferno reached him.

Nick sprinted to me. "Get on my back. Your boots are bloody."

"You could've killed him."

"He's already dead." Nick turned his back to me and hunched over. "Get on."

I wrapped my arms around his shoulders and hopped onto his back. He turned and dropped another fireball on my red footprints. He carried me into one of the alcoves at the end of the room. We hid under the only table pushed against a column holding up the galley above our heads.

Nick flattened his body against the floor.

A *whoosh* sounded from where we had just come. "What's that?"

"My fire ball going out," he said through heaving breaths. Another *whoosh*.

"That's the other one," he said, in case I didn't get it.

What sounded like heavy boots landed hard on the floor. I tried to count how many *thuds* I heard, but lost count. Ten. Maybe twelve.

"Do you think it's that Red guy?" I whispered, and tried to shrink myself into a ball beside Nick.

"Not just that Red guy," he whispered back. "He said *The* Red. Anytime there's a 'the' in front of someone's name, it's a bad thing. We are so screwed."

I reached for my side, but my sword wasn't there. It was

still on the display case with my shield. *What if they find it?* I crawled toward the other side of the column.

Nick nudged my leg with his foot, and I glanced over at him. "Where are you going?" he mouthed.

I pointed to my waist, indicating my missing scabbard, and brought my pointer finger to my lips to quiet him.

His eyes widened.

I continued crawling and peered around the column.

Several men and various creatures surrounded Antonio. In the middle of them, a man stood taller than the rest. His long, scraggily hair and beard were as red as fire. He had broad shoulders, a thick neck, massive arms, and a large snout that distorted his face, making him look more animal than human, like the Laniars I knew. He had to be The Red. I shuddered at the menacing sight of him.

"He started a fire," a man in street clothes said. "Why'd he do that?"

"An accident maybe," another man in Sentinel gear said. "But how come he wasn't burned? See here." He pointed at where my globe had blocked the fire from touching the carpet. "It's as though something covered him."

The Red examined Antonio. "Sentinels can't shield themselves, they can only block magic. This is indeed curious." He glanced down the long center of the room, directly in my direction.

I moved back into the shadows.

A scrawnier Laniar nudged Antonio's side with his boot. "He still breathes."

He's alive? Thank God.

The Red's gaze returned to Antonio.

"What shall we do with him?" a rust-colored man with horns rasped.

"Looky here," a stocky man with a partially bald head

and bushy sideburns said, holding my sword, breastplate, and shield.

My heart skidded to a stop. I held my breath, watching and hoping they'd think it was Antonio's gear.

"Where'd you get that?" the Horned Man asked.

"On one of the display cases. He must've set it down there."

The Red grabbed the shield from the man's fat hands. "This is not a shield belonging to a Vatican Sentinel. Their shields have crosses on them, not animals. And it's shaped like a woman." He dropped my shield on the floor. "Search the place. He wasn't alone."

I scrambled back under the table, clutching my knees to my chest and trying to make myself as small as possible. I glanced at Nick beside me. There was too much moonlight coming into the alcove. His face looked as freaked out as I felt inside. My stomach rolled, and my breaths sounded loud in my ears. Frenzied footsteps grew closer as the men searched the alcoves on either side of the reading room. Soon they would reach us.

"Red!" one of the men yelled from the other side of the room. "There's movement in the gateway. Sentinels. Coming here—"

A *swoosh*, then rustling of pages and boots thudding against the floor resounded through the library. Something came out of the book and knocked the man to the floor. The men searching for us turned and ran back toward the others.

The clash of metal mixed with thuds, grunts, and curses. I froze, listening. Every painful beat of my heart caused me to draw in sharp breaths. Nearly hyperventilating, I regretted our choice to hide in the alcove. We were sitting ducks there.

Get it together, Gia, I scolded myself, but then reasoned, *okay, you can do this. You've fought before. Don't overthink it. Just go!*

I hustled out from under the table.

Nick clamped on to my arm. "What are you doing?"

"I'm going to help." I yanked my arm from his grasp. "Are you coming?"

"Hell no!"

I left him there and bolted down the carpet runner. One of the Sentinels I'd seen in the Vatican Library before dropped a golden globe onto Antonio. The Sentinel studied him for a moment and then shouted something to a guy standing with his back to me before grasping Antonio by the jacket and jumping into the gateway book with him.

I tripped over the burnt separation of the carpet and landed on my hands and knees. And my heart slammed against my chest when I saw him.

Bastien. He was in danger. I had to help him.

He shot an electric charge at a Laniar with large ears and the tiniest nose I'd ever seen. The charge hit a display case, and shattered glass flew up in the air. Bastien's aim was off. He spoke another charm and studied his hands, the light slowly building in them. Two Sentinels quickly stepped in front of him, shielding him from The Red's gang.

It took several seconds before the fear holding me back subsided. I jumped to my feet and bounded up the charred remains of the carpet, heading for my gear lying on the floor. The scrawny guy in the group rushed me, spinning two small swords around him. I ignited my globe and catapulted it at him, knocking him to the ground. He scrambled on all fours for my gear. I dived for my shield at the same time the stocky man reached for it, but I was quicker and grasped the handle as I slid by. He clutched at my clothes and we crashed into the wall. I slammed the shield against his head, but he still clung to me. He punched my side hard, and I dropped the shield, gasping.

A flaming ball hit his back and his jacket caught fire. I

teetered to my feet. Nick grinned, wisps of smoke surrounding him.

I frowned at him. "Will you stop throwing fire already? We're in a library. There's paper everywhere. Why do you keep doing that?"

"It's my easiest conjure," he said. "The others take too long."

I picked up my shield and continued after my sword, pain shocking my side. I searched the area for Bastien. He was helping one of his men and didn't notice The Red heading for him. I uncurled my hand and created my battle globe, letting the pink sphere build larger than Sinead had warned me about doing. I heaved it between The Red and Bastien. The Red slammed into the pink wall and narrowed his eyes in my direction.

The energy whooshed out of me, and I slumped to the floor. Staring at the bottom of a bookcase nearby, I willed myself to stand, but I was too weak. Two huge boots stopped in front me, and their owner yanked me up by my ponytail. My scalp burned under the force.

A cry broke from my lips.

Panicked, I flailed my fist at him, coming up short. *He's going to kill me.*

"Let go," I screamed, trying to wiggle free, and came face to face with The Red. His glare was menacing, and another cry trapped in my throat. I extended my toes, trying to reach the ground.

Tears ran from the corners of my eyes. The pain was intense.

"Where is he?" His breath smelled like roadkill.

"Who?" I kicked his leg. The veins in his massive arm protruded like ropes under his pale skin as he lifted me up higher.

"Conemar. What did your people do with him?"

"My people?" I grabbed his arm and tried to pull his grasp away from my hair. "He's dead."

"You lie," he practically snorted out of his nose.

I tried to conjure my globe, but nothing happened. I couldn't concentrate with the pain searing my scalp.

"Tell me or I'll skin your friend."

I slid my eyes in the direction he was looking. Two of his men, Sentinels by the look of them, held Nick by the arms.

I swallowed. "I can't think with you pulling my hair."

He grunted and lowered me to my feet but kept his hold on my ponytail. "Now, where is he?" The scars running across his forehead and throat reminded me of those on Barnum, a slain knight who was Frankensteined back together by a wizard many centuries ago. He and three of his fellow warriors had been turned into monsters. The Tetrad. Connected by one soul, they were powerful. Conemar wanted it, and this freak of nature probably did, too.

"He's gone." I dug my fingers into his arm, but he didn't even flinch. "We used an ancient charm to send him to another realm or something. I'm not sure where."

An evil, feral snarl came from him. "So he's alive, then. I will find him." He let go of my hair, and I landed on my knees.

He stormed off toward the gateway book.

I glanced around the room through blurry eyes. Standing several heads taller, the horned man had his arms wrapped around Bastien. The French Sentinels' swords lay on the ground in surrender. Like a wet match, I kept trying to ignite my globe and failing.

"Stubs, your men take care of them," The Red said.

The Laniar with the small nose looked surprised. "But master, he's a Renard."

"We don't want them following us." The Red motioned

his other men to follow him before jumping into the gateway.

Stubs and four other Laniars remained.

I tried my globe again, and it finally sprouted. Focusing on Stubs, I lobbed the globe and it whizzed through the air hitting its target. It knocked him back and spread like a helmet around his head. He fell to the ground. Then rolled on top the gateway book, spoke the key, and disappeared. The French Sentinels snatched up their swords and fought the rest of The Red's men.

I readied another globe and faced the men holding Nick. They released his arms and ran down the room, toward the exits. I popped the globe in my hand, and flickers of light zapped around it. Two French Sentinels chased after the men.

I dropped to my butt on the floor and wiped the wetness from my eyes with shaky fingers. Nick gathered up my gear.

Bastien sat on his heels in front of me. "Gia, you're a bloody mess."

I glanced down. Antonio's blood stained my clothes, neck, and hands. My heart sank.

He handed me a hanky. "A hanky? What are you, ninety?"

"It comes in handy for situations like this," he said. "Are you injured?"

I shook my head. "No. Do you think he'll make it," I whispered, wiping my chin with the hanky.

"Who?"

"Antonio."

"I believe so. He's been in worse condition before."

"Worse than gutted?"

A sympathetic smile played on his lips. "It looked worse than it actually was."

"Huh?" I watched him curiously. "How do you know?"

"The Sentinel who took him scanned his wounds. Nothing vital was hit."

Nick placed my stuff beside me on the floor. "It's a good thing he didn't fry, then."

I wanted to smack the grin off Nick's face. "That was really careless of you, by the way. You could've killed him. And look at the place. It's a burnt mess."

"Hell, Gia, I didn't think it out, okay? You were leaving bloody footprints everywhere. They would've found us." Nick pushed his sweaty hair back from his face. "I'm sorry."

A tortured expression contorted his face, and I softened. "It's okay. I probably would've done the same thing. Where's your crystal?"

He slipped his hand into his pocket and walked off, nodding. The shadows in the dark room engulfing him as the distance between us grew.

"He's bad off," Bastien said.

"Yeah, ever since the curers released his power, he's been struggling with his emotions."

Bastien reached over and brushed the sweaty hair away from my face. "You're in need of a bath, or rather, a proper scrubbing crew." He sighed. "We should get you back home."

"Yeah, we should." I stood.

He looked down at me. "Are you all right?"

All right? I was scared shitless, but I'd never let anyone know it. I had to be strong, there was too much at risk to be weak. "Yeah, I'm good," I said.

His soft blue eyes surveyed my face.

That stare punctured me, sending chills through my body. I leaned toward him and quickly stepped back, all words and thoughts escaping me. *What the hell?* All I wanted was for him to hold me and make me feel safe. My heart pounded against my chest, and I felt weightless.

I'm just shaken up. I'd reach out to anyone right now.

He took a step toward me. "Gia, listen—"

I shook my head. "No, it's okay. I'm okay. All in a day's battle, right?" I turned and bounded up the carpet after Nick. I could hear Bastien's boots following. I tightened my hands into fists, trying to stop them from trembling.

What the hell was that? *You don't want him. You don't need him.*

Bastien caught my arm and spun me around to face him. He got real close to me. "You feel it just as I do. Stop denying your feelings."

"I-I can't." I pushed his hand away and shook my head. "I'm with Arik."

"You ready to go?" Nick said, coming out of the shadows. "Your pop is probably worried by now."

I lowered my gaze, avoiding eye contact with Bastien, and stepped around him. "I'm ready."

"You're a fool." Bastien caught my hand, stopping me. "Open your eyes. He's not the idol you've created him to be. He feels safe, that's all. There isn't the heat we have, and you know it."

"Leave me alone." I tugged my hand away from his grasp and charged up the burnt carpet runner. We passed Bastien's Sentinels and found the book still on the floor.

"That was intense." Nick gave me a curious eye and then glanced back at Bastien. "What's going on?"

"Nothing," I said, flipping the pages to the library in Branford. *"Aprire la porta,"* I said, and jumped into the gateway book.

CHAPTER SIX

The fog in my dream thickened like pudding around my body, making me gasp. Chills slithered up my spine. Dressed in a parka, a wool face mask, thick gloves, and boots, I clambered deeper into the dark frozen cave, balancing a light globe in my hand. Completely alone, trembling against the icy air, I weaved my way through the labyrinth of tunnels until I came into a massive cavity. Across the wide expanse from me stood a large metal door, large enough to fit an armored truck. There wasn't a handle, only hinges thicker than a man's leg. Seven holes formed a circle in the middle of the door.

I shivered out of the straps of a worn leather backpack and dropped it on the ground, sending a loud *clank* through the cave. After riffling through the bag, I pulled out seven metal rods and placed them at my feet.

I picked up a rod and said, "*Accendere.*" *Turn on.* The metal glowed blue, and I slid it into one of the holes in the door. The rods fit like puzzle pieces into the holes. When the last rod was securely inserted, I stood and took several steps back.

"*Rilascio!*" I shouted, pushing back the hood of my parka and staring at the door.

Nothing happened, so I called out again, "*Rilascio!*"

"*Rilascio!*"

Pounding on the door, the cold metal stung my hand. "Why won't it release?"

"You are not the one," a voice resounded from somewhere in my room.

"I am not the one..." Dream Gia's voice faded into the darkness as I woke.

I hugged one of my pillows. "I am not the one?" I glanced groggily at the alarm. "Shit." I sprang out of bed. We'd been going to school for nearly two months now, and being late was not an option for Deidre. She'd left me twice. Thankfully, I had showered before bed. Pulling on my jeans, I glanced out the bedroom window. Her new Jetta was still in the driveway, but there wasn't much time to spruce up, and I wanted to look my best today of all days. It was the day Arik and I were going public.

Seventh week of public school and I was just starting to adjust. It was definitely noisier than the private school I used to go to in Boston. The hall filled with excited chatter. The populace of Branford High weaved between gathered groups to get to their lockers or next classes. I shoved my English textbook into my locker and yanked my Marine Biology one out from the bottom of the pile.

"Hullo, ducky, ready for class?"

I jumped. "Lei! Stop sneaking up like that. You gave me a heart attack."

She leaned against the locker beside me. "Sorry, it's in

the DNA. It can't be suppressed."

"You know," I said, slamming my locker closed, "you don't have to wear those glasses when you're not in class."

"I like them. It's a fashion statement." She pushed them up her nose. The red frames were the right pop of color for her skin tone.

Lei and I had plenty of classes together, but Marine Biology was Lei's favorite. She had never seen an ocean before. The only bodies of water in the Mystik world were ponds, lakes, and hot springs.

"You'll forgive me later." She hooked her arm through mine, and we headed down the emptying hall to our class. "You can ditch whatever disagreeable lunch Faith packed. I brought an extra lunch for you. Sinead made oatmeal and raisin cookies, and your favorite Fluffernutter sandwiches, which by the way still makes my stomach roll. Who would eat peanut butter and marshmallow on a sandwich?"

"Me." I gave her a sharp look. "Anyway, thanks, it sounds delish."

Since Deidre practically ignored me and Afton was in Boston, Lei and I had become best friends, so to speak. Thankfully, since I helped Bastien save the world from Conemar's evil creations, she'd forgiven me for almost killing her boyfriend, Kale.

"Are you excited for lunch?" she asked before we entered the classroom.

"Yeah, I don't know how much longer I can handle eating Faith's cooking."

"Not that." She exaggerated a sigh. "*Remember?* Arik's going to ask you on a date in front of everyone so there will be no question when you two started your relationship. Maybe you'll get to snog in the hall like all the other lovebirds."

"Oh that." I'd been counting down the seconds for weeks

now. I was tired of hiding, and honestly, I didn't get the point. Why would it even matter to a bunch of high school students when we got together? They were too busy with their own dramas to care.

"Yeah, that," she said. "You don't sound excited about it."

"I am." I yawned. "I'm just so tired. I was up late talking Nick down from another episode."

"I thought he was improving with Professor Attwood's aid?" she whispered.

"He is. We're down to one call every few days." I yawned again. "After practice today, we have to search the libraries for the Chiavi. I just hope I don't drop dead before then."

She scanned the hallway for any eavesdroppers. "Who's guarding you tonight?"

"No one." I leaned close to her, keeping my voice low. "Carrig thinks, since Nick and I are shielded, we'd be safer if we go alone. A few Sentinels will watch us through the books and be ready to jump if anything goes wrong."

"Why didn't they ask us to go?"

"Because the Wizard Council thinks Conemar's allies are searching the Monitors for Sentinels from Asile. They're just being cautious."

Lei skirted around an underclassman. The boy's smile took up half his face, showing off his orange and blue braces.

"That boy is smitten." I nodded at him.

The glare she gave the boy caused him to turn quickly and collide into an open locker door. "Yeah, everywhere I go, he seems to magically appear," she said.

My stomach grumbled. "I think I may die of starvation. Seriously. Faith is the worst cook and she won't let anyone near the kitchen. I think she wants to feel useful."

"She's your house guard. That's not useful enough for her?"

"I guess not." My stomach roared this time.

She retrieved a granola bar from the front pocket of her backpack and handed it to me. "Well, at least stay alive until Arik professes his love for you. I can hardly wait to see the expression on Miss Snow White's face when he does."

"Emily? Why?"

We crossed an intersecting hall, and I practically skidded to a stop. Down at the end of it, Arik had his arm propped against a locker, his head resting on his palm. Emily was searching inside the open one beside him. She said something and Arik laughed. It wasn't a chuckle, more like a throw-your-head-back full-on howl. Their words never paused. She giggled and shoved him.

Emily glanced at her phone, said something, and they both rushed around the corner at the end of the hallway.

"Gia, you're staring," Lei said, tugging on my sleeve, urging me to step away.

I shuffled along with her, dazed. "Did you see that? Arik and Emily at her locker."

Lei yanked open the classroom door at the same time the tardy bell rang. "I did. They get along well."

"Ladies," Mrs. Greene called from her desk. "Are you joining the class or listening to the lesson in the hall?"

"She has two classes with Arik," Lei whispered as we found our seats, "and let's just say she doesn't hide the fact that she fancies him."

"I've never seen her flirt with him before, or noticed him act that way toward her." *Have I?*

I couldn't concentrate on Mrs. Greene's lecture of how pollution affects the marine ecosystems. How hadn't I known that Emily liked Arik? He seemed to like her, too. I replayed the times when I had seen the two together. Since I only had one class with Arik, and none with Emily, I didn't have much to work with. I'd seen her talking to him at lunch, between classes, and at an assembly. That was it. Emily was naturally a bubbly type, and I couldn't tell the difference between how she treated me from how she treated him.

Lei leaned over and whispered while Mrs. Greene was shuffling through her notes. "She flips her hair when she's with him. It's annoying."

I sent her a puzzled look.

"Stop obsessing. His heart belongs to you." She straightened at the same time Mrs. Greene looked up.

"Then why tell me this?" I hissed back.

Should I be worried?

The clock above the white board ticked agonizingly slow. Each click of the hands caused me to jump. The minute hand shuddered at 11:29 — one more minute — and I lifted, my butt hovering over the seat, anxious to get more details about Emily and Arik. The passing bell shrilled through the hallway. I sprang from my seat and dashed for the door.

"Miss Kearns," Mrs. Greene called before I was out the door. "May I have a moment, please?"

No. I looked over my shoulder at her, then glanced at the door. Lei waved from the hall for me to hurry. The tone in Mrs. Greene's voice had conveyed it was an order and not a question. I slumped and shuffled over to her desk.

She held up a piece of paper with red marks all over it. "I'm worried, Gia. You failed the last two tests. What's the matter?"

"I'm sorry. I haven't been sleeping well."

"I see," she said, following my eyes to Lei. "What's keeping you up at night?"

"A friend is going through some tough times."

"The D'Marco kid?"

"Yes. How did you know?"

"I've seen you with him. He's in my first class. I had to

send him to the office today."

I worried my bottom lip. Why hadn't he used his crystal?

"Don't be concerned," she said. "He told the principal he had just discovered he's adopted. The counselor will work with him."

Crap. The counselor? That can't be good.

I had to talk to Nick fast before he said something he shouldn't.

"Gia?"

I looked up. "Huh?"

"You know, if you're having difficulties, I'm sure you could ask your sister to tutor you. She's in my third period and has straight As."

Yeah. Not in this century. Besides, Deidre and the Sentinels cheated to pass their tests. Being from the Mystik world, they knew nothing about our education. The Council had provided them with glasses that had some sort of chip in the frame. They'd read a question and the chip would do a search and send the answer back on the lenses. They'd offered me a pair, but I refused. I actually enjoyed learning, and I was usually good at it when Nick wasn't distracting my studies.

"I will," I said instead.

She smiled. "You'd better go before Lei comes through the window."

"Thanks," I said before darting out the door.

Lei and I made a mad dash for her locker, grabbed the lunches Sinead had made, and headed for the lunchroom. "Remove your ponytail," she said. "And stop worrying about Arik. He only thinks of Emily as a friend. It's you he loves."

"You're right." The hair tie took a few strands as victims when I yanked it out. My fingers shook as I combed my messy curls with them. Why was I so nervous? Arik and I made out every day. So what if we were going public with it.

Lei grabbed my elbow before I entered the cafeteria. "Hold on there, you should be unsuspecting."

I paused and took several calming breaths before following Lei into the smells of fish sticks mixed with pine cleaner. The populace raced across the over-waxed floors, trying to find a bench at one of the many particleboard tables, their voices scraping against the whitewashed walls. And in the middle of all the chaos, standing beside our usual table, was Arik. Strong and confident, quiet and reserved.

Lei straddled the table's bench. "Hey, duckies, what are we talking about?"

"What kept you two?" Arik asked, giving me a once-over.

"Mrs. Greene made Gia stay after class." Lei shook her fancy juice bottle.

I plopped down on the bench. "Do you always have to tell everyone everything, Lei?"

She unscrewed the top. "Oh, I'm sorry, was that a secret?"

"Never mind. All the late nights are catching up with me. I have to do better on my tests." I took the brown sack Lei passed me and pulled out the oatmeal and raisin cookies and juice to get to the Fluffernutter sandwich.

"Oh," trilled Emily from across the table. "A Fluffernutter. I love those."

Where did she come from? What does a person do when someone does that? Ignore them? I had been looking forward to eating that sandwich. *The entire thing.* Sinead had even cut it diagonally for me.

I forced a smile and extended a piece to her. "You want half?"

"Really? Thank you." She snatched it from my hands and took a big bite. All while watching Arik.

It was like being in a sardine can with all the tables so close together. The benches were crowded with students.

Several I didn't know shared ours. Their eyes watching us, heads bent to listen to our conversations. We were the new kids. And the Sentinels were foreigners with hot accents.

"Gia?" Arik placed his hand on the table and leaned toward me.

I got lost in his deep brown eyes rimmed with thick black lashes. "Hmm?"

"I was wondering if you wanted to go see a flick or something with me on Friday evening."

Several faces turned in our direction.

A dark strand of hair fell over his eye and I fought the urge to brush it back. If we were alone or just with people who knew our true identities, I would've done it. In the corner of my eye, I could see Emily drop the uneaten part of the sandwich.

"Really? Me? I'd *love* to," I said, drawing out the word "love" and overfaking my surprise.

Arik raised a brow at my response. "All right, then. I'll pick you up at seven?"

"Sounds good."

He swung his leg over the bench, facing my side, then withdrew a wrapped Fluffernutter sandwich from his bag and placed it in front of me. "Here, I'm still full from breakfast."

I unwrapped the sandwich and took about the same size bite as Emily had before. "Yummy," I said around a sticky mouthful.

Arik gave me the "stop it" eyes. I shrugged a shoulder and took another bite.

"You two make the cutest couple," Lei was starting to sound like a true American teen.

A flash of hurt crossed Emily's face, and I felt bad. She didn't deserve us rubbing it in like that. Emily probably wouldn't have gone after him if she knew we were already together.

"So Emily," I said. "Heard you made the honor's list."

"Yeah." She didn't even look up, just picked at the crust of the remaining piece of her sandwich.

"Congratulations," Arik said.

Her head popped up and she smiled sweetly at him. "Thank you."

Lei gave me a puzzled look. "What are you doing?" she mouthed.

An awkward silence hung over us as we ate. Someone would try to drum up a conversation, but it would fizzle out and everyone would be quiet again.

The lunch bell rang mercifully announcing the end of lunch.

Arik walked me to my next class with his arm over my shoulder. The entire way, my thoughts were on Emily. I hated hurting her, but it was unavoidable. A murky cloud clung to my happiness at finally being able to show my affection for Arik in public.

CHAPTER SEVEN

I stood in the center of a room in the Monastic Library in Ulm, Germany, surrounded by statues resting on thick bases. Pink and green marbled columns surrounded them all. The columns had elaborate gold-leaf fittings that held up a gallery with a polished brown and black stone banister. There was so much to see, my brain went into overdrive. The books seemed lonely behind cages within the several bookcases standing between all the wonderful chaos of marble and gold.

A golden crown on one of the statues caught my attention. I measured my steps across the tile floor, wrenching the slip of paper Uncle Philip had given me out of my pocket. Even though I'd read the weird rhyme that was some sort of chart or treasure map for finding the Chiavi a thousand times, I read it again. My great-grandfather, Gian Bianchi, had it in a book charmed to find one of his heirs, which it did. Me.

Libero il tesoro—free the treasure—was the spell to release a Chiave from its hiding place. Not only did each Chiave piece together to form the key to release the Tetrad from its prison, but also each held individual powers.

A religious man's charm hangs from his vest.

That Chiave was a necklace with a cross pendant found in the Vatican Library by Gian. He had stuffed it into the handle of his umbrella before he was murdered. My mother, who hadn't realized he'd hidden it there, ended up with the umbrella. When she died, I had claimed it. I would've never found the cross if I hadn't been swinging the umbrella, causing the loose handle to launch off, almost hitting Afton in the face. The bearer of the cross could see things that had come before wherever they stood. I kept reading the list.

A school of putti, one of which sees farther than the rest.

Not found yet. Putti. Strange name. I had to look it up. It's another word for cupids.

Strong women flank the ceiling; the one in Sentinel dress holds an enchanted point small in size.

I had found that one after a battle in the Senate Library in Paris. Sinead was the one who spoke the key to release it. A warrior woman then came to life and handed her a sword. Its power could destroy all swords.

Behind Leopold he stands, one hand resting on a crown and the other holding a rolled prize. We were looking for this one now. Uncle Philip believed it would be in one of the libraries in Germany because of the mention of Leopold. This was the last library. We had searched them all and hadn't found it. And it definitely wasn't in this one, either. The others on the list seemed like a badly written poem or something.

With numbers in her mind and knowledge in her hands, on her brow a crown does rest;

In front of the world, he wears his honor on his chest;

Beneath destruction and rapine, he scribes the word, while time falls;

All these things are within the library walls.

All not found.

Uncle Philip was busy working out where the rest of the Chiavi might be from the riddles in the chart.

I stopped in front of the statue.

Nick shuffled into the room, his backpack shifting. Ever since we had that narrow escape from The Red, he brought his pack with him on our hunts, stuffed with provisions, survival gear, and a knife. "This place would be amazing if we were stoned," he said.

"Really, Nick?" I shook my head, not able to suppress the smile struggling on my face. He never had a filter.

"So you ready to go? We've checked this library twice. There's nothing here."

"There's maybe nothing we're looking for here, but I think this is a Chiave."

He came closer. "You don't say. What makes you think so?"

I pointed out the line on the chart. "This."

"With numbers in her mind"—he read it aloud and mumbled a few of the words—"knowledge in her hands...a crown." He looked up from the page and at the statue, a blank expression on his face.

I heaved a sigh. "You see, this is the room of knowledge. There's a statue for History, one for Natural Sciences, and this one is for Mathematics."

"I don't get it." He rubbed the back of his neck.

"With numbers in her head." I waited. He still didn't get it, so I added, "She has a crown on her head."

The light went on. "Oh, yeah. We found one!"

We found it? I let out an exasperated breath. "Yeah, whatever."

He eyed me. "Well, what are you waiting for? Do your magic."

"Okay, but we should stand back. No telling what will happen. I'm not sure what this pendant does."

We took several steps back.

I fisted the locket with Pip's feather inside and called, "*Libero il tesoro.*" Actually, it was more of a whispered shout, as if there was anyone around to hear me in the after-hours darkness of the library.

A strong gust of wind rushed through the room, whipping tea-colored strands of hair across my face. A cracking sound came from the statue, like bones snapping. The white plaster woman dropped a compass and paddle with letters and numbers on it she'd been holding.

The statue's eyes popped open. Nick and I gasped at once. Her sculpted eyes snapped in my direction. She hopped off the marble base, glided across the floor, stopping directly in front of me.

"Welcome, daughter of the Seventh. I am Mathematics." She removed the crown from her head and held it out for me. "The Chiave I offer you can render the owner invisible. But beware, for its magic doesn't last long."

I took the crown from her. "Thank you."

"May the heir go unnoticed into the blackness." She bowed her head, glided back to her pedestal, picked up the compass and paddle, and then hopped back up onto her perch. She repositioned herself, the wind dying the instant she froze back into place.

I glanced down at the golden crown in my hand.

"Well," Nick said. "That was weird and awesome at the same time."

"Here"—I pushed the crown into his hands—"put this in your bag."

He put it on his head. "Can you see me?"

I rested my hand on my hip. "Yes. Stop fooling around."

"It's broken?"

"Maybe you have to speak a charm?"

He took it off and examined the outside of the crown, and then the inside of it. "There's something etched inside."

"Let me see." I took it from him and read it. "*Nascondi.*" The crown glowed.

"Put it on."

I placed it on my head. "Am I gone?"

"Nope," he said. "The thing is broken."

"*Nascondi* means hide." I took the crown off and examined it. There was a crescent moon etched on the front of it. *It's like my brand.* "Maybe it doesn't cause invisibility," I said. "It must *hide* the wearer from the Monitors in the gateway. Kind of like how we're shielded from them."

"That makes sense. I bet you're right."

I took the crown off and handed it to him. "We'll have to look into it more."

"Okay," he said, slipping his backpack off his shoulder. "Should we take it to Asile?" He slid the crown into the opening then zipped the bag closed.

"No. Any Chiavi we find, we give to Carrig. He'll get them to the Wizard Council."

I tugged my phone from my front pants pocket and checked the time. "We have an hour or so left before we have to be back." I swiped down the photos of libraries I had saved on my phone. "I saw that Uncle Philip had listed a library in Austria as a possible location for the Chiave that mentions Leopold. He said he was some king or royal from ancient times. Maybe we could check it before we return home."

"I'm game. Anything to keep me out all night and away from my mom's disappointed frown."

"You should be easier on her, Nick." I looked up from the screen. "You know she loves you."

"I know. I don't feel normal around anyone lately, except for you."

"That would be a sweet sentiment if I treated you as well as everyone else does."

"Yeah, maybe if they were meaner to me, I'd be nicer to them." He smirked. "I'm so screwed up."

I chuckled. "You so are." I continued reading the list. "Here it is. The National Library of Austria. It's in Vienna."

"Cool. Let's do this." He swung the pack over his shoulder. "You want to jump first or should I?"

"I'll go. I have the sword."

"Good point."

I shook my head at him again, smiling. He was such an annoyance. An enduringly cute one, though.

The National Library of Austria, dressed in warm wood, was in complete contrast to the cold marbles and ornate decor of the Wiblingen library. The glossy wooden railings of the galley, giving access to the upper level bookcases, harmonized with the cream and brown marble on the walls and columns. Even the gold fittings didn't distract from the many bookcases reaching two levels high. Display cases, white marble statues, artwork, and world globes decorated the museum-like room.

The circular windows encompassing the cupola let in light from the full moon. Dust particles teased each other in the silvery beams. Everything had a quiet blue hue to it.

"Hello!" Nick called out, his voice resounding in the room.

"Nick," I hissed. "Stop it, someone will hear you."

"I just wanted to see if my voice would echo in this huge place."

"We don't have time for games."

"Okay, got it. No fun. Ever. You check this room," he said. "I'll search another one."

"Sounds like a plan." I pulled out my phone. "Or I could just Google it."

"If this dinosaur has wifi."

"Looks like it does." I tapped the key charm that unlocked wifi passcodes into my phone. They were emojis—*clap, clap, devil, punch*. The wizard techs were so clever.

Nick glanced at the screen. "It's a gamble you'll find anything. All my searches for the other clues so far have come up empty. Or I'd find a million things that matched it."

"Well, this time we have a location and a specific item—um—or person." I touched the internet icon, typed in a search for Leopold in the library, and waited. The connection took a long time. Nick and I both frowned at the screen as we waited for the results.

The page slowly loaded. "Here it is," I said. Something flickered in my peripheral vision, and I snapped my head in that direction. My stomach dropped as I peered into the shadows. "Did you see that?"

"What?" He spun around, looking in the direction I was.

"It had wings."

"Stop. You're going to give me a stroke." He sighed. "It was probably just a moth."

The page finished loading. "The statue is of the Archduke Leopold Wilhelm," I said. "It's somewhere in this room." I showed him the picture, and we drifted across the checkered floor, inspecting each sculpture we passed.

We walked by map display cabinets made out of intricately carved wood and passed between two enormous marble columns. I kept sneaking glances over my shoulder, looking out for whatever it was I had seen. Nick was probably right. It had to be a moth. The little creatures snuck in through open doors and windows all the time back home.

"You know, we really do have an interesting life now," Nick said, interrupting the silence of the library.

"Interesting? That's an understatement."

He suddenly stopped. "Well, hello, Mr. Leopold."

"We found it?" Excitement replaced my alarm.

"The dude's wearing a dress, and check out that honker."

"You're impossible." I stepped around the thick column to see the statue with his back to Leopold. Something whizzed by my ear and I swatted at it. "I don't think it was a moth, but a bee. It buzzed." I flailed my arms above my head.

Nick joined me on the other side of the column, searching the area for the mysterious bee. "It's November, it can't be a bee. So who's the spinster?"

"It's a man."

"How can that be? Look at his long hair. And it's curly. And the skirt."

"The men wore wigs at that time. And skirts. The website said he was part of the Hapsburg family." I retrieved my list and read it again. "Well, this has to be the statue. He's behind Leopold." I looked from the paper to the statue. A marble crown was on top of a marble stand beside the man. "His hand is resting on a crown. The riddle mentioned a rolled prize in his other hand."

"There's nothing in that hand," Nick said.

A creature resembling a girl, no bigger than my open hand, with a lanky green body, much like a praying mantis, landed on the statue's hand. "It's because this Chiave has already been taken." Her sharp voice startled us, and we both jumped back.

"What the hell is that?" Nick asked.

Deep red curls bounced against the girl's back and between iridescent wings.

"I know you," I said.

"Is she real?" Nick's voice trembled.

"I assure you I am most certainly real." She stepped over the statue's thumb.

Nick moved behind me, looking over my shoulder. "She's real—real freaky looking."

"You're one to talk. At least I haven't got a big nose."

"It isn't big." He rubbed his nose.

She raised a tiny eyebrow at him.

"You belong to Sinead," I said. "You helped us in Esteril."

"I'm not a pet. I don't *belong* to anyone." She gave me a wide sharp-toothed smile. "I aided Sinead in finding you that day in Asile when someone had drugged you. I am Atenae, daughter of Solitare, princess of the book faeries."

Nick edged out from behind me. "What does a book faery do exactly?"

"We protect the pages of books from things like book mites, fires"—her amber eyes watched Nick coolly—"and dirty human fingers."

"I'm a wizard."

"You smell human." She climbed the statue's arm and turned when she was eye level with us. "I've been watching you two. You're the protectors. Gian told me you would come. His heirs." Her gaze landed on me. "You're a tough girl. Gian would be proud."

My cheeks warmed, and I was about to thank her, but Nick spoke first.

"So are you going to tell us who took the scroll?"

"Gian discovered it, and now it's in a Laniar's possession." She flew up and hovered in front of Nick's face. "You know, for having a big nose, you are sort of cute—in a weird human way."

Nick stood straighter. "You're not so bad yourself—in a weird green insect kind of way."

She giggled and returned to the statue's hand, landing gracefully on the marbled knuckles. "I saw the statue come to life and give the Chiave to Gian. The statue said that it held the name of the one who can destroy the Tetrad. It had said, 'Blood of blood, flesh of flesh, only the heir of the one can stop the elements of the four. Whoever holds the scroll, guards the secret.'"

"Gia's the one," Nick said.

"No, I'm not. In a dream, I was in an icy cave, wearing a parka. I tried to release the Tetrad, but it said I wasn't the one."

Nick's shocked expression found mine. "I had the same dream."

"Stop fooling around, Nick," I said. "You couldn't have the same dream as me. It's impossible."

"I wouldn't say that," Aetnae said. "Haven't you learned? Nothing is impossible when magic is involved. A Spirit Seer could have given you both the dream. Whoever did, wants you to know there is another."

"So neither of us is the one?" I wanted this to be true, but wasn't sure I could trust Atenae. "Then who is?"

Atenae's wings began fluttering, and she lifted off the statue. "Only you two remain from the Seventh Wizard, and the one comes from his blood. That is, unless there is an unrecorded heir."

"Maybe that creature with the Chiave knows who it is," Nick said.

"His name is Toad. You can find him in the gallows under the Vatican Library." She flew off into the shadows. "But do not let anyone know that he has the Chiave, for he would surely die before the morning," she said from somewhere in the darkness. "Go alone. Toad won't talk to you if you bring any Sentinels along. He was instructed by Gian to only speak to an heir."

Chapter Eight

Faith paced her bedroom in the attic just above the room I shared with Deidre. Faith had an addiction to reality shows. I made sure to record them for her so she'd have a distraction while we slept at night. I waited for her pacing to stop before slipping out of bed and wiggling into my jeans. I decided to ditch the Sentinel getup. If Faith caught me sneaking out this late, at least I wouldn't tip her off to what I was actually up to by wearing my gear.

Wanting to travel light, I decided not to take my helmet and shield.

"Where are you going?" Deidre asked from her twin bed on the other side of the room.

Crap.

I paused in the middle of pulling my T-shirt over my head. "Um—I'm meeting Arik. Be quiet. Can't you just pretend to be asleep like I do when you sneak out?" I yanked my shirt down.

She sat up on her elbows. "You aren't meeting Arik. He's in Asile."

I shot a puzzled look at her as I slipped on my jacket.

"He is?"

"Ah-ha! I knew you weren't going to see him." Deidre swung her legs over the side of the bed. "I saw Nick texting you. What are you two up to?"

"Be quiet, Faith will hear you." I rushed over and sat on the bed beside her. "You promise not to tell?"

She nodded. "Promise."

I studied her face, wondering if I should trust her.

"Stop frowning like that." Her short bleached hair stuck out all over the place. "I may not like you, but I'd never rat you out."

I glanced at the door. "Okay, here's the thing. No one can know. Nick and I discovered the location of another Chiave, but it's in the gallows under the Vatican library. We're sneaking there tonight to find it."

"Why don't you tell Carrig?"

"I can't. The guy we're meeting would freak. He'll only talk to Gian's relatives. Nick or me."

She hopped off the bed. "I'm going with you."

"No you aren't." I popped up. "You're not shielded. It's not safe." Changelings had the exact same DNA as their Sentinels and could go through the gateway books. The doppelgangers weren't recorded with the Monitors at birth as Sentinels, wizards, and Mystiks were, but they still came up as nonregistered jumpers, and I worried her jump would cause alarm.

Deidre pulled on some leggings under her long *Dr. Who* T-shirt. "I'll go another way and meet you at the Vatican. They won't know who I am. And by the time they follow my trail, we'll be back here in bed. Besides, I know the Fey who work there. They run the gallows. Sinead used to take me along with her when she'd deliver care packages to the prisoners. I can get you in." She stuffed her feet into her pink

Doc Marten boots.

"He's picking me up on his motorcycle. There's no room."

"Three can ride a bike." She grabbed her leather jacket, snagged her hobo bag off the desk chair, and eased open the door. "You coming?"

I snatched my window rod off the desk and stuffed it into my jacket pocket. The rod—well, it was actually two pieces that snapped together—ignited a blue screen between them when separated. It was like video chatting to the Mystik world and would be handy if I needed to contact Uncle Philip in an emergency.

We snuck out the side door and crept alongside the bushes to the street. Keeping to the shadows, we trotted up the road to where Nick waited leaning against his bike.

He straightened. "What is she doing here?"

"Is that anyway to greet your girlfriend?" Deidre said, wrapping her arms around his neck and kissing him firmly on the lips. "I missed you, too."

Their kiss deepened and I stared at my Converse. "Hello, you guys, feeling awkward here."

They separated. "Sorry," she said.

"Now, seriously, why are you here?" Nick said.

"Because she can get us into the gallows," I said. "We'll explain later. Let's get out of here before we're caught."

"Yeah, okay." Nick straddled his motorcycle.

Deidre swung her leg over and scooted as close as she could to Nick's back. "Get on." She patted the seat behind her. "How are we getting into the library?"

"We told Miss Bagley that we're meeting Uncle Philip." I got on behind her.

Nick took off and my butt almost slipped off the back. I gripped Deidre's waist tighter.

...

The gallows were just as I'd imagined—similar to the medieval ones I'd seen in movies—dark and gloomy. The ceilings were arched and high, the walls rocky and slick, and the floors uneven and dusty. A rank smell stifled the air. Everything was caged in the gallows, even the lights dotting the walls every few feet.

A faery named Odran led us down a corridor that seemed as ancient as he looked. His pointy ears were hairy, wire tendrils of red hair surrounded the bald spot on his head, and he walked hunched over as if he couldn't straighten his back.

"I had a tough time getting you in," he said over his shoulder, "what with all the heightened security after the attack on the Vatican recently. But I owe Sinead my life, and if she needs something from this Toad then she shall have it."

"Thank you," Deidre said. "My mother has always thought highly of you."

"Why is Toad in the gallows?" I asked. "I thought it was for those sentenced to death. I read that he got life, not death."

"The gallows are for the criminally insane. Those who won't survive the Somniums. Not that anyone survives them, but it would be depraved for them not to have a fighting chance." Odran suddenly stopped, turned to a door, and unlocked it.

Nick practically choked. "We're going to see *him*? Alone."

"We'll be fine. I have my globe, and I'm sure you can't destroy anything here with your pyrotechnics. Everything is rock."

"Your magic won't work in the gallows." Odran pushed the door open. "The charms here disarm magic."

"Isn't that comforting," Nick muttered under his breath.

Inside the cell a gangly Laniar, with long salt-and-pepper hair and a matted beard, was on the small bed pushed against the wall. He sat with his feet on the thin mattress and his arms wrapped around his legs, his large sagging eyes darting around the room.

"You have visitors, Toad," Odran said, and then turned to Deidre. "I do this as a favor to your mother. You have fifteen minutes, no more."

"Thank you," Deidre said and motioned Nick and I with her eyes to go inside.

I went in first, followed by Nick, who cowered behind me.

"Um…Mr. Toad, sir," I said. "I was wondering if we could have a word with you."

"Only one?" He grinned, his teeth sparse and yellowy.

I took a step closer. "Sorry?"

"You said you wanted to have a word with me. That would be one. Are we done?"

I gave Nick a curious look. "That's just a— I meant, can I talk to you?"

"I don't talk to no one. Only the walls are my friends." He scooted around on his bed until his back faced us.

"I'm Gia and this is Nick. We're Gian Bianchi's great-grandchildren. I think you were expecting us?"

He spun back around. "What took you so long?"

"Well, first we had to be born," Nick said.

I elbowed him and hissed under my breath, "Leave it to me." I didn't want Nick's sarcasm messing things up. He didn't have a filter and not everyone got his humor.

The man scooted to the end of the bed and dropped his feet to the floor. He whispered something that I couldn't understand.

I stepped closer. "What?"

"I suppose you came for the Chiave," he repeated.

"Yes. Do you know where it is?"

Toad pulled at his beard.

"Don't worry," I said. "We know you didn't kill Gian."

His gaze went to mine. "But I did kill him."

"You did?" I gave Nick a look.

"Not by choice." He grimaced when he yanked a few hairs out. "I was compelled by a wizard. I tried to fight it, but I could not." He examined the hairs in his hands. "The wizard must've wanted Gian dead real bad to use up some of his life compelling me."

"Hurry up, time's running out," Deidre said from the door.

Toad shot up from the bed and paced frantically around. "Who is she? Go away. I only talk to Gian's heirs. No one else. Go!"

"She's my sister," I said, backing up with Nick.

He stopped and looked at her, and then me. "You twins?"

"Yes," I lied. I figured it was better than going into the whole explanation about her being my Changeling.

"Our time is almost up," I said. "How about the Chiave? Where did you put it?"

"Oh yes, oh yes, the Chiave." He shook his head several times, clenching and unclenching his fist repeatedly. "No one discovered it hidden in my waistband. Their magic did not pick it up. Chiavi are invisible to magic, they are."

He moved his cot away from the wall and dug his fingers into the cracks of one of the stones. The stone slowly moved, and he rocked it back and forth as he eased it out. After placing the rock on his mattress, he reached into the crevice and removed a parchment rolled around an ancient-looking metal spool.

"Time's up," Odran commanded from outside the hall.

"Take it." Toad reached the scroll out to me. "Only trust your own. Don't trust outsiders."

"I will." I grasped the scroll.

He didn't let go, his face sad and shadowed. "Dangers are everywhere."

"We'll clear you of this," Nick said.

"That is kind of you, but too late. I am beyond help." Toad released the scroll. He put the rock back in place, pushed the cot against the wall, and crawled onto his cot, pulling his knees to his chest.

I unrolled the scroll and read the name written on it. "Royston."

"Who's that?" Nick said. "Deidre, do you know someone with that name?"

"No," she said, her eyes darting from us to the corridor.

A siren sounded from down the corridor.

"Hurry," Odran urged. "There's been a breach. I must get you out through the back."

I didn't move, staring at Toad.

"Gia, come on." Nick grabbed my arm.

"We can't leave him." I looked over at Odran. "Whoever is coming is after him. Please, let us take him. He didn't murder Gian under his own will." My eyes pleaded with the man.

His hairy, pointy ears twitched as he considered it. He glanced from me to Toad and back to me. "Yes, yes. All right, then. We must hurry."

Toad hopped up from his bed. "I can go?"

"He said you could." I removed my jacket and put it on his shoulders. "Put this on."

He pushed his arms through the sleeves. My jacket fit him, except the sleeves were too short.

When Odran was out the door, I handed Nick the scroll. "Here, put this in your backpack. Guard it with your life."

"Come on," Nick said. "That's a little melodramatic isn't it? My life for a scroll. You do realize which one I'd choose, right?"

"If the wrong person got that name, every Royston alive would be murdered," Deidre said.

"My thoughts exactly," I said.

"Never mind Nick's life," he said under his breath.

"Well, are you coming or not?" Odran shouted from outside the cell.

We sprinted down the corridor and through a skinny door. Winding steps led up somewhere into the darkness. If it was The Red hunting us, I was not going to face him alone, not when I had other lives at stake. I tugged out my window rods and pulled them apart. The screen ignited, blue light ghosting Nick's body in front of me.

"Arik Baine," I said to the screen. It took several seconds for him to answer.

"Gia, what's the matter?" His eyes were half open and he had wicked bed hair.

"I'm in the Vatican. We're being—" My foot missed a step and I stumbled, dropping the window rod. One of the rods split in two. I quickly gathered the pieces and bounded up after the others, hoping Arik understood we needed help. The tight stairwell spiraled and spiraled a long distance up to another tight-fitting door. We single-filed through it, Odran leading the way into the Vatican Library.

"Follow me," he said and darted over the checkered tiles to a reading room with balconied stacks on one side of the room and arched windows directly across from them. Bookcases lined the walls between the windows. He slipped his hand between two shelves of one of the bookcases and pushed something. The case swung out. "Get inside. We must hide."

The secret door closed behind us, shutting out all light. I ignited my light globe. Disturbed dust swirled around the room. Antique shelves filled with volumes and volumes of record books lined the walls. My light flashed against the copper bases of several empty candle stands bunched in a corner.

"What is this room?" I whispered.

"It's the census records for the Mystik world. Every Mystik ever born is recorded in these books."

We sat there on the floor, not daring to move or talk for nearly forty minutes until we heard noise in the room outside.

Footsteps and muffled voices came from the other side of the bookcase. I popped the light globe in case its glow seeped through the cracks around the case. At one point, someone mentioned Nick and me by our names. How did they know we were here? The only people that knew we were going to the gallows were Atenae and those in the room with us. Deidre had library hopped through several gateway books before coming to the Vatican. There was no way all the Monitors could communicate her jumps to each other so fast.

Nick stretched his leg, knocking over one of the candle stands. We all froze when it hit the floor with a *clank*, holding our breaths, wondering if our pursuers heard it.

A light flickered under the door. "Did you hear that?" A man's deep voice came from the other side.

"Yeah, what was it?" another man asked.

"Don't know, but it came from behind this bookcase."

I leaned close to Nick. "Get your fireball ready," I said, barely audible. "After you throw it, I'll shield us. Okay?"

He nodded.

"It has to be a secret room," a woman's voice said.

The bookcase shook as if someone tried to move it. Books thudded onto the floor. It was only a matter of time before whoever was trying to get in would succeed. Something banged against the wood.

Bang.

Bang.

Crack. The tip of a sharp blade broke through the wood. Another *whack* and the head of an ax came through. A man's eye peeked through the slit.

"I can't see," the man said. "You have a light?"

"Sentinels are here," the woman said.

A fight broke out on the other side of the door.

"Gia!" Arik's voice called over the clangs of metal against metal, shuffling feet, growls, and grunts.

I pushed on the door and it wouldn't budge. Searching for a button or something to open it, I glared over at Odran. "Let me out!"

Odran pulled a lever on the wall and the bookcase swung open. Deidre seized my arm. "You don't have your sword or shield," she said, yanking me back.

Beside her, Nick had an electric charge building between his hands.

I stepped aside to let him pass. "What? No fireball?"

"I've been practicing. I wouldn't want to burn the place down." I sensed he was mocking me.

I glared at his back. "Just make sure to hit the bad guys and not one of ours."

"Give me some credit." He threw a glare at me before bolting out the door.

I turned to Deidre. "Can you stay here with Toad?"

"Yeah, go, and make sure Nick doesn't do anything careless."

My Converse squeaked across the floor as I chased after Nick. He abruptly stopped and lowered his hand. The electric charge died on the tiles. Arik, Jaran, and Demos, along with a few other Sentinels headed our way.

"What happened to the bad guys?" Nick asked, disappointment in his tone. He gave me a sidelong glance. "Guess we're late for the party."

"Remind me to send you an invitation next time." Demos nudged a man on the ground with the toe of his boot. "This one's out cold."

The bloodstain around the man grew wider as it soaked the carpet fibers. Luckily, the wizards had Cleaners to remove all evidence of the fight there.

"What do you think you're doing?" Arik bounded over to me. "Bloody hell, Gia, you can't just run off jumping in libraries and not tell anyone where you're going. It isn't safe."

I took a step back at seeing his angry face. "I had to."

Arik's jaw tightened before he snapped. "You had to? You had to risk Nick and Deidre's lives. The lives of those in the gallows? I don't know what to do with you anymore. You're careless and your rash choices will get someone hurt, again, or killed next time. You can't just act on your impulses."

He doesn't know what to do with me anymore?

His words slapped me, and a spark hit my chest. He had never lost it like this before. "I didn't ask for this," I said tightly. "And I'm going to make choices you won't like. I *had* to do this tonight. Don't forget who I am, Arik. If I hadn't come tonight, we would have lost a very important Chiave. I don't answer to you. I answer to the High Wizard of Asile. So you *don't* need to know what to do with me." I threw his words back at him with so much force it left me shaking.

Arik glared down at me. "I'm *your lead*. You do answer to me."

Demos got between us. "Okay, we're a little heated here. Let's all calm down."

Jaran put his arm around Arik. "We should let emotions simmer down before something is said that can't be taken back."

"Too late," I said, and turned my back to Arik. If I looked at him, I would cry.

"What were you two doing here?" Demos asked, returning his sword to its scabbard then adjusting the belt around his waist.

Deidre came out of the secret room with Toad and Odran. "We came to get him." She placed her hand on Toad's back.

Jaran lowered his arm. "Who is he?"

"This is Toad," Deidre said. "He murdered Gian, but not by choice. He had a Chiave. We had to get it."

I pushed past the others and headed for the reading room. I didn't want to talk. Not only was I mad, I was also tired. Of all people, I thought Arik would understand the burden I carried. With it came tough decisions. I had to do this without the Sentinels. If they had come with me tonight, forget losing a Chiave, Toad would've been dead before we arrived. And there was something innocent about Toad. Someone had compelled him to kill Gian, and I wanted to do whatever it took to clear him of the charges against him.

CHAPTER NINE

I hadn't spoken to Arik in two days. His reaction in the Vatican Library still upset me. I angrily tucked the blanket under my chin and curled up in my bed. I wanted to stay under the covers all day. Tears filled my eyes, making the room blur. When would he trust my judgment? I put all my faith in him. It wasn't much to ask for him to do the same for me.

The bedroom door opened, letting in all the wonderful smells that only Thanksgiving could bring. I tugged a pillow over my head.

"Go away, Deidre."

Heavy boots clunked across the wooden floor, and then muffled over the area carpet. "Are you going to hide out in your room the entire holiday?" Arik's voice startled me.

I sat up. "W-what are you doing here?"

"I was invited for bird and stuffing, whatever the latter is."

"I invited you before…"

His dark eyes surveyed my face. "Before what, exactly?"

"You know, you snapped at me."

He dropped down on the bed. "I believe you aren't used

to someone other than your father worrying about you."

"That was worrying? You used that whole *bloody hell* thing on me, which means you were angry. And you said many hurtful things."

He pinched his brows together. "So that's why you haven't attended practices the last few days."

"Well, obviously you didn't care. You didn't even check on me." I folded my arms across my chest. "So why are you here now?"

"If you would have answered when I rang, you would've known I wasn't around. I had a matter to settle before returning home."

"Who calls? You really need to learn how to text already."

He covered my hand with his and stroked his thumb across my knuckles, sending chills over my skin. "I could never ignore you, Gia. Couples fight all the time, and make amends afterward. I'm sorry it got heated."

His brown eyes full of sincerity were like probes melting my insides. The more time we spent together, the more I couldn't resist him. That concerned face of his was making me feel bad. Why was I always the irrational one in the relationship?

"I'm sorry, too," I said, ashamed, looking down at the pink comforter I wouldn't have picked for myself. Deidre had decorated our room.

He lifted my chin up and gently kissed my lips. "Truce?"

I nodded against his lips. But there was something different in his kiss—a lack of connection.

"Get dressed. The guest of honor should be brown and crispy by now." He stood.

"By the way, where did you go?"

He stopped in the doorframe. "I went along with Merl to attend the Wizard Council. There was a ceremony for the novices that made senior wizard. While there, we arranged a new trial for Toad. Asile is holding him until the proceedings, which shall be in a month's time."

Bastien. I wondered if he had made senior wizard, but for some reason I couldn't bring myself to ask Arik if he had.

"You did? A trial for Toad." Tears burned behind my eyes. "Really?"

He quirked a smile. "You'll be called upon to testify, but we can talk about the details later." He rested his hand on the doorknob. "I think Faith even baked a pie. Someone might want to tell her to use only the pulp of the pumpkin and discard the rind and seeds next time." He smiled and shut the door.

I wrapped a tie around my hair and pulled it into a messy bun, then touched up my face with some foundation and eye shadow. I picked up my root beer–flavored Lip Smacker and then dropped it into my bag.

Time to grow up, Gia. I snatched Deidre's red gloss off the dresser and swiped the wand over my lips.

"You look nice," Deidre said from the door.

I returned the wand into the barrel and put her lip gloss back on her dresser. "I'm sorry. I just thought—"

"Hey, no problem. You can use anything of mine you want." She smiled and crossed the room to the closet. "I have this shiny green shirt that would look fabulous on you."

Ever since we came back from the Vatican, Deidre had been super sweet to me, which made me uneasy. I was used to her ignoring me. She had definitely found her individuality. We hardly looked alike anymore. Maybe she didn't hate me anymore for taking over the life that should have been hers.

"Here, a nice pair of jeans and some ballet flats should do nicely."

I smiled at her. "Thanks."

"Don't mention it." She really had the American thing down. Deidre was like a chameleon, changing to blend in to her environment.

I dressed and met the others downstairs.

The Thanksgiving table was elegantly set with beautiful autumn themed centerpieces and various sizes of candles bunched together. Faith could decorate like nobody's business. Too bad her cooking wasn't as perfectly mastered. Thankfully, Pop had cooked the turkey and all the fixings while Faith slept.

Arik's knee pushed against mine. If we were alone I'd reach over and kiss his perfect lips, but since we weren't, I glanced at everyone instead. Pop had bought a folding table with chairs. The combined tables stretched all the way across the dining room and into the living room. There were twenty-four of us with all the Sentinels.

Carrig and Sinead leaned toward each other. Lei backed up against Kale, angling her iPhone to take a selfie with him. "Come on, love, smile," she said.

A slight grin pulled on Kale's face.

She nudged his stomach with her elbow. "Is that the best you can do?"

Pop and Miss Bagley were lost in their own conversation. They actually made a cute couple. Pop was happy.

Deidre was chatting up Mr. and Mrs. D'Marco while Nick studied his hands.

I missed Nana Kearns who was stuck in Boston due to a snowstorm that was heading our way. I'd never spent a Thanksgiving without her.

"That brown liquid stuff was delicious," Jaran said on my left. "What's it called again?"

"Gravy," I said.

Jaran's gaze fixed on Chane, who sat by the Sentinels at

the other end of the table. Jaran had been quiet lately. A sort of sad gloominess surrounded him.

"If you want, I can pack some in a container for you to take home?" Faith said. "Brian made tons."

His lips shifted into a smile, crinkling his eyes. "You needn't do that. Besides what would I put it on?"

"What would you put it on?" I feigned a shocked expression. "Why, everything. You could put it on eggs, vegetables, meat, French fries, um, well…maybe not everything. Like, you wouldn't want to put it on fruit or cakes and stuff."

Jaran laughed and this time it brightened his entire face.

Faith cut into a pie at the end of the table nearest the kitchen. "Who wants some? It's pumpkin."

"I do," Demos said eagerly, already picking up his fork. "I love this feast thing. The food just keeps coming, doesn't it?"

"I'm sorry, Faith, I don't like pumpkin anything," I said quickly before she had a chance to pass me a plate. I leaned closer to Jaran. "Be careful of the pie."

Jaran waved Faith off as she extended a plate to him. "Um, I think I'll just have some more of that red stuff."

"Cranberry sauce?" Faith frowned. "Well, all right. But you don't know what you're missing."

Faith offered a plate to Arik, and he gave me a sidelong glare as he took it. I squeezed his knee and he gave me a crooked smile, showing off his dimples.

"I couldn't have everyone refusing her," he whispered.

"You're such a do-gooder."

He flashed his almost perfect teeth at me before poking his fork at the pie.

"This pie is scrumptious," Demos said around a crunchy mouthful. He spit something into his napkin. "Is it supposed to have seeds?"

"Yes, studies have found the shell and seeds are good for

you," Pop said. "Great source of fiber."

Faith sat back in her chair. No one had the heart to tell her the truth about her pie. She'd worked so hard the night before making them. "You should add some whipped cream," she said. "It's homemade."

Arik dabbed his finger into the fluffy mound on his pie and licked it. He coughed and downed several gulps from his water glass. "It's...it's *salty*."

"Salt?" Faith's face twisted with concern. "It should be sugar. Drat it all. I think I mixed up the canisters again."

I tried to stifle a laugh, but it came out like a deflating balloon.

"Oh, stop it, I'm a mess." Faith folded her napkin with anxious fingers.

Carrig's name blasted from his pocket.

Everyone started. Forks clunked against plates among the gasps. Carrig reached into his pocket, retrieved his window rod, and pulled it open. Uncle Philip's face lit across the bluish screen. Both sides of the table could view him from either side of the rods.

"Good evening," Uncle Philip said. "Sorry to interrupt. Please accept my apologies. I wasn't able to get away to make the feast. Some rogue Mystiks attacked one of the havens in the early hours this morning. We've locked the gateway books and placed guards at the entries of the havens. All travel to the Mystik world has been restricted."

"What?" Miss Bagley scooted her chair back and rushed over to Carrig, leaning over his shoulder. "Who authorized this? No one warned me my book would be locked."

Demos leaned over the table, glaring at the screen. "First the covens, now the gateways. What's next? Segregation?"

Jaran patted Demos's arm. "Calm down. It won't do any good to get angry."

"Whatever." Demos flung himself back in his chair.

"There isn't anything I can do. The Wizard Council dispensed it." Uncle Philip's voice sounded static-y. "If you have to travel, you must put in a request to the Council to do so."

"What haven was attacked?" Carrig asked.

"Santara," Uncle Philip said.

"That can't be so, no?" Pia, one of the Sentinels from Santara, a haven in Spain, suddenly stood. Her chair fell back and thunked against the floor. "We must go to our people."

Uncle Philip heaved a deep sigh. "I'm afraid you must remain at your post."

Reya, the more sensible of the two Sentinels from Santara, placed a gentle hand on Pia's arm. "What damage did she sustain?"

His eyes flicked in Reya's direction. "There were many killed before help arrived. Several homes were set on fire, and the palace was destroyed."

"I request permission to return home so we may aid the victims." Reya's face held no emotion. Her back was straight, shoulders square. Beside her, Pia was slumped and worry distorted her face, tears stained her cheeks.

"I must deny this request," he said.

Arik threw his napkin down and stood behind Carrig. "If it were Asile, you could not keep us from returning, Professor. We can handle things here without Reya and Pia. Have some compassion and let them tend to those in need."

My heart squeezed at Arik's resolve. His eyes fixed on the window rod, his breath steady, sent chills across my scalp, to my fingertips, to my toes. He would never back down when he believed in something. I admired him for that.

"Professor." Sinead's soft voice calmed the room. "I know how you felt when Jacalyn was in danger once. You broke the rules to get to her. Look into your heart and do what is right here."

"But that was different." Uncle Philip lowered his head, and I wondered if he was remembering his love for Jacalyn, Nick's mother. And remembering how Conemar had killed her. Was he recalling past memories that now were bittersweet? Or was Sinead working her magic on him?

Uncle Philip raised his face to the screen. "All right. Miss Bagley?"

"Yes?" she practically barked, not able to hide the anger in her voice or on her face.

"See Reya and Pia to the gateway book. Carrig and Arik will accompany you. I will send guards to escort them to Santara. The gateway will open for a few minutes. Only those authorized to jump may go through. If the Monitor detects any other jumpers, the gateway will immediately shut, and those unauthorized will be stuck inside." He cleared his throat. "Am I clear?"

Miss Bagley's eyes narrowed at him. "Yes, but I do not agree with the Wizard Council's decision to lock the gateways. First restricted jumps, now this. For centuries, the gateways have always remained open, even during uprisings. Closing them makes us look weak to our enemies."

I hated to admit it, but I agreed with Miss Bagley. Why have Sentinels if you didn't have faith in them to keep the gateways safe?

Miss Bagley was thinking the same thing I was. "Why not just increase security around the entries to the havens instead?" she asked. "Decisions like this by the Council without thought or a vote cause our people to join Conemar's forces, and I don't blame them."

Uncle Philip looked sharply at her. "Be careful there, Kayla. What you say could be taken as treason. We are in the end times. We must take drastic measures to secure not only the havens and the surrounding Mystik cities, but also the human world. It's only a matter of time before rogues feel confident enough to attack humans."

"Mark my word, this action will do more harm than good." Miss Bagley's nose actually rose in the air as she stomped back to Pop's side.

"These attacks," Carrig said. "Do we know where the assailants retreated to?"

"The Monitors picked up their entries into the gateway but did not pick up their exits."

"What do you mean?" Jaran said. "They simply vanished?"

"We're not certain," Uncle Philip said. "It was as though their jumps were erased."

Demos pushed his chair back. "How can that be? The Monitors can see everything in the gateways."

"We haven't a clue," Uncle Philip answered. "Our finest wizards and representatives from the Fey nation have come together to sort it out." His eyes turned to Carrig. "You should be on your way."

Carrig nodded.

"Brian, sorry," Miss Bagley interrupted. "I must go. I'll send you a good night text later." Then she kissed him. On the lips. In front of everyone. Most importantly, in front of *me*.

Okay, I was ready for Pop to date, but not the PDA that went along with it.

"And Carrig," Uncle Philip was saying, "After escorting Pia and Reya, you and Arik are needed in Asile for a meeting with all the Sentinel leaders."

Reya and Pia said their good-byes before following Miss Bagley out the front door.

Arik stood and glanced down at me. "I'll ring when I return."

No kiss good-bye? He was definitely still mad at me.

"You could text." I was determined to get the boy to use modern technology. It was more private that way, especially since we both had shared bedrooms.

"What fun is that? Then I wouldn't get to hear your lovely voice." He winked.

Okay, maybe we're fine.

Carrig handed his window rod to Sinead, and then he and Arik departed after the others.

"Gia and Nick," Uncle Philip continued. "We will resume the search for the Chiavi after things settle down a bit. Miss Bagley will have some research books that you can use to search artifacts in the libraries of the world. I'll be preoccupied with Wizard Council matters and won't be able to aid you until situations calm down. Good evening, everyone."

"Good evening," Sinead said, and shut the rods.

Lei tossed her napkin onto the table. "I can hardly believe it. This is madness. I'm with Miss Bagley on this. With the gateways locked, we'll appear soft. Other groups will surely test our strength."

"Calm down," Kale said, rubbing her back. "There is nothing we can do about it. The Wizard Council is just trying to prevent further attacks."

"Well, its bullocks," Demos said, stabbing his fork into the empty pie shell on his plate. "We should be out hunting these rogues instead of hiding from them like babies."

"I'm inclined to believe," Jaran said, "if we hunt them, many innocents could get hurt. This way, we corner them, get them to come out of hiding, instead of them surprise attacking us all the time."

"It's still bullocks," Demos muttered under his breath.

"Shall we help Faith with the dishes?" Sinead said, picking up her plate.

Pop smiled at me. Not one of those smiles he'd give me when he wasn't too sure about all this other-world stuff, when he felt helpless, unable to protect me from the dangers my new life presented. It was more like a smile that said he was happy about them locking the gateways and that I'd be staying safe at home. He picked up several dishes and hurried off to the kitchen.

I picked up a button from the tablecloth. It looked like one from Arik's shirt. It must've fallen off. The antique-looking button had a lion's head etched into it. I went to the junk drawer in the kitchen, riffled around for a safety pin, and secured the button to my shirt.

Faith wiped the counter beside me with her dishrag. "Having a memento to remind you of a loved one is such a cherished thing." Her fingers went to her pendant. "It makes me happy to know that Ricardo kept my pendant."

"Yes, it is." I shut the drawer. "I already miss Arik."

"Gia, I'm happy they closed the gateways," she said, keeping her eyes on her task. "The Red is a dangerous Laniar. He has no heart. Laniars may not have a soul, but we have hearts. He has a dark one. Please don't go back into the libraries with him stalking them."

"Well, I can't now, right?" I stopped when I noticed the fear on her face. "What did he do to you?"

She looked at me, startled. "Why do you think he did something to me?"

"It's written all over your face."

"He…" Her lips puckered as she sprinkled cleaner on the counter, the heaviness of the truth weighing her shoulders down. "He killed my parents," she barely whispered, lifting up her shirt and showing me an angry scar running the length of her belly. "And then he gutted me…leaving me for dead."

The gasp escaped my lips before I could stop it. Tears

leaked from the corners of my eyes. "Oh, Faith," my voice cracked. "That's horrible."

"Merl saved me. I hardly remember it. I was so young." She turned her back on me and continued wiping the counters. "They say The Red was injured in a horrible battle many decades ago. He was on the brink of death. A demented curer tried all sorts of illegal experiments to bring him out of it. That is why his heart is black. Rotten."

Heat rose inside me. Angry heat. I wanted to drive my sword into The Red and gut him as he had done to Faith. The thoughts scared me. They were animalistic and cruel, and I wondered if I had the chance, would I do it?

"Faith?"

"Hmm?" She stayed focused on the counters, scrubbing the grout hard. The tile probably never had such a detailed cleaning before.

Thinking about The Red freaked me out, and Deidre tended to stay out late with Nick. I didn't want to be alone in my room. "Can I sleep in your room tonight?"

She paused mid-scrub. The corner of her mouth pulled slightly into a smile. "I'd love that, but you do know I don't sleep in the evening."

"Lately, neither do I." Sleep probably would elude me again tonight, knowing Arik and Carrig traveled the gateways while somewhere in the Mystik world The Red prepared for his next attack.

Deidre was touching up her face when I went to our room.

"Hey," I said, crossing to my dresser. "Are you going somewhere?"

"To Nick's for some real pie." She brushed mascara on her lashes.

I pulled out my pajama bottoms and a T-shirt from the middle drawer. "I thought you mentioned going over to

Emily's for a movie tonight."

"No. Those plans were canceled. We haven't been hanging out. I made new friends."

That surprised me. "What happened? Did you have a fight?"

She put her mascara down and sighed. "In a way. She keeps flirting with Arik in class. I told her to back off. That you and Arik are an item, that you're my sister, and that I couldn't be friends with someone who messes with you. But she wouldn't listen so, you know..."

I wanted to hug her. There was this connection building between us. Maybe it was because we shared a room or because we bonded during our covert operation at the Vatican the other night, but it was there. "Thank you," I said.

Her eyes met mine as she picked up her lipstick. "Don't get teary-eyed. You'll make me cry and mess up my freshly applied mascara."

"Okay. Well, have fun." I grabbed the new window rod Carrig had given me off the dresser and hugged my pajamas to my chest on the way to the door. "If you get back early, come upstairs and hang out with us."

She smiled as she swiped red across her lips. "Thanks. I might just do that."

I ducked into the bathroom and put my PJs on the counter, then pulled the two pieces of my window rod apart. The screen blinked on. "Bastien Renard," I said to it.

Almost a minute passed before Bastien answered my call. His eyes looked even bluer coming across screen. His hair was messy as if he'd been sleeping. "Hello, there. This is a nice surprise."

My lips twitched as I tried not to smile too big at the sight of him. "I just wanted to see how you were doing, and if you made senior wizard."

"I'm doing well, and yes, I graduated." He ran his hand through his dark hair. It was shorter than normal, as if he'd just had it cut. "And you? How are you, Gianna?"

"It's Gia, remember?"

"If you insist." His lips lifted with a smile. "But I'd rather call you by a name no one else uses. Besides, your full name is lovely."

I couldn't control it, my smile widened. "Well, congratulations."

"Thank you." He adjusted himself on what I could make out was a bed. For some reason, I felt uncomfortable with him lying down.

"I would have sent a gift, because that's what *friends* do in my world, but I didn't know how to get it to you." *Okay, that totally sounded obvious.* But I wanted to make sure he knew I was calling as a friend and not for any other reason.

"It's perfectly all right, *friend*," he said, mocking me. "We don't give gifts in my world for such occasions."

I glanced over my shoulder as if someone could see me from the other side of the bathroom door. "Well, anyway, I should go."

"Thank you for ringing, Gianna," he said.

"Um, okay." A short laugh escaped my lips. "Talk to you later, then."

"Good evening," he said, and I closed the rod.

Okay, that didn't go well. Was he flirting with me? I suddenly felt guilty for calling him, but he was a friend. We went to the play together. Fought Conemar together. Why should I worry? But there was something there, and I decided it was better not to call him again, out of respect for Arik.

After changing into my pajamas, I curled up on the futon in Faith's attic bedroom, cuddling under her thick cashmere blanket. Faith worked tirelessly to create a whimsical bedroom, using soft blue fabrics, white lacey window coverings, and a magical garden painted on the walls with fairies and butterflies.

I fingered Arik's button I'd pinned onto my tee, eyeing one of her fairies with deep red curls and large yellow wings. "That's a new fairy," I said. "You're almost done with all the walls. We should get you an easel and some canvases so you can keep painting. Maybe even sell some."

She pushed the netting covering her bed aside. "Really? You think I'm good enough?" She picked up a box from the bed and carried it over to me. Her lanky body moved gracefully across the floor. "Late at night, I've been going for walks, collecting leaves. I want to coat them with glitter and glue them on the trees I've painted."

"I think your work is amazing." I gazed at the bright yellow brush strokes forming a sun high up on the wall and taking over part of the ceiling. She had created day in her room. Unable to go out in direct sunlight, she existed in the shadows of storms and the darkness of night.

She sat beside me and smiled. "I painted this, too. It's my memory box."

The purple box had flowers, butterflies, and a fairy with yellow hair riding a unicorn painted on it.

"It's beautiful."

"I keep all my remember items in it."

"Remember items?"

She lifted the lid and placed it on the bed. "Yes. Things I kept from when I was a girl."

I ran a gentle finger over the lid, admiring her handiwork, then paused over the crown on the fairy's head. "The crown." I shot up.

"What about it?" She watched me curiously.

"The Chiave we found. It's a crown and can shield whoever

has it from the Monitors."

"But we have the Chiave," she said.

"Maybe another one exists or something like it does."

Or was found and replaced. Uncle Philip had told me once that there were spies everywhere in Asile. And if the rogues had a way to sneak through the gateway. No one was safe.

I wasn't safe.

CHAPTER TEN

Nick sped his motorcycle around turn after turn. My fingers grew numb gripping his waist and holding on with all my might. He slowed the bike when we approached the beach and parked by the curb. I swung my messenger bag to the side and slid off the seat. The slate gray sky blended into the water beneath it. Early morning joggers, diehards, trotted across the damp sand. Nick felt at peace here by the beach, his tense shoulders relaxing as we plodded over to his favorite bench.

"So your boyfriend still gone?" he asked in an attempt to make small talk.

Glancing up from digging through my bag, searching for my window rod, I frowned at him. "Yeah, he won't be back until late tonight. I won't see him until school tomorrow."

"What's wrong?" His breath formed a cloud in front of him, and he shivered against the cold. "Anytime I bring him up, you get down."

I found the window rod and pulled it out. "We just seem off lately. He was really mad at me that night in the Vatican, and we haven't had any time to talk about it. And it probably didn't help that I'd pushed him away."

He wrapped his arms around himself. "I wouldn't worry. You two will be back to normal soon."

Mine and Arik's plans for the Thanksgiving break were ruined. We were supposed to do normal teen stuff. Like shop the sales on Black Friday, see a new release at the theater on Saturday, and laze around on Sunday. It should have been a day with Arik, eating popcorn, watching old movies, and making out when no one was looking. Instead, I was with Nick, waiting for our scheduled meeting with Uncle Philip on my window rod.

Uncle Philip called my name through the rod, and I opened it. His face flashed onto the screen.

"Good afternoon, Gia. Are you alone?"

"Nick's with me. But yeah, it's just us."

"Hey," Nick said.

His eyes went to the silver knight pin on my jacket. "I see you have my gift. Did Nick receive his?"

Touching the pin, I said, "Yes, we got them. What are they for?"

"So you can pass through the spells locking the gateway books," he said. "You aren't to tell anyone about their purpose."

"We won't," I said.

"Very well," he said, tugging at his high collar. "Now then, several of our wizards in the lab investigated your theory about the Chiave. They found that there isn't a way to duplicate the crown without destroying one of the Monitors' globes, which is difficult to do. You see, the two are made of the same magical glass and it's practically unbreakable. Only a brand like yours could shield someone while in the gateways. And the charm to create one was lost when the recipe was ripped out of the ancient spell book found by your nana."

"Are they sure? How else could The Red just erase his and his men's jumps? And how did they use the gateways if they were locked?"

"I wondered that, as well. I had the Chiave tested. It's a fake."

"*Arrrk! No magic*," Pip, the Monitor for Asile, chirped somewhere off screen.

Uncle Philip looked to his side. "Yes, Pip. You've told me."

"It can't be a fake," I protested. "The spirit of the Chiave gave it to us."

"The Chiave we have is a replica. Someone switched it with the real one before it made it to Asile. When whoever stole it used the crown to jump through the gateway, it removed our spells locking it. Was the Chiave in your possession the entire time?"

"Yes—" I stopped. "It was in Nick's backpack."

"Yeah, I had it the whole time. I even gave it to Carrig myself."

Uncle Philip rubbed his chin. "And it wasn't out of your sight at all?"

Nick stared off at the water. The waves were picking up, and the clouds deepened into a darker gray. "When we all returned to the library in Branford, we went home. We didn't tell anyone that we had a Chiave, not until later."

"That's right," I said. "A book faerie told us about Toad, so we went home and snuck out later to go see him in the gallows about the scroll."

"What did you do with the pack when you returned home?"

"I left it on a chair by the front door," Nick said.

"Where were your parents?" Uncle Philip said.

"Watching some show in the living room." He combed his fingers through his tousled brown hair. "Emily Proctor stopped by to return my textbook she borrowed."

"You never told me that." I stared at Nick's profile, his jaw tight and his mouth a straight line.

"It was quick," he said. "She was only there for a few minutes then she left."

"And she was never left alone?"

"Only for a second. She sneezed and I got her a tissue." He rubbed his hands together. "You saw how gaudy and big that crown is. She couldn't have hidden it from me."

Uncle Philip leaned back in his chair. "And after you snuck out and returned later from the Vatican, where was the bag?"

"With me," Nick said.

"And the crown was with you?"

"Yes." Nick tapped his foot nervously. "I didn't want my parents finding the crown before I could give it to Carrig."

I rested my elbows on my knees, my arms aching from holding up the window rod. "When we returned to the library in Branford, Nick went to the restroom."

"And the bag?"

"I don't remember," Nick said. "I probably brought it in with me."

"Try to think." Uncle Philip's jaw tightened, Nick's lack of answers clearly beginning to wear on him. "What did you do with it?"

Nick's shoulders stiffened, and he folded and unfolded his hands before reaching into the front pocket of his pants, no doubt touching the mood crystal, hoping to calm the beast threatening to overtake him.

"Arik and the others waited with me in the lobby for him," I said, hoping to divert some of the pressure Uncle Philip was putting on Nick. "Miss Bagley was there, but she was busy turning off lights and doing whatever else she does to lock up the library."

"Well, from here on, after you retrieve a Chiave, you are to jump to Asile and bring it to me straightaway. No longer will you take it to Carrig."

"You don't think Carrig switched it, do you?"

"I suggest you trust no one," he said. "From here on out, only we three shall know about the Chiavi retrievals. You are to tell no one"—he looked directly at me—"not even Arik, about our findings."

"How could someone know we found the Chiave, make a copy, and replace the original without us seeing? If they even knew it was in Nick's bag, the possibility is unlikely. We didn't tell anyone we had it."

"Wizards can make doppelgangers out of anything, not just people," he said. "It would have only taken a matter of seconds for a wizard to create an identical crown. You could have been found out, and when no one was looking, a wizard could have snuck in and made the exchange. Nevertheless, there's a traitor in your midst. From here forward, we keep all matters of the Chiavi to us three. Are we clear?"

Nick nodded, and I answered, "Yes."

Snowflakes tumbled from the sky and vanished when they hit the window rod's screen. The wind shifted the waves, whitecaps sharply peaked above the ashen water, and buoys dinged their protests. Uncle Philip omitted the fact that if there was a traitor, then we weren't safe. Or possibly, he chose not to scare us by stating the obvious. Either way, I suddenly felt like every shadow cloaked an unknown threat.

"You have a storm." Uncle Philip's eyes darted around, watching the snow fall. "I will contact you when the search for the remaining Chiavi can commence. May Agnes guide you," he closed with the blessing from the patron saint of Asile.

The snow almost buried us on our way home. My bones

were still frozen when I cuddled under the throw I shared with Deidre on the couch. She was watching the movies I'd gotten for Arik and me. I couldn't focus on them as I replayed the events of the night Nick and I found the crown. I ran through every step in the Vatican to Toad's cell, following Nick's backpack in my memories.

Only Carrig, Emily, and possibly Miss Bagley were alone with the bag. There was no way it was Carrig. He knew what had happened to Conemar. If he were with The Red then his men wouldn't be searching for the evil wizard's whereabouts. Emily was human and didn't have any ties to the Mystik world, but she could be in disguise. I couldn't place Miss Bagley alone with the bag, just in the vicinity.

Whoever it was had to be working with a wizard to create a doppelganger of the crown.

I gripped the soft material of the blanket and sat up straighter. Then there was Nick.

"What's wrong?" Deidre tugged the throw back over her. "This isn't even the scary part of the movie."

Nick.

I suddenly felt colder. Could he be responsible for the switch? I shook my head. There was no way. All this crap going on was messing with my good senses. I slid down into the couch pillows, half watching the movie and half running things through my mind.

High school lunch rooms were strange places. The nondescript walls, lunch tables, and floor were a bland backdrop for the diversified students within. All shapes, sizes, and races mingled around the tables. Some kids rushed to grab unoccupied tables, others crept through food lines, and several flirted across the mayhem. My gaze kept going to the door as I waited for Arik to join us.

"They have fish sticks today," Demos said, dropping his tray on the table and shaking the bench as he sat.

I wrinkled my nose. The smell was horrible. "How can you eat that? Do you realize how processed it is? It can't even be real fish."

He stuffed one into his mouth. "It's delightful," he said around the breaded fish parts.

Lei threw her napkin at him. "Ugh, close your mouth. You're repulsive."

Demos snatched up the chocolate milk carton in front of him and took a long gulp.

"What's on your shirt?" Lei asked.

I inspected where her eyes were fixed, expecting to see a stain in the cotton blend. It was Arik's button with the lion's head. I'd pinned it on for luck. "Oh this," I said. "It's just a token. Have you seen Arik?" I switched the subject so she wouldn't ask me where I'd gotten it. "He's usually here before us."

"I saw him," said Kale, snatching one of Lei's cookies. "He had to stay after class to complete a project."

"Oh." I unwrapped my sandwich. That wasn't like Arik. He only did what he had to do to get a passing grade. To him, going to school was a cover and he didn't exert much effort on it.

My attention was half on the lunchroom door and half on ripping the crust off the sandwich Faith packed for me. She had torn the bread trying to spread a left-over cheese ball onto it. I smiled at her effort.

Demos continued stuffing his face with fish sticks. Deidre and Nick sat at a nearby table, their heads together, whispering and arguing about something.

"Why don't they just take a break?" Demos said, dipping a stick into ketchup.

"Because love can be torture sometimes," Jaran said. "But it's still love and hard to let go of."

Lei bumped his shoulder with hers. "You're so poetic, ducky."

Kale took another cookie from Lei's pile. The boy had a sweet tooth. "Love may be torture at times, but it shouldn't be like theirs. There should be give and take, sacrifice from both sides."

He had a point. Deidre and Nick's relationship had become one-sided, and Deidre was getting the short end of the stick. His statement gave me fresh eyes on my situation with Arik. I needed to apologize to him. Maybe that's why he'd been so distant lately.

Arik sauntered into the lunch room. I stood, climbed over the bench, and straightened my shirt. Lei snatched my hand before I could rush to him. I glanced at her, then at him and froze. It took me several minutes to process the image. He had his arm draped over Emily's shoulders, leaning close to her and whispering something into her ear. Her face beamed. My gaze narrowed in on her hand reaching up and holding his.

I must've looked like a moron standing there staring at them with my mouth gaped open. It was as if they moved in slow motion toward me. Emily's dark hair bounced on her shoulders, her lips glossed red split into a satisfied smile, and her porcelain skin, luminous under the florescent lights, caused all the guys she passed to stop what they were doing to stare at her beauty. But the only eyes I cared about were the deep brown ones checking out how the mounds of her larger-than-mine breasts jiggled with each of her steps. I thought it was against dress code to wear such a low-cut top.

What the hell?

I wanted to wake up from this nightmare. My stomach rolled, threatening to toss the half-eaten cheese ball sandwich onto the floor. All noise in the cafeteria thrummed in my ears.

Is this a joke?

I couldn't make out what Lei said beside me, and turned to her. "Huh?"

"What are they doing?" Lei said louder.

"I don't know," I muttered, my hands shaking at my sides.

Arik and Emily stopped in front of us.

Lei flung her long hair over her shoulders and put her petite body between me and the obvious couple. "What the bloody hell is going on, Arik?"

"Um..." He looked confused.

I glanced at the other confused faces surrounding me.

Jaran hurried to my side. "What are you doing, Arik?"

Demos dropped his fish stick. "Have you lost your bleeding mind?"

"I'm not seeing what I'm seeing," Kale said, giving Lei a confused look. "Am I?"

"Oh you are," Lei said. "And it's not right."

Emily angled closer to Arik. "Didn't you tell her, babe?"

I fisted my hands to keep them from shaking. "No, he didn't tell me. *Babe?*"

Arik gave me a puzzled look.

"Can we talk, Arik?" I held Emily's gaze. "Alone."

He turned his puzzled look to Emily.

"It's fine," she said.

"You need permission to talk to me?" This had to be a nightmare. I just had to wake up. There's no way Arik would be someone's lost puppy, only moving on her command.

He reluctantly followed me out into the hall.

I spun and faced him. "What's going on?"

I watched his beautiful face, waiting for him to drop the bomb on me, my heart breaking into pieces and cutting painfully against my chest. I couldn't breathe, my throat clogged with a scream threatening to blast out.

He lowered his head, unable to hold my glare. "I'm not sure how it happened. I…"

"Are you breaking up with me?"

"We never really made it official." He raised his head. "Did we? I've been trying to talk to you for days. But the moment never presented itself. You had to feel the distance growing between us as I had."

"I thought we were official." Emotion cracked over my words, and I couldn't stop the tears no matter how hard I tried. I took deep breaths. "Are you with her?"

"Yes," he said barely audible.

I stared at him through blurry eyes, waiting for him to take it back. Waiting for him to tell me that he was just playing a horrible joke on me.

Waiting.

Waiting to breathe again.

He just stood there. Head down, unable to look at me.

"I'm sorry," he finally said, digging the dagger of truth deeper into my heart.

"I don't even know how not to smash in your face right now—" My breaths rushed out and I tried to calm them, almost hyperventilating. My nails dug into my palms as I tightened my fist.

Arik took a few steps toward me until he was right in front me and whispered, "Listen, I'm sorry. I care deeply for you, Gia, but—"

Another sob escaped me and I shoved him away. I ripped the safety pin holding his button from my shirt and threw it at him. "Stay away from me!"

Unable to look at him anymore, I sprinted down the hall and bounded for the doors.

"Gia!" Jaran called from behind me.

I slammed into the doors and struggled to open them. Finally, they flew open and I slipped on the ice, landing on my butt and sliding down the steps.

Jaran dropped down beside me and pulled me into his arms. "It's going to be okay. I'm here. You'll get through this."

I sobbed into his chest. "How could he?"

"I don't know. This doesn't seem like Arik."

"But he did it. He lied to me. He led me on. He—He—He…" I gasped for air. It hurt to breathe. It hurt to think. It hurt so bad I thought I might pass out. It felt like shards of glass pumping through my veins, ripping me apart from the inside out.

"Shh… Just take small breaths." He didn't let me go. I sank into his warm arms, broken. For several minutes, he let me cry against him until my breaths matched his calm ones.

I shivered.

"How about we go inside and find a warmer place to talk?"

I nodded against his chest. I wanted to be anywhere but in the lunchroom. I never wanted to see Arik again. Not with her. And yet, I longed to see him at the same time.

Jaran helped me to stand. My legs shaky, I grasped his arm as we stepped carefully up the slick steps.

"In time, this wound will heal. You just have to keep going."

"How do you know it'll get better?" I snapped. "I just want to die right now."

"I know because I'm in love, but he decided to be with another." Jaran yanked the door open. "Someone who isn't afraid to come out. Someone braver than me."

"Oh, Jaran, I'm so sorry." I rested my head on his shoulder.

"We're a mess, aren't we?"

"Well, you definitely are, but my pain is calloused now."

"Why can't you come out?"

He smirked, but it wasn't a happy smirk; it was one full of regrets. "I come from an ancient world, one that doesn't accept my preferences. One that had betrothed me to a girl I could never love."

"Was the guy Chane?" I asked. Talking about his pain was relieving mine somewhat, which was totally messed up.

"No, that infatuation ended when we moved here. Besides he's more afraid of being discovered than I am." He led me down the hall. "The guy is Cole Jenson."

"Really?" I sniffled. "The student body president? I can see it. He's got style."

"And a new boyfriend."

"Sorry."

"Don't be. What do you say we just grab our coats and cut class?"

"Ditch? You?" I was surprised. He never broke rules.

"I'm not so rigid that I can't step outside the lines once in a while."

"Where will we go?"

"There's a movie I'd love to see."

"Anywhere dark sounds good to me." I wiped my wet eyes with my sleeve and let him lead me to my locker. If someone's soul could die, mine was withering with each painful step.

CHAPTER ELEVEN

The fluorescent lights hummed across the ceiling of the gym. I finished my stretches, my eyes locked onto Arik. He acted as if nothing had happened. That he hadn't crushed my heart into a pulpy mess. He stretched his arms above his head, cracking both sides of his neck. I wanted to break it.

A group of Sentinels from other havens walked by me, whispering.

Pia and Reya stopped at my mat. "How are you doing?" Pia asked.

"We heard what happened," Reya said. "I can't believe how cruel he was. Just showing up with that girl without ending things with you beforehand."

Great. The whole world, no, both *worlds know Arik dumped me.*

"I'm good," I said, punching the air.

The looks on their faces before walking off said I wasn't very convincing. I was dying inside.

I made a move to go pair up with Arik, and Jaran stepped in my way.

"Want to match up?" he asked.

"No, I already have a partner," I said.

He must've noticed the fury in my eyes because he shook his head. "I don't think that's a wise decision."

"Why? You think I'll kill him?"

"Actually, that's exactly what I'm thinking."

I released an exasperated breath. "He's more of a match for me."

Jaran acted wounded, placing his open palms across his heart. "Now, that just hurt my feelings."

"You know I didn't mean it as an insult."

He grinned. "I do know it, but still, I won't let you fight him. Your feelings are too raw. Someone will get hurt."

"Listen to him, ducky." Lei swung her wooden sword around, loosening up her swing. "How about we have a go at it?"

"Now you're both insulting me," Jaran said.

"I didn't mean I wanted to fight her"—she pointed her sword at Arik—"I meant him. I'll roughen him up for you." She waggled her eyebrows at me and then took off toward Arik.

Kale looked dumbfounded. "Now who's sparring with me?"

"Apparently, I am," Demos said.

Across the mats, Arik argued with Lei about something. Her braid bounced against her back with her exaggerated hand movements. My hand tightened around my practice sword. I wanted to fight him. I wanted to knock some sense into his thick head.

"Carrig!" Arik called to him as he crossed the gym. "Did you give the order to trade partners? I thought you matched us up by skill level."

"No, I not be giving any such order." Carrig looked around

at the pairings. "What is this, some kind of revolt?"

"Obviously, Gia cannot fight Arik," Lei said. "Not with their situation."

Arik raised a brow at her. "What situation?"

I'd had it. I marched across the mats and looked up at him. "Are you for real? You broke up with me. Remember?"

He actually looked confused. "We weren't obligated to each other. I apologize if you misunderstood my intentions."

I crossed my arms. "Misunderstood your intentions? Ha! Seriously? Kissing, fondling, and saying that you love me. Oh, right, I'm sorry, I totally misunderstood you there."

"I never…" He took a few steps back.

"You never what? Never loved me?" Tears pooled in my eyes, and I took a deep breath, trying to stop them. I swung my padded sword hard at him, hitting his shoulder with a *thwack*.

Arik winced and dropped to his knees on the mat. "Bloody hell, what was that for?" He grabbed his shoulder.

"For being an ass."

"Gia, back down!" Carrig stormed over to us. "No matter what has gone on between the two of you, we respect each other in the fight. We are Sentinels, and we live up to a higher code."

"I'm not a Sentinel. I didn't grow up in the code. I grew up without you, remember?" I wanted to take the words back as soon as they left my mouth. I *was* a Sentinel. It ran in my veins. I would die for all of them. But this pain was clouding my senses.

"Now you're just being mean." The disappointment in Carrig's eyes made me feel as tiny as a tick.

"I…I didn't mean it."

He came closer to me so that only I could hear him. "I know in me heart you didn't mean it. I felt such pain before.

You need to heal." He turned from me. "Jaran, could you please see Gia home?"

I dropped the sword and met Arik's eyes. "I would give my life for anyone in this room, including you. But I will never forgive you, Arik." I didn't wait for his response. I spun around and lumbered to the door, the shame of my actions weighing me down.

"Brilliant show," Jaran said, catching up to me.

"You think?"

He chuckled as we stepped outside into a winter wonderland of brand new snow. The brisk wind bit at my nose and cheeks, but the cold didn't bother me. I had been numb since the breakup.

Reading had become my new escape. After avoiding Arik and Emily during school hours, I'd come home, grabbed a bag of chips, thrown on my yoga pants, and hibernated in my room with a book. My greasy fingerprints marked the pages I'd already read.

Tears flowed again, dropping onto the page and spreading as the paper soaked them up. I wanted to call Arik. Hear his voice. Have him tell me it was all a mistake. Had he broken up with me because we really didn't have anything in common? Did he and Emily have more of the same interests? I should have seen this coming. But I hadn't. Or I'd ignored it, because I wanted to give us a chance to find similar likes.

After my outburst the other day, Carrig made me take a break from practices. I glanced at the clock. Jaran would be here in an hour to help me cope, so I only had to survive until then. The week was going excruciatingly slow. I had no idea how I would make it through the weekend.

Something mewed at my bedroom door and I paused mid-crunch to listen. The next mew drew out longer. I knew that sound.

Cleo? I saved my place with my bookmark before padding to the door. Cleo darted in as I swung it open and she jumped onto my bed. I hadn't seen her since Conemar's men demolished our apartment in Boston. Before moving to Branford, Pop and I had searched the streets around our neighborhood, but we couldn't find her.

"Oh my *God*," I squealed. "What are you doing here?" I picked her up and sat with her in my arms, nuzzling my nose into her fur. "Hey, squeaker, I missed you. How'd you get here?" *Baron?* Nana's cat pranced in and sat on the area carpet. Cleo leaped out of my arms and joined him. She lightly batted her multi-colored paw at him, and then bathed his black coat with quick licks.

"I don't think we could possibly separate them now," Nana said as she glided into the room.

I leaped to my feet.

"*Nana.*" I practically tripped over the love bath happening on the carpet as I rushed over and wrapped my arms around her. "You're here. You're actually here. How did you find Cleo?"

"Your neighbor, Mr. Navarro, was taking care of her."

Deidre charged into the room. "Is everything okay?" She stopped. "Oh, Mrs. Kearns you made it."

"I would've been here sooner, if not for the snow." She pulled back and studied me. "You're a snotty mess. What's this I hear about you and Arik?"

I stared at my hands; my nails were broken and the cuticles torn. "He's just not into me anymore."

"Well, isn't he a silly boy." She lifted my chin. "A Kearns

woman never sulks, dear. We never show a man he's gotten the better of us. Deidre, I think a mani-pedi is in order."

"I'll get my things," Deidre said, and dashed out of the room, probably to the bathroom to grab her arsenal of nail products.

"What's wrong with my nails?"

"They're atrocious," Nana said. "You could kill small animals with your toenails."

Baron hissed.

"I didn't mean you." She frowned at him. "The problem with familiars is...they understand everything you say. After we're done, we'll have dinner at this cute new Italian restaurant in town. It's opening night."

"The D'Marco's place?"

"You've heard of it?"

"Yeah, I've heard it mentioned around." I laughed and squeezed her again. "I'm so glad you're here, and that you could make it for the restaurant's opening."

"Well, I'm like the cavalry, dear. When all seems lost, I charge in." She patted my back. "We just have to get you through to Christmas vacation. Afton's coming to spend the holiday with us."

I could hardly believe it. Afton was coming, too. The excitement swelled in my chest. A thought hit me, deflating my excitement.

"Her parents are okay with that?" I asked. "Where are they going? Christmas is a big deal at the Wilson's house."

Nana frowned. "Sorry to say, her father moved out. Not a happy situation for Afton at the moment."

"Why didn't she tell me? We've video chatted all week and she didn't mention it."

"She probably didn't want to upset you, dear." Nana patted my cheek. "You've had such a hard time since the breakup."

"Yeah, I was basically crying the entire time." My shoulders slumped. "I'm such a horrible friend."

Deidre came back carrying plastic bins. "I'm thinking purple with confetti tips."

An hour later, with my nails done, soft waves in my hair, and dressed in Deidre's black dress, I felt like a new person. I caught my image in the mirror hanging in the host area of the D'Marco's new restaurant. I didn't look like a girl who'd just had her heart ripped out.

The place was crowded. Mrs. D'Marco spotted us and rushed over."Katy, I'm so happy to see you." She gave Nana a polite hug. "I have a wonderful table nestled in the corner for you. The others are already here."

Others?

I backed up toward the door. Nana quickly wrapped her arm through mine. "He's not here," she whispered.

For some reason that wasn't as comforting as it should have been.

As we approached, Lei patted the seat beside her. The overly big smile stretching her lips said it all. Arik wasn't here because he was with Emily.

I sat and said hello to the others. Nana took the empty seat at the head of the table, next to me.

"You look beautiful," Nick said.

"Why aren't you working?" I snatched the white linen, tented napkin perched on the plate in front of me, unfolded it, and spread it across my lap.

Deidre placed her hand on his shoulder and leaned forward to see around him. "'Cause he's too moody with the customers."

"I am not." He shrugged her hand off.

"Okay, whatever." Deidre rolled her eyes, and then leaned back into her chair.

"How do you feel?" Jaran asked from across the table. There was an empty chair beside him. and I instantly felt sad thinking Arik should be there.

"Wonderful, now that Nana is here."

"Well, you look amazing," he said.

"Thank you," I said, trying not to look at the vacant spot beside him.

Kale tore a piece from the loaf of bread in front of him.

"Stop eating all the bread," Lei said. "You won't have any room for your meal."

Carrig poured some wine into Sinead's glass. "I've been told the meatballs be grand here."

"They're the best," Pop said.

Miss Bagley rested her hand on Pop's hand. "I was thinking, um—"

"Lasagna," Pop finished for her.

"Yes," she said, grinning.

Pop beamed at her, taking her hand in his and gently squeezing it. "Good choice."

Miss Bagley and Pop had started finishing each other's sentences.

Nana caught my gaze and nodded toward Pop and Miss Bagley.

I shrugged my shoulders.

She gave me an understanding smile and took a sip from her water glass.

Mrs. D'Marco gave me a curious look as she poured water into my glass. She wiped a skeletal hand on the black apron tied around her tiny waist. "You doing okay, sweetie?"

"Yes, I can't wait to have your rosettes."

"I'll have Tony make them extra special for you tonight."

"Right behind you." Mr. D'Marco, Nick's dad and head chef, approached the table, balancing two large plates of antipasti salad in each hand. At their restaurant in Boston, he'd always smelled like meatballs and the familiar scent clung to him tonight.

Mrs. D'Marco grabbed one of the full plates of antipasti from her husband and placed it on the table between Jaran and me. "Now, don't fill up on this, or you won't be able to eat the main course."

Mr. D'Marco placed the other plate in front of Pop and Carrig. "And save room for dessert. We have something special tonight. But it's not as sweet as my sweetie."

"Why would you say something like that in front of the customers?" Mrs. D'Marco snapped, and stormed off.

"*Mia bella*, they don't mind. They're our friends," said Mr. D'Marco, chasing after her.

I chuckled and picked up my water glass.

"Good evening," Bastien said, standing beside Nana at the head of the table.

Water spurted out of my mouth. *Where did he come from?* I quickly wiped my mouth with my napkin.

"I'm sorry," he said. "Did I startle you?"

"Um…" *Awkward.* My cheeks heated. Not to mention I totally lost verbal capabilities at the sight of him.

Lei came to the rescue. "You made it! Have a seat by Jaran."

"Thank you." He folded himself into the chair, which happened to be diagonally across from me. "You look lovely, Gia."

All eyes were on us. I shrunk into my chair.

"Thanks. You look good, too."

How awkward.

He did rock his dark suit. It fit snugly around his toned body. His blue shirt enhanced the color of his eyes. He unbuttoned his jacket and draped his napkin across his lap.

Stop staring at him. I didn't want another guy messing with my emotions. What I needed was to get over Arik. It was like half my soul was ripped away from me. And I wasn't sure if I'd ever get it back.

"How did you get here?" Kale reached for the bread again. "I thought the council restricted travel through the gateways."

"I've come on council business," he said. "Carrig invited me to dinner."

Lei moved the breadbasket out of Kale's reach, and he frowned at her. "What business?" she said.

"I'm here to escort Gia and Nick to Toad's trial."

"Really?" I couldn't tell if the excitement I felt was for Toad or how Bastien's eyes on me glinted like sapphires against the candlelight. "He's actually going to get a chance to tell his side?"

"That he is." His full lips quirking into a smile creased the corner of his eyes. "Because of you, an innocent man may get another chance."

I grabbed a cherry pepper from the antipasti platter.

"When are we going?" Nick asked.

"Early morning," Bastien said. "Before the libraries open."

A foot brushed across my ankle right when I bit into the cherry pepper. Bastien smiled at me. I coughed on the spicy juice hitting the back of my throat and dropped the pepper onto my dress. It left a trail of oil behind. Was that an accident or did he touch me on purpose?

"That's unfortunate," Lei said.

"Excuse me." I stood and hurried to the restroom.

I leaned over the sink, scrubbing at the stain with a drenched, stiff paper towel. The more water I dabbed on the oil stain the more the wet spot spread. I eyed the wreckage in the mirror.

Great. It looks like I lactated.

I gave up on the stain and stepped out of the restroom. I was too busy shaking the neckline of my dress, trying to get it dry, that I bumped into someone.

"Excuse me," Emily said.

I didn't say anything, just stared, her presence not registering right away. It felt like someone had sucker punched me in the stomach. I looked past her and then sharply at Arik.

"What are you doing here?"

Emily forced a smile. "We're having dinner, of course. Why else does someone come to a restaurant?"

"Tonight? You knew we were coming here," I said to Arik, ignoring Emily completely.

"I wasn't aware you'd be here," he said. "You were absent from practice today."

Their hands were interlocked, causing bile to rise in the back of my throat. When would the agony of seeing them together end? Every time, it was a cut to the heart. I couldn't believe Arik and I had ended. Our relationship obviously didn't matter to him. And there I was standing there, not moving, making the situation even more uncomfortable.

Why can't I move?

"There you are," Bastien said, weaving around Arik and Emily to get to me. He slipped his arm over my shoulders. "The waiter would like to take our order. Are you finished here?"

"Yes, sorry. Arik, you know Bastien, right?"

"Of course," he said. His eyes seemed vacant. Not at all himself. Like he was an unemotional drone. What was going on with him? Had someone gotten into his head? Hypnotized him? The jealous fire he used to get in his eyes over Bastien was gone. Was he sick? Was he hit hard on the head during practice? I wanted any of my irrational reasons to be true.

When I noticed them all staring at me, I said, "Bastien,

this is Emily."

"Hello," she said, leaning closer to Arik.

"It's a pleasure to meet you," Bastien said, and then turned to me. "Shall we?"

I nodded, and he took my hand in his and led me away.

"Thank you for rescuing me," I said when we were out of ear shot.

"I'm always happy to lead you away from Arik."

I glanced back. Emily watched our retreat, a smug expression on her face.

CHAPTER TWELVE

The Wizard Council met in the Italian haven, Mantello. The hidden access into Mantello was behind a bookcase in the Riccardiana Library in Florence, Italy. The tunnel leading from the library to the outbuilding in the haven was tight, with a series of stone steps going up and down and twisting left to right. The skirt and heels I wore, along with my overstuffed messenger bag, made the trek somewhat difficult. Nick sweated in his suit in front of me, his dress shoes scuffling across the rocky floor. In the lead, Bastien took quick, regal steps downward.

The haven reminded me of pictures I'd seen of Tuscany. The gardens, stone pathways, and stucco cottages surrounded a palace that resembled a massive villa. We walked the pathway until we came to a town that looked frozen in an ancient time. Old cottages and buildings, vibrantly colored valances shading windows, and planters with colorful flowers lined the streets. Bastien brought us to an amphitheater-type room. We sat closest to the bottom on the stone benches. Just below us, a round antique table dominated the stage.

The men and women trickling in and taking their seats at the table seemingly came from all parts of the world, dressed in heavy red robes with shiny buttons and thick golden ropes tied around their waists. I counted twenty wizards on the council.

"Man, these benches are uncomfortable." Nick shifted. "Hey, that looks like King Arthur's round table. They totally stole the idea, didn't they?"

Bastien sat close to me. His arm brushed against mine, heightening my awareness of him being so near. "I'm not certain where the idea came from, but this table was made for the first Wizard Council meeting many centuries ago. The attending wizards were the original seven."

We waited several addled minutes after the last wizard took his seat before two beefy men brought Toad out. He'd had a bath, a shave, and his hair cut. I almost didn't recognize him dressed up in a tweed jacket and dark pants. The two men led Toad to a box seat just below the stone benches and to our right.

An older woman, with white hair swirling away from her pale skin and falling short under her ears, stood from one of the chairs around the table. "Your Highnesses," she said, nodding at them. "I shall start the proceedings. For the record, my name is Ellen Arkwright of Asile, and I will be overseeing the inquiry today. We gather this fine fall morning to hear the statements from Toad of the Laniar clan Darkdale, as pertaining to the murder of Gian Bianchi on the twentieth day of July in the year nineteen hundred and thirty-eight. Have the barristers advised the malefactor of his rights?"

A small man, barely five feet tall, with a balding head and thick glasses stood. "We have, Your Highness."

"Splendid. Toad, you may tell us your story, and afterward we will take statements from witnesses. You may proceed."

She sat down.

The barrister waved for Toad to stand. Toad glanced around nervously until one of his handlers nodded to him. Balancing on shaky legs, Toad held his hands behind his back and cleared his throat.

"I'm not certain where to start, ma'am... I mean, Your Highness," he said.

"Just start from your encounter with Professor Bianchi before the murder," she responded. "You were in the Abbey Library in Saint Gall, Switzerland. What brought you to that library?"

"The compelling did," he said. "Actually, I stalk Gian days in a row. No matter how hard I try, I could no release myself from the spell. Gian jumps to many libraries—searching for something. For traps, I am thinking, 'cause he does that thing with his hands, like he feels the air. I fight against the urge to attack him. Like a dog wanting a bone, I can no longer resist. I corner him in the Abbey. It's dark. I hardly sees him, but for that red umbrella he always carry."

He paused to wipe his eyes. It was strange how he spoke as if Gian was still alive and the events he spoke about were happening right then.

"I love Gian like a brother. He always takes care of unfortunates like me. I struggle and struggle to not overtake him, but I can no do it. I stab him. His face twists and he makes me bury the knife deeper until he falls. But he's not dead. There's a push from within me to finish him off. I fight it. I refuse. Miraculously, the power releases. I'm free, but Gian agonizes on the floor."

Toad lowered his head and brought his hands to his front, folding them as though he were praying. He looked up. "He gives me the scroll and I hide it in my waistband. Then I help him put the other Chiave...the cross, in the handle of that umbrella. We hear someone jump into the library. I try to move him and he shoves me away. I ran out to stop whoever comes for him. That is the last I see him alive."

Arkwright glanced up from the notebook she'd been jotting notes in. "Who did you encounter when you ran out from that room?"

"Conemar and a few Sentinels is there."

"And what happened next?" she pressed.

He gave a quick glance over his shoulder at me. "They drag me back to Gian. I won't finish him off, so one Sentinel stabs him several times. Then Conemar hits me over the head and all goes black. The sound of boots on the floor wakes me. Many guards wearing uniforms from Asile charge into the room."

The only noise in the amphitheater came from the ticking of an extremely large clock attached to the far brick wall as everyone waited for Arkwright's next question. "Was a copy of the jump records for that day retrieved?"

The other barrister stood. I assumed he was like a prosecuting attorney. "No, Your Highness."

"And what was the verdict?"

"Toad was found criminally insane."

"You don't say?" She scribbled something onto her notepad. "You may sit. Gianna Kearns, is she here?"

I looked sidelong at Bastien.

"It's all right," he whispered. "Stand and say who you are."

I eased up from the bench. "Yes, Your Highness."

"What is your relationship to the malefactor?" she asked.

"You mean Toad?"

She dropped her pen. "That is what I said."

Bastien popped up. "Excuse me, Your Highness."

"I wasn't aware you were here, Your Royal Highness. Do you have something to add?"

"I do," he said, giving my hand a quick squeeze before continuing. "Gia is unfamiliar with the dealings of the court. I am certain she hadn't understood the meaning of malefactor." He looked at me. "She means the defendant, Toad."

"Oh, okay," I said, feeling embarrassed.

Bastien returned to his seat.

"And why doesn't the girl know these things?"

"I'm new to the Mystik world, Your Highness. I am the great-granddaughter of Gian Bianchi. My mother was Marietta Bianchi. I was raised in the human world."

"Ah, I see, you are our missing Sentinel, Gianna Bianchi." All the wizards' eyes went to me.

"I am."

"What is this alias you go by?"

"It's the name I was given when I was born in the human world. I use my stepfather's last name."

"While in our world you must use your bequeathed name." Her stern look made me want to hide behind Bastien. "Now, I understand you helped Toad escape from the gallows. You do realize we could charge you and everyone else involved with this crime?"

"No. No one said I was in trouble." I looked nervously at Bastien.

She ignored my response. "Care to tell us why you went to see your great-grandfather's murderer."

I swallowed the lump forming in the back of my throat. "I went to ask him about a missing Chiave."

"A missing Chiave?"

"Yes. The one Toad mentioned in his statement. The scroll. You see, Nick and I are descendants of the Seventh Wizard. We're the protectors that the prophecy mentions—"

"We on the council are well aware of the prophecy," she interrupted. "The fact that you are a descendent of Gian is the only reason I don't have you thrown in the gallows. Now, explain the missing Chiave."

"We were informed that Toad had a Chiave and that he was in the gallows. So we went to retrieve it. Soon after we arrived, The Red and his men attacked the gallows. So we fled, and we took Toad with us to protect him."

Bastien stood again. "There is a correction to Gianna's response, which is in the statements from the Asile Sentinels. It was assumed to be The Red's men, but he was not with them during the attack."

Ellen Arkwright cleared her throat. "With all due respect, Your Highness. Only barristers may interrupt these proceedings."

"Perhaps if they would do their job, I wouldn't have to." Bastien sat.

The four barristers adjusted uncomfortably on their seats and gave one another looks.

"Noted." Her lips went into a straight line as she studied me. "Very well, you may be seated, Gianna." She read some papers on the table in front of her. "Nicklaus Roux Agard, please stand."

Bastien elbowed Nick. "She means you."

He hesitated before getting to his feet. "Yes, ma'am, I mean, Your Highness. But that is not my name."

She eyed him. "Your father is Conemar Agard and your mother was Jacalyn Roux, is it not?"

Nick swallowed hard. "Yes, but I was adopted by humans. My legal name is Nicklaus D'Marco."

"That may be your legal name in the human world, but it is not here in ours. You will have to file forms with the Mystik Registrar to change your name." She scribbled something on her paper again. "Tell me, how do you feel about your father?"

Bastien shot to his feet, again. "How does that have anything to do with this proceeding?"

She flashed a look at him. "You may be a royal, but you have no say in this arena. Sit down, Bastien Renard of Couve. I asked this boy about his father for good reason. There is a charm over the arena that compels everyone under this roof to tell the truth. I need to know where his alliance lies."

"I hate him," Nick blurted. "I want to kill him for murdering my mother. I *will* kill him. It's all I think about, and I definitely don't want to carry his name."

I reached for his hand but it was just out of my reach. My heart ached for him. It was hard to imagine what he must be going through.

Ellen Arkwright's eyes flicked across his face. "Indeed." She wrote something in her notebook. "Now, did you go to the gallows knowing you would free Toad?"

"No. We went to recover the Chiave. Then all the shit… oh sorry…*stuff* went down, and we ran. Gia was worried The Red and his men would kill Toad."

Arkwright's gaze traveled over Nick, and the smile on her face was haunting. She made some more notes and then glanced back at him. "Thank you, Nicklaus." Her eyes shifted toward the wizards surrounding the table. "I move to release Gianna Bianchi and Nikolaus Roux *D'Marco* from all charges."

"How come he gets to keep his name?" I muttered.

Bastien gave me a stern look. "They're showing mercy to Nick. Your name is well respected in the Mystik world. His is feared."

"Wait a minute." It registered just then that Arkwright mentioned charges against Nick and me. "Excuse me," I said. "Were we on trial?"

She expelled a long breath. "Miss McCabe we do not interrupt the head council without permission to speak. You are not on trial, but charges were filed as to yours and Mr.

D'Marco's part in Toad's escape. Now, may I continue?"

"Um, yes, sorry." I eased back onto the bench.

Arkwright cleared her throat. "The council will go into deliberation about this confession. We would like to have the jump records for the twentieth of July nineteen hundred and thirty-eight delivered to our chamber. We will meet again tomorrow at the same time to hand over our verdict. After our Highnesses depart the arena, all others are excused." She picked up her notebook, hugged it to her chest, and mingled with the other wizards as they shuffled out a side door.

"That was wacky," Nick said.

I raised a brow at him. "Agard?"

"And that's completely jacked. If they had kept calling me by that name, you might as well have painted a target on my back." He shoved his hands in his pockets. "So now what? We go home?"

"I'm afraid not," Bastien said, scooting by Nick. "You'll remain here tonight in case the council has more questions to ask you at tomorrow's proceedings."

"What are we going to do all day, stuck here?" I climbed up the steps after him.

"How about I show you around Mantello?" He glanced down at me, with a devilish grin playing on his lips. The twinkle in his light eyes stopped me, my breath swooshing from my lungs. Everything about Bastien was perfect, from his rock-star good looks to his easy, laid-back attitude. I could really see myself with him, but fear stopped me. How could I trust anyone after what happened with Arik?

"Sounds boring." Nick pushed on my back. "Why are you stopping?"

I twisted, causing his hand to drop away. "Don't shove me."

"It's anything but boring," Bastien said. "It's festival week.

There will be dancing, food, drink, and magical games."

"Still sounds boring," Nick said.

"The dancers wear little clothing," Bastien added.

Nick stepped around me. "Well, why didn't you say that in the first place? What's the drinking age here?"

"Drinking age?"

"He means, what is the *legal* age someone can drink alcohol?"

"We have no age limit. It is up to the parents to decide."

Nick hopped up the steps. "What if your parents aren't with you?"

"You're considered an adult at sixteen."

"This is my kind of village," Nick said.

The light burned my eyes when we stepped out of the arena and onto the cobbled street. People crowded the tight lane. Banners hung from the windows of the buildings crowding the road. The town had come alive while we were stuck inside.

Bastien guided us along the sidewalks. Women tossed flower petals from the windows above us. We spent the day shopping in the makeshift market, drinking fresh fruit juices, and eating fried breads.

Nick watched women in thin cotton outfits stomping grapes in long troughs. The women danced seductively, picking up grapes and rubbing them across their exposed midriffs. Nick's mouth hung open.

"This is awkward," I whispered to Bastien.

"Why? The women are seducing the grapes to yield their juices."

"That sounds so wrong. And they are definitely seducing Nick."

Bastien laughed and snatched my hand, making me dizzy. "Shall we leave him to it and find some mischief of our own?"

My heart flipped. "Um—I don't think…"

"Relax. I only meant there is a puppet show around the corner." He led me up the street. "I think you'd be more comfortable watching it instead."

"Oh. Yeah, that sounds less, um, revealing." I walked along with him. It felt good to be there, away from Arik and the pain of our breakup.

Bastien and I chuckled at the ridiculous actions of the puppets in the show. The puppet masters spoke Italian so fast I could barely make out what was going on. His hand would rest on my back, and then fall away with each laugh outburst, only to find its way back between lulls in the comedy. I caught myself leaning against him, then quickly straightened.

At the closing of the show, the crowd's applause exploded and echoed off the buildings.

It felt good to laugh as I practically floated down the street with Bastien, back toward where we left Nick. We weaved through the crowd surrounding the troughs filled with grapes. Nick, his pant legs rolled up and his shirt tied into a crop top, stomped on the grapes, among the women. One girl who seemed around his age held his hand and gave him flirty eyes.

Bastien sidestepped behind me and placed his hands on my shoulders, making my stomach do that flip thing again. "Are you having fun?" his voice tickled my ear, and goose bumps rose on my arms.

I twisted to look at him and flashed a smile. "Yes. This is great."

Just then, his face went serious and it looked as if he was going to kiss me, stopping my heart. My mind flashed to Arik and the pain of losing him, and I quickly withdrew from Bastien.

"I'm sorry. It's just—"

"You're not over him." His gaze drifted from me to the crowd then back to me. "He's chosen another over you, yet you still won't let him go."

Before I could say that wasn't so, that it was more about my fears, a man with a round belly and a rounder nose shoved a silver goblet of wine into my hand. I tried to give it back to him, but he waved me off. "No, no, *las mujeres beben a la vitalidad.*"

The women drink to vitality. Does he want me to drink this?

"I don't drink," I tried to say before the man handed one to Bastien and rushed off.

"It's only wine," Bastien said, his voice and his body language stiff. "It's just like drinking fermented grape juice. A few sips won't harm you. Besides, it's tradition."

The villagers didn't stop at one toast, they said many, and before I knew it, I'd downed the entire goblet. My head felt dizzy. The sky turned from blue to purple to black with sprinkles of stars twinkling against the darkness. Fireworks blossomed in the sky.

Nick danced across the street, buzzed on wine or just from all the excitement swarming around us. Grape splashes stained his white dress shirt and the corners of his mouth.

"We should find him a bed before he gets out of control," Bastien said.

I gasped. Nick teetered on a retaining wall as he tried to walk it like a balancing beam. "I think it's too late."

After coaxing Nick down from the wall, Bastien brought us to a room in a small villa. We tucked Nick into one of the beds.

"This way," Bastien said, leading me across the hall to another door.

I opened it and paused. "Where's your room?"

"I'm bunking with Nick," he said. "With the crowd visiting for the festival, I could only acquire two accommodations."

"Oh, I see."

He pulled on the back of his neck, avoiding eye contact. "All right, then. Sleep well."

I blew it. He wanted to kiss me and I screwed it up. Damn you, Arik.

I drew in a sharp breath. "Please don't be mad at me."

His eyes locked with mine. "I'm not angry, just frustrated."

He unbuttoned his shirt.

"What are you doing?"

"It occurred to me you don't have anything comfortable to sleep in." He slipped the shirt off and handed it to me. My eyes traveled over the fall and rise of his muscles under his tight undershirt.

"Night, Bastien," I said, wanting to say anything but good night to him.

He headed back to his room, and as I swung the door closed, catching one more eyeful of his well-defined biceps, he turned, catching my stare. He smiled before ducking into his room.

The door clicked shut, and I sighed. What was wrong with me? A totally too-gorgeous-to-be-real guy was across the hall, and I held on to the hope that Arik would tire of Emily and come back to me. It was absurd, and I knew it. I just couldn't help how I felt. I shut my door and turned the lock.

I removed my skirt and blouse, and put on his shirt, smelling the collar. A hint of his cologne filled my nose. As I stood there cursing myself for not inviting Bastien in, a small envelope slid under the door. I ripped it open and read it.

Leave Mantello tonight. Do not attend the proceedings tomorrow.

I yanked open the door and searched the hall.

Nothing.

I darted to Bastien and Nick's door and pounded on it. A few seconds later, it flew open. Bastien stood in the doorframe, his undershirt off, pants unbuttoned, and a toothbrush hanging from his mouth.

"What's the matter?" he said around foamy paste.

"Um—" My eyes scanned his bare chest. "Um—" I couldn't speak, so I held out the card.

After he read it, he peeked his head out the door, looking up and down the hall.

"Get inside." He moved back to let me in. "You'll sleep here."

"What do you think that means? Am I in danger?"

"No, it's only a ploy. Someone wants Toad convicted. They think having Gian's great-grandchildren at the sentencing will show support for him."

I glanced around. "There's no room for me here."

"Take my bed. I'll sleep on the couch." He shuffled to the bathroom, his eyes doing a quick inspection of my bare legs before he disappeared behind the door.

A familiar book with a highlighter beside it lay on the comforter.

The Secret Garden. He's reading it. I flipped through the pages, and many passages had been marked yellow. I smiled, moving the book and the pen to the nightstand.

Peeling back the covers, I hopped into the bed and tucked the comforter under my chin. A few minutes later Bastien returned. I could only make out his amazing silhouette in the dark. He took the extra pillow beside me and padded to the couch. The smell of his soap and toothpaste lingered after he was gone.

This was the definition of torture. I was scared about the note and, at the same time, scared about my growing feelings for Bastien. There was no way I would fall asleep. What was up with the excitement I felt every time he was near?

I'd been tortured enough witnessing Arik's and Emily's budding relationship. Maybe it was time to get distracted with someone new.

Seconds turned into minutes, minutes added up to hours. Nick snored in the bed next to me, and Bastien adjusted on the couch. My head ached and exhaustion finally took over, and I closed my eyes.

CHAPTER THIRTEEN

The dream overcame me like an invader in the night. I sat on grass, a vibrant red and gold skirt billowing around me, a leather-bound journal on my lap and a quill in my hand.

I was in Athela's head again. I'd been hopping in and out of it ever since I entered the Mystik world. Athela was my ancestor from an ancient time when humans and Mystiks lived together in what is now the human world. She was an enchanter and showed me things she felt I needed to know by having me relive her past. One problem, all the memories were like puzzle pieces that I hadn't put together yet.

An older woman in a plain gray dress, a dingy white shawl wrapped around her shoulders, sat beside me. A small boy with sandy-colored hair ran around a green field sprinkled with white flowers, playing with a wooden sword. He galloped across the grass, his eyes on me.

"There," Athela said. "Everything his protector needs has been registered."

"What shall we do with it?" the woman beside her said. "Spells as these are dangerous and will give someone too much power."

"It shall be hidden in plain sight. Not a soul shall suspect what it holds."

"See me, Modor?" the boy shouted.

Mother? He's her son.

Reliving her past taught me about the Tetrad and the horrible disasters it could cause. Good thing the monster was locked up somewhere and hidden from the world.

"Modor sees Roy-Roy," she called, closing the journal and returning the quill to the inkwell beside her. She leaned over and opened the lid of a basket in the middle of the blanket. "Come, I have delightful morsels for you, my sweet angel. Are thou not famished?"

"The boy has not come into his power," the older woman said. "It is feared your curse inflicted him."

"Then we shall teach him to fight." Athela removed a rolled up cloth, unwrapped a small grilled bird, and placed it on a plate. She then handed the woman a knife.

"Your brother's wife has borne a dead son." The woman sawed at the bird. "The high wizard lineage has withered like a dying limb on a tree. Esteril will no longer bear male wizards."

"It was my hope that Roy-Roy would inherit powers from his father. Instead, as I cursed my people, I have cursed him. He was born to die. I shall prepare him for the horrors I see coming for him."

The woman placed a severed wing on a plate. "There is a rumor spreading among the villagers that Mykyl has been murdered by the Seventh Wizard's heirs. Can we not return to Esteril now that your father is gone?"

"We cannot. I must protect my son." Athela reached into the basket. "Thou hast made a pie. We shall celebrate my son's life today, the day of his birth."

It was like someone pressed fast forward in my dream. The countryside went blurry and Athela and her son grew older. He was a man and she had graying hair. In a dark medieval-looking room, she sat at a table while he paced in front of her.

"I must go, Modor." His amber eyes pleaded with her. "The humans are killing Mystiks, burning their covens. They have attacked wizards."

"What of your wife? Your children? Who will protect them?"

He touched her cheek with a muscled hand. "Thou wilt watch over them. Modor, I must get our people to the safe boundaries."

"My father's people never aided us," Athela said.

"I am not speaking of your father's people. I speak of *my* father's people. Of Asile. Their wizards have sent the havens into another realm."

Athela nodded. "Then it is time. You must go. I fear, my dear son, this is the last moment we shall share together. You must bear this burden on your own." She handed him a rolled parchment.

He gave it a questioning look.

"Your destiny is written on it," she continued, tears glossing her eyes. "There is no cheating it. Your death will be the salvation for all living beings."

He read the words on the parchment and slumped to his knees on the floor. Athela rushed to him, wrapping her arms around him.

"I cannot suffer this," he said to the floor. "Remove this cross from me."

She rested her head on his. "My son, many nights have I prayed, many nights have I sacrificed the anointed, many nights have I cried, to no avail. There is no undoing what is already in motion."

What was she trying to tell me? Her son had to die? Why? I wasn't sure if the overwhelming sadness I felt was her emotion or mine. The dream slipped away from me until everything went black.

M y heels clicked against the cobbled streets, busy with people rushing here and there. The council hearing wasn't for another hour, so Bastien brought us to the square to eat breakfast. I took the last bite of the pastry he'd bought me. He and Nick searched a grocer's stand for something else to eat. While they smelled and squeezed fruit, I window-shopped, admiring the colorful clothes displayed behind the glass panes.

I absentmindedly moved around people, my mind on the dream I'd had and on the note slipped under my door. I hadn't had a dream about Athela since leaving Asile. Not since returning to the human world. I wondered if she could only invade my sleep in the Mystik world. It seemed to be a pretty solid theory. Bastien brushed off the note as someone trying to keep me from gaining sympathy for Toad. That made sense to me, but it still nagged at the corner of my brain, making me worry about the proceedings today.

I paused at a bookstore and stepped over the threshold.

"*Buongiorno,*" a very scholarly-looking young man with glasses and a bright smile said from behind the counter.

"Morning," I muttered, browsing the books on the shelf.

"*Americana?*"

"*Sì.*"

He straightened a stack of magazines on the counter. "Please to tell me if you're in need of *assistenza.*"

I nodded. "*Grazie.*"

I dragged my fingers across the spines of the books and stopped on one that caught my eye—*The Dangers of Compelling*. I bought the book with the coins Bastien had given me, and then found a bench by a fountain in the middle of the square.

Gingerly turning each well-worn page, I absorbed the information. Only a wizard could perform a compelling. The person under control would do whatever the wizard wanted. Wizards lived long lives. Compelling someone shortened a wizard's life. If the wizard controlled their victim too long, the wizard would age rapidly and die. If a wizard died while compelling a victim, the victim would turn evil and never go back to their normal state before the compulsion.

There were pages and pages of case studies on compelling and the results it had on the using wizard. The graphic pictures made the pastry in my stomach sour. Evil distorted the victims' faces, and their eyes were so light their irises were barely visible.

Part of me thought that maybe Arik had been compelled. Except for there was a feeling that surrounded someone who had been. I'd experienced it with Faith when she was under one to kill me while I was in Asile. The air had thickened around me and it was as if an ominous energy, like invisible creatures, crawled over my skin. I hadn't felt that with Arik.

Nick crossed the square to me while popping grapes into his mouth. "Hey, here you are. We've been searching all over for you."

"I've been right here for almost an hour." I closed the book. "I would think you'd be sick of grapes after last night."

"Funny. But seriously, I've never tasted a grape that tasted so grapey before."

Bastien rushed over. "Shall we go? The proceedings will start soon."

I tucked the book into my messenger bag. "Yep."

We made our way to the arena and took the same seats as we had yesterday. Unlike the day before, the place was filled with people. There was hardly any seating room. I felt uneasy waiting for the council to enter. The message still weighed on my mind. Toad rubbed the back of his neck several times. He couldn't sit still.

The Wizard Council walked single file into the arena and took their spots at the round table. They didn't sit, just stood there as if waiting for something. About a dozen guards with swords and shields surrounded the stage. The side door suddenly opened and two women and five men marched in then sat on some comfortable-looking seats directly across the arena from us. Merl was among the group.

"They look important," Nick said, inspecting the wizards. He pulled out a piece of bread and picked at it. "This is better than a movie."

I elbowed him. "Really?"

"Stop. You made me drop my bread."

"Well, act your age. This is serious."

"I am acting my age. You're not my mother." He picked up the slice of bread and brushed it off.

I turned to Bastien. "What's Merl doing here?"

"The high wizards from the main havens must attend all sentencings when death is a possible penalty. They will have the final decision and can pardon the prisoner if they feel the order is too harsh."

I gave Bastien a startled look. "I don't understand. How could they give him a death sentence when he didn't have one before?"

"He did have a death sentence, but because they believed him insane it was converted to life. Now that they know he was of sound mind, but possibly compelled, death is on the table."

"What?" I snapped. My outburst caused all eyes in the arena to find me. Merl frowned in my direction. I leaned closer to Bastien and hissed, "You mean to tell me, I got him out of the gallows only to risk him getting the death penalty?"

"Calm down." He glanced around the arena. "It's highly unlikely he'll get death. The evidence is in his favor, and they know he spoke the truth. No one can lie here or use magic. The charm will not allow it."

Arkwright stood and straightened her robe. Her hair slicked back from her face emphasized her wrinkles. After giving her opening statement, she turned to the high wizards.

"Welcome, Your Majesties. I trust you all have had the opportunity to review the recordings from yesterday's proceedings."

Merl stood. "We have," he said, and returned to his seat.

"The high wizards have the power to overturn any death ruling they deem unwarranted." She slipped her glasses on to read the paper in front of her. "Toad of Darkdale, please rise."

Toad shook so hard he could hardly stand erect. One of the guards grabbed his arm to steady him.

"Are you well enough to continue?" Arkwright asked.

"I am," Toad said.

"Are you aware of the possibility of death?"

"I am."

"Do you have any final words for the council?" she said.

Toad darted a look over at Nick and me. An ominous energy surrounded me. It was like invisible creatures slithered across my skin. "That I love Gian as brother, and I am sorrowful I can no prevent his death."

"The council has exonerated you of all charges." Arkwright removed her glasses. "You have suffered dearly for a crime you did not commit. The havens have agreed to compensate you for the time served. Asile has agreed to house you for the remainder of your years."

Something long and thin soared across the arena, and I flinched. An arrow punctured Toad's throat with a sickening, wet-sounding *thud*, and I inhaled a startled gasp. Blood sprayed out as the point pierced through the other side of his neck. Toad collapsed forward, falling over the stone barrier separating the seating from the stage. His lifeless body thumped onto the floor below.

I shot to my feet, my hands covering my mouth. *No, no, no, no. Toad!*

The arena exploded with screams. People scrambled for the exits.

Panicked breaths consumed me, and I practically choked on the air rushing into my lungs. *Don't freak out.*

Another arrow flew, then buried into one of the guard's chest.

Calm down. Breathe in. Breathe out. I concentrated until the fear and shock passed over me.

One by one, arrows staked the guards.

The next arrow found its way into one of the high wizard's stomach. He fell back against his chair, and the other wizards ducked down.

I tried to form my globe, but nothing happened. The charm over the arena prevented magic. I kicked off my heels and hopped over the bench in front of me.

"Gia, get down!" Bastien yelled.

"Get Nick out of here," I ordered, and swung myself over the banister onto the stage.

"Gia!" Bastien's panicked voice didn't stop me.

An arrow whizzed by, barely missing me as I jumped onto the stage floor. I dashed to the nearest fallen guard and picked up his sword and shield, then sprinted for the high wizards cowering behind the banister in front of their seats. They were sitting ducks. The barrier didn't offer much protection, since the arrows were coming from the highest point of the arena. Another arrow sliced into a red-headed high wizard. From where the arrows originated and how they were spaced apart, I knew there were possibly two shooters. What I didn't know was how many arrows the shooters had.

Spotting one of the archers at the top of the stairs, an arrow aimed at Merl. The archer released his bow and I scrambled over the barrier and jumped in front of the arrow soaring for Merl. I blocked it with the shield, and it ricocheted off.

"Move with me!" I yelled to Merl and the others. "We're going for that door." I nodded toward it.

I sidestepped toward the door, putting myself between the high wizards and the shooters. Another arrow whizzed for us and I sliced it off with the broad side of my sword. The arrow died on the ground. The next arrow missed us by a foot. We moved as quickly as we could. Just a few more feet and we'd reach the door.

I hissed as an arrow grazed my arm. Merl pushed the door open and the other wizards rushed through it. Before shutting the door behind me, I caught sight of the stage below. Arkwright was nailed to the table with an arrow and the man beside her lay back in his chair, an arrow sticking out of his chest.

Guards rushed in from all the doors, and I spotted the shooter trying to escape through a nearby exit.

Pia?

The guards overtook her and she struggled in their grasp. I followed where Pia's eyes were staring. Reya swung an arrow at a guard as she tried to get away. The guard lunged at her with his sword extended, burying the blade into her stomach.

"No!" Pia screamed.

Reya looked at her with sorrowful eyes. The guard pulled his sword out and Reya crumpled to the floor.

Pia collapsed in the guards' hold. "Oh, Reya!" She hung her head and sobbed.

I charged up the steps to her. "Why?"

She looked up at me, tears dropping from her cheeks. "I-I warned you not to come. We didn't want to hurt you or Nick."

"You sent the note?"

She nodded and tears splashed onto her shirt. "He's one of Conemar's men. Many of our people are dead because of Conemar. Women, children—" A sob cut off her sentence. "Our haven was attacked because of him. Toad deserved to die. You're a sheep, Gia. You trust too easily. You think there's only one threat."

"Why kill the high wizards?"

"Because the Council is corrupt. They stood by and let the Mystiks attack our haven. Our Sentinels sent out a call for help. No one came. No one came…" She lowered her head.

Bastien placed his hand on my shoulder. "Gia, come with me."

I faced him. "Why didn't anyone answer Santara's call for help?"

"The distress call was blocked," Bastien said. "The Monitors didn't receive it in time."

"That's a lie," Pia snapped. "The call was received. Someone chose to ignore it. There's a secret group of humans who want to end the Mystik world. They're connected to someone here. And because Santara has fought for Mystik rights, she was targeted by this group."

"The rumor of this group has been around for ages," Bastien said. "Do you have proof the call was received? Or proof that this group exists?"

"No." Pia lowered her head, defeated. "We haven't, but

that doesn't mean it isn't so."

"Then there's nothing I can do. You murdered many here today. You will go to trial for your actions." Bastien turned to the guards and nodded at Pia. "Take her away."

Pia pulled against the guards' hold. "Gia, The Red—"

The guards dragged her to an exit.

"Wait," I said. "What is she saying?"

Pia twisted her neck, staring at me with pain-filled eyes. "The Red didn't attack Santara. Someone else—"

The guards shoved Pia through an open exit and the door slammed behind them. She was gone.

"What did she mean?"

Bastien took my hand and led me down the stone steps. "She doesn't know what she's saying. She's gone mad. The Red jumped to Santara mere minutes before the attack. The Monitors recorded it."

He was probably right. No one in their right mind would kill so many people. Pia was delusional. But my heart ached for her and Reya. They'd become my friends. We trained together, shared meals, and hung out. But there were ways of protesting other than killing people, and I couldn't wrap my mind around what they'd done. Besides, The Red attacked their haven.

With him jumping into Santara so soon before the attack, it had to be him. And the thought of The Red sent shivers across my body. I never wanted to face him again. But my sinking stomach told me I would have to one day.

Curers rushed into the arena, tending to the victims. Blood filled the cracks of the floor around Toad. His face looked peaceful, as though he was finally free. I covered my face with my hands and cried. Bastien wrapped his arms around me.

"You scared me." His warm breath brushed my hair. "I

don't know what I'd have done if you were taken."

"I'm a warrior, remember?" My words sounded tough, but the quake in my voice said differently.

"Well, you certainly reminded me today."

Merl crossed the room to us. "Gia, are you all right?"

I untangled myself from Bastien. "Yeah, I'm good. Are you okay?"

"Yes, thanks to you." He smiled, but it couldn't mask the hurt in his soft gray eyes. "You saved lives today. So many more would've fallen if you hadn't been here."

I should have saved more lives, or prevented it entirely. When that note from Pia came, telling me to stay away, I should have alerted the council. Because of my inaction, several people were murdered. I hung my head and sucked back the emotions threatening to tear out of me.

"You're injured," Bastien said, freeing me from my haunting thoughts. "We should have a curer look at that."

"It's only a scratch." Blood trickled through a rip in my sleeve. "Where's Nick?"

"I had some guards take him to safety."

"I can't believe Pia and Reya did this." I picked a piece of my ripped shirt out of my wound. The pain finally registered in my arm and I winced.

"There's no telling what a person will do after seeing their home destroyed like they had," Merl said, motioning a curer to join us. "I've sent word to Professor Attwood. He's coming to see you and Nick home safely. Bastien, you are to escort Augustin back to Couve. He is a little shaken by the attack."

Bastien glanced at the new High Wizard of his haven before saying, "Yes, certainly." There was sadness in his eyes. Was it only because of what had happened in the arena, or also because he was thinking of his deceased father who had once ruled Couve?

I wanted to go to him, to ease his pain, but the curer, a small Italian woman with large hands and dark hair, was inspecting my cut.

There wasn't anything for the curers to do for the ones hit by Reya and Pia's arrows. They were gone. The weapons found their marks—the most damaging targets. The precision of the attack reminded me of the tree in the graveyard by the Sentinels' gym. The cuts were close together, probably practice shots from Pia and Reya. I didn't even know they had bows and arrows. I had never seen them.

The curer wiped my wound, slathered some gunk on it, and wrapped my arm with a bandage. A small girl handed me a tin cup filled with water.

I smiled down at her and she beamed up at me. "Thank you."

"You have a fan," Bastien said.

A guard rushed up to us. "Excuse me, Your Highness. The dead girl had a transmitter rod. We overheard orders given to someone over it. The person was instructed to intercept Professor Attwood. To use him to obtain the Chiavi in Asile's possession."

They were going after Uncle Philip.

I dropped the cup, my heart dropping with it.

CHAPTER FOURTEEN

I kicked off my shoes and ran through the cobbled streets. People darted out of my way. A girl carrying a sword and shield had to be scary for them. Heavy breaths burned my lungs as I sprinted down the hills and to the outbuilding. My bare feet, bruised and cracked from pounding against the stones, were on fire. Once in the tunnel, I created a light globe. The smacking of my feet against the puddle-covered, rocky ground resounded down the corridor. Clunking footsteps came from behind me.

"Gia!" Bastien called after me. "Wait for us."

"What are you doing?" Nick added. "We don't have any light— *Ow.* See? I just ran into a cave wall. *Shit.* And it's really jagged."

I didn't stop. I couldn't stop. Uncle Philip was coming for us and he was in danger. I hit the latch to the bookcase and it swung open. The Riccardiana Library was eerily quiet. I eased out, holding the sword in front of me, ready to strike.

A buzzing sound came from my side.

I whirled around. "Atenae?"

She bounced frantically on the air beside me. "He's this way. Hurry. Hurry, hurry, hurry…" her voice faded down the row of bookcases. Several faeries swarmed after her.

"Tell me the charm!" a man's voice boomed from the other side of the room.

I strained my eyes to see through the darkness. Moonlight lit up a beefy man holding a large machete and hovering over someone on the floor. Light shone on something above his head. The man wore a crown—the stolen Chiave.

"I-I don't know what charm you speak of," Uncle Philip said, his voice shaky.

I took a deep breath and held it, sliding my feet across the floor, easing closer, barely making a sound.

"You know the one," the man growled. "The one to unlock the gateways."

Uncle Philip quickly crab-crawled away from the man, but a bookcase behind him stopped his retreat.

The man took two powerful steps forward. "This is a waste. You will never give it up." The machete glinted as he pulled it back. Before he could swing it, I aimed my sword and threw it like a javelin. The blade flew through the air and punctured the upper left side of his back, making a sickening tearing sound as it broke through his flesh.

The man turned to me, a startled expression on his face, and took several unsteady steps toward me. He raised his machete and held it there for several seconds before dropping it. The machete clanked against the tiles. With a guttural moan, he collapsed to the floor.

Atenae flew up to me. "You look sick. Breathe."

I nodded to her and took several breaths as I held my side. Uncle Philip, bleeding from a gash in his head, pushed unsteadily to his feet. The concern in his eyes made me shrink to the floor. I sat there without moving. All the images of arrows and swords piercing and slicing people down overtook me. I sobbed into my hands.

Nick and Bastien stomped to a halt beside me.

Bastien dropped to his knees and pulled me into his arms. "It's over. You're fine."

Nick went to Uncle Philip's aid.

I shook my head hard. "I killed him. I killed him."

"If you hadn't, he would have killed the Professor." He pressed his lips to my temple. "It's his fault. He was a bad man. Can you walk?"

I nodded, and he guided me to my feet. My knees almost buckled, and he held me there until I was steady.

"I want to go home," I said, swaying.

Uncle Philip removed the crown from the man's head. "Are you all right?" he asked. "How did you know where to find me?"

"It was heard over Reya's transmitter rod," I said.

Uncle Philip gave us all a questioning look.

Bastien held on to my arm. "Pia and Reya attacked the hearing today. They killed many. I will fill you in on all the details later. I think we should get this cleaned up first."

"Yes," Uncle Philip said, taking in the aftermath of his ambush.

"Well, at least we have the crown back," Nick said, struggling with both his backpack and my messenger bag.

I looked around for Atenae and her faeries. They had vanished.

We waited with Uncle Philip until the Cleaners and a few guards came to take the body away. The Monitors had reported that the man was from Santara.

After the guards had secured the library, Bastien turned to me, taking my hands in his. "I must go. I have to escort Augustin back to Couve. You'll be okay with the guards here."

He blew out a frustrated breath. "Listen to me. You were fearless today. Saved lives. You can take care of yourself, can't you? Arik is daft if he doesn't see what I see in you. You did well today, Gianna. Stay safe." He kissed my cheek.

It was as if a rock plunked into my stomach as Bastien walked away. Something had shifted inside me. I wasn't sure what it was, but the moment he disappeared around the corner, I wanted him to come back. Even though I'd been the one to jump in front of the arrows today, I felt safe with Bastien around. Cared for in a way I hadn't been before, even with Arik. I might not want to admit it, but I'd felt that way since the day I'd met him.

Carrig met Nick and me in the library in Branford. When I finally reached home, Nana slathered me in all her healing concoctions before tucking me into bed.

She held a shot glass in front of my face. "Here, drink this." It contained her pain elixir. She then glared at Carrig. "You have to stop putting her in danger. She needs to be a normal girl for a while."

"I won't be arguing with you, woman." He shifted his feet. "I agree. Gia will be taking a rest for the time being."

I wasn't going to argue, either. I looked forward to being normal for a while.

I downed the shot. "Where's Pop?"

"He's at work. It's nearly eight in the morning. Now rest." She kissed my forehead, then closed the drapes before leaving, nodding for Carrig to follow her. "I'll be in later to check on you."

"Okay."

Everything hurt, but the worst pain wasn't physical. I wanted to cry. I killed a man. I'd killed before, but only beasts. Witnessing Toad, Arkwright, and the wizards die shook me. After several minutes, Nana's elixir soothed me and I fell fast asleep. No Athela dreams. No haunting images of arrows and swords piercing bodies.

Just darkness.

When I awoke, I felt a presence in the room and rolled over, thinking it would be Deidre. Instead, Nick sat in my desk chair, engrossed in a game on his phone.

I stretched my arms over my head, pain flaring up in my left shoulder. I winced and returned my arm to my side. "What are you doing here?"

"Babysitting." He tapped the screen.

"Very funny. Who asked you to watch me?"

"No one." He spun around in the chair. "You're the only one who likes me, so I was kind of hoping you'd recover."

"Who says I like you?"

He shrugged a shoulder. "You've been sleeping for ten hours, twenty-two minutes, and precisely ten seconds. Eleven. Twelve. Thirteen—"

"I get it," I cut him off, and pushed myself up on the pillows. "I think I could sleep for a week."

"Maybe you should take a shower. You kind of stink."

I smirked. "And you wonder why no one likes you."

"Dinner's almost done," he said.

I sniffed and whatever was cooking actually smelled delicious. "Hopefully, it tastes as good as it smells."

"It will. Nana's cooking."

I swung my legs over the edge of the bed. "Okay, I'll be down in a sec." My legs felt wobbly as I made my way to the bathroom. I stood under the hot water spurting out of the showerhead, letting the heat loosen my tight muscles.

Flashes of arrows, images of bodies falling into pools of blood, and the startled face of the man I had killed played through my memory. I squirted shampoo in my cupped hand and scrubbed it into my scalp, hard. The glass surrounding the shower closed in on me. Shampoo ran down my face, burning my eyes. My head pounded, my ears thrummed, and my body shook uncontrollably. I slid down the glass to my bare butt, pulling my legs to my chest. At first, I tried to fight the tears, but then gave up and cried. I cried hard, letting the water wash my tears away.

When I was done, I slid up to my feet and finished washing. The water had turned cold, and I shivered as I rinsed the suds from my hair. I slipped into my yoga pants and pulled on my hoody, then plodded down the stairs. Pop met me at the archway leading into the dining room. He gave me a bear hug, sending shards of pain down my arm.

I cringed and drew back from him.

"I'm so sorry." His face pinched with concern. "I forgot about your wound. You okay?"

"Yeah, it's not that bad," I lied. It was totally bad, and I kept my arm close to my side to keep from moving it.

Pop had set up the folding table from Thanksgiving at one end of the formal mahogany one. Lei, Kale, Jaran, Demos, and Arik took up one end, while Deidre, Nana, Faith, Nick, and Pop occupied the other. I eased into the empty chair close to the center between Faith and Nick.

I adjusted myself on my seat and inspected the plates on the table, trying to keep from looking at Arik. "Fried chicken?" My voice sounded scratchy.

It felt strange having Arik here. Uncomfortable. I fidgeted with the butter knife beside my plate. But it made sense he'd be included. He was part of our team. That would never change.

"And mashed potatoes," Faith added.

"Thought we should have a meal that would stick to your bones," Nana said, picking up the platter of chicken then passing it to Pop.

The bowl came to Faith and she plopped a huge spoonful onto my plate. "Nana's teaching me to cook."

"And she's become a pro." Nana poured gravy on her potatoes. "She could go on one of those cooking shows."

Faith brightened.

I ate two servings of everything on the table. I even had two slices of Nana's caramel apple pie. We lounged around the table, talking and laughing. I kept smiling, hoping to hide the fact that I felt awkward with Arik there. Thankfully, Demos and Jaran blocked my view of him. Anytime Arik spoke, everyone looked at me to see my reaction, which made things even more awkward.

When we were all tired of sitting, we cleared the table. I carried my plate and cup to the kitchen.

"How's the arm?" Arik came up from behind, startling me.

The glass slipped from my hand and shattered against the tiles. I dropped to my heels and reached to pick up the pieces.

Arik caught my wrist before I touched the glass. "Careful there, you'll cut yourself."

I looked up at him, our eyes locking. We stared at each other for several seconds before he let go.

I straightened. "Thanks. I wasn't thinking."

Faith rushed over with a broom and dustpan. She quickly swept up the pieces, darting worried looks from her task to me. "You needn't help with the dishes. Go rest."

I nodded and made my way through the kitchen into the great room.

"Gia?" Arik was right behind me.

I pretended I hadn't heard him.

"Gia, can I have a moment?" It didn't work. He wouldn't back off.

"Sure," I said. "What's up?"

He looked past me at the others gathering on the sofas. "Could we go someplace more private?"

"Sure." I followed him out to the porch.

We stood at the railing surrounding the porch and stared out at the yard. Patches of grass peeked out from the snow. The bare tree limbs rattled in the wind. I hugged myself, trying to keep warm.

"I believe there has been a misunderstanding about our relationship." It was so cold, his breath frosted in the air.

I wanted to yell at him that I understood our relationship perfectly. We kissed. We said things. It was perfectly clear to me. He used me until something better came along. But I didn't yell. I didn't say anything. I just listened. I was tired of fighting. I was tired of crying.

I was just plain tired.

He leaned against the railing and studied his hands. "I'm not certain how it all happened. Not certain what changed my feelings. I apologize for the way it all came about. I should have been a better man and explained it to you before showing up with her that day in the cafeteria."

"Are you happy?"

He gave me a sidelong glance. "Happy?"

"You know, does she make you *chipper*?" I used a word that sounded British to me. It sounded corny, but I was dying inside and humor always made things better.

He didn't even crack a smile. When I thought about it, I hadn't seen him smile in a long time.

"Yes, I suppose so."

That was odd. He supposes? It sounded like he was indifferent.

Stop looking for cracks in their relationship. I knew the drill. He was worried if he admitted he was happy, it would hurt my feelings. But knowing that didn't dull the pain.

Demos burst through the door just then and clomped across the decking.

I faced the yard, not wanting Demos to see the tears glossing my eyes.

"You ready to leave, Arik?" Demos said. "Carrig and Sinead should be back from Asile by now."

Recovered, I turned back around. "Why were they there?"

"They had a meeting with Bonifacio," Arik said, his face an unemotional mask. He certainly could turn his feelings on and off easily.

"And he is?" I said.

"He's the High Wizard of Santara," Demos said. "The meeting's agenda was to discuss how to handle their rebels. Apparently, Pia and Reya weren't alone. Others have risen up against the havens non-response to Santara's distress call."

Kale held open the door for Lei as they came outside. Jaran stepped out behind them.

"So, ducky, I heard you were a real badass in Mantello."

"We weren't going to bring that up," Kale reminded her.

"We said not around others," she protested. "The entire Mystik world is talking about it. You're a hero."

"Really? I don't feel like one. It was horrible seeing people die." I dragged my eyes away from them and stared back at the yard. When would I stop teetering on the edge of crying?

Jaran placed his hand on my arm. "It will get easier. Just take time to heal."

I forced a smile. "Thank you."

"Will you be at school tomorrow?" Lei asked.

"No, she's taking a few days off," Nana said from the doorway. "Gia, you should get out of the cold. You don't want to fall sick while healing from your wound." She stepped back into the kitchen.

"See you soon?" Lei hugged me, being careful not to hurt my arm.

"Definitely."

"Good evening," Kale said.

I buried my freezing hands into my armpits. "Night."

"I'll come by and visit after school," Jaran said.

"Sounds great," I said.

He skipped down the steps to catch up with Lei and Kale. Arik headed for the porch steps.

"Good night." I spun around and headed for the door.

"Gia."

I paused, keeping my eyes on the door. "Yes?"

"I did love you. I thought you should know that."

"I didn't need to know that," I said through clenched teeth, and fumbled with the doorknob, keeping my eyes on the Christmas wreath Faith had made and hung there.

Don't you cry, Gia. Don't cry. Not in front of him. The door clicked open and I slammed it behind me, leaving Arik standing alone on the porch.

He *did* love me. Meaning he no longer loved me. Emily could have him. I didn't care anymore.

I charged up the stairs, fell into bed, and wrapped the covers around me until I resembled a burrito. I wondered how long I could get away with hibernating in bed. Cleo slinked onto the bed and buried herself into an opening in the Gia burrito. Before long, Baron found her and the two trapped my legs between them.

Deidre tiptoed into the room and searched the drawers for her pajamas in the dark.

"I'm up. You can turn on a light."

Her lamp clicked on. "How are you feeling?"

"Like crap."

"I heard what Arik said to you."

"You were spying on us?"

She stepped into her red and green pajama bottoms. "No, of course not. I took the trash out the side door. I caught the tail end of his absurd apology for breaking your heart as I crossed the yard. If you ask me, he's been acting odd ever since they started dating. Maybe he's so in love with you, he's scared, so he decided to date Emily. You know, so he doesn't get hurt."

I contemplated pulling my pillow over my head so I wouldn't have to listen to her theories.

"It's like she put a spell on him, or maybe she has a voodoo doll."

"It could be the fact that she's beyond beautiful and a nice person." I nudged Baron with my toe to get him to move. He didn't budge. "That is, she's nice to everyone but me."

"She was nice to you before you publicly got together with Arik."

She had a point. Emily was friendly to me when we first moved to Branford. Guys always screwed things up between friends. Girls were too jealous by nature. I had to get over Arik. After all, there were more pressing matters to worry about than relationship dramas. We had to protect both worlds from whatever dangers were brewing in the Mystik realm. And things were getting bad.

"I think I'll go to school tomorrow," I said, fluffing my pillow.

"That's the spirit."

She clicked off the lamp.

CHAPTER FIFTEEN

I must've looked like a real creeper, peering around my locker door at Emily, gathering up my nerve. For two weeks, I stalked her, trying to gain courage to speak to her. She wore her blacker-than-black hair in a side ponytail, a modest skirt, and knee-high boots. I inspected my ensemble—jeans, T-shirt, leather jacket, and Doc Martens. It was something Nick would wear to ride his bike. I removed my hair tie.

"Hey, Emily," I said, approaching. "You have a minute?"

She glanced at her cell phone. "Actually, we have a few before class starts."

"I just wanted…" I wasn't sure exactly what to say. If she knew Arik and I were together before coming to Branford, she'd realize I wasn't trying to sneak in and snatch him up before she could. But if I wanted to move on from Arik, I had to make amends with both him and Emily.

"Well?" She glanced at her phone again. "Time's almost up."

"I just wanted to say that I had no idea you liked Arik when I agreed to go on a date with him. If I'd known, I would've said no." The lie tasted bitter in my mouth.

"Yeah, Deidre did say she hadn't told you I was interested in him." She swung the strap of her backpack onto her shoulder. "There're no hard feelings. I guess it all worked out in the end."

The bitter taste in my mouth moved to my stomach. The smug look on her face made me wish I hadn't come over to talk to her. It may have worked out for her, but it tore me to pieces, and I wasn't sure I'd be able to fit all the parts back together again.

"That sounded horrible," she said. "I only meant that it was good things ended with you guys before you got too attached to him."

Too attached to him? The breakup caused my heart to explode in my chest, leaving a hole the size of the Grand Canyon behind, that's all. I wanted to tell her we had been together for months before she entered the picture. But I bit my tongue.

The warning bell sounded.

She searched the ceiling as if she could see the bell somewhere. "Listen, I should get to class." She started down the hall, stopped suddenly, and stomped back to me. "You know, I'm sorry, too. I think it was just a matter of neither one of us knowing the other one had feelings for him. You're a beautiful girl, Gia. I'm sure your prince will find you soon."

Was she being nice or pouring salt in my wounds? Emily made a beeline for a girl with hair paler than her skin, said a few words to her, and then they dashed down the hall together.

I darted off to class. I was done obsessing over her and Arik. I'd been messing up in school ever since the big breakup, and I didn't need another tardy warning going home to Pop.

Everyone was already in their seats when I made it to English class. The tardy bell rang as the class door shut behind me. I slipped into my desk.

Jaran leaned across the aisle. "Where were you?"

"I had to take care of something."

"Are you feeling well?"

"I feel great."

He smiled, then straightened when the teacher addressed the class.

"Good morning, class." Mrs. Ripple sent a stack of books down each row. "We're going to read a book from a local author over the holiday break. I would have liked to have read it during Halloween, since it has to do with the local myth about witches in the area, but we had to wait for Mrs. Downey's class to finish with them."

The books made their way to me, and I grabbed one before passing the remaining two to the girl behind me. The title read: *The Witches of Branford*. The woman on the cover had black hair and piercing blue eyes, with flames surrounding her. A Celtic trinity knot hung from a thick chain around the woman's neck. I'd seen the symbol recently but couldn't place where.

Mrs. Ripple drew three intertwining ovals and a circle around them on the white board. "Does anyone know what the symbol on her necklace is?"

No one stirred.

"I take that as a no? Okay, then, it's the Power of Three symbol. It represents eternity and continuity. Many women in the 1600s, who used herbs to heal the body and mind, were considered witches."

A hand shot up.

"Yes, Becca?"

Becca tucked her short mousy hair behind her ears. "Just like in the Salem Witch Trials?"

"Well, sort of. Unlike Salem, the people of Branford aren't

aware of this bit of their history. It was hushed, and only recently did the author of this book publish the truth. He had found a diary of a distant relative that documented the event."

Becca studied the cover of the book. "It would be so cool to die a horrible death. Like this witch burning in the fire. I bet she was buried somewhere private. You know, the religious guys never let witches be buried in the community graveyards."

The girl was morbid. Or brilliant. The stories she came up with during creative writing were captivating.

Mrs. Ripple gave Becca a puzzled look. "Um, that is true. No one knows where these poor souls were buried. Possibly, their families hid their graves on their properties. Anyway, winter break starts tomorrow. Please have the book read before school resumes."

Becca's statement about the burial made me think of the graveyard behind our fencing club. And then I remembered where I'd seen the trinity knot recently. One of the gravestones had the same symbol on it. I had a sudden interest in reading the book and finding out more about the hidden cemetery. It would be a good distraction from the Mystik world and Arik.

Nana sat at the kitchen table, sipping tea, with Baron curled up on her lap. Cleo bathed in a patch of sunlight on the carpet by Nana's feet.

"Hey," I said, dropping my messenger bag onto the bench beside the kitchen door. I removed the book assigned in class from its front pocket. "How was your day?"

"Quiet." She placed her teacup down. "And yours?"

"Bearable." I took a seat at the table and pulled my legs

up into a pretzel. I slid the book across the table to her. "Do you know about the witches of Branford?"

She put on her reading glasses that hung from a chain around her neck and picked up the book. "I'm not aware of them. Are you sure this is a true story?"

"No. But this author says it's true."

She read the back of the book. "Sounds like an intriguing tale. Why do you ask?"

"There're some old gravestones behind the club." I pointed at the pendant on the cover of the book. "This symbol is on one of the gravestones."

"Take me there." She took another sip of her tea, stood, and placed Baron on the chair. "I'll get my coat."

The parking lot at the gym had an untouched layer of snow covering it. The tires of Nana's Lexus cut through the white lot. She slowed the car to a stop at the side of the building.

Nana stepped out, pulling up the faux fur collar of her jacket. Her boots crunched across the snow as she met me in front of the car.

"The gym looks impressive," she said, following me down the path. "Those artisans from Asile did a fantastic job fixing the place up."

Piles of snow weighed down the bare limbs of the trees, providing an icy canopy over the tiny cemetery. Soggy leaves clung to the bases of the trunks. Nana shoved her hands into her pockets, her gaze turned up to the tree branches.

"There's a dark aura around these woods," she said. "Something horrible happened here. Death and despair echo in the wind, whispers of a terrifying event."

I glanced at her. "Can you freak me out more?"

"I'm sorry. I thought you wanted to know what happened here."

"I do, but jeesh. Can you put more dread into your voice?

Seriously, you sound like that horror movie narrator. You know, the one in those old movies."

"Vincent Price? Dear, no one's voice can be as creepy as his." She stepped over a log.

I passed her, snapping twigs under my weight. The gravestones were lonely looking without the greenery hugging them; winter had left them exposed and unprotected.

Nana stopped suddenly. "Gia, wait."

I hesitated. "What's wrong?"

"You're in the circle."

I back-stepped to her. "What circle?"

"See those rocks surrounding the area?" She pointed them out. "It's a witch's circle. We must respect the women in those graves. Going into the circle is disrespectful and can bring you bad luck."

"That would've been good to know before Arik dragged me in there. I definitely have had bad luck lately. Can I get rid of it?"

"I have a few things we can try later." She lowered her head as if in thought. "No. Not women, but young girls were buried here. They were about your age. So much pain surrounds this place. Loss. Betrayal."

I took another step back. "You're scaring me."

"Sorry, dear, but it can't be helped." She took measured steps along the outer circle of rocks. "Can you go get my tote from the trunk of my car?"

"Alone?"

Nana Kearns held out her keys. "I'm sure you've faced scarier things than woods with a past."

She had a point, but ghosts and stuff like that were worse. How would a person fight off that kind of attack? I weaved through the trees and ran up the path to the Lexus, the eerie sounds in the woods chasing me all the way. The normal chirps and tweets of forest animals sounded more sinister after what Nana had said. The car trunk protested as it opened. I grabbed Nana's bag and slammed the trunk shut.

A shadow moved across the trees. I squinted but couldn't see anything.

Stop it, Gia. It's just a trick of the light, or a forest animal. But no amount of my reasoning could shake the feeling I had that someone was watching me.

I flew back to Nana. She was kneeling in a patch of dead grass and glanced over her shoulder when she heard me approach.

"I thought I saw someone back there," I said, trying to catch my breath.

"Most likely one of the girls buried here," she said. "Whoever placed these rocks wanted to prevent the graves from being disturbed. In doing so, it prevented the spirits from moving on."

"That's comforting."

She raised an eyebrow at my sarcastic tone and reached her hand out for her tote.

I handed it to her. "What are you going to do?"

"Release them, naturally."

"Naturally." I frowned down at her.

She took out baggies filled with an assortment of leaves and petals then placed her tote on the ground.

If a cop ever stopped her while driving, the baggies might look suspiciously like pot. Their smell was nothing like it, though. The leaves she tossed in the air while chanting a spell carried a minty, rosy scent.

"Help me move the rocks," she said.

We placed each one at the base of a nearby tree.

"Be free," she spoke to the grave markers. "May your journey home be swift, and may peace await you on the other side." She moved into the circle, inspecting each stone. She looked over at me. "There're six grave markers, but I only felt five spirits. A family member of one of the girls must've exhumed her body and buried her somewhere else. Most likely, a family lot in their church's cemetery, which if they were caught doing, was punishable by death."

I swallowed. There wasn't any fear in me anymore. Just sadness for what the girls must have gone through.

"Hmm." She returned her eyes to the markers. "The witches buried here were killed for practicing their craft. One was a Bane witch. I'm not certain which one, though."

A Bane witch? It was as if cold fingers crawled up my back. They were evil. Nana was a Pure witch and used her magic for good.

"Emily's last name is Proctor, like on that marker. Do you think she might be a witch and related to whoever was buried here?"

"You think she did something to Arik?"

"I don't know," I said. "But since they got together, he's not himself anymore."

"Is he not like himself around everyone or just you, dear? Maybe he's merely feeling guilty for hurting you."

"Maybe. But the others say he's changed, and it happened so fast."

"All witches are registered in the Witch Registry. Thankfully, my membership online is still active. I'll see what I can find."

"Thanks."

"If I do this and nothing comes of it, will you promise to forget what happened with Arik and move on?" Her soft green eyes held concern.

"I think I'm already moving on," I said. My thoughts drifted to Bastien. I wasn't sure what was going on there, but maybe it was worth exploring. "But if Emily is doing something, I owe it to Arik to help him. He was there for me when I was first pulled into the Mystik world." No matter how mad I was at Arik, I didn't want anything bad to happen to him.

We headed back to the Lexus, arm in arm. The cold bit at my face. The wind swirled around us, making me draw closer to Nana.

Thank you, thank you, thank you, thank you, thank you. The wind seemed to whisper.

I gave Nana a freaked out look. "Did you hear that? It sounded..." I trailed off, not wanting to admit I was hearing things.

"I hear it, too," she said. "The spirits are grateful we released them. They're on their way now."

I knew how the witches felt. Being trapped in this small town and unable to live in Boston sucked. I let out a deep sigh, the frosty air turning my breath into fog.

"You all right, dear?"

"I'm fine. It's just been an emotional day."

She gave me a questioning look. "If this girl is a witch and spelled Arik, the spell wouldn't last this long. She would have had to brand or tattoo the spell on him. Search him and see if there is a distinct mark on him."

"Yeah, that'll be easy," I muttered under my breath. Arik was hardly ever alone. Every time I saw him, Emily was attached to his side, and when she wasn't around, he avoided me. At practice, we were too busy trying to kill each other with our wooden swords to get up close. Plus, I'd have to get him naked to do a thorough search. Impossible.

"Excuse me, dear, what was that?"

"Nothing, just talking to myself." *And hating my life.*

CHAPTER SIXTEEN

The library in Branford was buzzing with small kids. With Saturday came Christmas art projects and story time for them, and there was no way to keep them all quiet. A stack of books sat on the table beside me. Researching artifacts in the libraries around the world made my eyes cross. I covered my ears to block out the noise around me. Since recovering the crown from the man I pinned with my sword in the Riccardiana Library, we had to find only three more Chiavi.

"Could there be any more cherubs in the world?" Nick groaned.

"They're *putti*, and the singular is putto," I said. "Maybe we should just call them cherubs. When you say putties, it just sounds so wrong. Like something you do in the bathroom."

He shook his head at me. "This blows. We could be at the shopping mall, people watching or pigging out on pretzels. There are millions of *cherubs* in the libraries. We'll never find the right one."

It did seem as if all ancient artwork depicted putti. We just hadn't come across one that could "see farther than the rest," whatever that meant. I assumed it probably had glasses, a magnifying glass, or something else that aided sight. Our search on the internet hadn't come up with any putti fitting our criteria.

"Oh, we didn't search for a telescope," I said.

"On it." Nick tapped the screen of his phone.

Miss Bagley walked up in flats and dress pants. She looked tired. "How's it coming?" she asked.

"We haven't found anything," I said.

Her lips pressed into a straight line of disappointment. "That won't do at all. Keep searching."

Nick slumped over the book. "For how long?"

"Another hour. I'll check back in a few." She glowered at two kids chasing each other in the lobby. "There's no running in the library." She rushed after them.

Maira, a volunteer at the library, sidestepped to our table and pretended not to speak to us as she darted glances over her shoulder. "Don't look at me. I'll get in trouble if I talk to you. Miss Bagley is a very strange librarian. Children annoy her, and she hasn't even read Jane Austen."

Look who was calling the kettle black. Poor Maira, though. I wanted to tell her that her suspicions were right. Miss Bagley wasn't a real librarian. The part about Miss Bagley not liking kids comforted me in a way, though. If she and Pop got married, then maybe they wouldn't have any. With Miss Bagley distracted, I decided it would be a great opportunity to hunt the library records for any information on the Proctors of Branford. Nana needed a full name of the witch buried in the woods to search the Witch Registry.

I reached into my messenger bag and took out the book Mrs. Ripples had handed out in class. "Maira, do you know if there's any information about the witches in Branford? The ones mentioned in this book? Actually, I'm not interested in the witches in this book, but the earlier ones. Maybe when the town first started?"

"There are some old newspapers from the seventeenth century on the computer in the reference room. Miss Bagley told me not to disturb you two. She wants you to finish whatever assignment you're working on." She darted a look over her shoulder. "Give me ten minutes, and then come join me there. Don't let her see you. Pretend you're going to the bathroom, in case she spots you."

"Okay, thanks," I said. Uncle Philip must've come down hard on Miss Bagley for her to enforce searching for the Chiavi today.

"What are you trying to prove?" Nick whispered. "Emily isn't a witch. And I highly doubt Arik would let her tattoo or brand him."

"Probably not, but I need peace of mind." I watched the lobby, waiting for Miss Bagley to leave. She lingered in the hall, cooing over a toddler, which made me nervous. Maybe she would want a kid. I guessed it wouldn't be too bad to have a baby sister or brother.

"You need to stop your obsession, already," he said. "I think they prosecute stalkers in this state."

Nick was right. It was most likely a long shot, but Emily's last name etched on that grave marker in the hidden cemetery was too much of a coincidence for me to ignore.

Miss Bagley finally climbed the stairs to the second level. "Be right back."

I didn't wait for Nick's warning. I charged across the lobby and into the reference room. Maira sat at a computer clicking on the mouse. "I found several articles of the time," she said. "I can email them to you."

"Wow that was fast."

"It's called modern technology." She quirked a smile at

me. "We've scanned all old documents into the computer. The microfiche is obsolete nowadays. Which ones do you want me to send?"

"I don't need a copy, just a name." I leaned over her shoulder and read the titles as she clicked through them. I spotted the names from the graves in large print on one of the articles. "That one. Can you make it larger? I can hardly read it."

She hit a few buttons and the page zoomed in.

I scanned the names for Proctor and found it at the end. Ruth Ann Proctor. She was born on the eighteenth of June in the year sixteen hundred and sixty-two, and the court had sentenced her to hang by the neck until dead.

"What are you doing in here?" I practically jumped onto the desk at Miss Bagley's sudden appearance.

Maira quickly clicked out of the page onscreen.

"She's just helping me do an internet search for putti with a telescope."

For not knowing what I was talking about, Maira kept her face expressionless.

"Did you find what you were looking for?" Miss Bagley asked.

"No, not yet." I made a move for the door. "Maybe Nick's had some luck." Putto. Something just clicked. The riddle mentioned a school of putti. We were looking for one cherub when we should have been looking for a group together. And a *school* of them, which meant they had to do with knowledge or something. "I think I just figured it out."

Miss Bagley tried to keep up with me as I hurried back to Nick. I plopped down on the seat beside him and started flipping through the pages of photographs.

Nick's eyes followed each flip of the page. "What's going on?"

"I think I know what we're looking for. Now we just have to find it."

A crowd moved like a wave into the lobby. Miss Bagley looked sharply at them. "Let me know if you find it." She charged off for the group.

"Hell, if I'll let her know," I mumbled. "Why does she have to know? What's up with that?"

"She's kind of pushy lately, isn't she?" Nick sighed. "It's like her panties are too tight."

I smiled at that. For once, Nick's inappropriate comment was spot on. I gave him the details of my discovery, and we searched the photographs. We found the school of putti in the Abbey Library in Saint Gall, Switzerland. I was hitting homeruns today—it was like Nana's good luck spell was working for me. I had the library for the Chiave and the name of the witch buried in the hidden cemetery in the woods.

Miss Bagley whirred back into the room. It was a busy day at the library and it showed on her appearance. Her hair was frizzy and her face drawn.

"Well, did you find it?" she snapped.

"No." I kept my eyes locked on her, not daring to look away or she might catch that I was lying to her. "We'll have to come back after Christmas. I have practice in fifteen minutes."

"After Christmas? How about tomorrow?"

"Uncle—Professor Attwood gave us permission to take a break. My best friend from Boston is arriving tomorrow and I'm going to spend time with her."

Nick and I shuffled around the tables, walked into the lobby, and glanced back before going out the library door. Miss Bagley's attention was back on the baby. Maybe she only liked babies and not kids that could run around and break valuable artwork.

...

I bent to my side, stretching my muscles. Not practicing regularly had caused them to feel petrified. Since I was early, I pulled on some gloves, then front-kicked the punching bag hanging down from the ceiling and connected to the floor. I backed up and performed a roundhouse, hitting the center with my foot, the chains rattling violently. Sliding my feet into a solid stance, I threw jab after jab against the bag, my gloves smacking loud against leather.

"Easy, lass, what harm has it ever caused you?" Carrig crossed the mats to me. "Good to see you at practice. You be ready for it?"

"Yeah, I didn't realize how much I missed hitting things," I said between heavy breaths.

"That's the spirit." He headed off for the equipment room.

I smirked at that. Deidre always said the same thing.

Carrig was a wonderful father to Deidre. I bet he missed her, since she had to live with Pop and me and pretend to be my twin. My heart was like a paperweight in my chest thinking about how it could have been if Carrig had raised me and if my mother had never died. But then I'd think of Pop, and I would never change a thing. People sometimes say that there's nothing better than a real parent, a biological one. I'd argue that Pop was my real parent. No matter how far away we were from each other, I always felt his love around me.

Lei and Kale ambled in, his arm resting across her shoulder, her arm around his waist. I kicked the bag harder then threw another series of punches at it.

"Whoa, Gia, I'd hate to have you ever get mad at me," Demos said, lugging his gym bag over his shoulder.

The Irish Sentinels, Aiden and Hugh, flanked him.

"She'd beat you senseless," Hugh said, elbowing Demos.

Aiden snickered. "You're one to talk. She'd easily take you down."

Arik swaggered in behind them. He was so gorgeous, even with his serious, expressionless face. I broke my trance on him and slammed my gloved hand against the leather again.

"Gia," Carrig called across the gym. "Show the bag some pity and gather with the group."

The other Sentinels trailed in. Jaran kept step with Abre, their heads together as Jaran showed her something in a magazine.

We all surrounded Carrig. "We will keep to our original pairings today." His stare found me.

I frowned at him.

"I don't want any complaining, so if you be inclined to protest your matching, make sure you be thinking about it thoroughly." He shifted his weight. "You be the hope of the worlds—keep your emotions under control."

The group broke up in their pairs. I faced Arik from across the mat, tapping my dummy sword against my thigh.

Carrig sounded his whistle, and I charged for Arik. He blocked my sword with his. The vibration from the hit almost caused me to lose my hold. My grasp was too relaxed. I tightened my grip and charged him again. He ducked my attack. As we sparred, I inspected his bare arms and exposed neck. There were no burns or tattoos.

"You really ought not to miss practices," he said, dodging my attack again. "You're getting soft."

Oh, no, he didn't just say that.

"I'll show you soft." I bolted down the mats, my boots slapping against the vinyl.

We fought for forty minutes, with small breaks between each round, and we were finally on our last fight. I had made it through practice without crying. Actually, I was numb.

Had I moved on? I had shut all doors to our past, except for one. And to do that, I needed to know he wasn't tricked into breaking up with me.

The whistle sounded again.

I swung my sword to his right, and he parried it left. I shuffled around, holding my sword parallel and readying for his next attack. He came straight for me, and I cut off his swing, my fake blade meeting his with a loud *thwack*. I threw blow after blow, and he blocked each one. He was on the defense and I was on the offense. We broke from each other, catching our breaths and eyeing one another.

His lips quirked at the right corner of his mouth, creating a dimple. There was something in his eyes for just a brief second that I recognized. Admiration. He had looked at me like that before.

Before Emily.

And just as suddenly as the glint in his eyes had appeared, it was gone. The joy rushed from me like water down an unplugged drain. Maybe I was wrong, or stupid to even try, but I had to find out if Emily had placed a mark on him.

The next time we were in range of each other, I grasped the neck of his shirt and yanked as hard as I could, hoping to rip it off him.

He wrenched from my grip. "Bloody hell, are you trying to choke me?"

All the Sentinels paused their fighting and stared at us.

Arik stomped off and tossed his sword into the pile by the equipment room.

Carrig sounded his whistle. "All right, then, take to the showers. I gave Sinead my word I'd be ending practice early today so you can get ready for the party tonight."

I weaved between the other sweaty Sentinels to Jaran. His short dreadlocks glistened and his forehead shined with sweat. Abre's dark eyes looked disdainfully at me, her short hair sticking to the wetness around her face.

"What?" I raised my palms at her. "You have something to say?"

"Why did you grab his shirt? You must keep your emotions out of the fight," she said, sauntering by, and added over her shoulder, "We only have each other when in a battle. Mistakes mean death."

Jaran wiped his forehead with his towel. "So why did you try to strangle Arik?"

"I wasn't choking him. I was trying to get his shirt off."

He dragged the towel around his neck and smirked. "You wanted to undress him here? Are you getting desperate?"

"No. Not like that. I was looking for something."

He pulled on his jacket.

"Aren't you going to shower?" I said.

"I'm missing my show. I'll shower at home."

"But can't you just shower here?" I rocked on my feet. "Plus you could stream it on your phone."

"I like it on the big screen."

I gave my best pleading look.

He studied me. "All right, what are you scheming?"

I told him everything about Emily, the hidden cemetery, and that she might have branded or tattooed a spell on him. In the end, he agreed to shower there and see if he could find anything.

I hurried to the girls' locker room and took the quickest shower I'd ever taken.

Lei watched me curiously as I raced to get my clothes on. "Where's the battle?" she said.

"I have to get home. You know, Afton is coming in at five."

She glanced at the clock above the mirrors. "It's only a little after four."

"I don't want to risk being late." I tied my wet hair up in a ponytail and bolted out the door.

Waiting, I pretended to search my bag for something. One by one, Demos, Kale, and the other male Sentinels trickled out.

"Who are you waiting on?" Demos said, hoisting up his bag.

"Jaran. Is he almost done?"

Jaran pushed open the door. "Yeah, I'm done."

The others walked off for the outside doors.

I dragged him across the mats toward the door. "Did you see anything on Arik? A burn mark or a tattoo?"

"Nothing. His skin is flawless. Not even a blemish."

I deflated. "Are you sure there wasn't any kind of mark?"

He dropped his bag in front of the doors and retrieved his jacket. "I saw every square inch of him. It was a difficult task. Trust me." His grin said it was anything but difficult.

I forced a smile. I really believed Emily had done something to Arik. That he hadn't rejected me. It was time to face it. He didn't want me anymore. "Thank you for doing it," I said, defeated.

"It was entirely my pleasure." He bumped my shoulder, the wide grin still fixed on his face. "Listen, why don't you just let him go already? When you do, you will open yourself up to new possibilities."

"I'm working on it." I leaned into his shoulder. "How about you embrace all your possibilities, too? I dare you to bring a date to the party tonight."

The grin slipped from his face. "I don't have anyone to invite."

"I heard Cole and that soccer player broke up." I jerked open the heavy door. The sunlight blinded us, and I squinted at him. "Plus, I caught him checking you out at lunch the other day."

"You're not teasing me, are you?" Jaran rushed after me as I crossed the parking lot to Pop waiting in his Volvo.

"Just call him."

"All right, I'll call him," Jaran said. "Only if you invite Bastien."

Pop lowered his window. "Hurry up. Afton's train will arrive soon."

I yanked open the door, glancing at Jaran. "I already did. He can't make it. See you tonight."

He waved as we drove off.

I buckled the seat belt, wondering if Arik would bring anyone to the party. My heart sank at the thought of him bringing Emily. I really needed to get a grip and let him go. But it was like telling my heart to stop beating. My lungs to stop expanding and deflating. My brain to stop working. I didn't know how to stop loving him.

CHAPTER SEVENTEEN

Falling snow created an icy confetti celebration for Afton's arrival at the train depot. We held each other in a tight embrace, not caring about the cold. "I can't believe you're actually here," I said, releasing her. "And I definitely can't believe you ditched the hair weave. You look amazing in short hair, like a young Halle Berry."

She stepped back, her eyes looking past me, past Pop. "I never thought we'd see each other again."

"He's not here," I said, answering the question on her face.

"Who isn't?" she said.

I slipped my arm through hers and pulled her along the wet platform. "Come on, it's me. I know you were looking for Nick."

"He didn't want to come and see me?"

"He's working at his parents' restaurant tonight. Said he'd come in the morning for breakfast."

We reached Pop. "Here, let me take that," he said, grabbing her suitcase.

We folded into Pop's Volvo. I let her take shotgun and

hugged the back of her seat to talk to her.

"How are the parents?"

"Not good. My dad and that woman broke it off, but my mom refuses to take him back." She fastened her seat belt. "She said their relationship is too damaged to fix. It's horrible. She cries all the time."

"I'm sorry I wasn't there for you." I leaned back and fastened my belt as Pop backed up the car.

He guided the Volvo out of the parking lot and onto the street.

"Maybe she could come down for Christmas Day?" I said.

"We'd love to have her," Pop added.

"I'll text her and ask, but she's sort of a hermit right now." She stared out the window, and I could see her sullen face reflected in the darkened glass.

Afton's family had always been the kind of family I dreamed of having—a two-parent home. She had a brother and sister, but they were ten years older than her and already out on their own. Afton was a surprise pregnancy. The Wilsons always had fun together, going to movies, plays, and just kicking back at long dinners. I never saw the breakup coming. I bet Afton hadn't, either.

I decided to change the subject. "The house is going to be full of life with you and Nana here. It'll be fun to have everyone together. Nana is staying in Pop's room, and Deidre offered to stay with Faith so we can share our room."

"That's nice of her. Are you two getting along better?"

"Yes, she's actually not so bad." The seat belt tightened against my shoulder as Pop pressed on the brake to make a turn. "Nana and Faith put together a party for your arrival tonight. They've been cooking all day."

The Volvo's headlights lit up the driveway to our house.

"Oh, they shouldn't have gone to—"

A light shone behind us and illuminated the inside of the Volvo. I twisted around to see who it was. "It's Nick's motorcycle."

Pop glanced in the rearview window. "I thought you said he had to work?"

"He does. I don't know why he's here."

Pop hit the remote to the garage door, and it wobbled a little as it raised. He parked the Volvo in the bay. Nick rolled his bike to a stop behind us. The headlights flashed off.

I popped open the door and met Nick in the driveway. "Hey, I thought you couldn't make it."

"Ma practically forced me to come," he said. "She said it would be rude not to be here on Afton's first night."

Afton bolted around the hood of the car and collided with Nick, wrapping her arms tightly around him. "I'm so happy to see you."

He hesitantly encircled her in his arms. The hard look that had been darkening his face ever since we came to Branford softened. His eyes crinkled in a smile and his shoulders seemed more relaxed.

They held each other until it became awkward—for me, not them. I wanted them to be together. They were perfect for each other, but I also cared for Deidre and didn't want her to get hurt. Thinking of my twin, I figured I should break the two of them up before she saw their inappropriately long hug.

"Afton, you should freshen up for the party," I said.

They released each other. "It feels good to have us all together again," Nick said.

She smiled and squeezed his hand. "I'll see you in a few."

In my room with Afton, it was like old times, primping for the party. She rejected each outfit I held up for her approval.

There was a quiet knock on the door.

"Yeah?" I said.

"It's Deidre. Can I come in?"

"Of course," I called at the door. "It's your room, too."

She seemed uncomfortable as she came in. The red dress she wore played up the rouge in her cheeks and on her lips. She had curled her short platinum hair, and she sort of looked like Marilyn Monroe. I wondered, as I watched my exact twin, if I could pull off the same look as effortlessly as she had. It was all about attitude, and Deidre had it in spades.

"You're not dressed," Deidre said, sitting on her bed.

"I can't find anything to wear," I answered.

Afton looked through the mirror at me as she crimped her eyelashes. "The only dresses she owns are summer ones. She doesn't even have a cocktail dress."

"I'll give you the perfect thing." Deidre popped up and searched her closet.

"Me wearing your things is getting to be a habit," I said.

"I don't mind." Deidre removed a hanger holding an A-line emerald-colored cocktail dress with a bell skirt made of taffeta and a beaded bodice. "How about this?"

Sinead loved shopping with Deidre. She had tried to get me to go a few times, but I'd always found an excuse.

"Ooh!" Afton squealed. "I love that. With a side bun you'll look amazing."

"Can I at least wear my ballet flats?"

Afton frowned at me for several seconds. "It would be nicer with heels. Maybe a better necklace. What is that thing you're wearing?"

I covered the glass locket with my hand, as if I could protect it from her dislike. "Uncle Philip gave it to me. It's important. I can't take it off."

"I think flats would work fine," Deidre said. "I have black satin ones."

Afton dropped the eyelash curler into her makeup bag.

"You're probably right, and she's a little clumsy on heels."

"*She's* right here," I said, "and *she* thinks she'll wear the heels."

Afton's lips turned up at the corners as she applied lip gloss, and I knew she'd just played me. All someone had to do was say I couldn't do something and it made me want to prove that I could.

I picked up my root beer–flavored Lip Smacker from the dresser and slathered it on. "Ready?"

"You haven't grown out of the lip balm, yet?" Afton stood and smoothed down her dress.

"Nude lips are classic," I said, as if I knew what I was talking about. "I'm wearing eye shadow *and* mascara—that has to count for something."

"You both look amazing," Deidre said, making her way to the door.

Trays of food and a large punch bowl sat on the dining table pushed against the wall, leaving a small area in the middle of the room for dancing. Deidre hooked up her iPhone to the speakers on the entertainment center, and music instantly filled the room. The entire house looked like the North Pole with all the decorations, figurines, and snow globes crowding every available surface. The perfectly decorated Christmas tree dominated the corner nearest the big bay window. The red and gold balls dangling from its branches glinted in the flashing white lights.

Arik, Demos, and the other Sentinels stood together by the table, holding tiny plates filled with appetizers. Kale had his arm wrapped around Lei as they leaned close to each other on two of the chairs lining the walls. Pop, Miss Bagley, and Nana were in deep conversation on a few chairs down at the end of the row. Missing from the party were Jaran, and thankfully, Emily.

Faith, wearing a human glamour courtesy of Sinead, carried in a tray of plastic champagne glasses. Her black shimmery dress skimmed her body. She stepped carefully over to Afton and me. "You two look amazing tonight."

"Thanks, and I like this glamour on you," I said. She had more curves than her normal illusion. She sort of looked like Jennifer Lopez.

"Too bad it doesn't last long. I have to keep having Sinead reapply it." She extended her tray toward us. "Take one. It's soda and sherbet. This, of course, is an alcohol-free party."

"Thanks. You've done a wonderful job with everything." I lifted a glass from the tray.

Afton took one. "Yeah, you should totally go into the party planning business."

Faith beamed. "That's so kind of you to say. Nana has taught me so much. I hope she stays with us forever."

Forever? I never thought about us hiding out forever. I had always thought of this as temporary. My stomach suddenly felt queasy. Boston was my home; I felt misplaced ever since we left. I couldn't imagine never returning, never eating at the North End, never walking the Common, and not being able to see Afton whenever I wanted.

The door opened, letting in an arctic wind causing the hair on my arms to bristle. Every gaze shot to the entry. Jaran strolled in with Cole Jensen beside him. He took Cole around and introduced him to everyone.

I smiled against my champagne glass at his courage. I smiled because of how everyone accepted them. I smiled because Emily wasn't there.

I smiled because Arik was checking me out as he headed over to us.

He sauntered up to me with his easy stride. His blue dress shirt and black pants hugged his body perfectly. He wore his hair longer nowadays, and it brushed his collar in the back. I preferred his hair shorter. He probably grew it out for Emily.

"You look lovely this evening," Arik said, stopping beside me.

"I bet you say that to all the ladies."

"Not all." Lately, whenever he wasn't with Emily, he seemed almost normal again.

"Where's the ball and chain?" I used something Pop always said to Nick's father as a joke.

He pinched his eyebrows together. "I don't understand."

The lights dimmed, the music turned up, and Deidre dragged Nick to the middle of the room to dance.

"Why isn't Emily here?" I raised my voice over the music.

"She went with her uncle to spend the holidays with relatives."

The music was too loud to keep up a conversation, so we stood watching our friends and family move across the tiny dance floor. To me, they'd all become family. And family came in many colors and didn't necessarily need the same roots to grow. It was in that moment I realized Arik would always have a piece of my heart, even if it were as a brother instead of something more.

The music slowed.

"Would you like to dance?" he asked.

I blinked. Did he just ask me to dance? I blinked again, not sure if I was hearing things. "What?"

He nodded toward the others. "Dance?"

"I don't think that's a good idea," I said.

"Why?"

Really? Why? I wanted to shake him. "Ask your girlfriend."

I missed him.

I missed *us.* But I wasn't sure what it was about us that I missed.

Tears trickled down my cheek and he brushed them away with his thumb. My startled eyes met his warm brown ones. The Arik I knew and loved was back. His hand cupped my cheek.

"Gia," he whispered.

I swallowed hard. "Arik—"

The door opened and winter rushed in again. I instinctively pulled away from Arik, backing up several steps.

"Hello," Emily's voice trilled into the room.

At hearing her, the warmth in Arik's eyes went cold.

She hurried to Arik, embraced him, and planted a kiss on his lips. "We couldn't make it through the storm, so I guess we're staying here for Christmas. I hope you don't mind, but I invited my uncle to the party." She glanced over her shoulder at a balding man with long legs and hunched shoulders.

"Of course not." Faith met him at the arched entry. "May I take your coat?"

"Yes, thank you," he said, removing it.

I was riveted to the spot. No matter how hard I willed my feet to move, they wouldn't budge. Emily practically groped Arik in front of me, and I still couldn't move. He had touched my cheek, his eyes had looked longingly at me, and he'd been about to say something. What was he going to say? My hands curled into fists, and my nails biting into my skin did nothing to make me move.

"Did you want something, Gia?" Emily's sculpted smile was so fake it could easily shatter if there were a small tremor.

Afton slipped a gentle hand in mine. "Gia, I thought you were going to show me Faith's room. I can't wait to see her artwork." Always the rescuer, Afton guided me away, my legs almost failing with each step up to the third level.

I plopped down on the futon in Faith's room. Afton examined the painted walls while I just stared off, thinking about that quick moment Arik had returned to me. It was an even quicker moment before he was gone again.

Afton faced me. "This is beautiful. She really is talented."

"She is." I finally found my voice.

"You okay?"

"Yeah, I think it's about time to let go of my hopes of Arik returning to me." I cleared my throat to hide the fact that my voice was getting croaky with emotions.

"Healing takes time," she said, sitting beside me, "and forgetting takes even longer."

"I'm so happy you're here."

"Good thing, since you're stuck with me." She patted my knee. "Come on, where's that warrior spirit of yours? Suck it up, put on a brave face, and let's enjoy this night."

I heaved a sigh. "All right. How much more painful can it get?"

She bumped my shoulder with hers. "That's the spirit."

We made our way back to the party, gobbled down some yummy food, drank some pretend champagne, and laughed with Demos until our sides ached. I surprised Afton, and myself, and danced with her, Jaran, and Cole for hours. I didn't even notice when Arik, Emily, and her uncle left the party.

I hugged Jaran close as we slow-danced together, my feet aching in the heels.

"Why don't you just kick them off already?" he said.

"Good idea." I pulled off my shoes, threw them to the side, and wrapped my arms back around him. "Are you happy, Jaran?"

"Happier than I've been in years." He kissed my head. "Thank you, friend, for giving me the courage to be me and to bring Cole."

"Ah, you always had it. You just needed a little shove."

He twirled me around the floor, and I got lost in his happiness. I was ready. Ready to live my life.

Arik-free.

CHAPTER EIGHTEEN

Bottles clinking and sounds of someone riffling through drawers woke me. I lifted my tired eyelids. Deidre was hunched over her dresser, searching for something. Afton sat up on her elbows.

"What's going on?" I asked in a hoarse sleepy voice.

"It's the last day to shop before Christmas," Deidre said. "I still have too many presents to buy."

I hadn't even started shopping, which now made me panic, but my body was too tired to react. We had stayed up late dancing.

"Who are you going with?" I rubbed my eyes. "If you wait, we'll go with you."

"I have a date." She paused and spun around. "Shit. I wasn't supposed to say anything."

I pushed up into a sitting position and glanced at my phone. "Nick never gets up this early."

"It's not with Nick."

"Okay. Hold on. I'm confused." I slipped my toes into my slippers. "If you aren't going with Nick, and you have a date, who is it? And what happened to Nick?"

"I ended it. He blew up again after the party. I can't take his mood swings." She tugged a purple-and-gray scarf out of the drawer.

"Why didn't you guys say anything?"

She wrapped the scarf around her neck. "We didn't want to ruin the holidays."

"Who broke up with who?"

"It wasn't working. His moods. Our differences. He's fine with it." She looked over at Afton. "I think there was always someone else for him."

Afton glanced down, breaking eye contact with Deidre.

"Anyway, there are no hard feelings between Nick and me. We're better as friends." She lifted her purse from the desk chair. "Okay, well, maybe we'll see you at the mall?"

When she was gone, I gave Afton a curious look.

"Guess I should shower," she said, her lips twitching as she tried not to smile. "We do have a lot of shopping to do."

While she was showering, I texted Nick and told him to meet us at the mall. A little matchmaking between friends was in order.

The two of them had horrible timing. Nick was smitten with her the first day she walked into ninth grade English. She thought he was a sarcastic show-off. Then the three of us settled into an easy friendship. Secretly, or rather not so secretly to everyone around him, Nick had a huge crush on her. He gave up when he met Deidre. That's when Afton realized her feelings for him were more than friendly. Between all their verbal sparring, Afton had fallen hard for Nick. With Deidre out of the picture, this was their chance to be together.

Christmas music played over the loud speakers. The mall was crowded with last minute shoppers. I snuck glances around the store while Afton tried on lipstick at the makeup counter.

As the minutes turned into an hour, I worried Nick hadn't gotten my text to meet us and wasn't coming.

"Who are you looking for?" She dabbed a glob of red onto her lip with a Q-tip.

I flinched, knocking over some lotion bottles gathered on the counter. Fumbling to stand them back up, I avoided her stare. "Huh?"

"Are you looking for Arik? I wish you'd forget about him already."

"I have. I was—"

"Hey, fancy meeting you two here," Nick said, and leaned against the counter.

Fancy? That wasn't at all moronic.

Afton dropped the Q-tip. "*Shit*, Nick. Why are you always startling us like that?"

Nick grinned at her reaction. "I like that color on you."

I decided I should leave them alone. Nothing crushes a budding romance more than a third wheel. "I have to get my shopping done. Nick, can you help Afton pick a color? I'm terrible at it anyway."

"Why certainly." He leaned closer to her. "I forgot to mention last night, but I really like that haircut on you."

"Really? I was so afraid it wouldn't work with my face." She fluffed the back with her fingers.

I made my exit, going from one shop to another, picking up items for everyone on my Christmas list. A figurine fairy for Faith, a few sweaters for Pop, a tweed messenger cap for Deidre, a bracelet for Afton, and some rose-scented lotion for Miss Bagley. I exited the shop and merged into the crowd. Nick and Afton sat on a bench between two planters. I weaved between shoppers to get to them.

Afton watched my approach. "Did you get your shopping done?"

"No, I have a few more presents to buy. Did you get your list done?

She smiled at Nick. "No. We got lost in conversation."

Nick pushed himself up from the bench. "Well, I have to get to work. My mom gave me another chance. I can't be late or she'll lose it. And it should be a busy night. I'll see you guys tomorrow."

Afton watched Nick's departure with a smile on her face. He had a little hop in his step. It was nice to see him happy for a change.

I tucked my arm around hers and dragged her toward the sporting goods store. "I want details."

"Why are we going there?" She wrinkled her nose at the sign.

"I have to get a little something for the Sentinels. I'm thinking either spandex shorts or water bottles."

The left side of my bed felt like it was tilting and I would fall off. I scooted back, trying to find a level spot.

"Are you going to wake up?" Faith sounded less than patient sitting on the edge of my bed. "It's Christmas morning, and I'm still awake."

I groaned and rolled over to face the wall. "Just another hour."

She stood and pulled on my arm. "Come on, get up. Everyone's downstairs. It's so fun. We're all in pajamas. Nana made cinnamon rolls."

"Why didn't you mention those before?" I slipped out of bed.

Faith was dressed in all green, with pointy-toed shoes,

and white fluff on her cuffs and collar.

"What are you wearing?"

"I'm Santa's elf." She even wore a pointy green hat. "What's this?" She picked up my slip of paper with Ruth Ann Proctor's name scribbled on it.

"Oh, that's mine, it's something for Nana. I must've dropped it." I shrugged into my robe and wiggled my toes into my slippers. Did the name even matter now? So what if Emily was a witch? She hadn't spelled Arik into falling for her. He fell on his own. I should do what Carrig was always telling us to do in practice: put on my big girl panties and just deal with it already.

She handed me the paper. "Guess what I made?"

I shoved it into my robe's pocket. "I'm not sure I want to know. It's nothing I have to wear is it?"

"No, but that would've been a great idea. I'll have to remember it for next year." I wasn't sure if she was teasing or not, and it made me uneasy. "I made reindeer pancakes," she said.

"Sounds awesome. You sure do like this whole Christmas thing," I said, pounding down the stairs after her.

"It's the best holiday. I wish it were Christmas every day."

Nana, Afton, Pop, and Miss Bagley sat on the sofas and chairs surrounding the Christmas tree. Deidre was absent. She'd gotten up early to spend Christmas morning with Carrig and Sinead. I had sent my presents for the occupants of the McCabe Boarding School with her because I didn't want to see Arik. I was getting used to the idea that we were over, and I didn't want to open any healing wounds.

I dropped onto the vacant chair, and Faith sat in front of the tree. Flames crackled in the fireplace—a perfect Norman Rockwell scene.

"Now that we're all here, we can open presents." Faith

picked up the nearest present and read the tag before passing it to Afton.

One by one, the presents were opened. My loot was piling up. I'd gotten a *Doctor Who* T-shirt from Faith, a black sweater from Afton, a stack of books from Nana, and a laptop from Pop. My other laptop met an untimely demise when Conemar's men destroyed our apartment in Boston.

"This is the last one." Faith stretched an impressively wrapped box, the size of a boots shoebox, out to me.

The package was heavy. I flipped the tag over. *Kayla*. "It's from Miss Bagley."

"Please call me Kayla." Her smile was bright, reaching all the way to her eyes. Pop's arm rested on the back of the sofa behind her. As they'd settled into their relationship, there was this easy comfort vibe coming from them. "I think we're close enough to go by first names, don't you?"

"Okay." I removed the bow and tore the wrapping away from the box. Inside was an early edition of *The Secret Garden*. My favorite edition. "How...how did you know?"

"I saw you in the library with it several times."

"You saw me?" Whenever Nick and I had a break from looking for the Chiavi in the reference books at the library, I'd find *The Secret Garden*.

It reminded me of when I first ran into Arik at the Boston Athenaeum Library. I'd been carrying that book and literally ran into him, dropping it. He had picked it up for me and quoted a verse from it. Each time I read that line, it gave me hope that Arik would come back to me. Just when I thought I was over him, something would remind me of what we had together. But not this time.

This time I actually felt done. There wasn't that hollow feeling I'd get when something would trigger a memory of *us*.

Kayla rested her hand on Pop's knee. "I hope you like it."

"Oh my gosh, yes. It's perfect. Thank you."

"I'm glad," she said.

Miss Bagley had been tough on Nick and me lately, but her thoughtfulness about my present made up for it. Being undercover, she most likely had to put walls around her feelings, but when she was with Pop, she showed a softer side.

"Shall we eat?" Faith jumped to her feet.

With the presents gone from under the tree, Baron and Cleo snuggled on the tree skirt together. The house was drafty. I shoved my hands in the pockets of my robe to warm them. My fingers touched the paper inside one.

Stopping Nana before she went into the dining room, I slipped the folded paper into her hand. "I forgot to give you the name on the gravestone. I don't think it matters now since there wasn't any mark or tattoo on Arik. But I'm still curious to know if Emily's related to the woman on that stone."

"I'm curious, as well." She stuffed the slip into her bra.

"Um…" I wasn't sure how to react to the whole bra-stuffing thing.

When it was obvious I wasn't going to say anything, she added, "I don't have my logins here, so I'll have to go online when I get home."

"Great, thank you," I said, trying not to look at her chest. "Have I ever told you you're the best grandmother ever?"

She patted my cheek. "You don't need to tell me, dear, actions speak louder than words. The honor is mine entirely."

I shuffled over to the tall bay window, my slippers scraping against the floorboards, and stared through the strings of Christmas lights Faith had nailed to the window frame. Emily's house was just down the way from ours. The old house stood large and stately. The windows were dark, and the only decoration was an enormous wreath with a red satin bow on the wide front door.

Was it just Emily and her uncle in the house this morning? A part of me felt sorry for her losing her parents and not having them for the holidays. The longing to have a Christmas with my mother still ached. I'd been so young when she died, and I couldn't recall a memory of her sitting around a tree and opening gifts with me.

A silver sedan eased over the slick driveway to our house. As it neared, I almost didn't recognize the driver's thin, sullen face. *Mrs. Wilson?*

"Afton, your mother made it," I called, my eyes stuck on the frail Latina woman as she held tight to a shopping bag and carefully stepped across the snow. Afton was a beautiful mixture of her mother and her father.

Afton bolted out the front door, not giving her mother the chance to climb the porch before hugging her. Afton towered over her petite mother. She got her height from her father. Just past them, I spotted Arik trekking up the drive, a poorly wrapped gift in his hands.

I stepped out on the porch.

"Happy Christmas," he said, climbing a few steps then stopping.

Afton and her mother returned the greeting and went inside the house, leaving us alone.

I leaned against the post, shivering in my robe and pajamas. "Merry Christmas."

"Thank you for the water bottle," Arik said.

"You're welcome. It's BPA-free."

"Is that a good thing?"

"Yeah, it is." Even this early in the morning, he was dazzling. "You on your way to Emily's?"

"I am." He glanced over his shoulder at her house. "I wanted to stop and give you this beforehand." He held up the package wrapped in gold.

"It's a book?"*Holy shit. Don't tell me he got me a copy of* The Secret Garden, *too. Wait. If he did, that has to mean something, right? That he still cares.* I wanted to rip the package from his hands, but I took a deep breath and composed myself.

His eyebrows pinched together, eyeing the present. "How did you know?"

"The shape."

"Oh, right."

Our fingers touched as I took the present from him. I wasn't sure my shiver was because of him or the fact I was freezing. It was almost zero degrees outside, after all.

"Open it." He had a giddy smile on his face. Obviously, he was proud of whatever book he'd gotten me.

I unwrapped it to find a monogrammed leather-bound journal. The initials GMB were embossed in gold on the front. The cover seemed fragile from age as I flipped it over and carefully thumbed through pages of handwritten text.

I gave him a questioning look. "A journal?" My body went numb. I was stupid to think he would give me a copy of the book that had brought us together.

"It's Gian's journal. I discovered it at an estate sale in Asile. That time when we escorted Pia and Reya before…"

Before you broke up with me.

He cleared his throat. "Before they attacked the Wizard Council."

"Oh." He meant that, not us. "They're selling his stuff?"

"No. This wasn't his estate sale. It was someone else's. Many items of Gian's were sold after he had died. Your great-grandfather's things are worth a considerable amount of money. This journal was mixed in with other books. The man overseeing the sale didn't realize what he had."

My eyes blurred. He bought it while we were still together.

When he was with Carrig in Asile, he was thinking of me. It was bittersweet, and the thought tasted rancid in my mouth. That was the thing about regret; it never fully went away. But it became easier to endure with each passing day.

Concern crossed his face. "You don't like it."

"I love it. Thank you."

"I should be on my way." He turned to go.

"Hey, Arik," I said, stopping him half way down the steps.

He glanced up at me. "Yes?"

"I'm glad we can be friends." And I truly was happy about that.

He smiled, his dimples pressing into his cheeks. "As am I."

The door opened and shut behind me, but I didn't turn to see who it was. My eyes followed Arik's descent. He slipped a little on an icy spot on Emily's driveway, recovering effortlessly and looking incredibly athletic doing it.

"You okay?" Afton said from behind me.

"I believe so."

She stepped up to my side. "I'm glad to hear that."

I pulled my attention away from Arik and turned for the door. "Come on. We have our traditional movie to watch."

And I needed to drown my sorrows in an oversize mug of hot chocolate with multi-colored marshmallows.

CHAPTER NINETEEN

My feet fell asleep underneath me. I had been curled up on the window seat in the living room for hours, reading Gian's journal. There were only three days left of winter vacation, and I just wanted to hibernate. After spending New Year's Day with Nick and me, Afton and her mother returned to Boston. I would've given anything to go back with them. At least I had Nana for one more day.

Nana sat on one of the high-back chairs, her feet propped on the ottoman, with Baron stretched across the back of the chair and Cleo on her lap. We both were still in our pajamas. She knitted a scarf she was making for Deidre, who was pouting in our room over her latest guy issue. She'd dated three guys over the break so far. Jaran and I had an ongoing bet how many she'd go out with before we got back to school. He'd said four, I'd said three, and it looked like I might lose.

Gian's journal was more of a record book than an actual diary. He'd registered library names, dates, and times on the pages. Some were dates before his time, as early as the seventeenth century. The word "slip" kept coming up on the page. I read one of the entries, trying to figure out what it meant.

January the fourth, ten thirty-three, evening, I encountered a slip under the "House of Books" in Gall. I tapped the laminated prayer card that had bookmarked the page against my leg.

"Stop frowning, dear." Nana looked over her teacup at me. "When you get to be my age, you'll have craters between your eyes. What's that in your hand?"

"It was stuck in the book." There was an illustration of an enormous, white church on the card. "It's a prayer card from St. Patrick's Cathedral in New York. Someone wrote 'prayer candle, seventh row, three in' on it. Strange. Do people register the prayer candles they light?"

Nana looped a string of yarn around her needle. "Possibly. People have strange habits sometimes."

I pushed the card between two pages in the back of the journal. "I just don't get the entries in his journal. He keeps talking about slips in the library. What's a slip?"

"Maybe it's a change in the air or something."

I picked up my window rod from the coffee table to contact Uncle Philip.

He answered immediately. "To what do I owe the pleasure? I trust you rang in the New Year with a great celebration."

"Yes," I said. "I hope yours was good."

"It was splendid. Quiet and uneventful."

"I'm sorry to bother you."

"You are never a bother to me." His voice sounded stiff, it always did, but this was different. Stressed.

"Arik gave me one of Gian Bianchi's old journals for Christmas. I found some recordings in it. Like dates, times, and names of things. A word keeps coming up—slip. Do you know what he meant?"

"It's an old term. Slips are what we practiced feeling in

the library. How one detects a trap. I'm curious to see this journal."

"I'll bring it next time we meet. What about 'House of Books'? Does that mean anything to you?"

"No. Why?"

"He mentioned this slip was between the 'House of Books.'"

He rubbed his chin as he thought. "Very interesting. I don't know of a trap registered as such. He must've been recording traps. Ones we haven't documented."

An explosion went off in the background. The window rod got static-y. Pip squawked madly on his perch. Uncle Philip listened to whatever the bird was saying. Another explosion sounded. Debris fell around Uncle Philip.

"Gia, inform Carrig—" The static increased. "Asile is being attacked. Send help—" The screen went black.

I shot to my feet, dropped the journal onto the coffee table, and snatched up my cell phone.

Carrig answered on the second ring. "Good morning, Gia."

My heart thumped in my throat. "We have to...we have to... Asile is under..."

"Calm down and tell me slowly."

"I was talking to Uncle Philip when explosions went off. He said to send help. Asile is under attack."

"Get your gear on. Is anyone with you?"

"Nana is."

"Have her take you to the library. We'll meet you there."

I slammed my phone on the coffee table and dashed upstairs to change. Nana hurried behind me. I grabbed the silver box Miss Bagley had given me to call her to the library. I pressed the crystal twice to say it was an emergency, and it glowed red.

Superman had nothing on me. I was out of my pajamas and into my gear in seconds. Nana was right behind me, which was even more impressive when you figure in the age difference.

I lifted my shield, attached it to my back, and buckled my scabbard around my waist. Nana passed my trench coat to me, and I tugged it on as we went out the door.

She fishtailed it all the way to the library, and I succeeded in not throwing up on her dashboard. We were there first and waited for the others.

The McCabe Boarding House van slid to a stop in front of the library. The Sentinels jumped out before Carrig turned off the engine. Under their trench coats, they were dressed in their biker-like knight gear—leather pants, boots, helmets, metal and chain chest plates, shields on their backs, and swords attached to their waists. Except for Kale, who wore his bladed gloves and wrist guards.

I met the Sentinels at the library door, leaving Nana behind in her Lexus.

"Where's Kayla?" Carrig demanded, bounding up the steps to us.

"I paged her," I said, slipping on my helmet and lacing my arm through my shield.

"Is she with Brian?" he directed to me.

"No, he's at work."

"All right, then. Arik, get us in the library." He faced Nana in her car. "Mrs. Kearns, can you let Sinead know what happened? She be at a movie with Deidre."

Nana nodded her agreement over the steering wheel.

Arik removed a thin card from his pocket and used magic to break us into the library.

"How are we going to travel through the gateway with it locked?" I asked Carrig as we headed for the book.

"I've always known the charm," he said. "I just never let on that I did."

Jaran fetched the gateway book.

Carrig waved his hand over it. "*Sbloccare il gateway*," he chanted. "This be a dangerous situation. We jump in pairs. We're odd numbers, so I'll go on me own."

"We'll go first," Arik offered. "Gia can protect us before we enter the library."

"Gia?" Carrig waited for my agreement.

"I'm fine with that." I was anxious to get to Uncle Philip. I prayed he was okay.

We grabbed hands.

"*Aprire la porta*," Arik said.

The book tugged at me, and I jumped with Arik into it. I felt at home in the gateway, the dark hugging me, the cool air brushing my face, but this time uneasiness fluttered in my stomach. I never knew what I'd see on the other side before, yet I wasn't as terrified as I was now, not since the first time I accidently went through one.

Arik created his fire globe on his palm as we plummeted. The orange and yellow glow flickering across his face made him look like he was on fire. I ignited my pink globe to a softball size. When we slowed, I tossed my globe in front of us and watched as it went through the gateway exit. Arik landed in the Bodleian Library first, with me right behind him. My globe had hit the floor and shot up to the ceiling, engulfing us in a protective shell.

"Release us," Arik said, steadying his globe.

I dug my fingers into the membrane of mine, popping it.

The library was quiet. I removed my sword from its scabbard and readied my attack position. We moved around the reading room, making sure the coast was clear. The others made it through, and we kept alert while following Carrig down the corridor of bookcases.

I flicked my gaze between the rows of desks sitting between each set of shelves and the intricately etched dark wood arches overhead, scanning for an attack from any direction. Shadows moved around us, and I flinched before realizing they were ours.

Carrig turned to face the third bookcase on the left. He pulled down the two wooden knobs on each side of the house-shaped box attached to the end of the bookcase.

"*Ammettere il pura*," Carrig said to unlock the secret passageway.

Nothing happened.

Carrig tried to open the bookcase several times before giving up. "Someone used a lock charm."

"Gia, try your globe," Arik said.

I nodded and created a small globe. I tossed it against the bookcase and recited the key. A pink glow spread across the wood, releasing the charm. The bookcase trembled as it slid across the floor to the left, revealing the staircase diving deep into the darkness.

The light from our globes bounced across the rocked walls as we sprinted through the tunnel to the end and up the steep stairs to the outbuilding. We dropped our trench coats on the floor. They'd only be in the way if we found ourselves in a fight. Carrig pushed the door open, and I froze alongside the others at the sight across the hills.

Asile was burning.

The screams echoing down the hill pushed us into motion. I raced up after the others, the pathway a blur under my feet. I was vaguely aware of the destruction around me. The people of the cottages surrounding the castle rushed around, drenching fires with water, aiding the injured, or huddling in corners stunned by the horrors around them.

Carrig chanted a charm behind us, locking the outbuilding. My thoughts were on Uncle Philip. I had to get to him. He had to be okay.

What if he isn't? What if he's—? I couldn't even think the word.

My feet pounded harder, my breaths rushing out painfully.

We broke into two groups. Carrig led a bunch of Sentinels from the other havens to the city beyond the castle. Arik took our Sentinels to the castle. I stayed on Arik's heels as we blew through the doors and into the wide corridors. Lei and Kale went left. Demos and Jaran went right. Arik and I went straight ahead to the education wing.

We climbed the stairwell to Uncle Philip's office. Bookcases were overturned, burn marks scarred the walls, and the books and folders on his desk were charred and wet. Someone must've doused the fire that had caused the damage. Smoke burned my throat with each breath, and I covered my mouth, stepping over the fallen bookcases and scattered papers. The Monitor's bird perch and globe had been tipped over, the glass sphere cracked in the middle. Something scratched under one of the bookcases. I stopped and listened.

"Arrrk! Help. Attack. Arrrk!"

"Pip!" I scrambled to the side of the bookcase. "Help me lift this."

Arik hoisted the case up, and I reached in, feeling around for Pip. He nuzzled his feathered head against my hand. I gently grasped him and eased him out. Pip's feathers were a little ruffled and smudged with soot, but he seemed okay. Arik righted Pip's stand and globe, and I eased the parrot onto his perch.

"What did they do to Uncle Philip?" I asked.

"Arrrk! Gone."

"I know he's gone, but where? Did you hear anything?"

Pip spread out his wings and rested them on his back. "*Chiavi. Arrrk! Hurry.*"

I looked over at Arik. "Where do they keep the Chiavi?"

He blanched. "Merl's vault."

He didn't even wait for me. After Arik's parent faery was murdered, Merl had become like a father to him. He clomped over all the stuff and flew out the opened door. My boots skidded across the floor as I tried to keep up with him around corner after corner, down and up staircases, and through corridors. As I ran, I snapped the shield off my back and yanked out my sword. Arik hadn't readied his fighting gear, his focus on Merl.

"Arik, get your shield and sword out," I yelled at him.

He darted a look over his shoulder at me and then unsheathed his sword, disappearing around the corner.

"Your shield, too! Damn it!"

A man tackled me from the side and we crashed to the floor, my head hitting against my shield, pain blossoming above my eyebrow from the blow. I grasped his jacket, yanked him over, and straddled him. His fist hit me square on the chin and I fell back against the floor. Before I could recover, he was on me, clutching my neck, choking me.

I dug my nails into his skin, trying to pry his hands from my throat. He butted his head against mine and stars erupted in my vision. Something hit him from behind and his face went slack. He teetered and fell off me to the side.

I coughed and wheezed as air rushed into my lungs.

Arik yanked his sword out of the man's back.

"What the hell? We stay together." I removed my helmet and dropped it on the floor, coughing. "We stay together!"

"I'm sorry, I wasn't—"

"Thinking? You weren't thinking?" I stumbled to my

feet. "Get your head in the fight, Arik. I need to trust that you have my back. Remember? Those are your words by the way, not mine." I picked up my sword and shield. "And slow down. We have to conserve our energy."

"I apologize. It's just—" He sighed.

I placed a shaky hand on his shoulder. "I get it. I'm terrified for Uncle Philip, but we have to stay calm. We can't let anyone down by making senseless mistakes. You taught me that."

This wasn't like Arik. I got that he worried about Merl, but he was trained to keep his feelings in check. I should be the one losing it, not him.

He took a deep breath and shook his head hard before saying, "All right, can you continue?"

"I feel like shit, but I can keep going."

"Right. We stick together. You watch one side, and I the other." He unhooked his shield.

A rust-colored man with horns and a stocky, bald Laniar charged down the corridor, swords in hand. Arik and I rushed for them, side by side. My steps didn't falter, even with fear twisting my stomach. I gripped my sword tighter and prepared for impact.

The Laniar's blade met mine and we slammed into each other. I backed up and brought my sword down on him again. He parried my blow, and I moved around him.

The Laniar bared his sharp teeth at me. "Put down your sword, little girl. You can't win against me. I'll eat you whole."

I shrank back.

What am I doing? Don't show fear. Stand your ground.

Straightening, I measured my stance and balanced my weight, aiming my sword at him.

Arik grunted to my right. I didn't dare take my eyes off the Laniar, though I desperately wanted to know how Arik was doing in his fight. I stepped over the debris from the damaged ceiling.

The devious grin on the Laniar's face made me want to recoil, but I took a deep breath and held my ground.

Focus, Gia. It's just like a practice match. Except bloody and deadly. I swallowed that hard fact down and kept my focus on my opponent.

He made a fatal mistake, and I smiled. The Laniar chanced a sideway glance at the horned man. I side-kicked his left knee, causing him to drop to the ground. The sword fell out of his hand, and a startled expression crossed his face. While he was down, I threw a knee strike to his face. He fell backward, and I slammed the hilt of my sword repeatedly against his head until he was unconscious.

I should have stabbed him, but I couldn't do it. I didn't want to kill people or creatures. That wasn't me. At the same time, I wondered if I was lying to myself.

Arik thudded to the floor beside me, and I spun around.

The horned man brought his sword down, and Arik rolled away. The sword clanked against the tiles, missing Arik by mere inches. I got into a ready position fast and delivered a roundhouse to the horned man's face. He stumbled back but recovered quickly. It was enough of a distraction for Arik to leap to his feet and drive his sword into the man's side.

The man staggered, lifting his sword. Arik sparked a fire globe to life, manipulating it into a fiery whip. The Laniar shifted on the floor, picking up his blade. He pulled his hand back, readying to throw the sword at Arik. I ignited my globe. The sword spiraled through the air, aiming for Arik. I pitched my globe, capturing the sword in a pink sphere before it met its target. It hit Arik's back and he stumbled forward. The globe dropped to the floor and busted, the sword clattering onto the rubble from the ceiling, the point sticking straight up.

Arik hit the Laniar across the chest with his fire whip.

The Laniar scampered down the corridor, vanishing through a broken part of the wall. Arik made to give chase, but then stopped. The horned man advanced, blood dripping from his side, his eyes fierce and his hand tight around his sword.

"Arik, watch out," I screamed.

Arik spun around, a fireball bouncing on his hand. He threw it at the horned man, hitting him smack against his chest. The man flew back and landed on his sword, the blade skewering through his back and out his chest. He jerked several times before falling silent.

I bent over, trying to catch my breath.

Arik dropped a hand on my back. "Are you all right?"

I nodded.

"We must keep going," he said.

I nodded again, straightening.

Arik picked his way through the rubble, and I followed.

He glanced back at me. "Where's your helmet?"

"Back there somewhere. Keep going. We don't have time to get it."

Once through the debris, we stayed silent as we booked it down the corridor and headed for Merl's chambers. Smoke filled the hallway, Asile guards lay lifeless on the ground, and water drenched the floor. The door to Merl's chambers was ajar.

Kale and Lei arrived at the same time Arik and I did.

The inside of Merl's chambers resembled the destruction inside Uncle Phillip's office. Arik eased in, with me close behind him. The vault was open and a man's hand stuck out of a pile of rock and mortar. I held my breath as Arik knelt beside the man and clawed at the debris. I dropped my sword and shield and joined him, removing bricks and clay, uncovering the man underneath.

I gasped.

Merl stared up at us, his eyes lifeless. Arik fell back with a guttural moan that resounded across the room.

With a painful sob, I covered my face with my hands. How could this happen? How could he be gone?

"No!" Lei screamed from the doorway.

My teary eyes found her anguished face. She collapsed into Kale's arms.

I dropped my hands and staggered to my feet. Arik was a mess. He wasn't recovering from the shock. It was so unlike him. But I couldn't worry about him. Or what was wrong with him. I had to keep going.

I had to find Uncle Philip.

The debris rolled under my boots as I climbed over the rubble and made my way to the door.

Kale let go of Lei, and she flew to Arik and cradled him in her arms.

"Where are you going?" Kale said. His eyes were red as he forced his feelings back.

I grabbed my sword from the ground, leaving my shield. I needed to move fast and didn't need the added burden. "I'm locking Arik in here," I said. "Something is really wrong with him. He can't get a handle on his emotions. If he fights in this state, he'll get himself killed. Are you staying or going with me?"

He glanced at Lei. "I'm going with you. Lei, watch him. Kill any foe that comes through this door."

She nodded as she wiped her eyes.

We stepped out into the hall and I closed the door. Kale recited a charm to lock the door.

"Only a wizard can release them," Kale said. "Hopefully, there's none behind this attack."

Another agonizing cry from Arik sounded from the other side of the door. I placed my palm on the thick wood, wiping tears from my eyes.

I'm so sorry, Arik.

CHAPTER TWENTY

Running through the destruction around us, I kept seeing the image of Merl's expressionless face, his body broken under the rubble. I couldn't lose Uncle Philip, he was my only connection to my mother, and I loved him. It would break me just like seeing Merl dead had broken Arik.

I pushed forward, a machine on a mission, catching up to Kale. "What is our plan?"

"I haven't one," he said.

It was growing dark outside. The corridors were silent. Everyone was most likely hiding, waiting for rescue. The Red had to be responsible for the attack. I vowed that before the night was over, I'd kill him.

We came up on the dead horned man on the floor, and I remembered the other Laniar crawling into a hole in the wall. I crouched in front of the opening, aiming my sword at the darkness, and then held up my hand.

"*Sia la Luce,*" I said. *Let there be light.* My globe ignited on my palm. I readied myself to crawl inside, but it wasn't a tunnel, only a cavity.

The Laniar was curled up against the wall. He squinted at the light.

"Tell me where they took Professor Attwood, and I won't finish you off."

"I cannot."

I pressed my sword against his neck.

He winced.

"I'm losing my patience with you."

He strained his neck back, trying to move away from my blade. "It would be my death."

"You're in a very tough predicament, then, aren't you? Because you can either die now or later." I nicked his skin, blood beading to the surface. "Or you could tell me where The Red is and hope I kill him before he gets you." The hatred boiled inside me and it scared me.

He stared at the light, not able to focus on me behind the glare. "It's not The Red I'm frightened of," the Laniar said.

"What do you mean? Who are you afraid of?" I glared at him. "It doesn't matter. Tell me where they took Professor Attwood."

"You're getting nowhere with this guy." Kale brushed me aside and tossed a globe on him. The Laniar froze, his breaths laboring. "You will tell us or I'll keep stunning you. It feels like drowning, doesn't it? We'll keep doing this until you tell us." He looked to me. "Remove my stun."

I dropped my globe on him. His stare was eerie looking in the pink glow. He gasped. "I can't—"

Kale threw another globe on him. He waited a little longer this time before he told me to release him again.

The Laniar coughed and wheezed. "All right, all right," he said through coughs. "He's in the village. A tavern. Something about a lonely lamb."

I straightened and looked to Kale. "Have you heard of that place?"

"I haven't. There are many pubs in Asile." He tightened the straps on the leather sheaths attached to his forearms. Blood stained the steel knuckles on his gloves. "We aren't letting him go, are we?"

"I don't think he'll get too far if he runs. Carrig charmed the outbuilding, so no one could come or go from Asile." I adjusted my scabbard and continued down the hall. Kale's boots clomped behind me.

The city lights that normally bathed the sky just above the hill were dark. The moon lit our way up the path to the Mystik city adjacent to the wizard haven. Werehounds and Sentinels patrolled the cobbled streets. It made me uneasy not knowing what faces to trust.

Two Sentinels cut us off. "State your name," the taller of the two ordered.

"I'm Kale and this is Gianna," he said. "We're Sentinels of Asile. You're in our territory, back down."

We skirted around them.

"Wait." I turned to the Sentinels. "Have you seen Carrig?"

"He's leading a search through the streets with the Emeritus," the more muscular one answered. "The entries into Asile are blocked. Those who attacked the wizards' castle are trapped in the city."

"The Emeritus?" I whispered to Kale.

"They're the older Sentinels called out of retirement after we went into hiding."

"Have you heard of a tavern with 'lonely lamb' in the title?" I asked.

"The Lonely Lamb Tavern?"

That was actually the name? "Yes, that's the one."

"Go up three blocks in that direction and turn right, and then it's five blocks down."

"Thanks," I said, and hurried up the road. The crooked cobbles threatened to twist my ankle. The road was steeper than the streets of Beacon Hill in Boston.

"Should we get assistance?" Kale labored beside me.

"It'll take too long. Uncle Phillip could be dead by then." My breaths deepened. "And too many guards would alert them to our arrival. I'm thinking we sneak in and surprise attack. You could stun most of them before they notice we're there."

"They possibly have him in a room or basement of the tavern. We have to be careful."

"You think? 'Cause I was just going to bust in and hope for the best."

He gave me a questioning look. "Are you being sarcastic?"

"Of course I am."

The streets were narrow. No cars ran across the roads because the havens forbade vehicles. It was a way to keep the havens pure, free of the things destroying the human world. People and creatures walked and pushed carts wherever they went.

We approached a sign hanging over the road. The tavern actually had a sad-looking lamb on the sign.

Kale pushed the buttons on his palms. A silver blade shot out from each sheath and stretched over the top of his encased hand. I eased down the tight alley between The Lonely Lamb tavern and a dress shop, searching the walls for an entry.

I wrinkled my nose. "Gross. It smells like pee."

"Drunks don't care where they relieve themselves," he said, walking backward behind me, keeping his eyes on the entrance to the alley.

Another alley ran behind the buildings. A heavy wooden door dominated the middle of the lean four-story building. Each floor had two windows surrounded by balconies.

Kale stared up at the windows.

"What are we doing?" I whispered. "Should we use the door or go through a window?"

"That's what I'm pondering. Can you climb?"

"Not sure. I haven't climbed anything since I was ten or so. Well, that's not completely true. I've rock climbed at a place before, but that was a year ago, and they had ropes and foot thingies." I was definitely nervous, because I was rambling and my hands shook.

Kale wasn't listening. "Then we're going by way of the door," he said, trying the handle. "Locked."

I shook my head. "You really thought it would just open, huh?"

We squatted close to the wall.

"Do you have one of those things that opens doors?" I asked. "You know like what Arik has?"

"I do, but I hadn't thought to bring it during the mad rush to leave."

"Guess we have to climb." I glanced up the wall to windows. "I'm thinking the drainpipe." The drain looked pretty iffy from here. "I don't think it'll hold you. I'll climb it and find a way to let you in."

He nodded. "Yes, all right. I'll stand below you in case you fall."

"You're going to break my fall? That sounds like a *lovely* plan." I slipped my sword into my scabbard and dried my hands on my pants.

I placed both hands behind the iron drainpipe and a foot on each side of it against the wall. Inching up, I walked the side of the building while gripping the pipe tight and pulling myself up. The pipe shook with each of my movements.

Don't look down. Don't look down. Shit. Why did I look down? I froze there for a moment, catching my breath, my muscles burning. *It won't kill me if I fall. I'll just break all my bones or something.*

I continued shimmying up the pipe. One of the clamps around it popped, and I leaned sideways to avoid it hitting me. I glanced down. Kale caught the metal before it hit the ground and alerted someone to our attempted break in.

A few more steps and I'd made it to the first balcony. I reached for the railing, my fingers barely brushing the metal. As I stretched for it, more clamps holding the pipe to the wall snapped, and I swung backward. I leaned my weight toward the balcony, causing the pipe to crash back against the wall.

Yeah, that didn't just wake the dead. This was going to end badly, I was certain. I grasped the railing and swung my leg over.

When I released the pipe, it fell away. Kale darted under it, taking a blow to keep it from chiming against the ground. It hit him hard, and I held my breath until he moved and waved at me that he was okay. I grabbed the railing with my other hand, boosted myself over it, and eased onto the balcony.

I got down low, crawled to the nearest window, and peered through the drapes. A few men I recognized from The John Rylands Library in Manchester, England with The Red when they'd tried to murder Antonio sat around a table, drinking and arguing over some game. They were so loud no one heard the ruckus I'd made getting up there. A couple of them flanked the far door. I didn't see Uncle Philip in the room. The ceiling shook with heavy footsteps on the floor above me. The Red's gang could be scattered throughout the tavern.

Making my way past the other window, I decided I had

to get to the next balcony up. When I reached the small strip of wall between the window and the railing, I slid up to my feet, mounted the railing, and balanced on the thin handrail, wrapping my fingers around the bars of the balcony above me. I towed myself up, hand over hand, to the next balcony.

The room was empty, so I raised the window and stepped inside. Blood stained the grungy sheet covering what looked to be a body on the bed, and the room stunk like death. My heart collapsed.

Please, no. Please don't be Uncle Philip.

I held my breath, dragged the sheet off the face, and stumbled back. The air punched from lungs, relief rushing over me. It wasn't Uncle Philip but a werehound, caught between forms—he was half man and half hound. The stench hit me stronger and bile rose in the back of my throat. I replaced the cover and crossed the room to the door. Easing it open, I peeked through the crack.

The place was active. A woman dressed in Sentinel gear walked by, and I leaned back. Kale had to get up here with me. I closed the door with a soft *click*.

I couldn't find anything in the room to use as rope. The dead body gave me the willies. There was nothing else. I tugged off the sheet, ripped it into thick strips, and tied the ends together, checking to make sure the knots were tight. It wasn't long enough.

The drapes. I yanked one down, tore it with my sword, and fastened the pieces to the sheet rope.

I crawled out the window, tied one of the ends to a railing at the far side of the balcony, and tossed the other end over the side. Kale latched onto the makeshift rope and scaled the wall to me. I helped him over the railing and he rested there, catching his breath.

"What's with the blood?"

I shrugged. "I took it off a dead guy. There wasn't anything else."

"Splendid," he said with acid in his voice. "What's the situation?"

"There're too many of The Red's gang wandering around to sneak out."

He slipped through the window and edged to the door, cracking it open and peering into the hall. He waved me over.

"There are two stairs," he said barely audible. "The main one directly in front of us and the back stairs to our right. When the chance arises, we'll make our move and go down the back one."

I waited behind him, keeping my breath steady. Minutes passed before Kale eased the door open just enough for us to slip out of it. I crouched low and stepped carefully after him to the back staircase.

He looked over his shoulder at me and mouthed, "Where?"

I pointed up. It was my best guess. Since each floor only held one large room, a bunch of The Red's pack occupied the second floor room, and a dead guy occupied the one we were in. By the sound of it, the rest of the pack was on the street level, probably on alert for an attack from the road. I only wanted to find Uncle Philip. That was, if he was still alive. We climbed the stairs as quietly and swiftly as possible to the fourth floor.

Kale stopped at the landing before moving into the hall. A baldheaded man who resembled a bat with thick dark skin and a flat nose with slotted nostrils stood guard by the door. A purple swirl appeared on Kale's palm, and he launched it at the man, stunning him. The man slumped to the ground.

The door flew open at the sound of the body hitting the floor. Kale tossed another stun globe that slammed into the woman I'd seen downstairs. We dragged the two into the room and quietly closed the door.

"Oh, thank God." I wanted to cry at the sight of Uncle Philip sitting bound to a chair with ropes. A rubber bar was stuck between his teeth, secured around his head with a leather strap, preventing him from talking.

I rushed over to him and pulled at the rope. The knots were tied tight. "Should we tie them up?" I said, nodding toward the two bodies on the floor. "If we don't counter the stun, they'll die."

"I don't care if they die." Kale's face held no emotion. "They chose the wrong side."

I removed the dagger from my boot and cut Uncle Philip free from the ropes and the leather strap around his head. He spit out the bar and coughed. I practically tackled him with a bear hug.

Kale kept watch through the crack of the door.

"Thank God, you're okay." I released Uncle Philip. The leather strap had left rashes on his cheeks. "Man, they really tied that gag tight."

"It was to keep me from using my magic."

"Are you hurt anywhere else?"

"Not badly." Soot and blood covered his face. "Merl?" His eyes looked hopeful.

I shook my head, not able to say the words, not wanting to hear them. Merl was gone. They'd killed him. Uncle Philip hung his head, breathing heavily as he tried to recover from the news. Tears burned the corners of my eyes, and I busied myself returning my dagger to my boot.

I sucked in a breath and released it before asking, "Can you walk?"

"I believe so." His arms shook as he pushed himself up from the chair.

"Do you know what they did with the Chiavi?" I said.

He looked at the table. "In that bag."

"Are you kidding me?" I laughed. "These guys are dumb. Who keeps their loot with their prisoners?" I inspected the bag for the four Chiavi—crown, scroll, cross, and sword—all there.

Uncle Philip opened his mouth, stretching out his jaw. "They probably thought no one could get by them to this level."

I crept out onto the balcony and looked through the railings. Two men were skinning an animal just outside the back door, and I wanted to vomit on their heads. I spotted his long, scraggily hair—its color like fire—as The Red stepped outside and spoke to them. He took out a pipe, lit it, and leaned against the doorframe. A small woman hobbled down the alley. The Red straightened and watched her approach.

The Red's voice vibrated up the building to me. "Hurry and finish up; the guide is here. We must eat before we leave."

"Crap." I blew my bangs out of my face. "We can't climb down. The Red and some of his men are in the back. There's a woman with them who has a long nose and feeler things wiggling from it."

I glanced over my shoulder at Kale and Uncle Philip. "What is she?"

"A Talpar," Kale said. "They probably hired her to escort them to the secret tunnels."

"Secret tunnels?" I repeated.

"Yes. The Talpars had dug those centuries ago. Only their tribe knows how to locate the entries into them." Kale turned for the door. "We'd better move. What's our strategy?"

"I don't know." I pulled my sword out of the scabbard. "While The Red is kicking back outside, we should blast his men in the lobby with our globes and get out the front. We don't stop. We just keep going, and they won't have time to react."

They both stared at me as if I'd just grown wings.

I frowned. "Okay, what's your plan, then?"

"I'm processing this thought," Kale said.

I slid the Chiave sword into my scabbard.

Kale eyed me curiously. "What are you doing with the Chiave?"

"It cuts metal. Plus, if they end up with the bag full of Chiavi, they won't actually have them all to gain world dominance." After putting my sword in the bag, I tied the drawstring and handed it to Uncle Philip. "You stay behind us. Just do what you can to help, but don't lose the bag."

Kale inspected the hall. "I haven't approved this plan."

"We don't have time for you to *process* it," I said. "The Red is distracted now."

"Gia's right," Uncle Philip said. "We have to act now."

"All right, if one of us falls, the others keep going." Kale opened the door wider. "We can't hesitate, just keep moving. Don't even stop for a second."

If he stalled any longer, my nerves were going to catch up with me. "Got it. Can we go already?"

It felt like I was in slow motion, even though I sprinted across the landing behind Kale and in front of Uncle Philip. We bounded down the back stairs. At the bottom, the moonlight coming from the back door lit up a small hall. I created my battle globe and tossed it at the entry; a pink membrane sealed the hallway and trapped The Red and the two men out back.

Kale tossed stun globe after stun globe as we burst into the tavern. Men sitting at tables slumped in their chairs. Men and women standing at the bar fell back onto to the floor. A man formed a green sphere on his palm, and I flung my pink globe at him, knocking him back and disabling his globe. I lobbed my globe at anyone who wore Sentinel gear, crippling his or her globes.

Turning to face the crowd in the tavern, Kale waved

me to go past him to the exit. I yanked open the door and pounded down the steps, with Uncle Philip close behind me. Kale slammed the door behind him and joined our race down the cobbled road.

Behind me, I could hear The Red's pack chasing us. A lightning globe exploded between Kale and me; bricks shot up in the air and pelted us, separating me from him and Uncle Philip. Another one exploded, almost hitting Kale and knocking me sideways. I slammed into a column of a building.

Kale made to come for me, and I screamed, "Get Uncle Philip to safety. I'll catch up with you."

The look on his face said he was going to refuse my order. "Go already!"

He gave me one last look of concern before he ran off.

I struggled to my feet, taking deep breaths, trying to push through the pain. When I felt steady, I hurried as fast I could down the alley to my right, weaving through breaks in buildings, like running through a maze. Several times, I came to dead ends and had to backtrack. Somewhere in the labyrinth of twisted alleys and small roads, I could hear The Red's pack, hunting me, getting closer. I had to get off the roads. Every door I came across was locked.

"Jeesh, doesn't anyone trust anyone around here?" I wasn't thinking rationally. Of course they would lock their doors during an attack.

Something hit my back, hard, and I sucked in a sharp breath. My skin glowed blue and my muscles froze. I fell over like a cut-down tree, smacking against the cobblestones as I landed, my head hitting a rock. I lay unmoving on the ground, pain cutting through my body, struggling to breathe.

CHAPTER TWENTY-ONE

It felt like boulders were on my chest, and I couldn't do anything about it. Sweat ran down my face, burning my eyes. My screams stuck in my mind, unable to release, burning inside me. A rock on the ground, I waited to die.

"Remove the stun," The Red said.

"Do you wish to kill her?" a craggily voice said. "She is the one of legend."

"No. She's Gian's heir."

Something dropped on my stomach and air rushed into my lungs. I rolled over and wrapped my arms around my stomach, coughing and wheezing, gulping at the air as though I was hungry for it.

"Where's the professor?" The Red said.

"He got away with that other one." The man's voice was ugly and deep.

Kale and Uncle Philip made it. They're safe.

"What should we do with the girl?" the bat-like man asked.

"Let her go," The Red's deep voice resounded against the buildings.

My gaze shot up to meet his. *Let me go?* Just like that? I slid my hand to the hilt of the Chiave. The handle was larger than the one on my sword.

"We must get out of here," he continued. "The alert is out. The Talpar will get us safely to Darkten."

Light globes lit up the alleys nearby. Carrig called out my name from somewhere in the maze of streets. I struggled to my feet and cocked an eye, trying to see through the sweaty, bloody blur, barely able to hold my head up. The pain across my body was almost unbearable.

The Red stared at me. "She'll be fine."

"Why—?" It felt like sand clogged my mouth. "Why did you kill Merl?"

"They near," the bat-like man growled.

The Red turned, but before running off with his men he added, "Not all is always what it seems."

"Wait," I said. "Faith. You know her?"

He shot a puzzled look at me.

"Why did you kill her parents?"

"She is my sister." He let out a kind of feral growl. "Where is she?"

What? He's her brother?

"Now, Master," one of his men urged. "They're nearing."

I stood there watching as The Red and his gang disappeared into the adjoining alleyway, processing his words, not knowing what to believe. The light from the Sentinels' globes as they entered the ally engulfed me. I slumped to the ground, unable to hold myself up any longer.

Faith.

•••

Athela stood at a window, the sky outside angry and dropping rain. She was older. Her hair streaked with gray, skin loose on her jawline.

"Milady?" I recognized the servant from the picnic. She looked nervous and unsure of approaching Athela.

"Has he been found?"

"No. I am truly sorry."

Athela turned from the window. "Do not be. He is safe from those who wish him dead."

I opened my eyes. Sheer curtains fluttered at the side of the window. Birds chirped on the trees outside. The dream, though confusing, was a welcome change to my nightmares of The Red. I adjusted my pillow. The past week had gone by slowly with my mandatory bed rest, but I was feeling much better.

I rolled onto my side. Faith sat on the fancy chaise across the room from the bed. She held a ripped envelope in her hand. I got out of bed and sat beside her.

"Is that the letter I sent you?"

She glanced at it. "It is. He said he was my brother?"

"He did," I said, uncertain at how to take the solemn look on her face.

Her fingers shook as she removed a faded photograph from the envelope. It was of a Laniar family. I recognized Faith standing next to an older woman. Faith must've been twelve or something. Beside the woman was a man, and beside him was a teen boy. The boy's facial features resembled The Red. So did his deep-set eyes and red hair.

She touched his face with her index finger. "This was my

brother, Falto. He's dead."

"Have you ever seen The Red?"

"No." Her voice was so tiny, her face drawn. At Merl's funeral, she wailed like an injured animal the entire service. I wasn't sure about telling her the truth, but she had to know.

"The boy in the picture is The Red."

Her head snapped in my direction, her eyes wide, and she strangled the envelope. "Are you certain?"

"I am."

"Then he's alive." She lowered her head. "But he's a monster."

"Yes," I said. Her face twisting with sadness and confusion broke my heart. Whatever she'd gone through the day her parents and coven were butchered must have been horrific. How could a person recover after witnessing that?

She stood and crossed the room. "I must go. There's a meeting for security today. Thank you for letting me know about my brother. I'm not sure what to think. He's been dead all these years to me. He killed my parents, left me to die, and I'd rather think of him as dead instead of as this monster."

"You need time to process. I get it."

Lei poked her head through the opening of the door. "You're up. Good. We have to get dressed."

"I'd best be going. We'll talk another time," Faith said, stepping around Lei then slipping out the door.

Lei shut the door. "You should probably bathe."

"Why all the fuss? You'd think someone was getting married." I stretched my hands over my head, trying to loosen my muscles. "Do we really have to wear long dresses?"

"Yes, you do. And a High Wizard coronation is like a wedding. It's too bad Nick couldn't be here."

"Yeah, too bad," I said.

Nick could've come, but after the humiliation at Toad's

trial, when Ellen Arkwright attached Conemar's surname to his, he feared the havens. Feared what the Mystiks thought about him. Feared they would think he was evil like his biological father.

Lei plopped down beside me. "I'll do your hair and makeup."

"Well, why didn't you say that in the first place?" I was all up for being pampered.

"This is the third ceremony," she said, twisting my hair. "And three funerals. There's so much unrest in the havens."

Talking with Faith about The Red reminded me of what Pia had said before the guards dragged her off. "Have you heard of a group of humans who know about the Mystik world and want to destroy it?" I asked.

Lei stopped braiding my hair. "Yes. How did you hear about them?"

"Pia mentioned them." I turned on the bed to face her. "So it's true?"

"No one knows if it's true. This rumored group has been around since the seventeenth century." She grabbed my shoulders, turning me to face the other way, and continued working on my hair. "It is believed the group hunts and kills any Mystiks they find in the human world. They used to kill witches, but that was centuries ago."

"I see."

"You needn't worry about them. The group is a myth. Probably started by parents wanting to scare their Mystik children into staying away from the human world. If they did exist, humans can't jump through the gateway books or enter the Mystik world on their own, so they can't reach us. Besides, we have spies out there who keep watch for any threats to our world."

"I see."

Maybe Pia was right. Why would the Council have spies watching out for this group if they were just a myth? And I didn't feel comfortable asking Lei if the Wizard Council was corrupted. I'd have to figure that out on my own.

When she finished, my hair was in tons of braids intricately arranged on top of my head in a beautiful design. My silver taffeta dress with a long, flowing skirt and beaded capped sleeves felt expensive. Lei wore a bright yellow dress, with her hair curled and piled high on her head. If she nodded, I feared she would tip over.

The colors of Asile, red and gold, flew from every window, decorated the walls, and clothed the guards. On the field of the Asile Academy, Mystiks, wizards, and Sentinels prepared to watch the coronation ceremony on the stage.

Sentinels from all the havens had descended on The Red's camp, but he had escaped before they got there. The rebels from Mantello had disbanded, their leaders arrested. Everyone spoke of peace. They believed the threat was over. I had my doubts, but I did enjoy the quiet.

Horns blasted through the murmurs coming from the audience. The high wizards of each haven walked onto the stage, wearing colorful tunics and capes representing their havens, followed by Uncle Philip. He was the youngest man up there.

"Isn't this amazing?" Lei said. "Why do you suppose Bastien is avoiding us?"

"He's here?" I spun around, searching the crowd.

"My point exactly. If you aren't even aware he's here, then he's dodging us."

I got on my tiptoes and strained to see over the people. He was sitting in a special reserved area for the high-ranking wizards. He wore a similar tunic as the high wizards on stage, but his was better suited for his muscular body compared to the older wizards' softer frames.

"Hullo," Arik said from behind us.

"Hey," I said, landing back on my heels.

He looked amazing in his elegant suit. It reminded me of an old uniform. Like a Red Coat from the Revolutionary War.

Kale, Demos, and Jaran were right behind him. All drool-worthy in their uniforms. Kale wrapped his arm around Lei's waist and nuzzled her neck.

"Gia, you're rocking that dress," Demos said. "Now that you're single, we should spend more time together." For some reason, when he tried to talk like an American, it sounded completely wrong.

"How about no," I said, keeping my eyes on the stage. I couldn't see Bastien over all the people.

"Well, when you're ready," Demos offered.

"It would be like dating a brother," I said. "Not happening."

"We should have come earlier," Lei complained. "I can't see a thing."

A man trying to get closer pushed Jaran into me.

"Hey, watch it. You needn't be rude," Jaran said. "You'd think this was a rock concert."

"It sort of is," Arik said.

Lei swept a strand of hair behind her ear that had come loose. "Yeah, Asile hasn't anointed a new high wizard in decades. Not since Merl."

Everyone's smiles slipped. We'd just buried Merl and here we were a week later celebrating a new high wizard. It felt wrong, yet right at the same time.

"Can you even hear them?" I said, trying to draw their attentions back to the ceremony and off Merl's death. "I can't make out anything they're saying."

Demos hopped up several times. "Can't see much, either.

We should be up front. After all, we protect this haven."

"Follow me," Jaran said, grabbing my hand and snaking through the crowd. "Excuse us, please, Gianna Bianchi coming through." He used my great-grandfather's surname, most likely because no one in the havens knew me as Gia Kearns.

It was like the sea of people split open in front of us. I glanced back to make sure Arik and the others were following. People touched me as I passed, mumbling words of gratitude and praise.

Uncle Philip was crossing the stage at the same time as we came out of the crowd to the front row. He sat down on a high-back chair in the middle. When he spotted me, he nodded slightly. I was his closest relative here. Well, except for Auntie Mae, who was asleep in the front row of the royals' box a few seats down from Bastien.

Bastien and I locked eyes. He mouthed something I couldn't make out because he was too far away. I could never read lips and didn't understand why people even tried to mouth words. I shrugged my shoulders at him. He frowned, leaned over, and said something to his mother. She riffled through her purse and handed him a pen and card. He scribbled something on it and passed it to the person beside him, saying something as he pointed down the row at me.

The new head of the Wizard Council, a lean man from the African haven, Veilig, approached the podium. After seeing many photographs of the beautiful haven, I wanted to visit there one day. The entry was through Port Elizabeth Public Library in South Africa. "We gather today to anoint Asile's new high wizard," the man's voice blasted through the speakers. "Philip Ralston Merlin Attwood, formerly Head Wizard of Education."

I watched the card make its way to me. An older man

handed it to Arik with a disdainful look, probably for distracting the ceremony. Arik gave the card a curious look before passing it to me. His eyes met mine, and I smiled. There was a look in his that caused me to pause.

Was he upset? No. That couldn't be it. I was imagining things. He probably was irritated at the disruption as the old man had been.

"Thank you," I said, shaking off my thoughts before reading the card.

You're a vision of beauty today. I must leave with my mother directly after the proceedings, but will come visit you soon.
Bastien

Feeling as if I'd lift off the grass and float away, I smiled at him.

He grinned and bowed his head slightly before returning his attention to the stage.

The head of the council said the anointment in Latin, and when he was finished, he handed Uncle Philip a jewel-encrusted baton.

"Inhabitants of Asile, I give you your new high wizard, Philip Ralston Merlin Attwood. May he govern with his head and show empathy to those he rules."

The field erupted in cheers. Many of the people and Mystiks surrounding me cried. The ceremony was a farewell to one beloved high wizard and a welcome to a new one. Many whispered that Uncle Philip would be better than any high wizard who had come before him. Uncle Philip moved among the people instead of distancing himself from them. I cared for Merl, but I didn't know him that well. He was standoffish. Uncle Philip had risked his life to save Asile. He would never hide behind the walls of the haven.

It was that thought that made my eyes teary. I looked over at Arik, his head hung low. He had known Merl better than most, and so had Faith. To those Merl had let in, he was a father.

I gave Arik's arm a slight squeeze to show my support.

A sweet smile twitched on his lips. He gazed into my eyes with the saddest look on his face. "All is how it should be. That is what Merl would say."

"I'm so sorry, Arik. He was a great man, and he was proud of you."

"I know. He made certain I knew his feelings. He would have been proud of you, as well. Because of you, there is peace," he whispered, his voice cracking. "I have never admired or respected anyone more than I do you in this moment. I will never fail you again, Gia."

"You didn't fail me."

"I did. I let my emotions at seeing Merl—" He sucked in a sharp breath.

My hand found his arm again. "Stop. If it were Uncle Philip it would have paralyzed me, too."

"You're too kind." He lowered his head and swiped the tears away from his eyes.

"Thank you." Uncle Philip had made his way to the podium. "It is with a heavy heart that I come before you today. My mentor, my friend, has gone to a place where those from both worlds reside. I revered him as a father. I trusted him with my wellbeing, just as each of you trusted his rule.

"Bounty hunters have captured The Red and his gang, and they have been sent into the Somnium. The Mystik world has entered a time of peace."

The crowd cheered.

His eyes traveled over the people and stopped on me. "I haven't always been a gentle or forgiving man."

The crowd laughed.

"It took a young woman with a fighting spirit to bring it out of me. I am thankful for her each day. If it weren't for her, we would not be here today. Gianna, *al caldo il mio cuore.*"

You warm my heart.

Tears broke free from my eyes, wetting my cheeks. I released Arik's arm and wiped my eyes with my fingertips. I wanted to tell Uncle Philip that he warmed my heart, too, but I could save it for later.

"There were many heartbreaks during the attack on Asile," Uncle Philip continued. "Today we shall celebrate those who have fallen and rejoice in our new beginning. May Saint Agnes bless us. Enjoy the festivities."

Bastien and his mother stood with the other royals and joined the cheering crowd. He whispered to her and she nodded. They weaved their way around the other royals and exited the boxed seats section. He led his mother behind the stage, and I couldn't see him any longer. It was like the ground had flipped over and I tumbled, falling and careening with nothing to stop me. I wanted to chase after him, stop him from leaving, and that feeling surprised me.

"Shall we eat?" Lei broke my trance on the corner where Bastien had disappeared. "I'm famished."

Dazed, I trailed after her.

"My stomach is eating itself," Demos added.

"It's too bad Faith couldn't make it," Jaran said, walking beside me. We headed for the tables covered by colorful canopies down the hill from the stage.

"Merl's death hit Faith hard," I said, recovering from the sense of loss I'd had watching Bastien go. "Pop's with her."

"I understand how she feels," Arik said.

I recognized a guy standing by himself, still staring at the stage as everyone broke off. The man had stringy blond hair hanging over a large forehead, a muscular and stout body, and a look of doom on his face.

"Edgar?" I hurried to him. I hadn't seen him since rescuing Carrig from Esteril. He was undercover there to gain information for Asile, and I had blown his cover. He had to kill a guard to save his and my life.

"Gia," he said, emotionless. "Causing more trouble, are you?"

"I'm not— Never mind. What are you doing here? I thought you were in Esteril, restructuring and stuff."

He had a look on his face that scared me. I knew there was tons of work to do in the Russian haven after Conemar had disappeared. The news was that the people were recovering as they took back control. Many hated Conemar's rule and were thankful to the other havens for their support.

"Yes, I am. It's going well. But there is still an underground group, angry about losing their high wizard. Angry about their entry into the libraries being closed. Angry at just about everything." He glanced at each Sentinel. "Never let your guard down, no matter how much everyone speaks of peace." He spotted the crowd thinning around Uncle Philip. "I must go. It was nice to see you again."

"Edgar, wait," I said, rushing over to him.

He stopped, glancing from Uncle Philip to me. "What is it? I must hurry."

I got close to him and lowered my voice. "There's a rumor that the Wizard Council is corrupt. Do you know if there's any truth in it?"

"Where did you hear that?" He grabbed my elbow and guided me a few more steps away from the others. Jaran watched us, concern on his face. I smiled at him so he would know it was okay. "There has been a changing of the guards protecting the Council members due to the recent high wizard murders," Edgar continued. "I'm not certain what's going on, but I'm here to assess the threat and head the Asile guards in finding the group responsible for ordering the deaths. You needn't worry. I will protect Philip with my life. Now, get back to the others. And be careful."

Unable to find my voice, I nodded, fear strangling my throat.

Edgar jogged off in Uncle Philip's direction.

Heading back to the others, I couldn't help but worry about Uncle Philip's safety. Someone was killing the high wizards, and now my uncle was one. He was in danger.

"He needs to lighten up a bit," Demos said, watching Edgar rush off for the stage.

"He's been undercover too long," Jaran said. "He may be in need of a break."

I worried my lip, watching Edgar weave through the crowd.

Arik came to my side. "Edgar dwells with the evils of our world. He doesn't know the good in the worlds. But it's always wise to be cautious."

"I think you are right," Kale said.

"Okay, but can we worry about this later," Lei whined. "Let's just enjoy the peace for tonight. I'm hungry."

Kale wrapped his arm around Lei. "I'm with her. We could all use some sustenance and enjoyment."

"All right," Arik said. "Enjoy the evening. We'll gather tomorrow to discuss this further."

We charged down the hill to the tents. I decided to forget about what Edgar had said until tomorrow.

The evening was full of roasted chicken, extravagant desserts, and laughs with Uncle Philip and the Sentinels. With Arik. As though nothing had changed between us. Except, now we were friends, and I was actually happy about that.

CHAPTER TWENTY-TWO

The lunchroom buzzed with its normal release after a long morning of boring lectures and tedious math calculations. Arik and Emily sat close together, sharing each other's lunches. Faith had packed me a Fluffernutter sandwich cut into a heart. The strawberries dipped in chocolate, the carrots and cucumbers arranged artfully on toothpicks, and a smiley face drawn on my water bottle had my lunch looking like it had been prepared on the Food Network.

"She really is into making lunches," Emily said over Arik as she opened a chocolate milk carton.

"Yeah, it's kind of extreme," I said.

My phone vibrated across the table. It was a text from Nana. She said she had something to tell me and that she would be coming for the weekend. When I asked what it was, she said we should speak in person. I couldn't think of what it could be. It could have to do with Pop's birthday coming up. Kayla, Faith, and I were planning a big surprise party for him.

Lei carried a tray over and sat down beside me. "Hullo, ducky."

I eyed her tray. "You bought lunch?"

"It's fish stick day."

I moaned. "Not you, too?"

"Demos was right, they're quite good."

"I told you," Demos said, placing two trays down in front of him. "No one ever trusts me."

Kale shuffled up and kissed the top of Lei's head. "Is the day over yet?"

"I wish," I said, groaning. "I have so much makeup work to do." Remembering Emily was present, I added the lie Pop wrote on my excuse slip. "They should give us a break when we're sick."

Emily lowered her milk carton from her lips. "I don't mind makeup work."

I was about to tell her she was joking, but I spotted Deidre across the cafeteria sitting at a table with the Sentinels from the other havens. Her finger hooked in Ludo's back pant loop.

I took a bite of my sandwich. "Is Deidre dating Ludo now? That would explain all the Italian food at home lately."

Lei glanced over at them. "Yes and how many is that now? She's quite lost, isn't she?"

"I think she's just trying to have fun after having such a tough time with Nick," I said. "Where is he, anyway?"

"I saw him eating outside," Jaran said, approaching the table and carrying his sack lunch.

I flung my leg over the bench and stood. "I'm going to check on him."

The moody winter weather had changed from snow, to mud, to sunshine. Nick basked in the warmth on the steps to the common area. The sun picked up the golden highlights in his chestnut hair.

"Hey, you. Why aren't you with the gang inside?" I sat down beside him.

"Just thinking."

"About a certain someone?"

He glanced at his phone. "Yeah, I really miss her. We're texting, so I didn't want to seem rude to the others."

"Please, all teenagers are rude. Our phones are an extension of our hands. Didn't you know?"

"You sound like your pop."

"Probably because I'm quoting him." I laughed and dug into my lunch. "You want a chocolate-covered strawberry?"

He took the strawberry from me by its stem. "She really is getting fancy with the lunches."

"Yep, love her." I popped one into my mouth and tried to chew it. The strawberry was too big for my mouth, and I nearly choked.

Nick chuckled, licking the chocolate from his fingers. "They're not bite size. You can't eat them whole."

"I know," I said around the mouthful. "Don't worry. Afton will be here for spring break."

"That's forever away." He took a big bite of his sandwich. A slice of ham pulled out with his bite and he shoved it into his mouth.

He seemed calmer since Afton's visit, even happy. "You can always video chat."

"I guess. Did she tell you we kissed?"

"No." I bumped his shoulder. "Details."

The old Nick was back, recounting the secret kiss. His descriptions always bordered on inappropriate.

"You ready to do some putti duty," Nick said.

"Very funny. I thought we were going with *cherub*."

"Putti is just so fun to say."

We ate our lunch. Just the two of us. Like it had been ever since we were born and before Afton had joined us. I missed our alone times. We had always been there for each other. He had snatched my baby bottle away from me in the playpen we shared when our mothers gossiped over coffee. He had punched that bully who tripped me in second grade. And he had held my hand whenever my mother's death saddened me. I never needed a biological brother growing up. I had Nick.

"You know I love you, right?" I said, pulling a veggie kabob out of my sack.

He ripped the crust off his sandwich. "Yeah, I'm kind of stuck on you, too."

Everything in the Abbey Library of Saint Gall was made of dark wood, polished until it shined like a freshly waxed bowling lane. Two-story bookcases with balconies surrounded the room. Gold Leaf accented everything and topped off the many wooden pillars between the bookcases. Several display cases around the area held antique books.

I drifted through the space, my face turned up to view the ceiling. The elaborate gold-trimmed frames encasing the murals on the domed ceiling reminded me of eggshell pieces from a Fabergé egg.

"What are you doing?" Nick broke the ceiling's trance on me.

"Taking a moment to soak up the beauty. You should try it some time."

"I took it in. I'm just a quicker looker than you."

I smoothed my hair down. "Ugh, I have helmet hair. You should have gotten that Bug your parents wanted to buy you."

"I look much cooler with metal between my legs."

"Oh, please, it's a rusty bunch of parts."

He grabbed his chest. "You wound me."

"Come on." I pushed his shoulder. "Let's find the Chiave, already."

"Putti!" Nick called, adjusting his backpack on his shoulder. "Here putti, putti!"

I gave him the look that said *quit it*. "Seriously? You're so juvenile."

"You *know* that was funny."

"You're hilarious." I rolled my eyes, fingering the locket around my neck.

The gateway book shook behind us. A man jumped out, and right after him came a woman, a boy, and a girl.

"Good evening," the man said.

"Hello," I said.

"Do you happen to know which bookcase leads to…" He looked at his map. "Greyhill coven?"

They were the fourth group of travelers we ran into in just the short time we'd been in the library. Since the Wizard Council had reopened the gateways and reduced the security alert to the lowest level, the libraries had become crowded after closing. The new system required all travelers to acquire a ticket at one of the havens. This prevented overloading the libraries.

"It's in that room," Nick said, pointing out the direction of the room. "It's the third bookcase on the east wall."

"Thank you, kindly." He ushered his family along.

"You think he was a Sentinel or wizard?" Nick asked.

"Neither. I think he's a guard out on vacation with his family."

Nick scratched the back of his neck. "Why do you think that?"

"They're going to visit the Greyhill coven," I said. "Wizards go to human places. They live long lives and get tired of the Mystik world."

The book bounced across the table again. This time, two women in their sixties jumped out.

Nick pointed in the direction he had sent the family. "That way. Third bookcase. East wall."

"*Grazie*," they said in unison.

"How did you know where they wanted to go?" I said.

"The brochure in the shorter woman's hand," Nick said. "There's some sort of festival happening in Greyhill."

"Nice catch."

He puffed out his chest. "I kill Demos every time in that *True Detective* game of his. He hasn't learned to stop challenging me. He owes me forty bucks already."

"He's from another world," I said. "Maybe you should take it easy on him. Come on. Let's finish this and get out of here."

We searched around for another fifteen minutes before Nick spotted the putti. Their painted wooden faces stared down at us. There were several of them occupying the many niches above the pillars. Each held a symbol of one of the arts and sciences.

"They're sort of creepy." Nick bent his head all the way back as he viewed the little statues.

"I think they're cute." My gaze stopped on the one holding the telescope. "And there's our little guy."

"Well, how are we doing this?" he said. "We don't want any interruptions."

"You should go hold the book closed while I get the Chiave."

"Good idea." He sauntered off.

"Yell when you're ready," I said.

"Sure thing." He dragged his feet as he crossed the floor.

I frowned at his back. "Maybe in this lifetime?"

A few minutes later, he yelled from the other room, "Got it!"

I stared at the putto. He held a telescope up to his eye as if he were viewing something on the ceiling. I was so hoping that the material draping his private parts wouldn't come off when he came to life.

I grabbed my locket and said, "*Libero il tesoro.*" Free the treasure.

The familiar wind that always came after reciting the charm swirled around me. The chill rushed across my skin, making it prickle. The putto lowered the telescope, the movement of his arm sounding like wood splitting. Thankfully, his loincloth remained where it should, and he bent his head to look down at me.

"*Benvenuto*, daughter of the seventh. I am Scopices, the keeper of the Chiave you seek. This telescope will allow the holder the ability to see through barriers." He tossed the telescope down, and I readied my hands. The putto froze back in his position. I was horrible at catching things. The scope spiraled as it flew down at me and slipped through my fingers, clanking onto the floor.

"Graceful." Nick snickered, crossing the room to me.

"It was a horrible throw. I'd like to see you try—"

The sound of another jumper coming through the book from the other room cut me off.

"Let's get out of here already." I handed Nick the Chiave to tuck into his bag.

"Surely, not all jumpers are a nuisance." Bastien kicked back against a column with his arms and legs crossed—a pose that belonged in one of those hot guy calendars.

"Oh my goodness, what are you doing here?" I sounded way too excited.

He flashed me a playful grin. "I just happened to be passing through. There's a festival in Greyhill. I have to make an appearance in my mother's stead."

Nick zipped his backpack closed and swung it on his shoulder. "I think I'll go explore a little. Take your time."

"The gateways have been busy lately," I said when Nick vanished around the corner. My eyes stuck on Bastien's. The blue in his shirt picked up their deeper hues. Like cobalt glass in the dark. His lower lip was fuller than his upper one. I hadn't noticed that before. There was a beauty mark over his left eyebrow. I hadn't noticed that, either.

My eyes were open now. I could see every wonderful thing about him.

He crossed the room to me, and the look on his face said he knew I was staring at him.

"I'm sorry. You just took me by surprise." I glimpsed him through my bangs. His amused expression made my entire body aware of him. I pushed my fingers into the tight back pockets of my jeans and tried to act unaffected by his nearness.

"So what do you say?" He kept coming closer, until he was so close I could smell the hint of cologne on his shirt. "Would you like to go to a festival with me?"

I strolled off, moving slowly along the bookcases. He followed me.

"I'm not sure," I said. "I have tons of homework tonight."

He caught my hand.

I faced him. My hand tingled under his touch.

"Have you ever had a peach so sweet it's euphoric?" he asked.

"No. But it sounds tempting."

He massaged my fingers. "Come for a little while. I'll have you back with enough time to do your work."

I didn't know why I hesitated. It was time for me to live, to be a girl, and enjoy my youth. I had been running from, running to, just running for way too long. I could get lost in

Bastien. Enjoy myself. Erase the pain. Maybe even erase the nightmares.

"I would love that." I slipped my fingers from his grasp and started walking again. If I kept moving, maybe he wouldn't notice how nervous he made me. "What about Nick?"

"Don't worry about me," Nick said. "I'm a big boy. I can find my way home."

"I think you're running out of excuses." Bastien kept pace with me, a smile pulling on his lips.

More people jumped in from the book. By the sounds of their voices, it was a group of girls.

Nick glanced over his shoulder. "Excuse me, I have doorman duty. Let me know what you decide."

"Well, what do you say?" Bastien said.

"Hello, ladies," Nick's voice traveled from the other room.

We ended up at a door. A plaque above it had an inscription on it. "I wonder what that says." I tried to keep the subject on anything but us.

He stopped beside me. "It's Greek. The translation is Sanatorium of the Soul or others have called it House of Books."

"Wait. What?" I took a step forward, glancing up at the plaque.

My head was so foggy I was vaguely aware of a charge snapping at my body. What I'd just felt registered when an intense cold overtook my skin. I spun around to push Bastien away, but he grabbed my hands. A puzzled look crossed his face.

"Let go!" I pulled my hands back but he wouldn't release them.

It was like shards of ice stabbing across my body. An intense suction gripped me, pulling me back. I stretched out my fingers, trying to break free from Bastien's grasp.

"Gia, what's happening?" Worry twisted his face and he tightened his grasp on me.

"It's a trapdoor. You have to let me go."

"No. Hold on to me. I won't let you fall." He tugged me forward but the suction was stronger than he was. "Nick!" he yelled, desperation lacing his voice.

"Please. Let go." My fingers slipped.

He was losing his hold.

Anger replaced the defeat in his eyes and he stepped forward, letting the trap suck him in along with me.

CHAPTER TWENTY-THREE

My cheek burned. Frigid air lashed at my exposed skin. I lay facedown on something hard. The surface felt slick, extremely cold, and wet under my fingertips. I shivered violently. It was as if I was in a walk-in freezer.

"Gia, get up." Bastien sounded far off somewhere. "Come on, we haven't time." He shook my shoulder.

I lifted my head, barely opening my eyes. The whiteness blinded me, and pain stabbed my right eye and shot through my head. I shut my eyes tight against the brightness.

"Wh-what happened?" My teeth clattered so hard together the vibration rattled down my spine. The flakes falling from the sky were like shards of glass stinging my skin.

"You tripped a trap." He grabbed my arm and guided me to my feet. I could feel the coldness of his hand through my sleeved arm. The breath panting from his lips hovered in an icy cloud in front of his face. "We have to find shelter or we'll freeze to death." He buttoned up his leather jacket.

I swayed on my feet, glancing up at a blue glow just above our heads. "What's that light?" Icy rocks turned under my feet as I tried to keep my balance.

His eyes went to where mine were looking. "It's where we fell through. It must be the trapdoor."

The land was flat. A frosty wind blew waves in the snow. He buttoned up my trench coat and then tied the belt tight around my waist.

"Shelter? There's nothing out there."

"Over there." He pointed across the field. I caught glimpses of a tree line between a break in the fury of ice obscuring it. "We have to keep moving. We must find shelter before it gets dark."

I nodded and staggered after him. Each step sank deep into the snow, slowing me. Ahead, Bastien struggled to get his foot out of the packed snow. My fingers were in so much pain. I tucked my bare hands in the pit of my arms to shield them from the freezing wind. The woods came into view the closer we got. Every joint in my body ached with each movement, the cold locking them, making it hard to push forward. I fell, sinking to my knees in the snow.

Bastien turned. "Get up. I know it's painful, but we can't stop, Gia. We'll die if we do. It's not that far."

I struggled to my feet, slipping and falling backward onto the snow. This was it. This was how I would die, in a barren wasteland, frozen into the ground. Daggers of pain shocked my breath. I gasped for air.

Bastien leaned over me, reaching out his hand. "You can't stop. It's not all that bad if you keep moving."

"Not bad? We're going to die," I panted, and took his hand.

He yanked me up. "You're a warrior. It's all a state of mind."

"Can't you use your magic or something?" I called after him.

"We'll try something when we get to safety."

"What do you mean? We're freezing to death. Do it now."

He didn't stop. "What we know about the Somniums is that creatures inhabit them, and they're usually not welcoming. We need shelter."

I glanced around, reaching for the hilt of my sword. The frigid metal bit my skin. My steps finally landed on solid ground. We stopped when we were safely within the trees. The branches were thick and the trunks crowded together, blocking the biting wind.

Bastien's head moved back and forth as we made our way deeper into the woods. He stopped when he came to two boulders, each nearly twelve feet tall and butted up against each other.

"This will work." He grabbed some broken branches from underneath the trees and piled them in front of the crevice. He commanded fire, and a flaming ball formed in his hand. He dropped the ball and the wood burst into flames. "Let's warm ourselves before we make our shelter."

I huddled over the fire, thawing my hands. "Why didn't you let me go? You should have. Now you're stuck here with me."

He rubbed his hands together. "I would never let you face this alone."

My heart heated up like a furnace at his words. His sacrifice surprised me. Most people would've let me go, saved themselves, because fear is that strong. It makes you want to live at any cost. A normal person would only give it all up for a loved one.

I swallowed hard. *Could he—?*

The snap of a twig brought my attention back to him. "We're going to be all right," he said.

"I hope you're right." The frozen air scraped the back of my throat, and I swallowed again. "How do we get out of here?"

He squatted and stretched his hands over the flame, his eyes holding mine. "If they can find which one we're in, the Fey can retrieve us, but…" He stared down at the flames.

"But what?"

"It's nearly impossible to find an untagged trap. The doors flicker. They open and close. Not counting the fact that there are hundreds of them."

My stomach shifted uneasily. "You're basically telling me we can never get out?"

"I've never heard of anyone returning from one."

I lowered my head, the fire heating my cheeks. "There has to be a way…"

Bastien shuffled over to me, still in a squat position, and wrapped an arm around me. "Hey," he said gently. "We have each other. All we have to do is survive. They'll look for us, and we must hold on to hope. Besides, we have that date to look forward to."

I smiled, appreciating his attempt to make our situation seem less bleak. "Okay."

"All right, then." He squeezed my shoulder. "We have to gather branches and foliage from the trees."

Bastien straightened and started breaking off lower branches that the snow hadn't blanketed. The trees looked to be evergreens, but instead of pine needles, their foliage was soft.

"What kind of tree is this?"

"I've never seen anything like it before. Its leaves are unusually thick."

I shivered and rushed around yanking off branches. When we finished, we had a pile up to our knees.

"Now what?" I rushed back to the fire and warmed my hands.

Bastien stripped a branch and gathered up the loose leaves. "Raise your arms."

I gave him a curious brow.

"I'm going to stuff your jacket with these for insulation.

Then you can do mine." He shoved some down the back of my trench coat. An unusual floral scent filled my nose.

"I hope this stuff isn't poisonous."

"I'll risk a little skin irritation to avoid death. Turn."

I did, and he slid some into the front of my jacket. His cold hands glided across my shirt and the rise of my chest. I sucked in a startled breath, my pulse kicking up.

"Oh, sorry." He smirked. "Maybe you'd best do your own front?"

"Yeah, best." I took the leftover leaves from him and slipped them inside my trench coat. "How'd you know how to do this?"

"I've taken survival courses. It's mandatory at the Academy."

"What's next?" My lower lip trembled. I wanted to hurry and get back to the fire. He handed me the leaves and turned his back to me. I stuffed his jacket with leaves. My fingers rose and fell across the muscles under his tight shirt as I withdrew my hand from his jacket.

Bastien shuddered. "Ah, your hands are icy."

"Pay back."

"Okay, grab some branches."

I snatched up several branches. He laid his bunch on the ground between the two rocks. Then took mine and leaned them against sides of the rock. It was our own little nest.

"May I have your sheath?"

"Why?"

He frowned at me. "I won't harm it. We need a container."

I unbuckled my belt, drew my sword out of the sheath, and handed it to him.

"Get in the crevice. It should be warm there."

I placed my sword on top of the branches by the entrance of our makeshift shelter and crawled inside. The fire was already heating it. Bastien packed snow into my sheath, then dipped the bottom of it into the fire.

"What are you doing?"

He looked over the flames at me. "We need to keep hydrated."

The firelight flickered over his beautiful face. His cheeks and nose were bright red. The way he held the metal casing so gently in his hands reminded me of his kindness. I felt safe with him. If I had to be stranded with someone, he definitely was a sexy distraction.

"You know Nick will discover us missing," I said. "There will be a full-on search for the trapdoor. We'll be rescued in a few hours."

"I truly hope so." His fake smile said he didn't think so. "Here. Sip this. Hold it at the top or you'll burn your hands." He handed me the sheath and crept in beside me. "Be cautious, it's hot." He waved his hand over the fire. It spread across the wood lining the entry of our shelter. "If there are creatures in this godforsaken place, they won't get past that."

I took a sip from the sheath. The heated water rushed down my esophagus and warmed my chest.

"I wish we had time to hunt for something to eat, but we'll have to wait until the sun is high tomorrow."

I leaned back and retrieved the energy bars I kept in the pocket of my trench coat for whenever I used my battle globe and passed them to him.

"Excellent. We'll share one tonight and save the other two for tomorrow." He unwrapped one. "I hope there's a mountain or some caves around here. We can't survive here without provisions."

"We won't be here long," I said. "You'll see. They'll find us before morning."

"I hope so. But we must prepare ourselves in case they don't find us."

He dragged a branch over us, and I did the same until the soft foliage buried us. The only sounds were Bastien's soft breathing and the crackling from the fire. There were no bug chirps or animal noises, just the murmur of the wind. I startled when Bastien spooned up against me and draped his arm around my waist. He tightened his hold to keep me from getting up.

"Relax. We have to get close to stay warm." His whispering tickled my ear.

I stilled. My body tensed. There was no way I could relax with him wrapped around me like that. Besides, this place made me uneasy. I could lie to him about them finding us, but deep down I knew the truth. I'd read a chapter on it in the book *The Invisible Places* by Gian Bianchi, Professor of Wizardry, aka my great-grandfather. It was nearly impossible to locate a trapdoor. They flickered open and shut so fast and infrequently, someone would have to be in the exact spot as the door and wait for it. A wizard must instantly tag the trap or it would most likely never be found again.

I couldn't stop shaking, my eyes wildly searching the gaps between the branches. There was only a small flicker of light coming from the fire. I'd faced dangers before, but not knowing what was out there in the dark frightened me. I wanted to cry but held it in. I refused to be weak in front of Bastien. Plus, I was sure my tears would freeze on my face.

Stuck in this frozen wasteland, we most likely would never leave, but I would spend every moment here searching for a way out. Find a way back to Pop, Nana, and my friends. To Arik. Even though he'd dumped me for Snow White, I still cared deeply for him and couldn't bear the thought of never seeing him again.

Bastien's breath beat softly against my hair. Through the branches, I watched the shadows under the trees grow darker with the setting sun. His warmth enveloped me, and my body slacked against Bastien's strong form.

"What if the fire goes out?" I whispered.

"It won't. There's magic in the flame. The wood is only an anchor."

"But how?"

"There's no explanation to magic. You just have to believe and trust—"

"Trust it. *Right*." I sighed.

I detected a chuckle in his expelled breath.

A distant howl shattered the silent wasteland, and my fingers crawled to the hilt of my sword. "Did you hear that?"

"Maybe we won't starve to death, after all," he said. "We'll hunt it tomorrow." He adjusted behind me, and I stiffened.

The howls went on through the night. I vaguely remembered dozing off a few times, but mostly I watched the blaze of the fire, my hand gripping my sword and my senses heightened on every movement Bastien made behind me. His deep, rhythmic breathing was soothing.

I played everything I read about the Somniums in my head. When the wizards had hidden their havens several centuries ago, the split caused hundreds of gaps between the Mystik and human worlds, creating the Somniums. There was a sort of magic sealing them from the two worlds.

"Bastien?"

He groaned. "You're not sleeping."

"How can you sleep in a place like this?"

"I've been prepared for situations like this my entire life." He removed his arm from me and stretched it over his head. I instantly felt cold where his arm had been. "The human world is protected from knowing such evils as the Mystik world lives with them daily."

"The book I read about the Somniums was kind of old,

but I recall there was a man who escaped the trap. Right?"

His arm found my waist again, and my stomach jumped to attention.

"There was a man who escaped quite some time ago. He said he jumped the trap, but he died of injuries he sustained from an attack by one of the creatures before his experience could be documented."

"But then, there is a way out."

"Possibly." He leaned over me, his mouth so close to my cheek. My skin there pulsed under his nearness. "Get some sleep. Once we tackle our survival issues, we'll search for an escape."

I closed my eyes and tried to quiet the noise in my head. The corners of my mind slowly darkened, like the shadows under the trees until everything went entirely black.

When I awoke later, it was to birdsong and heat. Extremely hot heat. The area around my waist under Bastien's arm was now sweaty. I pushed the branches off me and sat up. The fire still gobbled at the wood, not even marring it. The snow had melted, and the woods were alive with birds and small scurrying creatures. The winter wasteland had vanished and been replaced with full-on spring.

"What the hell?"

Bastien came out of the branch pile and yawned. "This is odd."

"You think?" I gave him a *duh* look. "Talk about extreme conditions. Can you take down the wall of fire?"

"Oh, right." He waved his hand, and the flame disappeared.

I crawled over the branches and stepped across the still-warm sticks. Bastien followed me, twigs crunching under his weight. We stood there, mouths wide. The vibrant green, the colorful flowers, and the cute, furry animals running from tree to tree, all seemed surreal.

"It's as if we found Eden," Bastien said.

"Then what was yesterday? Hell?"

A light chuckle sounded under his breath. "Possibly."

I took off for a tree with birds swarming it and picked one of the oval-shaped purple fruit weighing down its branches. It was bigger than a grape and smaller than a plum. The skin popped when I bit into it, releasing a sweet juice tasting like honeyed cherries.

Bastien rushed over and knocked the fruit from my hand.

"Hey, why'd you do that?"

He frowned down at me. "You're a city girl, aren't you?"

"You say that like it's a bad thing."

"One doesn't eat the vegetation when one doesn't know if it isn't poisonous."

"Please." I rested my fists on my hips. "We *city* girls aren't stupid. I checked. The birds are eating it, and they aren't dying."

He inspected the birds. They bounced from branch to branch, pecking at the fruit. "They could have immunities to it." He looked sternly at me. "Let's make a ruling."

I stretched taller and stuck my chin out. "Ruling? You may be a high-wizard-in-waiting in Couve, but you aren't here, and you don't rule me."

"I didn't say *I* in that statement, I said *let's*, which is a contraction for let us. As in, *let us* make a ruling."

"Really." I sauntered over to the next tree. "I know what a contraction is, but it was your tone that told me that there wasn't any *us* in it." I stretched my arm high, reaching for another fruit. "And besides, I haven't died yet." I plucked it from the tree. A mass of birds squawked in harmony, taking off for the sky. Several oval balls rained down on me, popping against my head and shoulders, squirting juice over my hair and skin.

Bastien let out a whooping laugh, his face lit with amusement. I picked up a fruit in each hand and threw one at him. It hit his leg. *That was horrible.* My battle globe had always found its target, but a piece of fruit, total failure.

Sinead had said the globe was connected to my mind and that all I had to do was to think of where I wanted it to go, and it would go there. Right now, I wished the fruit were on mind-control. I pulled my arm back, gingerly cradling the fruit in my palm, and hurled it. The fruit bomb exploded against his chest, and the juice sprayed his neck and chin.

"You're going to wake a sleeping beast." He chuckled, and it was so sexy, I had to hit him again.

I went for a fruit dangling just above my head. Bastien's eyes went wide. I smirked. "Chicken?"

A growl sounded behind me, and I froze.

CHAPTER TWENTY-FOUR

I grabbed for my sword at my waist, but it wasn't there. I stayed perfectly still, too freaked out to turn around. Behind me, several paws padded against the drying ground. I found Bastien's eyes. He mouthed for me to stay still, a fiery ball swirling in his hands. The sunlight glinted on the blade of my sword in the shelter. Once Bastien threw the ball at the creatures, I decided I would make a break for it.

The growling got fiercer. Bastien flung the fire ball toward the source of the growls. I dashed for my sword, stealing quick glances over my shoulder. The tree was on fire. Two of the creatures' matted coats were smoking. I skidded to a stop. Bastien was on the ground, holding the ears of one creature, trying to keep the animal's long teeth from his neck. I snatched up my blade and sprinted toward them. When in reach, I swung my sword and sliced the beast's throat. Blood showered down on Bastien.

He groaned, pushing the creature off him.

Five of the creatures circled us, baring their teeth. They looked to be a cross between a huge cat and an extremely large wolf with saber teeth. Their hideous eyes, almost hidden behind their long snouts, stared us down. I raised my palm ever so slowly and ignited my pink globe. The animals sprung for us, and my globe shot up, engulfing Bastien and me with its protective shield. The sphere swayed against the impact, and I cried out, trying to keep it up with all my might. My sword slipped away and thumped onto the hard ground.

The animals slammed against the pink membrane, cutting their saber-teeth across it. I could feel the globe slipping from me. I dropped to my knees.

"Are you okay?"

"Grab my sword! I'm going to lose the globe."

Bastien plucked up my sword. "I doubt one sword will take care of that pack." In his free hand, he formed another fire ball. "You can do it, Gia. Don't give in."

I clenched my teeth so hard, my jaw was about to break from the force. My arms shook, weak and about to buckle under the force. Another creature rammed the globe. I fell back on my heels but kept the sphere intact, barely. Ripples ran down the sides, the membrane thinning. Several bursts of light flashed outside the globe. Animal wails, agonizing yelps, and retreating paws faded into the woods. The globe burst, and I dropped onto my back.

I couldn't move. Snow floated down and landed on my face. I watched the flakes glitter against the sun. An old man, with scraggly gray hair and a matted beard, blocked the sun and glared down at me.

"No time for resting," the man said, his voice raspy. "The beasts are gone. Get up. The change shall happen fast."

I lifted my head. "Who are you?"

"No time." He paced, his eyes searching the woods around us. "No time. Must get back. Good thing you caught that tree on fire. It alerted us."

Bastien knelt beside me. "She needs time to recover from her globe."

"She must get up." The man stopped his pacing when a loud scraping sound came from the other side of the purple-fruit tree.

A younger guy guided a sled made out of odd-shaped branches and logs, pulled by two goats with long hair and stubby legs, between the trees. Furs and woven baskets filled with colorful fruits loaded down the sled.

"Tie the dead beasts to the back of the sled. We'll have to drag them," the old man said to the other guy, then nodded at Bastien. "Put the girl on the sled." He glanced up at the sky. "We have less than an hour, I'd say."

Bastien lifted me in his arms.

"We can't go with them," I protested, wrapping my arms around his neck. "They could be dangerous."

"They saved our lives," Bastien said. "I doubt they'd risk theirs just so they could kill us instead of those beasts."

He had a good point. My mind was too exhausted to think straight. A spark of light caught at the corner of my eye.

"My scabbard and sword," I practically whined, stretching my arm out for them as if I could will them to me.

Bastien placed me on the furs draped over the sled. He paused and removed a strand of hair caught in my eyelashes, his thumb brushing my cheek.

"Hush," he said. "Just rest. I'll gather our things."

The wind picked up. A flurry of snow rushed across the woods. Chilly air nipped at my skin. When the guy finished tying the beasts to the back of the sled, the old man clicked his tongue. The longhaired goats tugged on the ropes harnessed around their chests, and the sled bumped after them. The storm got angry, blowing snow in my face.

"What's up with the weather," I called out to the old man.

"It was just burning hot, and now it's getting so cold."

"It is this Somnium's cycle," he spoke over the shrieking wind. "It's warm only a few hours each day. The rest of the time, it is dangerously cold."

Bastien handed me my trench coat, and I struggled to put it on, my arms feeling like there were no bones supporting them. The sled bouncing over rocks and roots heightened the level of difficulty, but I managed to get it on and wrap it tightly around me.

The woods resembled one you'd see in a horror film. The wind whistled eerily through the trees. The animals and bugs were silent once again. Shadows moved under the wind's touch. The trees remained green, the unusual leaves seemingly mocking the arctic madness swirling around them.

Our sled came out of the woods and tilted up as it climbed rocky foothills to the base of a cliff that soared into the sky, the top of it hidden behind angry dark clouds. The younger guy rushed to the front of the sled and grabbed the rope tied to the goats. He tugged them around a large boulder and stopped the sled in front of a cave opening.

"This way," the old man said, heading into the cave.

My legs struggled to hold the rest of me up as I followed the old man and Bastien into the dank cave.

The other guy stayed behind and worked at untying the goats from the sled.

Inside the cave was a long tunnel. The man took a torch off the wall and lit it with his magic.

He's a wizard.

The old man wobbled down the tunnel. On the left was a smaller cave. It stank like a porta-potty. There were dead grass and leaves on the floor. The area must've been a sort of stable for the goats. The tunnel banked right, and we came into a large cavern.

It was like the Swiss Family Robinson's tree-house in Disney World, except for it being a cave. Kind of like a hunting cabin. Furs draped the walls and covered the floors. A table made of logs took up one side. Two benches flanked its sides, with plates and cups whittled out of wood on its top. Two wide chairs made of wood, with furs as cushions, sat beside a fire pit. Between the chairs were stacked books.

"Come, come, and make yourselves comfortable." The man went to the pit and held his hand over the flame. No smoke rose from the fire.

"You're a wizard," Bastien said, stating the obvious. He stood by the man and warmed his hands over the wizard's fire.

I dragged my feet across the fur-lined floor and plopped down on one of the chairs. I was starving and weak. "Do you have anything to eat?" I asked and crossed my arms, trying to stop the quakes.

Bastien retrieved one of the energy bars from his coat pocket and gave it to me.

"What's your friend doing outside? It's freezing." I tore the wrapper open with my teeth and pulled the fur draped on the back of the chair around my shoulders.

"He's sheltering the animals and storing our supplies," the man said. "He won't be able to skin the two dead beasts until it warms again."

"Gross." That had to be a bloody business. I could never imagine skinning an animal. How did someone get up the nerve to do something like that?

Bastien reclaimed his spot by the fire. "How long have you been here?"

"A moment of nothingness in and of itself is difficult to bear, but to add them together would be complete agony." The man crooked his head and watched Bastien. "I have been here too long to count, and my friend has been here even longer. It is something we choose not to speak of, a sort of taboo, you might say."

His words sank to my stomach and mixed around with the energy bar, making me queasy. "Have you tried to get out?"

He glanced over his shoulder at me. His brown eyes hooded with bushy eyebrows and folded skin held sadness. "I've tried every spell, every bit of magic I know, and the trapdoor remains closed."

I stood. "So you just gave up?" The fur slipped off my shoulders, and the cold instantly rushed over me. I hurried to Bastien's side and hovered over the fire pit.

"No, I just ran out of options." The man stared at the flame, and a frown pulled down his face, the wrinkles deepening around his mouth. "Being in this wasteland for such a long time has caused me to forget my manners." He straightened and faced us. "Please forgive my transgressions. We haven't been properly introduced. I am Gian Bianchi from the Mantello haven."

My mouth gaped as I took in what he said.

My great-grandfather? He can't be. He's dead. They said he was dead. How can this man be him?

"You can't be." Bastien voiced what I couldn't. "He was murdered."

"I assure you, I am. I had used a wizard's illusion to fake my death." He placed his hand over the fire and raised it.

The flames shot up, the warmth encircling me. I was sure he did that to emphasize the wizard thing.

I cut a puzzled look at Bastien. "A wizard illusion?"

Bastien opened his hand, and a perfectly red apple appeared on it. I reached for it, but when my fingers touched it, they went through it. A cool, tingling sensation prickled across my skin.

Bastien lowered his hand. "Wizards can create illusions.

Objects from their memories."

"This is un-fricking-believable." I stepped closer. "How can you be alive? It's been over seventy-five years since…"

"It's been that long, huh?" He swallowed. "And my wife? Is she gone?"

I nodded, tears shocking my eyes at the sight of his glossing. "I'm…um…I'm your great-granddaughter. My mom named me after you. I'm Gianna, and this is Bastien from Couve."

He paused in the middle of reaching for a clay pot on the table and stared at his hand. "I should make us some tea," he finally said, and grabbed the pot. "It'll warm our bones, it will." He peeked over his shoulder. "You do like tea, yeah?"

"Yes. I'd love some," I said, watching him carefully.

He started his task, pouring water from a carafe made of wood into the clay pot.

I gave Bastien a curious brow. Either Gian was in shock or he was indifferent to me being his relative. My bet was that he was trying to gather his emotions. He probably thought all this time that his wife was still alive.

"So," Bastien cut through the silence, "you used an illusion to fake your death? Why?"

"I had been searching the libraries with a recovered Chiave," Gian said, adding some leaves to the pot. "A Laniar ambushed me and buried his dagger into my chest. I had tagged the slip to this Somnium before, so I knew it was there—"

"It's tagged?" I blurted. "So they could find us."

Gian shook his head. "No. I hadn't registered it. No one knows it exists, except me."

My shoulders slumped, deflated. The second of hope I'd had crushing like a dried flower between the pages of a book.

"But he didn't get the scroll," Bastien said.

"I had given it to Toad and begged him to hide it. When Conemar was busy searching my things for the Chiave, I created a doppelganger of myself and slipped into the trap."

I wanted to cry. Here was my great-grandfather. Alive. In front of me, and he didn't seem to care that I was here.

Bastien took my hand and squeezed it. "What were you searching for in the libraries?"

"I was following someone's path. I had found jump recordings in an old book. This person will change both worlds. Our salvation. When the presages come, whomever they may be must protect the one who will stop the Tetrad." He hooked the woven handle of the pot to a pole rigged across the fire. "I must get him back to the havens. He has to be protected at all cost."

"Who is it?" Bastien asked.

"My companion. The boy outside." Gian looked over his shoulder as if to make sure he hadn't come in. "Royston."

"Royston?" I stumbled back and fell onto the chair. Could it be? It was the name written on the scroll we had retrieved from Toad. "How did you know where to find him?"

He went to the stack of books and pulled out a tattered blue linen journal. "In this. Agnost's notes." He placed it back on the pile. "An heir from the Seventh Wizard is our salvation. I discovered in old records that Royston's guard witnessed him vanish through a slip. I knew if he were still alive in one of the Somniums, he would be the nearest heir, and our salvation. It became my quest to recover him."

"I haven't heard of this book," Bastien said. "Did you not show it to the Wizard Council?"

"No. I suspect there are those on the council with ill intentions." There was a limp to his step as he crossed the room. "I am the guardian of secrets, I suppose. Secrets that others can't be trusted to know."

He went back to the fire, picked up the pot, and strained the liquid through a cloth into the wooden cups on the table.

"If only I were able to record the slip, I wouldn't have been trapped here. Pip would have picked up the tag in his globe, and my jump into the Somnium would have been recorded.

"But there is hope. Each month the blue lights of the trapdoor turn silver for several days. I've managed to open it for a few seconds. I've seen into the library, but there is never enough time for us to jump through. The next one is in three weeks. We might have a chance to hold it open long enough with two wizards. It may take several attempts, but we could escape eventually. We have time to get Royston out before the end times begin."

"Gian," I practically croaked out his name. "Um, you see...I'm the presage. Your granddaughter was my mother. She and my father were both Sentinels. The end is already in motion. We have to get back fast."

"Who's the other?" Gian wiped his hands on his pants.

Bastien and I gave each other confused looks. Nothing phased this man. I just told him I was his great-granddaughter and that I was the presage and I got nothing from him. No tears. No wide eyes. No emotion. Nothing.

"There are two protectors." He picked up a cup and passed it to Bastien. "One will stay true, the other will not. Has the other showed him or herself?"

Nick.

"You have a great-grandson from your affair with Anise." I wanted to take back the part about the affair. My mother and Jacalyn had discovered it after Gian's disappearance.

"I see my memoirs were found." He gave me a cup.

I eyed him as I took the cup. Still nothing. "He's Conemar's son."

He picked up a cup and took a sip. "Now that is unfortunate. Conemar has a son who can find the Chiavi and release the Tetrad for him."

The look of doom on his face scared the crap out of me. "Well, Nick is on our side. He hates his father for killing his mother. He'd never help Conemar. Besides, Bastien sent Conemar into an untraced or untagged, whatever, Somnium. He's basically in prison."

"The prophecy is in motion," Gian mumbled into his cup. "Did you use an ancient charm to send him away?"

Bastien shifted nervously. "Yes. But—how did you know that?"

"It's in the prophecy. In that blue book over there."

"At the time, I didn't know it would put him some place where he'd gain power. I was just trying to save Gia and the others."

Gian took a sip from his cup. "I couldn't find any reference in Agnost's journals about where that place might be. All I know for certain is he will return."

"Lovely," I muttered under my breath. "And we're stuck here."

Royston shuffled into the cavern, with six ferrets running after him. Blond matted hair framed his face and covered his jawline. His icy blue eyes surveyed my body like I was a steak or something. The guy was built, with wide shoulders, but he sure was hairy, and dirty. I stepped a little bit behind Bastien to avoid Royston's stare. It was like he'd never seen a girl before.

That's because he hasn't seen a girl in centuries. I mentally slapped my forehead.

One of the ferrets came up to my toes and sniffed. "Oh, how cute. Where did they come from?"

"They were here. They are friends," Royston said. "We feed them, and they alert us when the beasts are near."

Gian clunked his cup onto the table. "I say we eat dinner, and while we eat, I think you two should fill me in about all that's happened since I've been away. We shall turn in early and wake in time for the next warm spell."

I searched the cave. It was one room, which meant the sleepover would be co-ed, with me being the only girl.

Wonderful.

CHAPTER TWENTY-FIVE

It felt as though someone was staring at me, so I popped open my eyes. Royston was leaning over me, his face so close to mine I could smell his majorly stinky breath. I sat up fast and bonked heads with him. I tugged a fur up to my chin, which was stupid since I still had all my clothes on.

"What *are* you doing?" I gave the crouching guy a sharp look and felt for my scabbard.

Bastien sprung up. "What's the matter?"

"You hungry?" Royston grunted, rubbing his head where our heads collided. "Gian says to eat. The sun is rising. It is the warm time. You must hurry." He scampered off and straddled the bench at the table.

"What I wouldn't give for a toothbrush and paste," I said. "And a bath."

Bastien snickered. "We both could use one. My skin is sticky from that fruit. I wonder if there is a body of water nearby. We could get a little skinny-dipping in before the next arctic blast hits us."

"I am *so* not skinny-dipping around here."

"Let me understand this, if we were somewhere other than here, you would skinny-dip with me?" He tickled my side.

"Stop it." I dodged his next attack. "I'd never be naked around you."

"Never say never." He took a spot on the bench beside Gian.

I slipped onto the bench across the table from Bastien. There were eggs, jerky, and fruit on our plates, and cups of steaming tea beside them. "This looks great."

Royston sat next to me.

"Eat quickly," Gian said. "The freeze will end soon and we'll have little time outside."

After breakfast, Gian gave us each a task and a ferret to look out for danger. I went about picking only the dark purple berries from the bushes in the foothills, staying away from all the other color berries that Gian said were poisonous. The sun glared at me and sweat trickled down my back, my shirt sticking to my skin. My guard ferret's furry white body circled my boots, threatening to trip me.

"We can't play, I'm working." I leaned over to pick a berry, but the ferret snatched it before I could reach it. I swear the furry nuisance was laughing as it darted off between the rocks.

I spotted a crevice between the cliffs and peeked in. Flashes of sunlight teased the greenery and sparkled on a body of water. I squeezed through the crevice and moved down the rocks until I came out on the other side. High cliffs and thick-leafed trees surrounded a pristine pond.

I searched the area and found I was alone, except for my ferret companion who followed and nipped at my heels. I sat on a rock, yanking off my boots, then socks, and rolling up my pant legs. Warm water welcomed my toes when I dipped them in. I removed my scabbard and placed it on the ground before skinning out of my pants and shirt, leaving on my undies and bra, then dove into the tepid water and swam out a ways. The ferret darted in and out of the shallows.

"I should give you a name," I called out to the ferret. "It doesn't seem right not to have a name, don't you agree? How about Momo? I like that name. It's from a show I used to watch." I leaned back and floated on the water, letting the waves ripple against my skin and closing my eyes at the sun's angry stare.

Something plunked into the water and I shot upright, wading in the middle. "Did you hear that, Momo?" Her cute, furry face just watched me. "Aren't you supposed to warn me of danger or something?" I spun in a circle, inspecting the area surrounding the pond.

Strong arms encircled me from behind.

"Bastien, I told you I wouldn't skinny-dip with you," I squealed, and twirled in his arms to face him, then gasped.

"Royston?" I pushed on his chest. "Let go of me!"

"Do you like me now?" He kept his grip on me. "I finished my duties early and shaved with my knife. Cut my hair to look like your companion."

I stopped struggling when I recognized his face. It was him. From my dreams. Athela's son.

Stay calm. I took a soothing breath. "You look nice. Now, will you let me go?"

He released me, and I pushed away from him.

Questions flew through my mind. How did he get here? Should I ask him about his mother? *No. Not now.* This wasn't the time.

A squawk sounded high above us, and I shot back to him.

He laughed, holding me against his bare chest. "It's just a bird."

"Are you naked?" I wiggled away from him again, my

eyes stuck on his muscled chest. And I froze. There was a scar the shape of a crescent moon on his perfectly defined pectoral muscle.

Just like mine. Someone shielded him.

"Isn't that how you take a bath?" His face was serious.

"Well, yes, but in private places only," I said, wading in the direction I had dropped my clothes.

"This was my private bath until you invaded it." Royston launched past me and stood. "You are so beautiful."

I rolled my eyes. "Coming from a guy who hasn't seen a girl since the Stone Age, I'll take that as you're very horny."

"Will you wed me?"

I paused. *What the hell?* "No. Thank you for the proposal, but I'll have to decline."

"Are you betrothed to someone else?"

I thought of Bastien; in the Mystik world we were technically betrothed. "Well, actually, I am. Besides, you do realize you're like my grandfather a hundred times removed or something. There has to be some sort of ancestor taboo thing there. I consider that incest."

"My mother married her cousin."

"Eww. You know, they've discovered that inbreeding causes birth defects."

"Your speech amazes me." He stood when his feet touched the bottom. It was like watching a Russian god emerge from the depths. The water stopped just above his pelvic bone. His well-defined abs and oblique muscles glistened in the sun. "I have desires, and need a wife."

I bet you do. He definitely had been trapped in the Somnium for far too long. I sucked in a breath and turned my back. "I'm too young to marry."

"How old are you?"

"Sixteen."

"It's a perfect age to marry."

"Probably back in your time, but not in mine. How old are you?"

"I am in my twentieth year," he said. "I'd make a good husband. I have experience. I was married before I fell through the trap. She gave me a son."

"You were *married* and a father? Oh, this just gets better."

His eyes were stuck on my chest, so I wrapped my arms around me to cover my bra.

"I am certain they are dead now," he said. "I realized it when Gian told me the year he left behind."

"I'm sorry for your loss," I said. "It's late. We should return to the cave. Go ahead and get out. I'll wait until you leave."

"I would never harm you, Gianna. But we should discuss my proposal later."

"There's nothing to discuss. I'm promised to another."

"You heard her." Bastien stood at the side of the pond, holding my trench coat. "She's betrothed."

"Are you betrothed to him?" Royston sized Bastien up.

"*Yes*," I said a bit too eagerly.

"I have more to offer than him. I am from royal blood."

"Um, so is he," I said. "Bastien's next in line to be High Wizard of Couve."

Royston trudged out of the water, and I caught a glimpse of his bare ass as he slipped into his pants. That ass could win contests.

The two of them were so incredibly hot standing beside each other, I wished I had my camera phone to take a picture and send to Afton. Royston's eyes were still on me like a hungry wildcat.

Bastien ignited an electric ball on his palm, expanded his chest, and took a step toward Royston. "Don't look at her. If you go near her again, I'll fry you."

The blue light illuminated Royston's face, but he showed no emotion. "My apologizes. I did not know she belonged to you." He bowed his head before disappearing through the crevice.

I paddled over to the shallow end, ran to Bastien, and snatched my trench coat from his hand. "Thank you," I said, shivering. I wrapped the coat around me like a blanket. "And thanks for rescuing me from that Neanderthal."

"What were you doing with him?" There was anger in his eyes.

"I was here first and he just showed up." I pulled the trench tight around me. "Are you mad?"

"Not at you," he said. "At him. I'm sure you could've handled yourself."

"Well, I was in a vulnerable position. I didn't have my sword."

"Well, he definitely had his." He laughed, sparks igniting in his eyes.

"Not funny."

His face went serious. "Gia…"

"What?"

He stepped closer to me, lifted my chin toward his lips, and kissed me. The trench coat slipped from my grasp and tumbled to the ground. He pressed my half-naked body hard against his taut frame. My heart thundered in my chest when he parted my lips with his tongue. The warmth of his mouth tasted like berries.

"You ate my berries," I protested around his tongue.

"Hush," he said against my lips. "I've waited a long time for this."

I wrapped my arms around his neck and kissed him back. Every nip, suck, and kiss, gentle and full of passion. It felt good to let go. To forget. Forget where we were. Forget the dangers. Forget Arik's rejection.

Bastien stopped and studied my face. "I want you fully. Without Arik in your heart."

"He's no longer there."

And he believed me. His mouth found mine again. His hands ran over my curves. His kiss faded all the memories of me watching Arik with Emily, them making out in the halls before classes. All the pain. All the tears I cried at night. Bastien wanted me.

Snow fell from the sky and a frosty breeze sped around us. Bastien stepped away from me.

"We'd better go," he said, breathless. "Get dressed."

Perfect. This place had a way of interrupting everything good. I yanked on my clothes and shoved my feet into my boots.

"I hate this moody weather." I shrugged into my trench and fastened my scabbard to my waist. "If we stay here much longer, I'll lose my mind. I swear."

Momo and Bastien's ferret let out earsplitting screeches, alarming us that those beasts were nearby.

I removed my sword from its sheath, metal crying against metal. "Where are they?"

"I can't see them," Bastien said, studying the cliffs. "Hold on, there they are, on the ledge."

I looked where Bastien's eyes were set. At the top of the cliff, three beasts paced, staring at us. "They can't get down from that height, right?"

"Who knows what they can do."

"Well, don't just stand there." I bolted for the passage through the cliffs.

I sidestepped through the opening until reaching the end of the crevice and peered out. Nothing moved around the foothills. Momo darted out, and then the other ferret followed.

I eased out of the opening, my sword readied, glancing around as I climbed down the foothills in the direction of the cave. Our boots clunked over the rocks.

Something dropped to the ground behind us. I reeled around. A saber-toothed beast stalked forward, its eyes narrowing. Electricity sparked between Bastien's hands, and then he released it. The charge zapped the beast and knocked him back, matted fur smoking. I'd seen the wizards' electric charges hit Mystiks before. It had done more damage than what it just did to that beast. It was back on its feet quick and the zap had only succeeded in pissing it off.

What the hell? That should've killed it.

A few of its friends decided to join the fun.

"That worked out nicely," I said sarcastically, securing my footing.

Bastien picked up a rock. "Get back."

"No. You get back." I held my sword tight in one hand and ignited my battle globe in the other one.

"*Gia!*"

I ignored him.

One of the animal's weight shifted to his back legs as it readied to spring. I tossed the globe at the same time it lunged. A pink membrane engulfed the animal. It crashed to the ground and rolled down the foothill. The globe busted against a rock, crushing the beast's skull.

Bastien tossed a fireball, and it caught the brush between the creatures and us on fire. With them contained behind the wall of fire, we scrambled down the rocks. Stealing quick glances over my shoulder, I hoped the beasts would stay contained. A brave one jumped through the flames and charged after us. Bastien tripped over a rock and nose-dived down the hill.

My heart raced, fast and furious. I centered myself as I waited for the attack. Snow blew across the rocks, and the wind slapped my face. The freeze was coming. I focused on the creature, watching its legs, waiting for a sign of which direction it would come at me. The creature hinted right, and I adjusted my stance.

The thing propelled itself off a rock. When it was within range, I lunged forward, my sword sinking into its stomach. It crashed to the ground and slid across the rocks, knocking me onto my back. Momo ran anxiously around as if she could help me up. I hustled to my feet. Bastien struggled to stand, his face scratched and bleeding.

Three of the beasts came at us from different angles. I lobbed a series of globes at them, but one dodged the pink barriers and reached me before I could get another globe ignited. I spun, just barely dodging its claws. It came at me again, but Royston charged the beast, stabbing it several times with a long dagger. The beast yanked away and scampered off, kicking pebbles into the air that pelted my face.

"Shit." I swiped the dirt from my eyes.

Sprawled across the ground, Royston stared up at me, a look of amusement on his face.

"Get up." I shouted at him, peeved that he would risk his life like that. If he died, there would be no hope for the worlds. "You could've been killed. What were you thinking?"

Electric lights blasted the other two beasts from different directions. Bastien's came from behind me, and Gian's came from the side. The beasts careened down a footpath, yelping and howling, their fur sparking and smoking.

A sheet of wet snow surged across us, the icy wind racing over the land. I lifted Momo, tucked her into the front of my trench coat, and fought the blizzard with the others. The frigid conditions stung my exposed skin, and I was on the verge of hypothermia. I never thought I'd love a cave as much as when we made it into its shelter.

We thawed in front of the fire, not a single word spoken between us. I looked sidelong at Royston. I couldn't imagine living like this for centuries or even seventy-five years. Fighting to live for a few hours of warmth each day. I vacillated between disbelief that this guy could save our worlds to believing he was the only one who could. How could it not be him? He'd survived so much. He was strong and fierce. No wonder he was a little bit odd. I felt my sanity slipping just the short time I had been in this godforsaken place.

Momo moved inside my jacket, so I took her out and put her on the ground. My thoughts spun out of control. This had to be some kind of mix-up. Someone had to have read that stupid prophecy wrong. There was no way I could protect Royston. He didn't need my protection. I figured the only way I could help him would be to teach him about the worlds he'd left behind so many centuries ago. Things were way different now from anything he knew or could ever imagine.

"Now then, how about we warm up with some tea." Gian broke the silence, going for his clay pot.

Royston crossed his arms. "The beasts are getting braver. I have never seen them venture such a distance from their dens. They've never come into the cliffs before."

Gian looked up from his tea preparations. "Those were my thoughts, as well."

A howl sounded outside, and I flinched.

Royston perked up. "They're still out in this weather?"

"I fear they're evolving," Gian said. "They're acclimating to the extreme weather. It happened when I arrived, and it has now increased with Bastien's presence here. The world changes when our magic enters it. We must get out of here. We can't fail the next jump."

"We won't," Bastien said.

CHAPTER TWENTY-SIX

The sun thawed hours of cold from my body. It had been three weeks since we entered the Somnium. I never appreciated the sun so much as I did now. My head rested on Bastien's abs as we lay basking in the sun on a large boulder outside the cave. Momo curled up to my side. There were no chores today. We waited for nightfall to trek to the trapdoor. Supposedly, the silver lights would show tonight.

Being there was like being on a bad vacation that never ended. If it weren't for Bastien, I totally would've lost it. I rolled over and faced him. At my movement, Momo darted down the boulder after one of the other ferrets.

"Have I ever told you how handsome you are with a scruffy beard," I purred.

He rubbed his chin. "No, just how much it scratches you when we kiss."

I reached up and pulled my fingers through his long hair. "You should keep your hair longer; it really is hot."

"You're on the frisky side this morning."

"I'm just happy we'll be home soon."

He slipped his hands under my arms and pulled me up to sit on his lap. "I'm not too sure I'm as happy as you are." His mouth found mine and he gave me a passionate kiss before pulling back. "I kind of like having your full attention."

I sighed. "Well, don't you miss your mother?"

"I do, very much so, but…"

I knew what was weighing on his mind. He worried that when I saw Arik, I wouldn't want him any longer.

Arik was a distant memory now.

Bastien's strength was my security. We took care of each other. Fighting off beasts. Foraging for food. He wouldn't let go of me when I was falling through the trap. When he knew he couldn't pull me out, he had jumped in with me. That kind of sacrifice meant a lot. And I would never let him go.

Bastien caressed my cheek with his strong hand. "When that look is on your face and your lip shudders like that, I know something is weighing on your mind. What is it?"

I love everything about you. Your blue eyes looking at me with concern. Your dark hair falling over your forehead.

I turned my head and kissed his hand. "It's nothing, just worried about tonight, aren't you?"

He pressed his lips against my temple. "Whatever we face, we won't give up. I'll be right next to you. Besides, you are quite fierce with a sword. There's nothing more attractive than a girl who can decapitate a beast."

I laughed. "So you like the violent type."

He quirked a mischievous grin. "There's nothing better."

Gian came out of the cave and gave us a stern look. I scrambled off Bastien's lap and fidgeted with my hands. My great-grandfather didn't like public displays of affection. Even if we weren't exactly in public.

"Good morning," Bastien said all chill-like. Though he didn't act entitled, he did have an air about him that said he was royal. Gian's disdainful attitude never bothered him.

"Let's hope it remains that way," grumbled Gian. "Gia, may I have a moment?"

I gave Bastien a confused look.

He shrugged.

"Certainly," I said, and slid down the side of the bolder and followed him. "You're going kind of far from the cave, aren't you?" I teased. He'd forbidden any of us from going past the boulders surrounding it after one of the beasts had snatched a goat from the entrance two days ago.

"Here will do." He stopped abruptly, catching me off guard and causing me to take a few steps ahead of him.

I turned to face him. "So why all the secrecy?"

"You are special, Gianna. You've handled yourself well in the face of adversity. I know I don't always show my emotions."

Like never.

He shot me a glance and I wondered if he could do that mind thing Uncle Philip could.

"Yes, I too am as intuitive as this professor you think of, except I might look like I'm in my fifties, but—"

More like sixty.

My thought must've interrupted him, because he laughed, which I've never seen him do the entire time we've been here. It looked good on him.

"How we view ourselves does not always agree with how others see us," he said. "Does it? I'm a few hundred years old, so my intuitive skills are more enhanced. Your young Romeo has the skill, as well."

"Bastien? He *knows* what I'm thinking?" I peeked over my shoulder at Bastien kicking back on the rock as he watched us intently.

"He feels things, but isn't sure what they are. He's young, not even a senior wizard yet."

"So you can hear all my thoughts?"

"When I choose to listen."

My cheeks warmed. *Shit. Did he read my thoughts about Bastien?*

"Those are thoughts I choose to ignore." He chuckled, a deep guttural sound. "I will say, though, suppressed feelings are never fully buried. They are merely seeds planted deep in the soil of denial that will sprout when the truth nourishes it."

I tried to keep my thoughts blank, but I knew he was referring to Arik. But he was wrong. I was over him.

I sighed. "You didn't drag me out here to talk about my love life, did you?"

"No. I wanted to tell you how proud I am of you." He slanted his eyes at me and smiled. "I wish I had known your mother. Her mother, my daughter, Rosetta, was a toddler when I disappeared. My first girl. I truly loved my second wife. You look very much like her, Gianna."

"You were married before her?"

"Yes. Terrible woman, that one. It was an arranged marriage. We never had any children. She passed away young, and I was free to follow my heart and marry Constance. She gave me a beautiful girl. What became of my daughter?"

I couldn't tell him my grandmother and mother were both dead, but apparently, my silence said more than words.

"I see. There will be time to talk of such things when we are free of this place." He lowered his head. "I am thankful, I have you. I hope in time we will grow closer. Forgive me for my oddity. I once was a jovial man. I've been in this place too long, I'm not sure how..." he trailed off, looking across the valley.

The freeze was moving in. I wrapped my arms around my chest to ward off the chill.

"I would like to learn more about my great-grandson."

"Nick? What do you want to know?"

"His powers. Has he mastered them, yet?"

"His powers were suppressed until recently," I said.

He twisted the end of his beard between his fingers. "I see. How about his temperament? Is it controlled?"

I cut him a curious eye, wondering where he was heading with that. "He hasn't been the same ever since he discovered Conemar was his father and the curers released his magic. He gets angry easily."

"Keep a watch on him. I'm aware you care for him, but don't trust him. He could turn on you."

"He won't."

"Heed my warning," he said. "Conemar is devious. Stay alert and don't let your guard down around Nick."

"Okay, but he won't."

"That isn't why I brought you out here. I wanted to talk about tonight." He heaved a deep sigh. "No matter what happens, you must get Royston through the trapdoor. For everyone you love in the worlds, you must get Royston to safety, even if it costs you losing Bastien—or me."

I swallowed hard. "I can't—I won't leave you guys behind."

"It is your destiny to protect the one. To protect Royston. If you fail, many will die. A split second decision could cost you more than what you'd lose in that one choice."

I nodded, tears forming in my eyes. But if it came down to that, I wasn't sure I could do it. Leave them to this world. Leave Bastien?

And in that moment, between anxious thoughts of Bastien lost forever, I knew my feelings. I was falling for him, and I would do anything to save him.

"When Bastien and I open the door," Gian continued, "you jump with Royston. It may only open for seconds, and not all of us will make it through. You are not to look back."

"Why can't Royston help? Isn't he a wizard?"

"Royston's mother was an enchantress. After her father betrayed her, she placed a curse on her haven, Esteril. Every wizard thereafter was born without powers. She never realized it would affect her own child. Royston is her son. He was born without magic."

"Wait. Do you mean Athela?"

"You've read of her?"

"Actually, she's haunted my dreams." A blast of brisk air raced across the valley and hit me, blowing tea-colored strands wildly around my face. I pulled the tie off my wrist and tied up my hair. "Her father was a real narcissist. He used deceased warriors to create the Tetrad."

His startled glare surprised me. "Are you certain?"

"I'm not certain about anything. It's a dream I had. Uncle Philip said it was from a spirit seer or something. It felt like I was actually Athela."

"Athela was a powerful enchantress. Some said she had the gift of the Seers." He slanted his eyes at me. "Her spirit found you. Most likely to show you truths."

The wind slapped my face and I sucked in a startled breath. "That means Barnum is Royston's father. Oh my God, that's awful."

"Why is that bad?" he asked.

"One of the warriors used to create the Tetrad was Barnum. That's why Athela cursed her father and his haven. I wonder if Athela ever told Royston about his father's fate."

"If so, he's never mentioned it to me. She must've wanted you to know this for a reason."

"Royston has to kill his father. Athela had a painting of Barnum with her when she fled her haven. Royston grew up knowing his father's face."

Royston's words from one of my dreams rang in my ears.

I cannot suffer this. Remove this cross from me.

"She prepared Royston to sacrifice himself to destroy the Tetrad."

Gian surveyed the sky. A cloud just above his head was a crescent shape. "You must find a way to save him."

Our brands. Royston's and mine. Athela showed me her writing in a journal while picnicking with Royston and her maid. *Nana's ancient charm book must've belonged to Athela. She wanted me to have it. There must be clues in it.*

"We should go inside, and you can tell me more about the dreams while we wait for the sun to set." He headed back to the cave.

Tell him more? He read my thoughts again.

I stayed behind for a brief moment, thinking about Royston and our joined fates, and the possibility of having to leave Bastien behind.

There's no way. We're all getting out. I can't live knowing Bastien is here in this hell without me. He wouldn't be here if it wasn't for me.

Bastien came up from behind and wrapped his arms around me. "Hey, *mon amour*, what are you doing?" I rested my chin on his arms. "It's time to go inside."

"You know, I care about you," I whispered, needing to tell him in case these were our last hours together. It might have been love, but I wasn't sure. I loved many people—all in different ways—Pop, Nana, Afton, Nick, Uncle Philip, and even Arik. I just didn't know where Bastien fit in the spectrum of it.

"I feel the same about you." A deep sigh expanded his chest against my back. "Care to share what Gian told you?"

I twisted around to face him. "We just discussed the jump. He wanted me to make sure to help Royston. He said it's my destiny to protect him."

"Whatever happens, we'll survive it." He kissed my forehead. "Follow Gian's instructions."

I just nodded, staring at Momo and the other ferrets darting in and out of the crevices between the rocks. I hoped he was right.

Before we started out for the lights, Royston let the goats loose. It saddened me to think what might become of them. We couldn't leave them tied up in the cave or they would die. Out in the wild, they most likely would become a meal for the beasts. As soon as Royston had untied them and shooed them down the hill, the goats moseyed back to the cave.

I clopped across the snow in Royston's handcrafted snowshoes. The guy had talent. He could whittle or tie sticks together to make all sorts of useful things. My bones felt tight against the cold. The blue lights of the trapdoor flickered just above the hills. It reminded me of the Northern lights I'd seen in a geography video Mrs. Anderson had played for our class.

The ferrets darted around us, Momo sticking close to me. I wondered what would happen to her, my heart imploding at the thought of leaving her behind. My thigh muscles strained with each heavy step forward. The darkness grew bright and a blue hue danced over the white snow as we approached the lights.

Gian halted directly under the lights and right in front of where they touched the snow. For being old, the man could really move. Struggling to survive each day did build muscles. My biceps were fierce and my thighs more defined from all the laborious work. It was good cardio, too, since we had to complete all chores within the few hours of warmth each day.

The blue lights flickered and began to turn silver.

"It's happening!" Gian yelled over the yowling wind. "Remove your snow shoes!"

I struggled against the force spinning around me. It felt like weights were on my arms. I finally got the contraptions off my feet and treaded through the snow to the others.

"Bastien," Gian hollered over the howling wind. "Instead of us hitting a force of energy in the middle, aim it at that side"—he pointed it out—"and I'll blast it from the other side. Gianna, stay with Royston in the middle. When the trap opens, you'll feel a pull much as you feel with the gateway books. Jump with the feeling and the energy will take you up. And don't turn back." He looked sternly at me. "You hear me? Whatever happens, don't turn back."

I nodded and tramped over to the lights with Royston. Momo scurried after me and jumped at my legs. I bent and picked her up, then tucked her into my jacket. How could I leave her behind? She had watched over me. It was the least I could do to pay her back. Besides, I sort of loved the little thing.

Bastien and Gian's electric charges hit the side of the lights, an image flickering in and out with each blast. I could barely make out the library on the other side. The next impact tore a hole in the lights and the library was right there.

An intense energy pulled at me. "Now!" I yelled over the howling wind, gripping Royston's arm tight. We jumped and flew through the door, hitting hard against the marble floor and then rolling until we collided into a display case.

I scrambled to my feet and slipped across the floor to the trap. The roars of many beasts came from the other side of the door. Bastien and Gian battled the deep snow, the beasts coming at them from all sides. The trap flickered.

"NO!" I screamed, as if I could stop it from closing.

Royston slid to my side. "We have to help them. Those animals will maul them."

I didn't have time to think. My battle globe formed on my palm and I tossed it at the door. A pink membrane bathed the opening. A blast of light boomed across the library, rattling the bookcases and pushing display cases across the tiles. The floor shook violently and the windows exploded.

Royston and I huddled together, covering our heads from the shattered glass spraying across the reading room. I fell backward, my arms and legs shaking out of control.

Bastien and Gian jumped into the library, a beast on their heels.

CHAPTER TWENTY-SEVEN

"Close the trap!" Bastien yelled.

"Why isn't it closing?" I threw another globe, knocking the beast back but not closing the door.

Two other creatures jumped into the library. Bastien zapped one with his charge. The other one tackled Gian. Royston jumped on its back, barely avoiding a long, sharp tooth. He pulled a dagger from the waistband of his pants and stabbed the animal in its side.

"Bastien, block the trap," Gian panted, holding tight to the beast's saber-teeth, straining to keep it from chomping down on him. "Conjure an electric cage."

Bastien kindled a charge between his hands and casted it out like a net at the trapdoor. An energy screen covered the gap. Royston stabbed the beast again, and the animal collapsed on top of Gian. He pushed it off him and it flopped onto the floor.

Bastien ran his fingers through his hair, surveying the damaged library. "For going utterly wrong, this actually worked out." He spotted me trembling on the floor, darted over, and dropped to his knees beside me. "What's wrong with her?" He looked to Gian for an answer.

"I'm not certain." Gian stared down at me, his bushy brows pushed together as he studied me. "That was a very powerful surge of energy. Her globe must've removed the trap door's charm."

"Please m-m-make this stop," I forced out. It was difficult to speak with the tremors quaking my body.

"We must get her to a curer," Gian said.

Bastien touched my cheek. "I'm going to pick you up, all right?"

I nodded, wrapping my arms around his neck. He lifted me into his arms.

"Gian, the gateway book is in that bookcase over there." Bastien nodded toward it.

I leaned my head against Bastien's chest and closed my eyes. His clothes smelled of smoke and outdoors, the beat of his heart soothing me as he carried me through the gateway.

The curers' chamber in Asile reminded me of an old Frankenstein laboratory. Beakers and bottles lined the shelves, stacks of heavy leather-bound books stood in tall piles on the tables, and several bubbling pots rattled on top of an old stove. The aroma swirling around the room smelled of sulfur and rubbing alcohol.

I sat up against the pillows and stretched my arms out. The uncontrolable shaking had stopped. I was in a glassed-off room with two hospital beds. One window let in bright light. Everything in the glass room was white and clean, and everything outside was brown and worn.

An older woman, hunching over one of the tables, looked

up. "Ah, you're awake." She hobbled over using a knobby cane to keep herself upright. "The boy will be delighted. He's stopped by so many times to check on you."

Bastien. I smiled.

"How long have I been here?"

"Just barely two days now." She smiled wide, her teeth crooked and yellowed. "You must be thirsty, dear. Something to eat would do you well, eh?"

"Yes, please," I said. "I'm starving."

"I won't be a moment," she said, and hobbled away. The door opened before she reached it. "Ah, we speak of the boy and he appears. The girl is awake. Looks mighty fine, she does."

I almost fell off the side of the bed. Standing in the doorframe wasn't Bastien but Arik. I didn't know what to say. He'd been the last person I'd expected to be "the boy."

He walked cautiously over to the glass room. "You do look well. Everyone's been worried about you. I should have never given Nick a window rod. He's been ringing constantly for updates on you."

Nick. I wanted desperately to see him.

I choked back my emotions. "Where...where are the others?"

"May I?" He indicated that he wanted to sit on the foot of my bed.

I nodded.

"Bastien was summoned to Couve. Gian and Royston are here being treated for small ailments they acquired while in the Somnium. Royston had an abscessed tooth and bunions. Gian had lice. They were taken in secret to a curer outside of the havens to protect them."

"What month is it?" I asked.

"It's the fourteenth of March."

"It feels like I've been gone for an eternity." I scratched at my scalp.

He quirked a smile. "You have no lice."

"Thank God." I sighed. "And Momo?"

He gave me a confused look.

"The ferret I had with me?"

An enlightened look crossed his face. "Oh yes. Royston is caring for the creature."

"So they're all safe, right?"

"Yes, they're being well cared for." He smiled. "Your father and the others will be happy to have you back. I'll take you home in a few days."

There was something different about him, but I couldn't place what it was. Maybe it was me who was different. I didn't have that gut-clenching feeling I used to have around him.

"I can't wait," I finally said. "Is everyone okay there?"

"Everyone is fine. They're relieved to have you back. We thought—" He cleared his throat. "I can't stay long. I have to get back to the human world. When you used your globe on the trapdoor, it released all the charms on the traps, leaving them all opened. We've closed them and captured most of the creatures. But we're having a difficult time locating all the prisoners that escaped."

I covered my mouth with my hands. "Oh no, did they hurt anyone?"

Sadness shadowed his face. "Unfortunately, there were some casualties."

"It's my fault. People died because of me." I sobbed into my hands. "I should've listened to Gian. I didn't listen."

Arik scooted closer to me and rested his hand on my shoulder. His touch startled me, and I pulled away. "You didn't know what would happen. You saved Gian and Bastien. You brought Royston back. We have hope to defeat the Tetrad now."

I glanced up at him. "I want to help."

"You should rest."

"I'm fine," I snapped. "Don't tell me I can't. You're the same as me. You would want to make it right. So don't keep me from doing what I was born to do."

His deep brown eyes held my gaze for several beats of my heart. "All right. Yes. You should eat something, though, while I get you some gear."

"Thank you."

He made to get up but stopped. "Gia, we must talk about Emily. I didn't mean to hurt you—"

"You don't have to say anything," I cut him off. "I'm over it. I hope you and Emily will be happy together."

"About that." He reached for my hand, and I jerked it away. A hurt expression twisted on his face again before he hid it with a smile. "It can wait."

I stared at the blanket, picking off little balls of white lint. "No. I'm sorry. Go ahead and tell me."

"I wasn't myself."

I scowled at him. "Yeah, I'd say."

"Are you going to interject sarcasm after everything I say?"

"No." *Maybe.*

"I *literally* wasn't myself." He stopped and frowned at me when I rolled my eyes. "I had been spelled by a witch. Your nana discovered it. She believed my actions were unusual, and was certain it was a side effect of a love charm."

I sat up straighter, his words processing slowly in my head.

"Your nana enlisted Lei to search my body for any signs of a spell. Lei found a tattoo on the back of my neck"—he rubbed at the spot for emphasis—"hidden in my hairline. It was a love charm. Your nana removed it."

"Emily is a witch, then?"

"Yes. Your nana found her name in the Witch Registry."

He was still rubbing at his neck.

"How did she tattoo you without you knowing it?"

"Your nana believes Emily drugged me first."

I stared blankly at him.

He scooted across the bed and slipped his arms around me. "Oh, Gia, I was quite certain I'd lost you forever. I was a complete madman, agonizing over the thought of what dangers you faced."

He kissed my head, his warm breath sending shivers across my skin. A hollow feeling settled in my stomach, and I swallowed the lump forming in the back of my throat.

His words were like daggers of betrayal cutting my heart into pieces. Images of Arik and Emily together flipped sporadically through my mind. How could Emily have done this to us? I wasn't sure what to think. Or worse, how to feel.

"The last memory I had was of you at practice," he whispered into my hair. "You were so angry. I tried to run after you, but my feet wouldn't move. I wanted to tell you something wasn't right, but I knew not what it was. I had this intense desire to be with Emily. To do whatever she asked. It made my insides feel rotted and decayed, like a death eating me from the inside out."

"I will kill…," I muttered so quietly I was surprised he could hear me.

"She's been punished and repented. We should feel sorry for her—"

"She repented?" I leaned away from him and glared. "To who? To you? She ruined my life. I will *never* forgive her. What loser does something like that? And I will *never* feel sorry for her."

"Gia, she hasn't ruined your life. We're here together now." He rested his palm on my cheek, and I shook my head against it, tears slipping from my eyes and landing on his arm.

"Arik, I have something to tell you—"

The door banged against the wall, and the curer plodded in, carrying a tray heavy with meats, fruit, and cheeses. The jug on the corner of the tray almost toppled over with each of her uneven steps.

"The cook must think you need to make up for lost time," she said. "As though you could eat a month's worth of food in one sitting, no matter what I say. Told him it was too much."

Arik pressed his lips against mine and kissed me quickly. "Whatever is troubling you can wait. You should rest. I'll return shortly with some clothes." He bounced up and squeezed past the curer at the door. "Isn't it a lovely day, Morta?"

"Lovely?" she crowed. "There's a war going on. Did you get your head clobbered? Shall I check it?"

Arik turned before leaving. "Ah, even in the bleakest times, love shines light." He bowed then ducked out the door.

My heart thudded to my stomach. I should have told him about Bastien and me.

I'm not one to starve even when things weighed on my mind. I was a stress eater. I dug into the food on the tray, shoving bite after bite into my mouth. After only consuming beast jerky and strange berries and fruits for the past month, bread and cheese tasted sinful.

I decided to tell Arik about Bastien when he brought my gear. The sooner he knew the better. Dread settled over me, rumbling the food around in my stomach. I leaned back against the pillows, trying to figure out what I would say to him. Would he forgive me? After all, it was Emily who tore us apart.

The door opened across the room. I set the food tray on the nightstand and smoothed my hair down.

"What's this?" the curer asked.

"Delivery for the patient, ducky." Lei continued across the curer's area without stopping.

"She can't leave yet. She's not strong enough."

"I'm just following orders from higher powers than you." Lei reached my room, carrying a pile of clothes, boots, and a scabbard.

I slumped. "Where's Arik?"

"Something came up. He's organizing the Sentinels. He asked that I bring you these." She placed the pile on the bed beside me. "How are you feeling?"

"I'm good, thanks."

"Glad to have you back," she said, her lips twisting slightly at the corners. "I'll wait outside while you put those on."

My muscles were like petrified wood, every movement I made stiff and painful. I shucked off my nightgown and slipped into the black leather outfit. The boots were a little snug, but they'd do. I eased out of the windowed room and crossed the laboratory-like room.

"Thanks, um…?" I searched my memory for the curer's name. "Morta."

"You should rest," she grumbled under her breath, not looking up as she mixed something in a big pot. "If you must go, don't use your battle globe. It's out of whack or something. No telling what it will do." She dipped a ladle into the pot and poured the liquid into a metal vial. "Here." She handed the vial to me. "If you feel weak, sip this. Just a sip, mind you, it's powerful."

"Okay," I said, examining the thick blue liquid before slipping the vial into the breast pocket of my jacket.

She held a tin shot glass out to me. "Drink this. It's just more of the same. It'll get you going."

I took it, drank the liquid down, and grimaced at the bitter taste. "Thank you for taking care of me."

"It was my honor."

I strapped on my scabbard and trudged into the hall where Lei was leaning against the wall, waiting.

"I didn't think grandma would let you out to play." She laughed and led the way down the hall.

"Where are we going?"

"The libraries," she said over her shoulder. "We've captured the creatures from the Somnium, but we're still tracking down the Mystik prisoners. We have some recorded disturbances in the gateways. We'll follow all the leads. Kick some naughty Mystik bums, and return them to their rightful hells."

"Nice way to put it."

As we passed the education corridor, I thought of Uncle Philip. "Do you mind if I stop by Professor Attwood's office?"

"He's not in. There's a Wizard Council meeting in Couve today. He did check in on you, but you were asleep."

"How do you know that?"

"I was there reading."

"Really, you don't say?" my voice sounded as surprised as I was. "Aww, you care."

"I was on duty," she said, rounding a corner. "Did Arik tell you what that beastly little neighbor girl did to him?"

"Yes, he did." I watched my feet, not wanting her to see the confusion on my face. What was I going to do? I sucked in a breath, my ribs protesting.

She glanced back at me. "You all right?"

"Yeah, just hurts to breathe."

When we arrived at the Bodleian Library, Arik was in a huddle with Demos, Kale, Jaran, and a few Sentinels I didn't recognize. They all had their battle gear and helmets on. I clutched my helmet and the strap attached to my shield tight. The metal banged together, alerting the group that I was there. A grin split Arik's face, and he took long strides crossing the room to me.

When he reached me, he wrapped an arm around me and pulled me against him. His lips found mine and he gave me a passionate kiss.

"Don't mind us," Demos said. "Public displays of affection aren't at all awkward."

I yanked away from Arik. "Please don't."

His eyebrows scrunched together, a puzzled look on his face. "What's the matter?"

"Listen, Arik, we have to talk."

"Okay, I'm listening."

I glanced at Lei, then Demos, and then the others. "Somewhere private."

The gateway book rattled on the table and everyone's eyes shot to it. Bastien jumped out of the book, followed by the French Sentinels. He landed on the floor and surveyed the group around him before he discovered me in the crowd.

"Why aren't you in bed?" Bastien bounded over to me and encircled me in his arms. "I've missed you. I'm sorry I wasn't there when you woke." He kissed my forehead. "I only escorted my Sentinels in order to see you."

"What's going on here?" Arik snapped.

I untangled myself from Bastien's arms. He kept a hold of my hand.

"You didn't give me the chance to tell you." It felt like I was under a spotlight. Lei frowned at me. Demos, Kale, and Jaran's eyes bounced from me to Arik to Bastien.

"Wait a minute," Demos said. "You two are together?"

"Which two?" Kale said. "I'm confused."

"Gia?" Arik took a step toward me.

I met Bastien's gaze. His blue eyes worried around the corners. "This is only about you, Gianna," he said. "About your feelings and what you want."

I nodded and willed the threatening tears away.

"I have to return to Couve," Bastien said to Arik. "I'll leave my Sentinels to aid you."

I squeezed Bastien's hand as a silent reassurance for him. He gently touched my cheek and gave me a warm smile before he jumped into the gateway book.

"Arik, can we have a moment alone?" I walked down the row of bookcases, heading for a smaller reading room. The sound of Arik's boots clapping against the floor followed me.

Once inside, I spun around to face him. "I tried to tell you, but—"

"But I wouldn't let you," he finished for me. "You and Bastien?"

"You were with Emily. It tore me to pieces. Bastien and I got close in the Somnium. I thought we'd never return."

"Are you in love with him?"

Tears pricked at the corner of my eyes. I did love Bastien, but my heart was aching for Arik, too. I stared at him, tears tumbling down my cheeks, unable to answer him. Afraid to answer him.

"You love me. A love like ours doesn't end. *Admit it*," he said it with so much emotion it broke me and I wanted to crumble to the floor.

"Arik—" my voice cracked over his name.

Arik ran his fingers through his hair and studied me, tears glossing his eyes. "Oh, Gia. You do love him."

I took a step closer to him. "I'm so sorry."

A sad smile hinted on his lips. "I am, too. It's not your fault. You weren't aware of Emily's devious deed. I was told how difficult it was for you to watch her and me together. But you must know it wasn't my fault. I had no control over it."

A sob left my throat. "It was a living nightmare. I don't

know what to do, but I have to give him a chance."

"I hate to see you torn." He hugged me and I rested my cheek against his chest. "Though this breaks my heart, I'll step aside. For now. Bastien is an upstanding bloke, but he's not the one you're meant to be with. You'll see. Our hearts are intertwined. We belong together."

"I'm so confused." I sniffed.

He petted my hair. "Follow your heart, Gia. It will lead you where you belong."

It was like déjà vu. Bastien had said the same thing. I couldn't hurt him. We had survived so much together. "I have to see this through. I owe him that."

"Just know that you own my heart and it will not falter again." He backed away and turned his back to me. "We have a difficult undertaking ahead of us." He swiped his sleeve across his face. "Are you certain you're up to it?"

"I've faced worse."

"No one is certain what came out of the Somnium. You may discover a new worse." He started for the other room and turned back. "And whatever you decide, I won't blame you. I love you, Gia." He walked away.

I sucked in a sharp breath, unable to breathe as I watched Arik's strong figure disappear into the shadows of the tall bookcases. I could've sworn I heard my heart crack in two as I sobbed into my hands.

CHAPTER TWENTY-EIGHT

Books, papers, and plaster littered the floors of the New York Public Library. The long rows of tables lay on their sides, lamps crushed under their weight. Arik slid his sword out of his scabbard. I did the same with mine and held it out in front of me. Sweat slicked my palm, making it hard to hold on to my shield. Whoever's helmet I wore didn't fit me. The eagle head rocked and pressed against my nose with every movement.

"What came through here?" Kale stepped over a broken chair, the blades in his gloves fully extended, the silver visor of his helmet shading his face.

"One of those beasts from the Somnium," Arik answered, peering at me through the eyeholes of his helmet. With each tilt of his head, the wings on the side glinted against what little light emitted from dimmers surrounding the room. "We killed it over there."

My eyes went to the spot. The dried blood still stained the floor. "Why haven't the Cleaners been here?"

"There aren't enough of them to clean up all the attacks,"

Arik said. "They've abandoned the effort. News reports have already covered the mayhem. The Cleaners are just disposing of all evidence of the creatures. Our leaders spread a rumor over social media to the humans that the attacks are from a terrorist group, and they've urged people to stay inside."

We moved down an open row between the desks, circling to make sure each direction was clear.

"It went viral?"

"Yeah," Kale said. "We're using fear tactics to keep people away from the libraries we haven't gained control over. The thing is we haven't found many escaped prisoners. It's as if they all vanished. Possibly hiding somewhere. Some say they were eaten by the beasts. When you blew the traps, most of the Monitors died. There were so many jumps when the incident happened, they tangled together and couldn't be read."

My gut knotted. "Pip?"

"He survived," Arik said.

I frowned. It just kept getting better. Now I was responsible for killing Monitors. "So what are we doing here?" I said.

"Pip picked up a prisoner's jump into this library nearly fifteen minutes ago." Arik inched forward, moving his head left to right, readied for an attack.

"How do they know it was a prisoner?" I said.

Arik stopped. "Before incarceration into the Somnium, a chip is implanted that tells the Monitors they're prisoners."

Something chimed above our heads. A man wearing a tan trench coat, water goggles, and heavy boots, with yellow skin and small leathery wings, balanced on one of the large chandeliers. He had an arm wrapped around the chains holding the light fixture to the ceiling.

"What is *that*?" I practically spit out.

"It's a Malailes," Kale said. "They're extinct. We've found many escaped species that were believed extinct."

"All right, enough with the history lesson." Arik aimed his sword at the thing, which totally pissed the creature off. The Malailes dove off the chandelier and flew around the room.

"Kale, go left," Arik barked. "Gia, right." He rushed down the middle row, chasing after the creature.

I found a gap on the right side of the desks and dashed down it, hurtling chairs and other items out of my way as I went. At the end, I squeezed through a double door that had been left ajar. It led to a small gift shop, with displays and a counter off to the side. Directly in front of me, the Malailes was perched on a balcony railing.

"*Et nolo pati ut noceret*," the creature's voice grated against my bones.

"Sorry, no *comprende*, dude," I said and crept closer. "Come on. If you come quietly, I won't hurt you."

His bloody, beady eyes watched me intently. "*Alium gressum… et occurret vobis cultro.*"

"*Gesundheit.*" I took another step. *What the hell is he saying? Is that Latin?*

He swooped down, tackling me to the floor and then straddling me. My sword flew from my hand. *Gia, don't harm him,* Athela's voice sounded in my head. *He is a friend. His name is Cadby. Royston's guard.*

What the hell? How are you in my head? Out here?

I'm not certain. Her thoughts were soft, as if she was miles away. *I think it happened when you tossed your globe at that trap.*

Sure, I thought. *That makes so much sense.*

Tell him ego sum protector, *and he knows English, the flying rat.*

Cadby looked at me curiously before wrapping his thick hands around my throat.

"*Ego sum protector*," I choked out, grabbing his hands and trying to pull them away from my neck. "Cadby, *ego protector!*"

His grip loosened.

"Yeah, that's right. And I know you can speak English. Athela told me."

"Athela told you?" His voice was so deep it was scary.

"Yes. Her spirit is speaking to me."

Cadby straightened to his knees. "You say you are the protector?"

"Yes, I am."

He stood and offered me his leathered yellow hand. I ignored it and pushed myself up.

Tell him you found Royston.

"Okay, but will you stop talking in my head, already. It's kind of freaky."

Cadby chuckled, which sounded more like a growl. "She's persistent, isn't she?"

"That's an understatement. She wants me to tell you I found her son."

His wings fluttered. "Where? He went missing long ago."

"He was in one of the habitats of the Somnium. When I freed him, I accidentally released all the trapdoors."

Arik and Kale stormed the room with their swords outstretched.

"You're late." I moved in front of Cadby to shield him. "If he wasn't an ally, I'd have been dead before you got here."

Arik stepped cautiously forward. "How do you know he's an ally?"

"A birdie told me." I blew out an exasperated breath. "It was Athela. She said he was Royston's guard. His name is Cadby."

"We know he's his guard," Arik said. "He was imprisoned

for Royston's death."

I frowned at him. "And Royston's alive, so obviously he was framed."

Kale glanced at Arik. "She's right on that one."

"The Wizard Council must exonerate him," Arik said.

"This place confuses me." Cadby waved his arm around the library. "I keep jumping in and out of gateway books and end up in these places."

"It's the twenty-first century," Kale said. "The entries have changed."

Cadby looked confused as he digested Kale's words. "I knew it had been some time since I was sent to prison, but not so many centuries. I am happy to go to the Council. I have something to tell them."

Arik relaxed his grip on the hilt of his sword. "Why? What do you need to tell the Council?"

"There was an evil man gathering all the convicts from the Somnium prison I was in. He promises wealth and power to those who join him. He's taken those who agreed to follow him to Esteril. He had creatures with him even more terrifying than myself."

Kale turned to Arik. "It has to be Conemar."

"That is his name," Cadby said.

"Crap. This is bad." I paced. My foot kicked my sword, and I snatched it up. "We have to warn Carrig."

"There's more," Cadby said. "He is after his son, who's also a protector. A witch gave Conemar his whereabouts. A place called Branford."

I dropped my sword and it clanged against the floor. "*Shit.* Do you have any other details? Like when are they going?"

"Calm down," Arik warned.

Cadby's wings twitched on his back as he watched me. "He and his men were here. That is why I was hiding on the ceiling. They are just ahead of you."

I grabbed my sword from the floor again and stomped out of the shop, fuming.

"Where are you going?" Arik rushed after me. "Don't lose your head. Why are you always charging into situations without thinking it through first?"

"Why are you always wasting time when it's a life or death situation?" I shouted over my shoulder. I would not fail Nick. He would do the same for me.

"Gia," Kale called after me. "Stop!"

I paused and turned. "What?"

"Arik is right. We have to think this through before acting."

I looked past Kale and sharply at Arik. "Don't tell me to calm down again. I have every right to be mad. We have to hurry before he finds Nick."

"Your hotheadedness will get us all killed," Arik said. "We can't just rush into an unknown situation."

"I think we must rush into it," Cadby said. "There's no time to waste. This boy is a protector. If Conemar gets his hands on him, he will find the Chiavi."

Arik stared off, mulling something in his head.

I grew impatient watching him. "Maybe we should go like in *this* century?"

Arik ignored my sarcastic comment. "Kale, gather the other Sentinels, and we'll wait here for you."

"Wait here?" My face heated. "We have to get to Nick *now*."

Arik stopped right in front of me and stared down into my eyes. "I know you don't trust my decision on this—we've been here before—but I am your lead Sentinel. You haven't a choice but to listen to me or face an infraction."

"Oh really? Like I care if I get an infraction." I glared at him. "I'll go without you, then."

"Ugh, you are the most stubborn girl," he growled. "It hasn't crossed your mind that Conemar will track you down while he's in the neighborhood? You think he'd let you live when you could lead us to the Chiavi? Besides, Nick is hardly ever at his own home. He spends most of his time at yours, riding his motorbike, or at the beach."

"How do you know that?"

"I've spent a lot of time with him while you were gone."

He was right. I was easily disposable to Conemar, but I wasn't backing down. "We have to find Nick before Conemar does."

"Bloody hell, Gia, you will kill me one day." Arik threw his hands up. "All right, Kale, get the others and meet us at Nick's house. Send Demos and some guards to protect Royston."

I sheathed my sword. "What are we going to do with Cadby?"

"I go with you and fight," Cadby said.

I wasn't going to argue with him. When facing a possible battle, I figured having a winged nightmare on your side was always a good thing.

Kale departed for Asile, while Arik, Cadby, and I jumped into the gateway book. The cold air rushed at me, whipping my hair around my face. When I landed in the library in Branford, the book wasn't in a bookcase. It was on the floor, as if someone had used it before me. It wasn't even three p.m. yet and darkness cloaked the library. All the lights were off and the blinds shut.

Arik came out of the book behind me, followed by Cadby. The only noise in the place was our breathing and the occasional flutter of Cadby's wings.

"Is that a nervous tick or what?" I whispered over my shoulder at Cadby, eyeing his wings.

"It takes some effort to keep them still," he said.

"This is strange." I cautiously weaved in and out of the bookcases with Arik and Cadby trailing me. "The library never closes early."

"Is it an American holiday?" Arik was so close behind me I could feel his breath tickle the back of my neck.

"No," I said.

We reached the front door. Locked.

"I think we're too late." I turned the locks then paused before pushing open the door. "Are you ready to freak people out? I'm sure the good people of Branford will be thrilled to encounter a bird creature."

Cadby gave Arik a quizzical look.

"It's called sarcasm," Arik said. "No one will be thrilled to see you."

I opened the door and the alarm beeped a warning. "That's unfortunate. We don't have the code, so we should probably run." I darted down the steps. There weren't any cars or people on the streets. No movement at all. I slowed my steps.

Cadby thumped up from behind. "I will take to the sky and get a breadth of the situation." He sprinted up the street and took off into the air.

"Keep your eyes on the right," Arik said, coming up on my side. "I'll watch the left."

I caught movement in the corner of my eye. A curtain settled in place in one of the windows of an apartment building. "It's like the Rapture around here."

We trotted through the business district into neighborhoods until we found ourselves on Nick's street. The front door to his house was hanging on its hinges, glass blown out of several windows, and the yard trampled and torn.

Arik and I yanked the broken door aside and stepped

over the debris. We searched room after room for Nick and his parents. The place was vacant.

My boots crunched across the doorframe on my way to the porch. "Now what?"

"We can check the school or your house," Arik said.

Cadby swooped off the roof and alighted onto the sidewalk. "Conemar's legions surround a house to the north of here."

"My house." I flew down the steps and sprinted across the lawn, hopping over the stout white-picket fence surrounding Nick's yard. My boots pounded hard against the pavement. The fear of something bad happening to Pop, Deidre, and Faith surged me forward.

"Gia!" Arik yelled after me.

I ignored him, picking up my pace, my hand clutching the hilt of my sword. My heart beating loud in my ears. My heels hitting the ground shook my bones. The street with the crooked sign came in view.

A burst of air hit my back and Cadby landed in front me. I veered left to avoid running straight into him, booked it up the couple of houses to my street, and rounded the corner. I could make out the pointy turret of our gray Victorian house through the trees. Passing Emily's house, I spotted several figures surrounding the outside of mine—Conemar's men.

I raised my hand and ignited my globe. I skidded to a stop. On my palm sat a clear iridescent globe. It was heavier than my pink one.

Arik trotted to a stop beside me, his eyes wide as he inspected my globe. "What's that?"

"I don't know. I think my battle globe broke when I threw it at the trapdoor." There were so many creatures and Sentinels on my front yard. "Why aren't the police here? Someone had to call them."

"See that blue light overhead?" Arik pointed to the sky above my house. "It's a charm. A shield. It controls noise and prevents phones from working."

A few men with Conemar spotted us. One had to be a Sentinel. The tall, broad man wore a black trench coat and balanced a smoky globe on his palm. He threw it in our direction. It exploded at our feet, throwing up dirt and grass clumps over us. I covered my face with my free arm to protect it from the spray, and then fired my globe at the man. The globe grew in size as it flew, expanding its sphere. The Sentinel dodged it. The globe sped across the yard, knocking several creatures to their knees until it busted against a rock in a cloud of glass and smoke.

"Okay, that was strange." I squared my stance and unsheathed my sword. Adrenaline stabbed through my veins and twisted my stomach as I readied myself for an attack.

The Sentinel sprinted for us. Arik conjured a fire globe, turning it into a whip. He lashed it at the Sentinel, wrapping it around the man's arm and burning through the sleeve of his trench coat. The man screamed in agony. His yells alerting the rest of Conemar's gang.

Mixed in with the Sentinels, hunters, and wizards were Mystik creatures. Some I'd never seen before and some I'd seen in books. A bald, blue-skinned man clutched a battle-ax. Thumping a rolled whip against her leg, one of the Fey with pointy ears and pink hair stared me down. A buff man with one eye smack in the middle of his face towered over them all. Several of Conemar's creations, the demon-like Writhes, slithered between them all.

A thin membrane, glimmering in the light, surrounded the house, and I knew it was Sinead's magic. I strained to make out the figures behind the windows but couldn't see who was in the house. Conemar just stared at us as if in shock. Beside him stood Veronique, a French Sentinel who turned traitor and joined Conemar's side. On her other side, Bastien's brother, Odil and Veronique's puppet, manipulated a fire orb in his hands. Our presence must've finally registered, because an evil scowl flared across Conemar's face.

"Why are you just standing there?" he yelled. "Take care of them."

A hunter broke from the group and charged for us. Cadby plunged from the sky, snatching the man off the ground and then climbing high before dropping him. The hunter crashed to the ground, crumpled and broken.

The others made to stampede Arik and me but then paused, their eyes fixed on something behind us. I glanced over my shoulder. Kale raced up with Lei, Jaran, and the other Sentinels. Behind them, Gian and Uncle Philip hastened up the driveway.

Several seconds of confusion went by, everyone taking in the situation, before the front yard exploded into a battle. Metal slammed against metal, fists connected to skin, screams and cries sounded out into the neighborhood. The ground shook and dust fogged the air.

Carrig and Nick bounded out of the house, with Sinead and Faith chasing after to join in the fight.

I ran for the faery with pink hair. She snapped her wrist and the whip in her hand unfurled. She cocked her arm back and flicked the whip at me. I raised my shield to protect my face, the leather fall snapping around the edge and grazing my neck. My skin burned where the whip struck me. Before she could pull it back, I caught the thong, yanked it hard, and fell to my right knee, pain exploding in my kneecap. The faery stumbled forward, keeping her grip on the handle.

Jaran tripped over me while fighting off another Sentinel.

"Shit," I yelped as his elbow slammed into my jaw and his

foot kicked my sword from my hand.

"Oh, dreadfully sorry." He slipped over the wet grass and leaves, then balanced himself and tore off after the bald blue man.

The faery pulled out her dagger and narrowed her eyes on me. I scampered on my hands and knees for my sword and shield. She snagged my ponytail, dragged me upright on my knees. She thrust her dagger at me, and I shut my eyes tight, readying for the blow. Something pulled her off me, and I swung around to see what it was.

Vines from the fence surrounding the property wrapped around the faery. All the vines that crawled up the fences and house were in motion, snaking across the ground, wrapping around limbs and ensnarling bodies, making several of Conemar's men immobile.

I looked over my shoulder.

Emily's hands were up and her fingers danced as she manipulated the vines.

Chapter Twenty-nine

"Get up and fight," Emily ordered from behind me.

"I should kill you for what you did," I snapped.

"Fine. You can do it later." She waved her hand to send a wall of soil from the flowerbed at a charging Writhe. "Right now, you'll have to trust me, and you might want to go help your daddy in the meantime."

"Trust you? You told Conemar where we were hiding."

"I did not."

"Yes you did. Cadby said a witch tipped Conemar off." I snapped up my sword.

"Well, it wasn't this witch." She blew a strand of black hair from the corner of her mouth. "Did you hear me? Your dad needs help."

My eyes darted to where she was looking. Pop was in front of Deidre, holding off a Sentinel with a two-by-four. I ran for them, creating my freaky battle globe and then pitching it in their direction.

"Pop, get out of the way!"

He glanced up to see my globe heading for him. He dived

off the porch. The globe smacked into the Sentinel and blew him into the house. Deidre hurried to Pop and guided him to his feet.

Sinead clambered up the steps to Deidre and grasped Pop's other arm to help.

"Gia, we have to get out of here," Carrig said, running for the porch. Blood stained his shirt.

I glanced at the carnage happening around the early spring marigolds. *This is bad. This is so bad.*

I pushed my fears aside. "Take Pop and the others through the back. Pop's Volvo is in the garage. Don't wait. Just get them out of here."

Across the street, an older couple that normally kept to themselves peeked through their drapes, horror written on their faces. I wondered what our other neighbors were doing.

Carrig herded Pop, Sinead, and Deidre into the house. "Stay alert. I'll be back once they're safe."

"Gia, be careful," Sinead said before she ducked through the door after them.

I nodded, surveying the battle and trying to decide my next move. And that's when I spotted him. The Red charged up the street with five of his men. Fear stabbed me in the chest. The fight was already leaning in Conemar's favor, and now it would be suicide for our side.

Faith? What would happen when she saw him? I glanced around, trying to find her.

Across the yard, Arik matched his sword against the Cyclops man's ax. The man bled from many wounds but didn't stop. He kept swinging his enormous ax at Arik. My breath hitched in my throat, and it was as if everything stopped around me. *Arik.*

I have to help him.

Cadby circled the skies above my head before diving for

a demon Writhe. He lifted it up into the sky and let go. The Writhe clawed at the air as it plummeted to the ground. It landed almost too close to Uncle Philip, who tossed a ball of fire from one hand to the next, taunting a Laniar with long black hair and dressed in a suit from the nineteen-twenties or something.

Faith had Veronique in a headlock. Veronique slipped out of the hold and slammed her fist across Faith's jaw. Faith stumbled back and Veronique kicked her to the ground and ran off for Conemar.

Uncle Philip and Conemar danced around each other, firing magical currents at each other and blocking the other's attack. Kale threw a series of globes at two demon Writhes slithering after Lei. The globes hit the creatures and they dropped to the ground, stunned. Lei turned and shot her lightning globe. It struck another Writhe, blowing a hole through its chest and coming out the other side.

My foot landed on a clump of grass and I twisted to the ground, straining my ankle. Faith pounced in front of me. She reached her hand out. I grasped it and hopped up. Across the yard, Arik was still fighting the Cyclops.

Faith patted my cheek. "Are you okay?"

I nodded, my breaths heavy. "Yeah, yeah, I'm fine. Your brother is here."

"He's here? To help Conemar?" Her eyes narrowed on a spot in the middle of the yard.

The Red and his men were fighting Conemar's men.

"He's with *us*?" There was hope and uncertainty in her voice.

I couldn't believe it, either. "It looks like he is."

Faith got into her attack stance and bared her teeth. "We must get back in the fight." She spotted Veronique and sprung off on all fours.

I shuffled around trying to decide where to go next.

Nick shot electric currents into a buff girl hunter. The hunter crumpled to the ground, her body sparking and smoking. His menacing scowl looked as if he were enjoying it. I shook off the thought and limped as fast as I could over the lawn.

I made it to Arik at the same time the Cyclops' fist slammed into his face. Arik fell like a cut tree and landed hard on the ground. The man's meaty arm slammed against Arik's back. A sharp breath punched out of Arik's mouth with the blow. Before the man's fist came down again, I swung my sword, severing his arm at the elbow. The creature roared in pain. He spun around, swinging his good arm at me, and I ducked.

"*Shit...*" I quickly backed away. Once out of reach, I adjusted my sweaty hands on the handle of my sword. He pounded toward me.

Patience, Gia. My heart hammered with anticipation.

He was getting closer, blood squirting out of his amputated arm. I swallowed hard.

Wait for it.

He raised his fist to hit me, and the second he stepped in my zone, I stabbed his eye with my sword. The creature roared, twisting and turning, punching at the air. I ducked his blow and dashed for Arik, dropping to my knees beside him.

Oh no. Oh no. You can't be dead.

"Arik?" My voice was shaky and the back of my eyes burned with tears. He coughed several times, glancing up with those deep brown eyes, and my breath hitched in my chest.

Thank God. He's okay.

"I'm fine," he said. "Just got the wind knocked out of me. Help the others."

"Well, don't just lay there, then," I said, straightening. "I can't keep coming to your rescue."

"You still owe me a few more rescues." He quirked a smile and struggled to his feet. I caught his arm and helped him up.

"I don't know," I said. "That dude should count for a few of them."

"He was ugly, wasn't he?"

"That's an understatement." I smiled. "See you on the other side."

"Of what?" He watched me curiously.

"It's a saying...never mind. Just watch yourself," I said, darting off into the fray, looking over my shoulder at him. His beautiful face a dirty mess. His eyes widened.

"Watch out," he shouted.

I turned to find a mace swing for my head. I dropped low, extended my leg, and swiped it against the shins of a hunter. He banged to the ground, smacking his head hard. Three vines came from different directions and ensnarled the man.

I found Emily standing nearby.

"You can thank me later," she said, and returned her focus on the vines.

"Okay, I won't kill you, but I'm still pissed at you." I took off in the direction of Nick. I had to get him out of here, to Carrig and the Volvo. He hadn't learned how to control his magic. Left in battle he'd surely get himself killed.

"You're welcome," Emily said as I passed, assuming that not killing her was my way of saying thank you.

I skidded to a stop when I spotted Conemar behind her. "Emily," I yelled. "Watch out!"

She spun around, and Conemar grabbed her neck.

His clutch on her throat reminded me of the time he had grabbed me so many months ago in the Senate Library in France. I darted for them.

"You disappoint me, Ruth Ann," Conemar said.

Ruth Ann?

Someone locked my arms behind my back and stopped me. "Hold on, Chosen One," Veronique hissed in my ear.

"My name is *Emily*." She dug her nails into his arms.

He grimaced but didn't let go, just stared her down as he lifted his other hand in front of her face.

I struggled in Veronique's grasp. "What happened to your accent? Lost it on the way to Evil Island?"

She pulled my arms tighter together. "You noticed. Charm tattoos are all the rage. Even Arik had one, I've heard."

Emily's head fell back as Conemar's open hand hovered over her. "I told you to never cross me or I'd take back the power I gave you."

"Leave her alone." I struggled against Veronique's hold. "What is he doing to her?"

"He put the spirit of a Bane witch inside her to make her more powerful," Veronique said. "Now he's taking it back to punish her. I don't know why he's wasting his time. After I kill you, I'm going to kill her next. But he loves a good torture. And that will definitely torture her."

A horrific-sounding scream came from Emily.

Conemar pulled something dark and sinister from her. He released her, and she crumpled to the ground. There looked to be a face within the black smoke he transferred to a long vial. After sealing the vial, he slipped it into the breast pocket of his jacket.

"Now that you're done with the witch," Veronique called to him, "I have another present for you."

A blue globe hit Veronique's back, hard, knocking me down with her in a flush of water.

Veronique screamed. "That stings." She rolled onto her back and glanced up. Jaran stood over her and slammed another glob against her face. She choked on the mini-tsunami.

Jaran grabbed my hand and yanked me to my feet. He pulled his sword out of his scabbard. "I've got her. You go."

I spun around, my wet hair slapping my face. Conemar was gone and Emily lay on the ground, not moving. My boots slapped across the mud as I ran over and fell to my knees beside her.

"Emily?" I brushed her hair away from her face. She moaned and her eyes blinked open. "You're alive."

"Yeah, I guess so," she said, sitting up.

"I don't know what just happened here, and we don't have time for a talk," I said. "So get to your house and lock yourself in. Okay?"

I gripped my sword and surveyed the battle.

Conemar and his legion of creeps were losing the fight.

Car tires screeched on the road. Miss Bagley's black Subaru jumped the curb and spun across the grass, coming to an abrupt stop. The door popped open and she slid out, glancing around the yard, stunned.

Great. What is she doing here? I decided I should probably save her, since she and Pop were dating. I darted in her direction, ducking attacks and hopping over fallen bodies.

I tackled a hunter going at Faith from behind. The hunter rolled me over and pinned my shoulders with his knees. I wiggled one arm free, quickly formed a globe, and smashed it against his head. He toppled, and I pushed him off me. I lumbered to my feet and froze.

Two of Conemar's Sentinels had Nick by the arms. Miss Bagley waved the Sentinels over. A girl Sentinel stood guard as the men dragged Nick to the car then tossed him in the back. Miss Bagley searched the yard, our eyes meeting. A sullen expression crossed her face and she shook her head at me. So slight that I almost hadn't noticed it.

What is she doing?

"Conemar," Miss Bagley yelled. "You're losing the battle. Come on, I have your son."

I took off after them. Nick struggled in the back seat.

Gian was on his knees in front of Conemar, his head down, his body beaten. Blood rushed down the side of his face. On the ground beside Gian, Uncle Philip twisted and turned in pain, his shoulder torn and bleeding from where his arm used to connect to it.

An electric charge burst to life between Conemar's hands. He aimed it directly at Gian.

"No!" I screamed, and knocked one of the French Sentinels out of my way.

"Stop, Gianna," Conemar yelled. "Or I will kill him."

I froze. "Don't hurt him."

Conemar's eyes shifted from me to Gian then back to me. "Have you grown so close to him already? When will you learn that caring for someone makes you weak? You can't stop me. All I need is Nick and the Chiavi to release the Tetrad. There will be a hell like none have ever known and all souls in the Mystik and human worlds will bow down and revere me." The sparks in his hand lit up his twisted face. "Don't you see? They all need me. You need me. After culling those who denounce me, there will be a peace."

"You're sick." A mix of anger and fear burned through my veins. "I will stop you. I was born to stop you."

"Gia, get away from here," Gian shouted.

"You can't have Nick." My battle globe warmed just under the surface of my palm.

"He's my son," Conemar said. "He belongs with his father. Join us."

"Never," I snapped.

His lips stretched into a menacing grin. "Are you certain

you're on the correct side, Gianna? For there's a gray line between the forces around you. Good and evil are bedfellows. You'd be wise to examine the agendas of those you trust." The electric ball between his hands grew brighter.

"Wait," I pleaded. "Don't do it."

The light blazed in his obsidian eyes. "It's you or him."

Gian's head slowly lifted and turned my way. His eyes were peaceful. And he smiled at me. "I choose me." Gian stood and lunged at Conemar.

Conemar released his charge before Gian reached him. The charge hit Gian square on the chest and he flew backward.

"*NO!* I'll kill you, I swear," I screamed, and ignited my globe, tossing it at Conemar. It shattered like glass on the ground beside him. My feet and legs felt numb as I sprinted for him, gripping my sword tighter.

Conemar created another electric swirl in his hands and sent it my way.

Strong arms wrapped around me and slammed me to the ground, covering my head with red-haired arms.

"Pop?'

He rolled off me. "You okay?"

"You have to get out of here."

"Not without my girl." He stood.

I pushed myself up, my eyes going to Gian's lifeless body. "He-he..." I couldn't breathe. "He killed him."

Pop grabbed my shoulders. "Take a breath. You're okay. We have to get out of here."

Pop looked over my shoulder with a stunned expression on his face. I glanced to where he was looking. *Miss Bagley?*

"Kayla?" he called out to her, stepping around me. "What are you doing?"

She glanced at him and there was sadness in her eyes. *She's with Conemar?* Her betrayal stung like a blow to the face. The look on Pop's face said it was more like a wrecking ball to his.

A tall man in Sentinel gear beside Miss Bagley raised his hand, and a flash of silver caught my attention as he threw something.

"Look out," Faith cried.

A large dagger soared in our direction. Faith tackled Pop to the ground at the same time the blade hit her back.

"No!" The scream tore from my throat.

Conemar scrambled into the passenger seat of Miss Bagley's Subaru. She ran around the hood and hopped into the driver's side.

A roar cut through the yard. The Red charged for the Subaru.

The girl Sentinel formed a bright globe on her palm and shot a lightning bolt at The Red, hitting him in the chest. He flew back, landing a few feet from where Faith lay. His hand reached out for her, but fell a foot short.

The girl and men Sentinels scrambled into the Subaru, and the wheels squealed as Miss Bagley backed the car off the curb and sped down the road.

Faith lifted her head, spotted The Red, and cried out. "Falto."

The Red crawled to Faith and pulled her into his arms, her head resting in the crook of his arm. "Sister."

"Why?" She coughed. "Why did you kill our parents? You left me to die."

"No, no, no," The Red growled and there was desperation in the tone of it. "Your memory fails you. Our parents were dead when I returned from hunting. There was a raid. I saved you from a Sagar. Its tusk speared you, not I."

She touched the scars on his face. "You were hurt, too. I see it now. Please forgive me for losing faith in you. I was a young pup."

He rested his head on hers. "It is I who needs forgiveness."

Tears blurred my vision, and I fell to my knees beside her. "Faith."

"I'm fine," she said. "Go. They have Nick."

Snap out of it.

They had Nick.

I spotted his motorcycle lying on its side in the driveway and darted for it. I fought to get the heavy piece of junk upright and balanced against my side. After replaying in my head the push-start lesson Nick had given me, I twisted the key to the on position, dropped the gear into first, held in the clutch, and pushed it down the hill. The bike roared to life, and I hopped on, straddling the seat.

You can do this. Think of Nick. I clenched my teeth and shoved my fear of driving and extreme speeds down. The engine revved as I sped down the road in the direction Miss Bagley took the Subaru.

Behind me, I could hear Pop and Arik yelling for me to stop.

The motorcycle shook at the highest speed. My arms hurt as I tried to keep control of it, taking corner after corner as fast as I could. I was gaining on the Subaru when the Sentinels in the backseat leaned out their windows and tossed battle globes at me. I swerved to avoid a flaming globe and splashed through a water one. It almost knocked me off, and I straightened in the seat. I attempted to form my globe, but each time I took one of my hands off the handlebars, I lost control of the bike and quickly grabbed the handle to control it.

Nick turned in his seat and stared out the back, a look of despair on his face. He mouthed, "I'm sorry," before the girl Sentinel pushed his head down.

The man Sentinel on his other side leaned out the window, flames bouncing on his hand. He threw one globe after the other, the swirling firebombs coming straight at me. Something hit me from the side and lifted me off the bike. *Cadby.* He flew low with me in his arms.

The fire globes hit the motorcycle and exploded, tossing the bike over our heads. Cadby lost his grip on me, and I nosedived into the ground. I crashed into the grass and rolled down the ravine until a bush stopped me, knocking the breath from my lungs. Pain throbbed across my back and shoulders. My knee was on fire.

I lay there, gasping for air. Cadby rushed down the ravine toward me. I rolled over and clawed my way up the hill, then lumbered to my feet. The Subaru disappeared around a corner.

Cadby wobbled up to my side.

"They're gone," I muttered, tears and dirt stinging my eyes. "Nick's gone. Can you fly after them?"

"My wing is broken."

I slumped to the ground and covered my face with dirty hands. The sobs came hard and my body shook out of control.

Cadby stood stoic as he waited for me to finish.

I shook my head hard, wiped my eyes, and stood. There was no time to mourn. I had no idea what was waiting for us back at my house.

"We should attend to the others," he said, deep and soft.

I gave him a slight nod and followed him, both of us limping and looking like we'd been through a war.

The front yard of my home was now a triage unit. Pop, Sinead, and Emily mended the injured. Bodies had been covered in sheets, blankets, jackets, and unused trash bags. Carrig and Jaran lifted Uncle Philip in their arms.

I met them. "Can I help?"

"No," Carrig said. "We're loading him in Brian's vehicle.

We must get him to Asile."

"I'll be fine, Gia," Uncle Philip said. "Help the others."

I leaned over and kissed his cheek. "Take good care of him," I said to Jaran.

"Of course," Jaran said, his eyes red and his jaw tight, as though he struggled to keep his emotions at bay.

I spotted The Red. He was alive. Sinead was attending to him.

"Where's Faith?"

Arik crossed the lawn to me. "Gia…"

I threw my arms around his neck and cried into his chest. "Where's Faith?"

Arik looked to three bodies covered with sheets.

I searched his eyes through my blurry ones. "Who…who else—" my voice cracked.

He stared off, unable to look at me.

My stomach twisted. "*Who* else?"

He didn't answer me.

I unwrapped my arms from his neck and dragged my feet over to the bodies. I eased down to my heels beside the first one. My hand shook as I slipped the sheet from the person's face.

Faith.

I choked out a sob. Her face was like plaster; she was hardening just as Ricardo had when he died pinned to the tree in Esteril. Small cracks etched her beautiful features. Just as her face began to shatter, so did my heart. It felt as though jagged edges were tearing up my insides. I covered her face, not able to watch her turn to dust.

I went to the other body. I knew who lay under the sheet before I uncovered him. Gian looked peaceful under death's hold.

"I'm so sorry," I said to him. With the tears flooding my

eyes, I could hardly make out his face. "You survived so much, only to lose here. I'm so thankful I met you. I won't let you down, Gian. Royston will fulfill his destiny. I'll make you proud." I leaned over and kissed his cold cheek.

I stared at the third body, and then glanced around, wondering who it could be. I knew Jaran, Carrig, and Arik were alive. I found Sinead and Deidre handing supplies to Pop. I couldn't find Kale or Lei. I looked back at the covered body.

"No. Lei?" I crawled over to the body and wrapped my fingers around the cotton material, strangling it in my hand. "God...please." I dragged the sheet off.

Kale's beautiful face looked so serene, as if he were sleeping. His slightly parted lips were blue, his hair still damp from sweat. I hugged the sheet, curling up beside him, and sobbed, pain stabbing my heart. I gasped for air, convulsing with each sharp and painful breath. I tried to suck in the air. A frightening groan came from deep within the darkest place of my soul.

I shook my head hard. "No, no, no, no, no. Oh, please, no! Where's Lei?"

Arik towed me into his arms, and I clung to him.

"How did he die?"

"Veronique," he said, his voice holding as much pain as I felt.

"Lei." I coughed on the sobs rushing out of me. "Lei. Where is she?"

"They took her to Asile," he said, swallowing hard. "She's distraught. Shocked."

I buried my head into the warmth of Arik's arms and cried. Now was the time to mourn, but I made a secret pact to Kale, Faith, and Gian. I would stop Conemar. I would get Nick back. And I wouldn't stop until there was justice for what was taken that day.

CHAPTER THIRTY

The days went by in a blur of funerals and healing. The sunsets in Asile were beautiful, a watercolor painting of blues, reds, and oranges. The vibrant sky was in deep contrast to the heart heavy in my chest, varying shades of black and gray.

I stared out the window, fingering Faith's charm around my neck. It was all I had left to remember her. The Red had disappeared after the battle, and I wondered where he was hiding. There were so many unanswered questions I had. He was against the Wizard Council, but he had helped us fight Conemar. Why? And why had he jumped to Santara right before it was attacked? I would never get my answers unless I sought him out.

I was vaguely aware of the pendant clanking against the glass locket with Pip's feather in it. A depressive fog separated me from the world.

A search for Nick turned up no leads. There were no sightings of Conemar traveling the gateway books or entering any of the havens or Mystik cities. Conemar and his legion of creeps seemed to have disappeared into the human world.

Hundreds of prisoners from the Somnium had escaped to Esteril. Fear grabbed hold of every creature in the Mystik world. The Wizard Council fueled the fear by holding siege on Esteril, surrounding the haven with charms to keep its people from leaving. The innocents were locked in with the villains. Protests erupted around the havens to free the innocents of Esteril.

During the fight, the man posing as Emily's uncle fled. Emily was an orphan. Several years ago, Conemar had stolen Ruth Ann Proctor's spirit from the secret graveyard and put it into Emily, a descendent. She was the only one who could host Ruth Ann's Bane witch powers. Emily had been born a Pure witch, like Nana Kearns. When Emily crossed Conemar and sided with us, he removed the spirit from her. Now Emily was weak, her health failing. Nana had taken her in and was working to find a cure.

Emily had spelled Arik and I wasn't sure if I could forgive her. But really, what did it matter? The damage was done. Just as a river couldn't change its course, I couldn't change the direction my heart was heading. Even if a tiny part of me still longed to rush back to Arik.

Bastien's strong arms wrapped around me from behind and he rested his chin on my shoulder. "You're in deep thought, *mon amour*. Tell me what's troubling you. I sense a struggle inside you." Bastien kissed my neck, sending prickles across my skin. "I will remove all your worries if you let me."

I turned to face him. "I'm just sad. I can't believe Faith and Kale are gone...and...Gian."

Tears trickled from the corners of my eyes. Bastien cupped my face and wiped them away with his thumbs. His touch was gentle and full of love. His best quality was compassion.

"One day there will be happy times again." His beautiful blue eyes held so much warmth in them I couldn't look away. "All of this will be over, and we'll have celebrations. We'll love and be loved. For now, we grieve those we lost, and when we're done, we'll emerge stronger than we were before. In the memory of our dead, we will strike down those who killed them."

He lowered his head, and I tilted mine to meet his lips. The warmth and softness of his kiss sent all my doubts about us flying away. He smoothed the hair away from my face and cradled my head in his hands. I pressed my body against his. My nerve endings ignited, sending sparks across my body and melting the coldness festering inside me.

A light tap came from my door. I ignored it, kissing him as though he could remove all the pain rotting my soul. It hurt to think. It hurt to remember what had happened to my friends. What happened with Arik wasn't fair, but I belonged with Bastien.

The door clicked open.

"Gia?" Afton sounded uncertain about entering the room.

Bastien slipped out of our embrace, and coldness reclaimed me. I tore my gaze away from his hypnotizing blues.

"Hey." I gave Afton a welcoming smile.

"I'm sorry," she said. "I can come back?"

"No, no, we were just saying our farewells." Bastien kissed my cheek. "I must get back to Couve. Augustin has fallen ill. My people need me. I will return soon, or maybe you can come and visit for a time."

"I'd love that." I hated lying to him. We were going into hiding, and I wouldn't be able to make that trip.

I wasn't safe there.

The protestors outside the castle wanted me arrested. Said it was my fault that every prisoner in the Somnium had escaped. That the lives those criminals took fell on my head.

So Carrig was taking me into hiding. Not even the Wizard Council would know where we went.

Carrig had made me promise to keep our plan from Bastien. It would be better for him if he didn't know we were running away. He could get in major trouble keeping such a secret, especially since he was next in line to be Couve's high wizard. I watched him take long strides to the door, knowing that I might not see him for a while. "And Bastien?"

He turned. "Yes?"

"Know that while we're apart, I'll be thinking about you."

A sweet smile reached his eyes. "And I, you." He moved past Afton and closed the door behind him. I turned and faced the window to regain my composure.

Afton crossed the carpet and stood at the window with me. "It's quiet today."

"Yeah, guess the protestors needed a break."

"Are you doing okay?"

"I've been better." I fixed a smile on my face.

"Carrig wanted me to tell you to get ready." She stared at an old leather knapsack in her hands. "You leave tonight. Professor Attwood—I mean, High Wizard Attwood— Or do we call him Philip now, like we called Merl by his name? I'm sorry. I shouldn't have mentioned..."

I slipped my hand into hers and squeezed it lightly. "I think everyone gets confused about that. You should call him Philip, I think."

She nodded and looked at her hands. "Anyway, he will remove Pip to clean his perch. That's when you'll all go."

"Are you sure you want to stay here?"

Afton's hesitation told me she wanted to say something other than what she would say. "I'll be fine here. So will your pop."

"You're going to face a lot of heat if they discover you had anything to do with us running away."

"What are they going to do?" She smiled. "Ground me? Come on"—she bumped my shoulder with hers—"I'll help you pack." She held up the knapsack. "It's Professor, um, Philip's bag. It's all I could find."

"It'll do." I bumped her shoulder back and took the bag. "You and Pop are leaving soon, right?"

"Yes. With Nana." Her smile was like a whisper on her face, soft and barely there. "Pop will be fine. He'll be with Nana. They're going to a witch's safe house."

"I know. Nana will take good care of him until—" Thinking about all the possible outcomes, I couldn't finish my sentence. Instead, I inspected the bag.

"Promise me something, okay?" she said.

I looked up from searching the pockets. "Sure."

"Bring Nick back." She strolled over to the wardrobe and started riffling inside it. "I can hardly think or eat since he was taken. I don't think I can live without him."

I dropped the knapsack on the bed, then shuffled over to her and towed her into a hug. "I won't stop until I find him."

She buried her nose into my shoulder and sniffled. "I worry about what that monster is doing to him."

Me, too. But I didn't tell her that. Instead, I just held her and let her cry. Pushing my fears and worries where they belonged—out of sight.

I n the early morning hours, when all of Asile slept, a band of Sentinels, a faery, a Malailes, and a Changeling jumped through the gateway book into the Trinity College Library in Dublin, Ireland. Because I was shielded, I was last, in case

Pip was returned to his perch before we all could transport. I didn't bother igniting a light globe, letting the dark and cold envelop me. I glided through the blackness with my arms outstretched and my body weightless. The dim light of the library shocked my eyes as I landed out of the book and onto the glossy floor.

The heels of my boots *click-clacked* down the long corridor between the tall bookcases lining each side. Our trench coats rustled in the quiet. The white busts of men were like bodiless ghosts floating in front of the tall black bookcases.

Sinead pulled her bucket hat down over her ears. Cadby's wings made a hump under his trench coat. With the knit beanie on his head, he sort of resembled a heavyweight boxer with yellow skin. Deidre bit her lip. She hadn't said much since Nick had been captured. I understood her worry. I was also scared. If he ever came back, would he be the same old Nick?

Arik and Jaran flanked us, on alert for a possible threat. Lei took up the rear, her back straight, her face expressionless. She had struggled with the loss of Kale, but kept her Sentinel demeanor. She avoided speaking about him or talking at all, really. Jaran said the curers had given her something to help her deal with the loss.

"Where's the entry into Tearmann?" I asked Carrig when we stopped in front of a heavy wooden door.

"We won't be going to Tearmann," he said, removing a thin gold rod from the inside pocket of his trench coat. "There be no way to keep you safe in the havens. Our little hideout be some place no one knows about. A secret place of me own. It'll be grand, you'll see."

"Don't let him fool you," Deidre said. "It's a cottage. And it's not at all grand."

Sinead frowned at her. "Don't listen to her, Gia. It's quaint."

"As long as we don't get killed before we arrive there," Jaran said, adjusting his backpack, "it could be a flea's nest, for all I care. A tent and a warm fire would suit me fine."

Arik's hand brushed against mine, and he leaned close. "It doesn't matter where we are, so long as you are there." His whisper tickled my ear, and my pulse raced. There was no place I'd rather him be than beside me. We were a team. Trained to fight together and guard each other's backs. Whatever internal battles we had didn't matter. Our mission was to stop Conemar, destroy the Tetrad, and save both worlds. Or die trying.

A shudder ran up my spine, and I fastened the top button on my trench coat.

A light drizzle welcomed us as we stepped outside. Dublin was asleep. The brick roads slick and quiet, only a few early risers passed us. The buildings hugged the roads, and their doors and frames were painted vibrant colors. Not many lights shone throughout the city at such an early hour. The sun wouldn't make an appearance for a few hours, and Carrig wanted us to be out of the city before then.

We moved quickly through the business and residential blocks, weaving our way to the outer limits of the city. Soon the city streets turned into country lanes. Rolling green hills spread out for miles, dotted with white rocks. Dogs barked at each other off in the distance. The muddy ground sucked at my boots and slowed my steps.

My feet were killing me. "We've been walking for almost an hour. Why aren't we driving?"

"There wasn't time to arrange it," Carrig said.

I grabbed at a pain in my side. "How much farther do we have to go?"

"Do we need a bit of rest or do you want to continue?" Carrig shielded his eyes from the sun with his hand. "We're merely miles from our destination."

"We should continue on," Arik said. "The sooner we get Cadby out of sight the better."

Deidre clomped up and kept step with me. "Are you doing okay?"

"I'm hanging in there, and you?"

"Worried. About Nick. It's good that you're back," she said. "We were so concerned. Pop was beside himself." She watched her steps. "Besides, the room's kind of quiet without you."

I cut a sidelong glance at her and smiled. "I missed you too, sis."

She walked alongside me for a while. We talked about Faith, musing over the silly things she had said, and about how her cooking was horrible. When we had nothing more to say, she trailed off to offer everyone the scones she had taken from the kitchen before leaving.

I picked at mine and kicked rocks off to the side of the bumpy road. My steps slowed, and I was a little bit behind the others, watching the clouds drift in front of the sun, then drift away.

Arik trotted back to me. "Is there something wrong? Do you need a rest?"

I glanced up. The others were far ahead of us. "I'm fine. I just got lost in my thoughts."

A beam of light escaped the gray clouds, and he squinted against its light. "About Bastien?" he asked.

"Yeah. And other stuff."

We locked stares for several seconds before his mouth curved into a smile. "Follow your heart. That is all I ask. If it leads to Bastien, I will step aside. Now, don't fall too far behind." He winked and picked up his pace, leaving me alone to digest my thoughts.

Carrig led the way down a road shielded by trees. I

couldn't pull my gaze from Arik's back. The shadows danced across his muscled frame, and every few strides he'd move into a patch of light that hit the golden strands hidden in his dark hair. How did I draw the long stick to have two guys, whose hearts were just as beautiful as they were, want me? I worried my lip.

The sun hit me as we came out of the trees. I lifted my face to the sky, soaking in the warmth on my skin. I climbed up a hill after the rest of the group, pushing my thoughts and worries from my mind. Carrig and the others paused at the top of the hill and stared down at the valley below. I stopped in between Deidre and Carrig.

Nestled in the valley between two hills that seemed familiar to me were three small cottages. One of which had smoke snaking from its chimney. Rocky walls cut through the green pastures in a disarray of patterns.

"I've seen this before," I said to Carrig. "It's from the memory you showed me of your past. You practiced your fighting here. This is where you grew up, isn't it?"

"Yes, it is." He patted my back. "Now yours, as well. I lived here with your mother once. It was one of the happiest times of me life."

"That was before we met," Sinead teased, and headed down the hill. "And now, every day is his happiest, so I like to believe."

Carrig chased after her. "I wasn't meaning that our time together hasn't been just as happy."

She wrapped her arm around his back, and he encircled his around hers. "You big oaf," she said. "You forget I'm Fey. I know your true feelings. If I didn't, comments like that would have chased me away long ago."

Royston came out of the cottage. He had his shirt off, which didn't surprise me.

Deidre's mouth gaped. "Who's that?"

"Thor," I mumbled.

"Huh?" She flipped me a quizzical look.

"That's Royston."

"You mean *the one*?"

I watched her suspiciously. "Yeah, apparently he's going to save all human and Mystik kind."

"He looks like a god," she swooned, and clambered down the hill.

Demos came around the corner of the cottage, spotted us, and waved.

Arik scrambled down the hill and paused just below me. His brows pushed together as he gazed at me curiously, reaching his hand out. "Are you coming?"

As I stared down at the glorious site of the Ireland farmland, I knew what I had to do. I was surer of my feelings than ever before.

I ignored his hand and scrambled down the hill. Arik kept pace beside me.

Wherever my chosen path took me, I knew it would lead me to where I belonged.

ACKNOWLEDGMENTS

Thank you to my agent, Peter Knapp, my strength during moments when I was weak, especially when I had tough decisions to make about this series. I'm so grateful for all the support and kindness you extend me. This book wouldn't be in the great hands it's in now if you hadn't helped it get there.

With that said, an abundant amount of gratitude goes to my publisher and editor, Liz Pelletier, whose hands it did land in. Without you, this story wouldn't be the one it is today. Thank you for believing in this story and working tirelessly to help make this book and series the best it can be.

A special thank you to Stacy Abrams for helping with edits. Your talent and eye for details amazes me. I'm so happy you had a hand in shaping this book. A warm thanks to Lydia Sharp for your additional edits. You have a sharp (pun intended) eye for details. I so appreciate it.

And many thanks to the entire Entangled Publishing team that worked on this book from editing to cover design to marketing and everything in between. Thank you for making my books pretty and getting them into readers' hands.

Thank you, Jami Nord for the critique of this book. You are always so good to me. To Pintip Dunn for reading this book and for always being there when I need a shove to keep writing or an ear to hear all my concerns and fears. To Heather Cashman for reading this book and giving me your honest opinions. A huge thank you to Marieke Nijkamp for her early notes on this story. You are simply the best and it was greatly appreciated.

To Laura Jayne and Sabrina Simmonds for beta reading this book and giving me great notes and warm fuzzies. I'm so glad I've gotten to know you both. Thank you for making me smile often!

To my writer friends here in Albuquerque who meet for coffee whenever we can (we miss you Veronica Bartles), to the wonderful Pitch Wars community, and my online friends, thank you for keeping me company and just for being genuinely awesome.

Thank you to my family and friends for all your support and for reminding me each day what really matters.

And to my amazing husband, Richard Drake, for all that you do for me so that I can follow my publishing dreams. I am so thankful we met over soup and not only became the best of friends, but also fell deeply in love. You are my home.

And finally, to you, dear reader, thank you for reading Gia's story. I hope you enjoy it as much as I enjoyed writing it.

DON'T MISS WHERE GIA'S STORY BEGAN

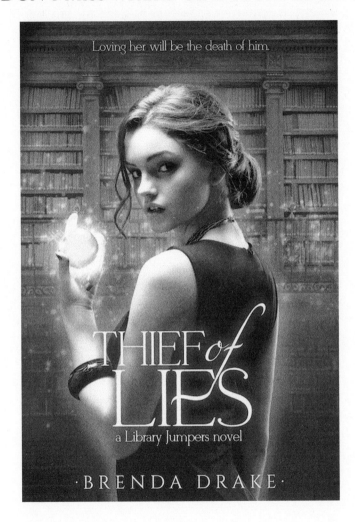

Loving her will be the death of him.

THIEF of LIES

a Library Jumpers novel

·BRENDA DRAKE·

GRAB THE ENTANGLED TEEN RELEASES READERS ARE TALKING ABOUT!

ISLAND OF EXILES
BY ERICA CAMERON

On the isolated desert island of Shiara, every breath is a battle.

The clan comes before self, and protecting her home means Khya is a warrior above all else. But when obeying the clan leaders could cost her brother his life, Khya's home becomes a deadly trap. The council she hoped to join has betrayed her, and their secrets, hundreds of years deep, reach around a world she's never seen.

To save her brother's life and her island home, her only choice is to turn against her clan and go on the run—a betrayal and a death sentence.

INFINITY
BY JUS ACCARDO

There are three things Kori knows for sure about her life:

One: Her army general dad is *insanely* overprotective.
Two: The guy he sent to watch her, Cade, is *way* too good-looking.
Three: Everything she knew was a lie.

Now there are three things Kori never knew about her life:

One: There's a device that allows her to jump dimensions.
Two: Cade's got a lethal secret.
Three: Someone wants her dead.

Secrets of a Reluctant Princess
by Casey Griffin

At Beverly Hills High, you have to be ruthless to survive...

Adrianna Bottom always wanted to be liked. But this wasn't *exactly* what she had in mind. Now, she's in the spotlight...and out of her geeky comfort zone. She'll do whatever it takes to turn the rumor mill in her favor—even if it means keeping secrets. So far, it's working.

Wear the right clothes. Say the right things. Be seen with the right people.

Kevin, the adorable sketch artist who shares her love of all things nerd, isn't *exactly* the right people. But that doesn't stop Adrianna from crushing on him. The only way she can spend time with him is in disguise, as Princess Andy, the masked girl he's been LARPing with. If he found out who she really was, though, he'd hate her.

The rules have been set. The teams have their players. *Game on.*

Spindle
by Shonna Slayton

In a world where fairies lurk and curses linger, love can bleed like the prick of a finger...

Briar Rose knows her life will never be a fairy tale. Most days it feels like her best friend, Henry Prince, is the only one in her corner. But then a mysterious peddler offers her a "magic" spindle that could save her job at the spinning mill. When her fellow spinner girls start coming down with the mysterious sleeping sickness, Briar will have to start believing in fairy tales...and in the power of a prince's kiss.